SHIVERS III

EDITED BY RICHARD CHIZMAR

SHIVERS III

EDITED BY RICHARD CHIZMAR

CEMETERY DANCE PUBLICATIONS

Baltimore
❖ 2004 ❖

SHIVERS III
Copyright © 2004 by Cemetery Dance Publications

Cemetery Dance Publications 2004
ISBN: 1-58767-117-4

All persons in this book are fictitious, and any resemblance that may seem to exist to actual persons living or dead is purely coincidental. This is a work of fiction.

Dust Jacket Art: © 2004 by Gail Cross
Dust Jacket Design: Gail Cross
Interior Art © 2004 Chris Trammell
Typesetting and Design: David G. Barnett
Printed in the United States of America

Cemetery Dance Publications
132-B Industry Lane
Unit 7
Forest Hill, MD 21050
http://www.cemeterydance.com

10 9 8 7 6 5 4 3 2 1

First Edition

UNDERNEATH

"This is a joke, right?"

Dean Lovell shifted uncomfortably, his eyes moving over the girl's shoulder to the stream of students chattering and laughing as they made their way to class. Summer played at the windows; golden light lay in oblongs across the tiled floor, illuminating a haze of dust from old books and the unpolished tops of lockers. Someone whooped, another cheered, and over by Dean's locker, Freddy Kelly watched and grinned.

Dean forced his gaze back to the girl standing impatiently before him. Her eyes were blue but dark, her jaw slender but firm.

"Well?" she said.

He cleared his throat, dragged his eyes to hers and felt his stomach quiver.

Her face...

Down the hall, an authoritative voice chastised someone for using bad language. Punishment was meted out; a groan was heard. At the opposite end of the hall, heated voices rose. A body clanged against a locker; someone cursed. Laughter weaved its way through the parade.

"It's not a joke. Why would you think it was?" he said at last, aware that he was fidgeting, paring slivers of skin from his fingernails, but unable to stop.

KEALAN PATRICK BURKE

The girl—Stephanie—seemed amused. Dean met her eyes again, willed them to stay there, willed them not to wander down to where the skin was puckered and shiny, where her cheeks were folded, striated. Damaged.

"Since I've been here, only one other guy has ever asked me out. I accepted and showed up at the Burger Joint to a bunch of screaming, pointing jocks who called me all kinds of unimaginative, infantile names before giving me a soda and ketchup shower and pushing me out the door. *That's* why."

"Oh." Dean squirmed, wished like hell he'd stood up to Freddy and not been put in this position. Defiance would have meant another long year of taunts and physical injury, but even that had to be better than this, than standing here before the ugliest girl in the school asking her out on a date he didn't want.

Then *no*, he decided, remembering the limp he'd earned last summer courtesy of Freddy's hobnailed boots. A limp and a recurring ache in his toes whenever the weather changed. *Inflammatory arthritis*, his mother claimed, always quick to diagnose awful maladies for the slightest pains. But he was too young for arthritis, he'd argued. Too young for a lot of things, but that didn't stop them from happening.

The remembered sound of Freddy's laughter brought a sigh from him.

Ask the scarred bitch out. See how far you get and I'll quit hasslin' you. Scout's honor. All you gotta do is take her out, man. Maybe see if those scars go all the way down, huh?

"So?" Stephanie said, with a glance at the clock above the lockers. "Who put you up to this? Is it a bet, a dare, or what?"

Dean shook his head, despite being struck by an urgent, overwhelming need to tell her the truth and spare her the hurt later and himself the embarrassment now.

That's exactly what it is, he imagined telling her, *a bet. Fuck-face Freddy over there bet that I wouldn't ask you out. If I chicken out, he wins; I lose, many times over. The last time I lost he kicked me so hard in the balls, I cried. How's that for a laugh? Fifteen years old and I cried like a fucking baby. So yeah, it's a bet, and now that you know, you can judge me all you want, then come around the bleachers at lunchtime and watch me get my face rearranged. Ok?*

But instead he said, "I just thought it might be fun...you know...go to the movies or something. A break from study...and...I hate to go to the movies alone."

She smiled then, but it was empty of humor.

"Sounds like a half-assed reason to ask out the scarred girl. You must be desperate."

"No," he said, almost defensively, "I just…" He finished the thought with a shrug and hoped it would be enough.

"Right."

"Look, forget it then, okay," he said, annoyed at himself, annoyed at Freddy, annoyed at her for making it so goddamn difficult to avoid getting the living shit kicked out of him. He started to walk away, already bracing himself for Freddy's vicious promises, and heard her scoff in disbelief behind him.

"Wait," she said then and he stopped abreast of Freddy, who was pretending to dig the dirt from under his nails with a toothpick. As Dean turned back, he saw Freddy's toothy grin widen and "go for it, stud," he murmured.

Stephanie was frowning at him, her arms folded around her books, keeping them clutched to her chest.

"You're serious about this?"

He nodded.

She stared.

Someone slammed a locker door. The bell rang. No one hurried.

"All right then," she said. "I'm probably the biggest sucker in the world but…all right."

For the first time, he saw a glimmer of something new in her eyes and it made his stomach lurch. He recognized the look as one he saw in the mirror every morning.

Hope.

Hope that this time things would work out right. That he would make it through the day, the week, the month, without pissing blood or lying to his parents about why his eyes were swollen from crying.

Hope that there would be no hurt this time.

Way to go, Dean, he thought, *nothing quite like fucking up someone else's life worse than your own, huh?*

"Okay," he said, with a smile he hoped looked more genuine than it felt. "I'll call you. Maybe Friday? Your number's in the book?"

"Yes," she said. "But Friday's no good. I have work."

She worked the ticket booth at the Drive-In on Harwood Road. Dean saw her there almost every weekend. Saw her there and laughed with his friends about the irony of having a freak working in the one place where everyone would see her. Secretly he'd felt bad about mocking her, but after a while the jokes died down and so did the acidic regret.

Now, as she walked away, her strawberry blonde hair catching the sunlight, he realized how shapely her body was. Had he never seen her face, he might have thought she was a goddess, but the angry red and pink blotches on her cheek spoiled it, dragging one eye down and the corner of her mouth up. This defect was all that kept her from being one of those girls every guy wanted in the back seat of his car.

"I gotta admit, you got balls, shithead," Freddy said behind him and Dean turned, feeling that familiar loosening of his bowels he got whenever the jock was close. Such encounters invariably left him with some kind of injury, but this time he hoped Fred would stick to his word.

"Y-yeah," he said, with a sheepish grin.

Freddy barked a laugh. "Give her one for me, eh Bro? And be sure to let me know how that 'ol burnt skin of hers tastes."

As he passed, he mock-punched Dean and chuckled, and though Dean chuckled right along with it, he almost wet his pants in relief that the blow hadn't been a real one.

«« — »»

The sun was burning high and bright. There was no breeze, the leaves on the walnut trees like cupped green hands holding slivers of light to cast iridescent shadows on the lawns around the school. Dean sat with his best friend, Les, on the wall of the circular fountain, facing the steps to the main door of the sandstone building, from which a legion of flustered looking students poured. The fountain edge was warm, the water low and filled with detritus of nature and man. The bronze statue of the school's founder stared with verdigris eyes at the blue sky hung like a thin veil above the building.

"You've got to be kidding me," Les said, erupting into laughter. "Stephanie Watts? Aw Jesus…"

Dean frowned. His hopes that Les would understand had been dashed, and he quickly realized he should have known better; Les couldn't be serious at a funeral.

"Well, it's worth it, isn't it? I mean…if it keeps that asshole off my back?"

Les poked his glasses and shook his head. "You're such a moron, Dean."

"Why am I?"

"You honestly think he'd let you off the hook that easy? No way, dude. He just wants to humiliate you, wants to see you hook up with Scarface. Then, when you become the joke of the whole school, he'll look twice as good when he kicks your ass up to your shoulders. Trust me—I know these things."

Before Dean had moved from Phoenix to Harperville, Les had been Freddy's punching bag. The day Dean had showed up, he'd bumped into Freddy hard enough to make the guy drop his cigarette. Les's days of torment were over; Dean earned the label "Fresh Meat." It had been that simple; whatever part of the bullying mind controlled obsession, Dean's clumsiness had triggered it.

"What's worse," Les continued, "is that not only will this not keep that jerk off your back, but now you've put yourself in a position where you have to *date* Stephanie Watts, and for a girl who's probably desperate for a date, God knows what she'll expect you to do for her."

"What do you mean?"

Les sighed. "Put yourself in her shoes. Imagine you'd never been with someone. *Ever.* And then some guy asks you out. Wouldn't you be eager to get as much as you could from him just in case you're never that lucky again?"

Dean grimaced, waved away a fly. "I never thought of it that way."

"I don't think you gave this much thought at all, hombre."

"So what do I do?"

"What can you do?"

"I could tell her I can't make it."

"She'll just pick another night."

"I could just *not* call her. That'd give her the hint, wouldn't it?"

"Maybe, but I get the feeling once you give a girl like that the slightest hint of interest, she'll dog you to follow through on it."

Dean ran a hand over his face. "Shit."

"Yeah." Les put a hand on his shoulder. "But who knows? Maybe all that pent-up lust'll mean she's a great lay."

"Christ, Les, lay off, will ya? If I go through with this, it's just gonna be a movie, nothing more."

"If you say so," Les said, and laughed.

«« — »»

"Who are you calling?" Dean's mother stood in the doorway, arms folded over her apron. A knowing smile creased her face, the smell of freshly baked pies wafting around her, making Dean's stomach growl. The clock in the hall ticked loudly, too slow to match the racing of Dean's heart.

"Well? Who is she?"

Dean groaned. In the few days since he'd asked Stephanie out it seemed the world was bracing itself for the punch line to one big joke, with him at the ass end of it. More than once, he'd approached the phone with the intention of calling the girl and telling her the truth and to hell with whatever she thought of his cruelty. But he'd chickened out. Trembling finger poised to dial, he would remember the flare of hope he'd seen in her eyes and hang up, angry at himself for not being made of tougher stuff, for being weak. It was that weakness, both mental and physical, that bound him to his obligations, no matter how misguided, and made him a constant target for the fists of life.

"Just a girl from school," he told his mother, to satisfy her irritating smile. He hoped that would be enough to send her back to the kitchen, but she remained in the doorway, her smile widening, a look of *there's my little man, all grown up* on her face.

"Did you tell your father?"

He shrugged and turned away from her. Frowned at the phone. "Didn't know I had to."

She said nothing more, but a contented sigh carried her back to her baking and he shook his head as he picked up the phone. They were always in his business, to the point where every decision he made had to be screened by his own imagined versions of them before he did anything. It angered him, made him sometimes wish he could go live with his Uncle Rodney in Pensacola at least until he went to college and was free of their reign. But Rodney was a drunk, albeit a cheerful one and Dean doubted that situation would leave him any better off than he was now. Overbearing parents was one thing; waking up to a drunk uncle mistaking you for the toilet was another.

Shuddering, he jabbed out the number he'd written down on a scrap of paper after using Stephanie's address (he knew the street, not the exact location, but that had been enough) to locate *Julie & Chris Watts* in the phonebook.

Perspiration beading his brow, he cleared his throat, listened to the robotic pulse of the dial tone and prayed she didn't answer.

"Hello?"

Damn it.

"H-Hi, Stephanie?"

"No, this is her mother. Who's speaking, please?"

The woman's voice sounded stiff, unfriendly and he almost hung up there and then while there was still a chance. After all, she didn't know his name, so he couldn't be...

Caller I.D.

Damn it, he thought again and told her who he was.

"Oh yes. Hang on a moment, please."

Oh yes. Recognition? Had Stephanie mentioned him to her mother?

A clunk, a rattle, a distant call and the muffled sounds of footsteps. Then static and a breathless voice.

"Hi. I wasn't sure you'd call."

Me neither, he thought. "I said I would, didn't I?"

"So we're still on for tomorrow night?"

There was a challenge in her voice that he didn't like. It was almost as if she was daring him to back out, to compose some two-bit excuse and join the ranks of all the cowards her imperfection had summoned.

"Sure," he told her and cursed silently. His intention had been to do the very thing she'd expected, to back out, to blame a family illness on his inability to take her out. He'd already come to agree with Les's assessment of the situation, and figured it really was a case of *damned if you do, damned if you don't.* Whatever happened with the girl, Fuckface Freddy had no intention of stopping his persecution of Dean. That would be too much fun to abandon just because he'd shown some balls in asking out the school freak. Now, not only would he suffer the regular beatings, he'd also have school rumor to contend with. Rumors about what he'd done with the scarred girl.

"You still there?"

"Yeah." He closed his eyes. "So when should I pick you up?"

«« — »»

The night was good to her.

As she emerged from the warm amber porch light, Dean almost smiled. In the gloom, with just the starlight and the faint glow from the fingernail moon, she looked flawless. And beautiful. So much so, that he was almost able to convince himself that she was not marred at all, that the scars were latex makeup she wore as protection against the advances of undesirables.

But when she opened the door of his father's Ford Capri, the dome light cast ragged shadows across her cheek, highlighting the peaks and ridges, dips and hollows, and his smile faded, a brief shudder of revulsion rippling through him. He felt shame that he could be so narrow-minded and unfair. After all, she hadn't asked for the scars and he should be mature enough to look past them to what was most likely a very nice girl.

Christ, I sound like my mother, he thought and watched as Stephanie lowered herself into the seat, her denim skirt riding up just a little, enough to expose a portion of her thigh. To Dean's horror, he felt a rush of excitement and hastily quelled it.

You're being an asshole, he told himself, but it was not a revelation. He knew what he was being, and how he was feeling. He'd become a display case, his shelves filled with all the traits he would have frowned upon had someone else been displaying them. But it was different, and he realized it always was, when you were an outsider looking in. Here, in the car with Stephanie, he was helpless to stop how angry and disgusted he felt.

13

It was just another event in his life engineered by someone other than himself and that impotence made him want to scream, to shove this ugly, ruined girl from the car and just drive until the gas ran out or he hit a wall, whichever happened first.

"Hi," she said and he offered her a weak smile. Her hair was shiny and clean, her eyes sparkling, dark red lipstick making her lips scream for a long wet kiss.

Dean wanted to be sick, but figured instead to drive, to seek distractions and end this goddamn night as soon as possible. He could live with the whispers, the speculation, and the gossip forever, but he needed to end the subject of them sooner rather than later.

"So where are we going?" she asked when he gunned the engine to life and set the car rolling.

He kept his eyes on the street. Dogs were fleeting shadows beneath streetlights; a plastic bag fluttered like a trapped dove on a rusted railing. A basketball smacked the pavement beyond a fenced in court. Voices rose, their echoes fleeing. The breeze rustled the dark leaves, whispering to the moon.

Dean's palms were oily on the wheel.

"The movies, I guess. That okay?"

In the corner of his eye, he saw her shrug. "I guess."

"We don't have to, if you have something else in mind."

The smell of her filled the car, a scent of lavender and something else, something that filled his nostrils and sent a shiver through him that was, alarmingly, not unpleasant.

"Maybe we could go down to the pier."

"What's down there?"

"Nothing much, but I like it. It's peaceful."

And secluded, Dean added and remembered Les's theory on what she might be expecting from him.

"Sounds kind of boring to me," he said then, aware that it was hardly the polite thing to say but wary of letting the night slip out of his control.

To his surprise, she smiled. "I used to think that too."

"What changed your mind?"

"I don't know. The fire, maybe."

Oh shit. It was a question he knew everyone in school wanted to know, that he himself wanted to know: How did you get those scars? And now it seemed, she would tell him.

"The fire that…" he ventured and saw her nod.

"My brother started it. Funny."

"What was?"

"That he set it trying to kill me and our parents, but he was the only one who died. Hid himself in the basement thinking the fire wouldn't get him down there, and he was right. But the smoke did. He suffocated. I burned."

"My God."

She turned to look at him then and in the gloom, her eyes looked like cold stones, the light sailing over the windshield drawing the scars into her hair.

"Why did you ask me out?"

He fumbled for an answer she would believe but all responses tasted false.

"Someone dare you?"

"No."

"Threaten you?"

"Haven't we already been through this?"

"That's not an answer."

"I told you: No."

"Then why?"

"Because I wanted to."

"I don't believe you."

He rolled his eyes. "Then why are you here?"

Another shrug and she looked out her window. "I'm hoping some day someone will ask me out for real. Until then, I'll settle for trial runs. When you look like I do, being choosy isn't an option, even if you're almost certain you're going to end up getting hurt."

"Hell of an attitude," he said, but understood completely and both hated himself for being exactly what she suspected and pitied her for having to endure the callousness of people.

People like him.

"Maybe. I figure it'll change when I meet someone who doesn't think of me as a freak."

He knew that was his cue to say something comforting, to tell her *I'm not one of those people*, but he was afraid to. It would mean fully committing himself to her expectations and they would undoubtedly extend far beyond this night. It would mean selling himself to her and that was unthinkable, because in reality, he was everything she feared—just another guy setting her up for heartbreak, and as guilty as that made him feel, it was still preferable to making her think he was really interested in her. Neither were palatable options, but at least there was escape from the former.

"I don't think you're being fair on yourself," he said instead, and silently applauded his tact. "I think you look good."

She snorted a laugh, startling him and he looked at her.

"What?"

"Nothing," she replied, but kept looking at him, even when he turned to watch the road; even when he found himself angling the car toward the pier; even as he felt his own skin redden under her scrutiny. The smell of her was intoxicating, the remembered glimpse of thigh agitating, a persistent itch somewhere deep beneath the skin.

This is *a dare*, he reminded himself when he felt a faint stirring in his groin. *I'm only doing it because I don't want to get my ass kicked through the rest of high school. And never in a million years would I have asked her otherwise and why the* fuck *is she still staring at me?*

He brought the car to a squeaking halt, its nose inches from the low pier wall, the black water beyond speckled with reflected stars, the moon gazing at its shimmering twin. Boats danced on the end of their tethers, bells clanking, announcing every wave. A rickety looking jetty ran out to sea and vanished under the cloak of night.

And still he felt her eyes on him.

After a moment in which he screamed to announce *well here we are!* he turned to ask her why she was staring—he couldn't bear the sensation of those eyes on him any longer—but when he opened his mouth to speak, she leaned close and crushed them with her lips, her tongue lashing away the memory of them.

Dean's eyes widened in horror.

Oh Jesus.

She shifted her lips, just a little and the side of her cheek grazed him. Hard skin. It was as if her nails had scratched his mouth. He recoiled; she followed, her hands grabbing fistfuls of his shirt. He moaned a protest but it only spurred her further. Her hands began to slide downward and oh God he was responding—even in the throes of horror he was responding and his hands were sliding over her blouse, feeling the softness there, the small points of hardness beneath his fingers and unbuttoning, tearing, freeing her pale, smooth unblemished skin. She made a low sound in her throat and broke away and for a terrible moment he thought she was going to stop, even though he wanted her to stop because this was a nightmare, but instead she sloughed off her blouse and smiled and now she was wearing just a bra and it was all he could see in a world full of pulsing red stars that throbbed across his eyes. She reached behind her and slowly, teasingly removed her bra and replaced it with his hands. His breath was coming hard and fast, harder and faster, an ache in his crotch as his cock stiffened even as his mind continued to protest *stop it stop it stop it you can't do this you don't* want *to do this* and she was on him again, her hair tickling his face, her mouth crushing, exploring, tearing at his clothes and he moaned, begged her, kneaded her soft, perfect breasts, then released them as she moved lower, lower, her wet lips tasting his nipples, his stomach, her fingers hooking the waistband of his pants and…

…and then the passenger door was wrenched open and disembodied white hands, large hands, leapt forward and tangled themselves in her hair, wrenching her head back to show a face with surprise-widened eyes and a gaping mouth too stunned to cry out.

Dean could do nothing, the lust that had swelled to bursting within him quickly turning to icewater in his veins. *Oh God, no.* He watched in abject terror as Stephanie was torn screaming from the car, the breasts he had held not moments before crushed beneath her weight as she was thrown to the ground face first. She whimpered and for a moment it was the only sound apart from the steady clanking of the bell.

And then Fuckface Freddy's sneering face filled the doorway.

"Surprise, shithead," he said.

《《—》》

It took only a moment for Dean to gather himself, but he did so with the awful knowledge that he was probably going to die and that awareness lent a sluggishness to his movements that saw him all but crawl from the car to see what Freddy was doing to the girl.

It was worse than he thought, because as he straightened himself to lean against the car, he saw that Freddy was not alone. Lou Greer, the principal's son, track-star and all-round sonofabitch was with him, giggling uncontrollably into his palm and shuffling around Stephanie, who was now sitting up, a shocked expression on her face, her arms crossed over her bare breasts.

Freddy was smiling, a feral smile that promised hurt.

"I'll be damned," he told Dean, "you're just full of fuckin' surprises, man. I was only kiddin' you about bonin' Scarface and here you were about to let her gobble your rod. That's really somethin'."

The bell clanged on, ignoring the hush of the tide.

Somewhere far out to sea, a ship's horn sounded.

The ground around the car was sandy, a thin layer scattered above concrete. Pieces of broken glass gleamed in the half-light from the streetlamps that peered between the canopies of box elder and spruce. This also provided a perfect shield from the road. Few cars would pass by tonight and those that did would not see much should they deign to look in this direction.

"Don't hurt her," Dean said, knowing as he did so that anything he said would only bring him more pain at the hands of Freddy and his comrade.

"That sounded like an order to me, Fred," Greer said, and giggled. It was the contention of most people who knew him, that the last time the principal's son had been lucid, Ronald Reagan was taking his first spill over a curb.

Stephanie was shivering, her pupils huge, the scarred side of her face lost in shadow, and while Dean was filled with terror, he couldn't stop himself from reflecting back on what they'd been doing before Freddy had come along.

But then Freddy stepped close enough to drown Dean in his shadow and the memory was banished from his mind.

"Since when do you give a shit about her?" Freddy asked, somehow managing to sound convincingly curious.

"I-I...I don't know."

Freddy nodded his complete understanding and turned back to Stephanie. She watched him fearfully.

"You do know he set you up, right?"

Greer giggled and muttered "oh shit, that *sucks*" into his hand.

Stephanie looked at Dean and he felt his insides turn cold. There was no anger in her eyes, no disappointment; just a blank look, and somehow that was worse.

"That's a lie, Stephanie," he said, stepping forward, "I swear it's—"

In one smooth move, Freddy swiveled on his heel and launched a downward kick into Dean's shin. Dean howled in pain and collapsed to the ground.

"Shut the fuck up, weasel," F4reddy said, and drove his boot into Dean's stomach, knocking the wind out of him. Dean wheezed, tears leaking from his eyes. When they cleared, he saw Stephanie, her arms still crossed across her breasts, her face drawn and pale but for the angry red on her cheek.

I swear I didn't he mouthed to her but knew she didn't understand, knew she couldn't understand because the look in her eyes told him she wasn't really here any more, that she'd retreated somewhere neither he nor Freddy and Greer could reach her.

Greer stopped giggling long enough to ask: "What'll we do with her, Fred?"

Freddy shrugged and turned back to face Stephanie.

"Can't fuck her," he said, as if he were talking about the weather, "they'd swab her scabby ass and I'd be off the football team."

"Please, leave her...alone," Dean managed, though every word felt like red-hot hooks tugging at his stomach.

"If you don't shut up, we will leave her alone, and do all the unpleasant things to *you* instead," Freddy said, over his shoulder and for a moment Dean stopped breathing.

Do it, his mind screamed. *Tell them to go ahead and beat the shit out of you. At least they'll leave her alone!*

But he said nothing, merely wept into the sand.

He didn't want her to get hurt, but he had been hurt so much himself that he couldn't bear the thought of more. Even if all of this was his fault. Even if the memory of the way she was looking at him haunted his sleep for the rest of his life.

He.

Couldn't.

Do it.

He squeezed his eyes shut, kept them that way until he heard a grunt and Greer's manic giggle and his eyes flickered open. The world swayed, stars coruscated across his retinas, then died.

Stephanie was no longer kneeling.

She was lying flat on her back, breasts exposed with Greer holding her wrists in his hands, as if preparing to drag her over the broken glass. As Dean watched, heartsick and petrified, Freddy grinned and straddled the girl. Still, she would not take her eyes off Dean. He wished more than anything that she would and "please" he moaned into the sand, sending it puffing up around and into his mouth.

"How did she taste, shithead?" Freddy asked and, setting his hands on either side of Stephanie's midriff, leaned down and flicked his tongue over her left nipple. As Greer giggled hysterically, Freddy sat back and smacked his lips as if tasting a fine wine.

"Charcoal, perhaps," he said and that was too much for Greer. He exploded into guffaws so irritating that eventually even Freddy had to tell him to cut it out.

And still Stephanie stared at Dean.

Oh fuck, please stop.

"I'm sorry," he whispered, and knew she didn't hear.

"Then again…" Freddy tasted her right nipple, repeated the lip smacking and put a thoughtful finger to his chin. "Maybe soot. You wanna taste, Greer?"

He didn't need to ask twice. They exchanged positions, Stephanie never once breaking eye contact with Dean and never once trying to struggle against what Freddy and Greer were doing to her. She said nothing, but bore the humiliation in expressionless silence.

Dean, unable to stand it any longer, scooted himself into a sitting position, his back against the car, drew his knees up and buried his face in the dark they provided, surrounding them with his arms. In here, he was safe. All he could hear were the sounds.

It lasted forever and he wept through it all, looking up only when a sharp smack made him flinch.

Greer was on the ground, his giggling stopped, a hand to his cheek.

Stephanie was in the same position as before, but her jeans and panties were rolled down almost to her knees, exposing her sex, a V-shaped shadow in the white of her skin. Freddy towered over Greer, one fist clenched and held threateningly at his side.

"I said *no*, you fuckin' retard."

Greer looked cowed, and more than a little afraid. "I was just goin' to use a finger."

"Get up," Freddy ordered and Greer scrambled to his feet. They stood on either side of the prone girl, the threat of violence in the air.

"You do as I say or fuck off home to Daddy, you understand me?"

Greer nodded.

"Good, now pull her pants back up and go get the car. We're done with this bitch."

Another nod from Greer.

The sigh Dean felt at the thought that it might all be over caught in his throat when Freddy turned and walked toward him. Dean's whole body tensed, anticipating another kick, but Freddy dropped to his haunches and smiled.

"Do we need to have this conversation?"

Dean said nothing; didn't know what he was supposed to say.

"Do I need to tell you what will happen if you tell anyone what happened here? Not that anyone will believe a little fucked up perv like you anyway, and I have ways of making sure the finger gets pointed in your direction if you start making noise. Capisce?"

Dean nodded, tears dripping down his cheeks.

"Good. Besides, we didn't hurt her, now did we? We were just havin' some fun. Harmless fun, right?"

Dean nodded.

Freddy's grin dropped as if he'd been struck. He leaned close enough for Dean to smell the beer on his breath.

"Because you open your fuckin' mouth, shithead and two things are gonna happen. First, we'll have a repeat of tonight's performance, only this time we'll go all the way, you know what I'm sayin'? We'll fuck that little burnt-up whore 'till she can't walk no more and then I'll get Greer to do the same to you, just so you don't feel left out, understand?"

Dean nodded furiously with a sob so loud it startled them both. Freddy laughed.

"Yeah, you understand," he said and rose to his feet, taking a moment to dust the sand off his jeans. He looked over at Stephanie, still lying unmoving where they'd left her, and said to Dean: "She's not much of a talker, is she?"

Dean was silent.

"Pretty fuckin' frigid too. Must be your aftershave got you that itty bitty titty, shithead."

Greer's Chevy rumbled to a halt a few feet away.

Freddy glanced back over his shoulder, then looked from Dean to Stephanie.

"Well folks, it's been fun. I hope you've enjoyed me as much as I've enjoyed you!"

He turned and walked to the car, his boots crunching sand.

With a whoop and a holler, Greer roared the engine and they were gone, the Chevy screeching around the corner onto the road behind the trees.

Night closed in around the pier and there were only the waves, the clanging of the bell and the soft sigh of the breeze.

««—»»

"Stephanie?"

He had brought her clothes, gripping them in a fist that wanted to tremble, to touch her, to help her, but when he offered them to her, she closed her eyes and didn't move.

"Stephanie, he said if I asked you out, he'd quit picking on me. He scares the shit out of me and I'm tired of getting my ass kicked and creeping around worrying that he'll see me. So I agreed, like an idiot. I'm sorry. I really do like you, even if I wasn't sure before. I do like you and I'm so sorry this happened. I swear I didn't know."

There was an interminable period of silence that stretched like taut wire between them, and then she opened her eyes.

Dark.

Fire.

Slowly, she reached out and took the clothes from him.

"Wait for me in the car, I don't want you looking at me," she said coldly, but not before her fingers brushed the air over his hand.

"Okay," he said and rose.

She stared, unmoving.

"I am sorry," he told her and waited a heartbeat for a response.

There was none. He made his way back to the car and stared straight ahead through the windshield at the endless dark sea, ignoring the sinuous flashes of white in the corner of his eye. Echoes of pain tore through his gut and he winced, wondering if something was broken, or burst.

When the car door opened, his pulse quickened and he had to struggle not to look at her.

"Drive me home," she said and put her hands in her lap. Her hair, once so clean and fresh was now knotted and speckled with sand and dirt, obscuring her face. "Now."

And still the smell of lavender.

He started the car and drove, a million thoughts racing through his mind but not one of them worthy of being spoken aloud.

When they arrived at her house, the moon had moved and the stars seemed less bright than they'd been before. There were no voices, no basketballs whacking pavement, but the breeze had strengthened and tore at the white plastic bags impaled on the railings. Stephanie left him without a word, slamming the car door behind her. He watched her walk up the short stone path with her head bowed, until the darkness that seethed around the doorway consumed her.

Still he waited, hoping a hand might resolve itself from that gloom to wave him goodbye, a gesture that would show him she didn't think he was to blame after all. But the darkness stayed unbroken, and after a few minutes, he drove home.

«« — »»

He awoke to sunlight streaming in his window and birds singing a chorus of confused melodies in the trees.

A beautiful morning.

Until he tried to sit up and pain cinched a hot metal band around his chest. He gasped in pain. Gasped again when the pain unlocked the memory of the night before, flooding his mind with dark images of a half-naked scared girl and maniacal giggling.

The clanging of a bell.

oh god

He wished it had been a dream, a nightmare, but the pain forbade the illusion. Real. It had happened and the light of morning failed to burn away the cold shadow that clung to him as he recalled his cowardice.

Jesus, I just sat there.

When his mother opened the door and spoke, startling him, he exaggerated his discomfort enough to convince her to let him stay in bed. He endured her maternal worrying until she was satisfied he wasn't going to die on her watch, and then cocooned himself in the covers.

When she was gone, he buried his face in the pillows and wept.

I just sat there.

He wondered if Stephanie had gone to school today, or if, even now the police were on their way to Dean's house, to question him. The momentary thrum of fear abated with the realization that he had done nothing wrong. Freddy and Greer were the ones in trouble if the authorities were brought into it. And still he felt no better. Doing nothing somehow made him feel just as guilty as if he'd been the one holding her down, or pawing at her breasts, mocking her.

He wanted to call her, to try to explain without panic riddling his words, without fear confusing him, but knew he'd lost her.

But what if I hadn't lost her? he wondered then. *What if Freddy hadn't interrupted us and we'd ended up having sex? What would that mean today? What would that* make *us?*

He saw himself holding her hand as they walked the halls at school.

He saw himself holding her close at the prom as they danced their way through a crowd grinning cruelly.

He saw the look of need in her eyes as she stared at him, the possessive look that told him he was hers forever.

He heard the taunts, the jeers, the snide remarks but this time they wouldn't be aimed at Stephanie alone. This time, they'd be aimed at him too for being the one to pity her. For being blind to what was so staggeringly obvious to everyone else.

What the fuck is wrong *with me?*

Pain of a different kind threaded its way up his throat.

He didn't like the person his feelings made him.

He didn't like who he was becoming, or rather, who he might have been all along.

I just sat there...

As the light faded from the day and the shadows slid across the room, Dean lay back in his bed and stared at the ceiling.

Watching.

Waiting with rage in his heart.

For tomorrow.

«« —»»

"Mr. Lovell, we missed you yesterday," a voice said and Dean paused, the only rock in a streaming river of students.

The main door was close enough for him to feel the cool air blasting down from the air conditioner, the sunlight making it seem as if the world outside the school had turned white.

Dean turned to face the principal, a tall rail-thin man who looked nothing like his son. Small green eyes stared out from behind rimless glasses. His hands were behind his back, gaze flitting from Dean's pallid face to the object held in his hand.

"Yeah," Dean muttered. "I was sick."

"I see," Principal Greer said, scowling at a student who collided with him and spun away snorting laughter. "Well this close to exams I would expect you'd make more of an effort to make classes."

"It couldn't be helped."

Greer nodded. "Where are you going with that, may I ask?"

Dean lingered, his mouth moving, trying vainly to dispense an excuse, but finally he gave up and turned away. He walked calmly toward the main door.

"Excuse me, Mr. Lovell, I'm not finished with you."

Dean kept moving.

"Mr. Lovell, you listen to me when I'm talking to you!"

Now the scattering of students in the hallway paused, their chattering ceased. Heads turned to watch.

The doorway loomed.

"Lovell, you stop *right this minute!*"

Dean kept moving.

"You…you're parents will be hearing from me!" Lovell sounded as if he might explode with rage. Dean didn't care. He hadn't really heard anything the old man had said anyway.

The hallway was deathly silent as he passed beneath the fresh air billowing from the a/c, and then he was outside, on the steps and staring down.

At where Fuckface Freddy was regaling two squirming girls with tales of his exploits.

"I swear," he was saying, "the bitch told me she got off when guys did that. I mean…in a goddamn *bowl* for Chrissakes! Can you believe that shit?"

It took four steps to reach him and when he turned, he squinted at Dean. Sneered.

"The fuck *you* want?"

Dean returned his sneer and drew back the baseball bat he'd taken from his locker.

He expected Freddy to look shocked, or frightened, or to beg Dean not to hurt him. But Freddy did none of those things.

Instead, he laughed.

And Dean swung the bat.

«« — »»

His parents, talking. He lay in the dark, listening. They were making no intent to be quiet.

"Did you talk to him?"

"I didn't know what to say. He says he's sorry."

"Sorry? He gave the guy a broken jaw, a busted nose and a concussion! Sorry isn't going to cut it."

"He was upset, Don."

"Oh and that's supposed to get him off the hook, huh? Did you ask him what the hell he's going to do now? Greer *expelled* him. You want to appeal against that? Just so our darling son can beat the shit out of the next guy who's dumb enough to cross him? Everyone gets upset, Rhonda, but not everyone pisses away their future by taking a bat to someone. I can't wait to hear what that kid's parents are going to do. They'll probably sue us."

"He says the guy was picking on him."

"Oh for Christ's sake."

"Well I don't know…you go talk to him then."

"I'm telling you…if I go up to that room, it won't be to talk."

"Then talk to him tomorrow. He's obviously got some problems we didn't know about. You being angry isn't going to help anything."

"Yeah well, jail isn't going to do him much good either, now is it?"

He lay in the dark, listening.

Smiling.

«« — »»

Over the next few days he was dragged to meetings, and heard the tone, but none of the words. Voices were raised, threats were issued, and peace was imposed. There were questions, different faces asking different questions, all of them threads connected to the same ball: *Why did you do it, Dean?*

Had he chosen to answer those blurry, changing faces in all those rooms that smelled of furniture polish and sweat, he would have told them: *I just sat there.* But instead he said nothing, and soon the faces went away, the slatted sunlight aged on the walls and there was only one voice, a woman, speaking to him as if he were a child, but still asking the question everyone wanted to know and which he refused to answer because it belonged to him, and him alone.

"Dean, I want to help you, but you have to help *me*."

That made him smile.

"Tell me what happened."

He wouldn't.

"Tell me why you did what you did."

He didn't, and when she shook her head at some unseen observer, standing in the shadows at his back, he was released. No more faces, no more voices, just his parents, expressing their disappointment, their frustration. Their anger.

It meant nothing to him.

«« — »»

In the dark of night he awoke, unable to breathe, his body soaked in sweat, panic crawling all over him.

I'm sorry I'm sorry I'm so sorry

Look at you now, a voice sneered in his ear and when he turned toward it, Fuckface Freddy was grinning a smile missing most of its teeth, his nose squashed and bleeding, one eye misshapen from when Dean had knocked it loose. His breath smelled like alcohol. *Look at you now shithead.*

Dean clamped his hands over his eyes, into his hair and pulled, screamed, a long hoarse tortured scream that made lights come on in more houses than his own.

Look at you now...

«« — »»

"These sessions will only be beneficial to you, Dean, if you open up to me..."

«« — »»

Look at you now...

«« — »»

"He starts at Graham High in the fall. Let's hope he doesn't fuck that up."

"Don't talk like that, Don. He's still your son."

"Thanks for the reminder."

«« — »»

Stephanie kissed him, her head making the covers ripple as she worked her way down his stomach. He moaned, filled with confusion and desire. Surely it couldn't all have been a dream, but if not, then he was thankful at least for the respite, this neutral plain where no harm was done and no one had been hurt.

Not here.

And when he ran his hands through her hair, she raised her face so that he could see the scars. So that he could touch them, remember them. But there were no scars. Only a wide gaping smile from which Greer's giggle emerged...

«« —— »»

Almost a month later, his parents left him alone for the weekend. They'd asked him to come with them to Rodney's farm; his uncle was sick, and they claimed getting away from the house for a while might do Dean some good. And Rodney would be just tickled to see his nephew.

Dean refused, in a manner that dissuaded persistence, leaving them no option but to leave him behind, but not without a litany of commands and warnings. Then, on Friday evening, his mother kissed him on the cheek; he wiped it away. His father scowled; Dean ignored it. Then they were gone and the house was filled with quiet, merciful peace.

Until there was a knock on the door.

Dean didn't answer, but his parents had not locked it and soon Les was standing in the living room, hands by his sides, a horrified expression on his face.

"Dude, what the fuck are you doing?"

"Venting," Dean said, drawing the blade of his mother's carving knife across his forearm. He stared in fascination as the cuts, deep and straight, opened but remained bloodless and pink for a few moments before the blood welled.

"Hey...don't do that okay?" Les said, his voice shaking as he took a seat opposite Dean. "Please."

"It helps," Dean said, wiping the blade clean against the leg of his jeans. Then he returned the knife to an area below the four slashes he'd already made. Blood streaked his arm and Les noticed a spot of dark red was blossoming on the carpet between his legs. Dean had his arm braced across his knees, as if he were attempting to saw a piece of wood. Face set in grim determination, eyes glassy, he slowly drew the blade back, opening another wide pink smile in the skin.

"Jesus, Dean. What are you doing this for?"

"I told you," Dean said, without looking up from his work, "it helps."

"Helps what?"

"Helps it escape."

"I don't get it."

"No. You don't," Dean said and grit his teeth as he made another cut.

«« —— »»

There were dreams and voices, the words lost beneath the amplified sound of skin tearing.

And when he woke, he knew his arms were not enough.

27

SHIVERS III

«« — »»

Summer died and took fall and winter with it, a swirl of sun, rain, snow and dead leaves that filled the window of the Lovell house like paintings deemed not good enough and replaced to mirror seasons that surely could not move so fast.

A somber mood held court inside. A man and a woman moved, tended to their daily routines, but they were faded and gray, people stepped from ancient photographs to taste the air for a while.

And upstairs, a room stood empty, the door closed, keeping the memories sealed safely within.

Another year passed.

«« — »»

"Two, babe," the kid said, running a hand over his gel-slicked hair and winking at the pretty girl in the ticket booth. On the screen behind him, garish commercials paraded across the Drive-In screen and the meager gathering of cars began to honk in celebration.

The kid glanced over his shoulder at the screen and looked back when the girl jammed two tickets into his hands. Using her other hand she snatched away his money, offered him a dutiful smile and went back to her magazine.

"Chilly," scoffed the kid and returned to his car, his shoes crunching on the gravel.

The movie previews began and the honking died. Crickets sawed a song in the field behind the screen.

The moon was high, bathing the lot in a cool blue light.

"One," said a voice and the girl sighed, looked up at the man standing in front of her and began to punch out the ticket. Her hand froze.

"Hi Stephanie," Dean said.

He moved his face closer, so the amber glow fell on his face and Stephanie barely restrained a grimace.

"What are you doing here?" she asked after a moment, then tugged the ticket free and slid it beneath the Plexiglas window.

"I wanted to see you."

"Oh yeah, for what?"

"To apologize."

"Apology accepted," she said testily and glared at him. "That'll be two dollars."

He smiled, said, "You look amazing," and passed over the money.

And she did. The scars were gone, with only the faintest sign that they'd ever been there. Perhaps the skin on her right cheek was just a little darker than it should have been, a little tighter than normal, but that could be blamed on makeup. Without the scar, she was stunning, but then, through all his nights of suffering and the endless days of rage, he'd come to realize that even *with* them, she'd been beautiful. It was he who'd been the ugly one, on the inside.

She stopped and stared at him, the look he remembered, the look that had haunted him, but then it was gone; exasperation replacing it.

"What happened to you?" she asked.

He put a hand to his chin, to the hard pink ridges of skin there and shrugged. "I had to let it out."

He expected her to ask the question so many people had put to him ever since the day his father had kicked in the bathroom door and found him lying bleeding on the floor, his face in ruins, his mother's carving knife clutched in one trembling hand, but she didn't. She simply shook her head.

"You destroyed yourself."

He nodded. "For you."

Her laugh was so unexpected he staggered back a step, the scars on his face rearranging themselves into a map of confusion.

Someone honked a horn at the screen. A chorus of voices echoes from the speakers.

Stephanie looked ugly again. "You almost killed him you know."

"Who?"

"Freddy."

"I know. He deserved it."

"No, he didn't."

He watched her carefully, watched her features harden and a cold lance of fear shot through him.

"What do you mean? After what he did—"

She frowned, as if he had missed the simplest answer of all. "I *asked* him to do it."

On the screen, someone screamed. For a moment, Dean wasn't sure it hadn't been himself.

"You used to see Freddy hanging around all those cheerleaders and blonde bimbos at school, right?"

He nodded, dumbly, his throat filled with dust.

"Did you ever actually see him out with any of them?"

He didn't answer.

Ominous music from the speakers; footsteps; a door creaking loud enough to silence the crickets.

"He had an image to maintain, Dean. He had to fit the role of the high school stereotype. He was a jock and that meant he should be seen with a certain type of girl. But that's not the kind of girl he *liked*." She smiled, and it was colder than the night. "He liked his girl's damaged, as if they'd been through Hell and returned with tales to tell, as if they had scars to prove they were tough and ready for anything. The Barbie doll type made him sick."

Dean shuddered, jammed his hands into the pockets of his coat; wished he'd brought the knife.

"I was his girl," she said, a truth that wrenched his guts surer than any blade. "No one knew because he still had his pride. Why do you think he hit Greer for trying to fuck me? That was going one step too far. 'Course that dumbass Greer knew nothing about it and still doesn't."

Dean stared, his body trembling, his hands clenched so tight the scars on his arms must surely rip open and bleed anew.

A joke. It was all a joke.

"We didn't think you'd freak out like you did and beat seven shades of shit out of Freddy. Christ. You nearly killed him, you asshole."

But Dean didn't hear her. An evil laugh filtered through the speakers, followed by a hellish voice that asked: "Where's my pretty little girl?" And then a scream to make Fay Wray proud.

Where's my pretty little girl?

"How…" Dean began, before pausing to clear his throat. "How did you…?" He indicated his own mangled face with a trembling forefinger.

"Surgery," she said airily. "It's why I'm still working in this fucking dump. My mother refuses to help me pay for it. Too busy buying shit she doesn't need on the Shopping Channel. Of course, when I lost the scars, I lost Freddy too. I was tired of him anyway."

The sound of unpleasant death, of skin rending, gurgling screams, and bones snapping, filled the air.

"Hey," Stephanie said with a shrug, "it's all in the past, right? No hard feelings?"

Look at you now, shithead.

Dean nodded, licked his lips. "Yeah. Right. No hard feelings."

Stephanie nodded her satisfaction. "Good, so are you going to watch your movie, or what?"

Look at you now.

HORN OF
PLENTY

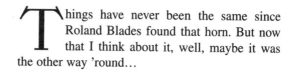

Things have never been the same since Roland Blades found that horn. But now that I think about it, well, maybe it was the other way 'round...

«« — »»

Hold it.

Let me take five, and get you all up to speed. Tell you about the group, and stuff like that. We called ourselves the George Thurston Quintet because way back when we got started, that was the wizard thing to do—if you were the boss, you named your group after yourself. And since my name is George Thurston, the engine pullin' this train...well, I think you can dig it.

We were never the bullet at the top of anybody's charts, but we've always been cool. Albums. CDs. We've had a few. And we've opened for most of the Greats. I ain't the best ivory, but hey, I don't embarrass myself either. We've played the college circuit, big clubs in the small cities, and small ones in the bigs. And every once in a while, our agent would get us the warm-up for the main heat.

The George Thurtson Quintet was The Real: five good jazzmen. No Gillespies or Coltranes in

THOMAS F. MONTELEONE

our bag, but we were *good*, Jack. We were professionals, and sometimes we had our moments, if you know what I mean.

Like when that chemistry-thing would just happen with Satchel Ross, our sax-man, and Roland "Razor" Blades, our trumpet. I never tried to say who between 'em was better on his axe. Never wanted to.

Blade played a horn that was sharp, so clean that you'd swear his sound could make you bleed. His solos could cut through the noisiest crowd, make them shut up, and start to really listen. He didn't flirt with the high notes like Ferguson, didn't have that throaty, mellow stuff like old Jack Sheldon, and never was much for that far-out phrasin' that Miles pioneered, but Roland could make the old standards jump up and do tricks.

On his sax, Satchel had lightnin' in his fingers, if you know what I mean. He could get them in a blur and the notes would pour from his alto like a waterfall. Would've made The Bird proud.

And we went on like that for years. Town to town. Gig to gig.

Until like I said, Roland found that horn.

Never forget it. We were the closing act in a K.C. club called The Oracle. It was a typical cow-town night in July and even with the air conditioners grindin', the humidity had the crowd sweatin' out every note. When we finished our first set, we all felt like we'd been workin' a sauna. We couldn't wait till we could head out the stage door for some open space and smokes.

And right there on the floor under the EXIT sign, Roland saw an old instrument case—fake alligator and frayed stitching and a cheap plastic handle. Pawn shop stuff.

"Looky-here," he said. "Somebody forgot their axe."

So he popped the latches, opened the case, and got a big surprise. Instead of a piece of beat-up brass, he found the most beautiful horn any of us had ever seen, Not to say it wasn't strange lookin'—it *was*. Never seen a trumpet like that before. First thing you noticed was its color—a blue so deep, it was almost black. And polished up like ten coats of lacquer on a Chinese table. It not so much reflected the light as it kinda swallowed it up, then let it leak back out to whoever was lookin' at it.

Weird, man.

You had to assume it was made of *some* kind of metal, but it just didn't *feel* like it—it was light and airy, yet dense and heavy too. Oh yeah, and no matter what the temperature or the season, that horn was always cool to the touch. Hard to explain.

Anyways, nobody showed up to claim it that night, or any other, and when it was time to get on the bus for our next engagement, that horn went along with us. Finders keepers, plain and simple.

So while we were on the road to Saint Louie, Roland took it out for a test drive of his own. We were all dozin' as he coaxed a few improvs out the bidness-end. And I'm tellin' you—as soon as the notes started to flow, we all woke up like a bunch of bears in a cave. We just caught a whiff of honey. The music was thick and sweet and hot, and like a woman gettin' excited, it grabbed us by the ears and wouldn't let go. We sat there in the bus, listenin' to Roland Blades play a horn like he'd never played in life. It was like that horn became a *part* of him—growin' outta his hands and his lips

He played on into the night, and time fell away in lazy coils of sound.

When Roland put that horn away, he was smilin' like I never seen him. "Looks like I got me a new axe," he said.

And he did.

He became the best, plain and simple. And he dragged us along with him.

And on those nights when everything was just cool, when everybody was cookin' with gas, Roland and Satchel would hit on it. They would play off each other's line like it was rehearsed, but I'm tellin' you it was some of the bee-boppin'est two-man improvs I ever heard.

I mean it was *sweet*.

And we all knew it was because of Roland and his horn of midnight blue.

«« — »»

For the next year or so, we got hotter and hotter. Like a cheap laser, Jack. Up the charts we went. CD's started sellin' like they never had, and we were gettin' the best gigs in the biz. We knew what had changed us, but nobody talked about it, and Roland wasn't the kind of dude to make a big deal out of it anyway. We played, and the world paid. It was that simple.

'Course, we'd all been around long enough to know it couldn't last. You get hot…then you're not.

So we made the most of the extra bread we were slicin' and decided not to worry about what might come next. Worst I figured was we'd slide back to where we started, which wouldn't be so bad.

But I was wrong.

«« — »»

At first, I figured it might be the increased travel schedule, or the lures of playin' the big shows in places like Vegas and Monaco and Paris. Or maybe the chicks, juice, or the jack… I mean, what I'm tryin' to say is that we all human and Roland Blades was just as much a man as any. We all had our fun, but it looked like it was catchin' up to him faster than the rest of the Quintet.

As the months went by, Roland started to lose weight like he was at one of them farms, you know what I mean? Not that he was a big, rolly, guy from the jump—not like me and my extra hundred. But now Roland was lookin' positively lean, man. Horn players got big puffy cheeks; it comes with the chops. But Roland's was fadin' away, sinkin' (like his eyes) into his face—which was lookin' long and kinda like a horse's head. And his complexion was changin' too—going from that nice warm, chestnut-brown, to this sallow gray. He looked a like an old Navy boat needin' some paint.

In other words, he looked like he was checkin' out time shares at one of Death's condos.

One night, after an absolutely smokin' gig in London's Brougham Club, we were ridin' the limo back to the Savoy, and I looked at Roland as he fixed himself a whiskey and water from the bar.

"Okay, you wanna tell me what's up?"

"Well, George…it sure ain' my dick."

He smiled, and there was so much of his teeth showin', it was like I was gettin' of preview of what he'd be like as a skull.

"C'mon, Rol, you know what I mean."

He looked around the limo. Satch and the other guys were zoned out, but Roland whispered anyway. "Somethin' got me, George. I can feel it. Cancer or somethin'."

"Man, don't be talkin' like that."

He didn't answer me right away. Just sipped his whiskey, stared out the window as the big stretch punched a hole in the night.

Then: "Okay, I'm-a give it to you straight, but you gotta hear me out, square biz?"

"You got it," I said.

Noddin' towards the old beat-up case holding his horn, he hinted at a small grin. "Now ain' none of us dummies," he said. "Even though we ain' talkin' about it, we all know I didn't start playin' my ass off till that horn joined the act."

He was right about that. It was one of those things nobody ever seemed like they wanted to bring up. Didn't make it any less true.

So I just said: "Okay…"

"Well, as far as I can see it," said Roland. "Here's the fack, Jack: that horn plays *me*…a lot more'n I play *it*."

He downed the rest of his whiskey, let its sweet sting slide all the way down. Then he went on: "Every time I put that thing to my lips, I feel it.

It's like it's alive somehow, and it…*attaches itself* to me…like them funny fish we saw on the Discovery Channel that time, remember?"

I nodded.

"Anyway, that ain' all. I've figured it out—somehow, that horn reaches into me and pulls out all the things I've been carryin' 'round all my life, then plays it back out, puttin' it into the tunes. All the hurtin', all the laughin', all the times I been pissed off and all the times I got my nut with a broad, and all that shit in between."

"That's a lotta shit," I said softly. "In between, I mean."

"Straight," he said. "But it's The Real, Georgie. And here's the final line of the contract: I know I can't keep lettin' it do this to me, cuz sooner, or sooner, there ain' gonna be nothin' left."

"Man, you know what you're sayin'?"

Roland smiled. "Like I said—we ain' no ventriloquist act. Ain' no dummies here."

"We gotta do somethin'," I said. "Get rid of the axe."

"No fuckin' way, Jack."

"Somebody else did."

He shrugged. "Maybe. Or maybe it was lookin' for a new…what they call it on the show?…a new *host*. Yeah."

"Roland, you talkin' shit now." I reached for the whiskey, poured a couple fingers, neat. Reloaded my old friend too. "You talkin' like that horn's alive."

"Not 'zackly, but close. Here's what I think—I think that somethin' of every man's ever played it still *is* alive…hangin' out in all the curves and twists of that horn. Man, I don't just think it…what'm I sayin'? I *know* it."

"I take that as a no…" I tried not to focus on what he was really tellin' me.

"Can't chuck the axe, Boss," he said. "Never know what else we'd be dumpin'."

"Or *who*," I said.

"Which brings me to Part Two," said Roland.

"Of what?"

"Of what I've been figurin' I has to say sooner or later."

"Go on," I said.

"After I cash, I want you promise me—my axe stays with the band."

"What you talkin'? Without you, there *ain'* no band."

Roland smiled, and again it was like a bony preview of what was comin'. "Yeah, like y'all gonna take up hobbies after I'm gone."

"I don't wanna be thinkin' about shit like that right now," I said. "We in London, ridin' the high hog."

"Yeah, right, Boss…just promise me, okay."

"Okay," I said after a pause. "We solid on that."

"Solid," he said with small, tight grin.

«« —»»

And that was the last we talked about any of that stuff.

Months ticked by, and Roland got thinner and weaker till we could almost see right through him. 'Cept when he was onstage, when he burned like a road flare. And I don't think any of was all that surprised when a hotel maid in Frisco found him one morning—all curled up like one them little mummies they find in them urns once in awhile. (Yeah, we saw that on the Discovery Channel, too…)

«« —»»

So there we were without a horn man. Not just a trumpet player, but a Horn Man. 'Cause that's what Roland was. For awhile, even the thought of replacing him seemed silly. We weren't the same without him, and never would be.

It wasn't like I'd never had to replace a part of the Quintet. We've been through some drummers over the years, and I've changed bass players more than my socks, but it was gonna be different with Roland. Without him, it seemed like Satchel had nothin' to play off of, makin' him sound like just another second-line alto.

I couldn't stop smilin' as I'd remember what it was like to have them both up there in the spots. I could just ride the keys and smile, watchin' them trade solos like hot potatoes, forcing each other higher and higher and you'd think their cheeks would explode, and then suddenly they would weave a melody together by some wicked impro, and they would both come out on top of it. It was a thing to *hear*, if you know what I'm sayin'.

Long story short: we went through three trumpet guys in a year. Turned out they all played their licks from a can, and the audiences could notice it too. We started losing the big gigs, and I knew that our edge, our special sound, was gone.

Some nights, when I couldn't get away from that truth staring me in the face, I'd be in my room and pull out my steamer trunk. Big ugly-ass thing full of crap I couldn't deep-six. Posters from the primo gigs, newspaper clips, snapshots, letters from some old girlfriends, some stuff from childhood and even mom. And stuffed in the bottom left corner, Roland's horn in the cheap case. I couldn't bring myself to open it up, touch it, but I would look down at it the way folks come to a grave and stare at the marker.

Things kept going downhill like they were on roller-skates, and it didn't seem like anything was going to get better. It got to be about a year and a half since Roland died. We were in Cleveland, doing the small-club-and-poetry circuit when my latest trumpet told me he was leaving us for dead, going back to the Apple for studio work.

After talking to Satch about it, I decided to give it one last try. As you might calculate, I'd been thinking of folding our tents. Only Satch talked me out of it cause he *hated* session-work in the studios more than I did. I figured to hit some of the other clubs in Cleveland, just to see who was available.

The first club I hit was real down. The piano player was so mechanical you could have put on one of those paper rolls with holes punched in, and you'd never have known the dude was gone. The bass-man struggled to keep a good line, but he was totally overshadowed by the homeliest female vocalist I'd ever seen, *or* heard. Off-key, lotta muggin'. I needed a drink.

Club to club I rambled; the night got old and the music worse. It was like every no-talent horn knew I was coming, and blew his brains out the minute I walked in the door—just to make *sure* I was hip to how bad he was. Finally; I checked into a small, dark place—known for its progressive/fusion stuff by the locals. I'd been avoiding the joint 'cause the George Thurston Quintet is strictly traditional, you know? I mean, I got no kick with the progressive people—hell, years ago, traditional jazz *was* progressive.

But, dig, you got to be a damn fine musician to play the new stuff very well. A lot of the youngbloods get tempted, and use progressive as an excuse for not learning their chops. Like a dude trying to write some free verse before he learns rhyme and meter. Or some phony in Washington Square throwing cans of paint on his canvas, and he ain't never done a still-life.

Right…

Lotta the progressive guys—they all talk about how they gotta "express themselves." Most of it sounds like a buncha yak farts…

Paul Desmond, many years ago now, told me: "I'm becoming an arch-conservative, George. Too bad it's gotten so fashionable to sound bad."

Yowza, Paul. These 'bloods wanna play the new stuff cool, they better be damned good.

Anyway, I'm in the joint watchin' more fuzzy-faced kids "expressin'" themselves. Opening a new pack of Chesterfields, I ordered a highball from the waitress (after I explained to her what it was) and sat back to listen.

The first two groups were heavily into synthesizer stuff and they sounded like a hundred others who'd tried it before them. The next group was a trio: electric bass, keyboards, and trumpet. The bass player was less experimental than I'd clocked him for, and the guy on the Fender Rose was self-indulgent—but he had some chops.

When the trumpet player started, I began to really listen. Instead of the usual collection of random squeaks and squawks, he came on with a smooth, liquid-like melodic line that almost seemed out-of-place, out of synch with his partners. Even the crowd picked up on it. They acted like they didn't know whether they should like it or not—I mean, it was like *pleasin'* to listen, not exactly the "in" sound these days.

I caught their whole set, and the skinny black kid with the horn was like a lighthouse in the fog, if you can dig it. After they closed to less than overwhelming applause, they moved offstage to pack up. I made my move towards them, and all three watched like alley cats caught in the headlights. What's this short, going-to-fat-and-balding grand-pop want?

"Excuse me," I said, looking at the trumpet player.

He said nothing, but started to assemble a hostile face.

"You play some nice horn," I said quickly. "What's your name?"

He stared at me for a moment, adjusted the doo-rag on his head. "Steele. Malcolm Steele. Why? Who wants to know?"

"Me. I'm George Thurston." I extended my hand to shake.

Steele's brow furrowed a little deeper, he looked at me a little harder. "George Thurston? You ain't the man with the Quintet?"

I smiled. "That's me."

Steele took my hand, shook it vigorously. "Hey, I'm sorry, man! Didn't recognize you, you know? You liked us, huh? Hey, that's the shit!"

I smiled again. Even though I was old, I was one of them.

"I liked your stuff, especially." Then I looked at the other two musicians, tried to smile.

"Yeah?" he asked.

"I don't wanna be rollin' no hand grenades under your door," I said. "Just this."

I pulled my card from my jacket pocket, and scribbled our hotel number on it. "Here's a number. If you wanna talk."

"Yeah? 'Bout what?"

"Later," I said. "You got the number."

I turned and split as fast as I could. I didn't need to hear what Steele would be saying to his partners.

I wondered whether or not he'd call, and I had to smile when he phoned later the same night.

I told him that I needed a horn man, and he said he was interested. So I invited him to sit in with us at rehearsal the next afternoon.

"There's one problem, though, man," he said softly into the phone.

"Don't worry about it. If you can play that new stuff, you can play our kind of music." I laughed lightly.

"No, it's not that…"

"Well, we can talk about it when you come by."

The next day we were all set up and had run through a few tunes, just warm-ups, really, and Malcolm Steele hadn't posted. Satch was giving me a I-told-you-so look, and I'm thinkin' like I been had. Maybe I *should* have asked him what the problem was while he was still on the phone…

"Excuse me."

Swinging around from the keyboards, I saw him standing in the doorway. Instead of the three-sizes-too-big T-shirt and the baggy pants of the night before, he was wearing the uniform of a parcel delivery driver, his hands deep in his pockets.

He explained that he had some trouble getting off work early, and I fumbled through some introductions to the rest of the group.

He looked nervous and very young and not very hip at all. Big difference from the previous night. I invited him to sit in on a few tunes and he just looked at me. That's when I first noticed that he wasn't carrying his horn, and I asked him if he had changed his mind.

"Oh no, that's not it at all. It's the hitch I tried to tell you last night…" He looked around at the rest of the group awkwardly. "Hey, can we talk about this…like alone?"

"Take five, guys," I said to Satch and the others. They did a quick fade to the bar in the front of the joint and I looked at Malcolm Steele as I fired up a Chesterfield. "So give, kid."

"I ain't got no axe, man."

"What was I seein' you play last night, a sweet potato?"

He grinned nervously. "Hey, no, man. That was Tyrone's, the bass player. He plays a little horn, too."

"You mean you don't *own* a piece? Well, why didn't you just bring your friend's?"

"No way, man. When I gave Ty the dope, he told me to fuck off, man…"

I had figured this was the rap, but I didn't say anything for a minute. Just kind of concentrated on the smoke from my cigarette. Now you know well as me what I was thinkin'. Thing was—did I really wanna do it? Did I wanna give this kid that kind of choice?

"So I guess I'm no good to you, Mr. Thurston."

"Don't talk like that. And call me George."

He nodded.

"I might have somethin' you can use."

His face brightened for a second, then he caught himself.

"For real?"

I nodded, told him to sit tight, and listen to the guys jam for a while. After a quick ride to the hotel for Roland's horn, I was back.

When I handed it to him, he smiled for the first time since I'd seen him.

"I've never seen a horn like this."

"Don't think nobody ever has," I said.

All he said was "thanks," and continued to stare into the depths of the horn's midnight surface.

"Do you know Lullaby of Birdland?" I asked as I sat down behind the keys.

He nodded.

"Okay, then let's run it through. One, two, and…"

We rode him through the melody twice just to give him a chance to warm up, and even though he sputtered a few times, he managed to recover nicely. Then we slid into one of Satch's solos, which he piped out with no real enthusiasm, before handing it over to Malcolm Steele. The kid picked up on it and started to improvise, and he sounded different than I'd remembered. The liquid smoothness was still there, but it was being pushed by a leading edge that suggested power, bite. Steele played on, getting some confidence once he could feel us cookin' with him; and it became a sweet thing to hear.

I looked up at Satch just as he was takin' a breath, and he shot me a quick smile. Then he played with some juice, the best I'd heard since Roland frogged. I rode the keys while Satch and the kid took a night-flight to a place where the rest of couldn't go. I was getting a little weepy when they finally came back, and we closed out with a run of the melody.

But everybody was all smiles after that, and I wiped away a tear or two. We played half a dozen more numbers—the last two being stuff that Malcolm claimed he didn't know.

Yeah, but he played 'em like he'd *written* them. With style and passion and little something more—that touch of liquid that I'd heard on Roland's best nights.

When we took a break, we knew we had a Quintet again. You could tell without saying a word, and I didn't have to tell Malcolm Steele either. The kid knew he was in, and looked like he was glad to be there, glad to take off them delivery man's rags. The other guys congratulated him, shook his hand, and led him off for a beer at the bar. I just sat there behind my keys, looking at that horn, laying on the kid's chair.

One night Roland had held it up to the light, and peered into its business end, and grinned. Then he spoke to it: "I think I'll call you the 'horn of plenty.'"

I remembered it like it was five minutes ago.

Slowly, I got up and turned to join the others at the bar. But I paused for sec, looked back at that horn, layin' there like some sleek jungle cat, waitin' for its next meal to come saunterin' by.

And I knew I had a *big* decision to make.

BECOMING MEN

It was like fire in his mind, in all their minds, it was a great bonfire reaching up to the sky, and Ralph knew that when it reached the sun, he'd wake up from it—a fever dream. The night had seemed to last forever, and they would all remember it for years to come, they knew, if there were years ahead of them and not mere hours. Shadows flickered around them, the darkness itself illuminated by a brilliant moon grown hazy with the canvas that stretched above their heads. The smells were sweat and farts and hidden tears—the fear was in all their mouths, in their nostrils, like smoke from a catching fire. The bunks and cots were shadowy with the other boys, some of them moaning in real or imagined pain, others huddled together like the small group Ralph found himself in, a circle of boys sitting up on two cots and sprawled on the wood floor of the Hut.

A match lit, the tiny yellow flame illuminated the circle of boys, casting their faces in flickering. It was like camp, that's what Ralph thought, it was like camp only it wasn't camp, it was the nightmare of what camp was to children much younger than them. Part of him felt as if he were still four years old and he'd been left all alone at the playground, his mother had not come to get him after school,

DOUGLAS CLEGG

and all the other children were gone, no one needed him enough to be there. No one wanted him enough. No one cared. But he was older now. He had to let the memory of that turn to ash. He needed to tell what had happened. He had to break the silence so the other boys around him could break theirs, too, so they could find relief from this night.

Ralph went first, his breath coming slowly because he still hadn't recovered from the way they'd held him down, his asthma had kicked in slightly and they'd taken away his inhaler so he had to be careful. Slow, deep breaths. His eyes hurt just from the memory of the interrogation's bright lights and then the bitter tears that followed his confession. Was he still crying? Even he wasn't sure, but he tried to hold it in as much as possible, to hold in the little boy inside him who threatened to burst out and show the others that he was what he'd always feared himself to be: a weakling. The darting matchlight slapped yellow war-paint on all of their features. They were Indians in a sweat lodge. He closed his eyes and began, "I had just barely gotten to sleep—halfway in a dream and it was all kind of like a dream when I heard all the shouting, it was my dad, he was shouting like crazy."

Jesus DeMiranda, the smallest boy of thirteen that Ralph had ever seen, said nothing, but his eyes widened, and he had a curious curl to his lips like he was about to say something, even wanted to, but could not. There was something compelling to his face, something withdrawn yet very proud. Ralph tried not to only look at him, because it made him feel little and ready to break down crying again, so he laughed like it didn't matter, "And my dad is such a loud son of a bitch."

Jack jumped in, "My dad didn't say a word. The bastard."

Hugh coughed. "My dad went nuts, he was just shouting, and my mom was crying, but even when the big guy grabbed me—"

"The big black guy," Jack added, then glanced at the others. The match died. Another one burst to life immediately; Ralph and his matchbook again.

"A big white guy," Marsh said, slapping Jack across the top of the head.

"Yeah, a big white guy, wearing camouflage shit and his face was all green, it was freaky, I tell ya," Ralph continued, holding the piss-colored fire in his hands like a delicate small bird in front of the others so they could all see their own fear, "and I was so scared I pissed my underwear and my dad, when I saw him, he was practically crying but since I could tell they weren't beat up I knew somehow that they had something to do with this, and it had something to do with that thing with my cousin from three days before and maybe with the fire that burned down this old shack, but I never really thought they'd do something like this, I mean, shit, this kind of Nazi bullshit—"

"It's scary," Marsh said, and his voice seemed too small for his six-foot tall frame. He grasped his elbows, leaning forward on his knees. "I just smoked some pot. That was it. Not half as much as my friends."

"What did you do that got you sent here?" Ralph asked Jack.

A silence.

Match died.

"Ralph," someone said in the dark, Ralph wasn't sure who it was, but he waited in the dark for a moment because the ghosts of their faces still hung there, photographed by the last light of the match.

Scraped another one against the matchbook.

Marsh continued, "With me, I thought they'd killed my folks and my sister and they were gonna do something terrible to me. And then I wished it was a dream. All of it."

"They hit you hard?" Hugh asked, nodding towards him.

Marsh shrugged. "They hit me. That's all. I barely felt it by then. I just figured they were gonna kill me. I figured if I just concentrated or something it would all happen and then it would be over. I thought it was because of the time I bought pot and got more than I paid for. That's what I thought. I didn't even think. I just figured that was it. It was over."

"And it's worse than that," Jack said. "You know what I heard my mother say when they put the blindfold on me? I heard her say—"

"No one cares," Ralph spat. "They all lied."

The boys fell silent for a minute.

"I thought it was gonna be like ToughLove or something."

"They sold us up a river."

Jesus opened his mouth as if to speak, but closed it again. Fear had sealed his lips.

"They did it because they love me," Jack said, but he was crying, he was fourteen and crying like a baby and Ralph decided then and there that he didn't care what the others thought. He leaned over and threw his arm over Jack's shoulder. It reminded him of when his little brother got scared of lightning or of nightmares, and even though Jack was his age, it seemed okay, it seemed like it was the only thing to do. Jack leaned his head against Ralph's neck, and wept while the others watched, not shocked, not confused, but with longing for someone to let them cry on his shoulder, too.

Jesus DeMiranda wept, too, softly. Ralph asked him why, and he said it was because he was afraid of the dark. Ralph gave him one match to keep. "For an emergency," he said, and all the boys watched as the little DeMiranda boy put it in his pocket, as if the match were hope and someone needed to keep it.

Ralph kept lighting his matches as other boys gathered around in the darkness and told their stories of woe, and wept, and gave up what fight they had in them.

By the time Ralph's last match had died, morning had come, and with it, no sound until the foghorn blasted its wake up call.

«« — »»

TO BE A MAN
YOU MUST KILL THE CHILD
YOU MUST BURY THE CHILD
YOU MUST GROW UP
YOU MUST ACCEPT RESPONSIBILITY FOR YOUR ACTIONS
YOU MUST TAKE ON THE RESPONSIBILITIES OF OTHERS
YOU MUST BURN
YOU MUST FREEZE
YOU MUST GIVE YOURSELF TO US

The words were emblazoned on the side of the barrack wall, and every morning, Ralph knew, he would see those words, every morning, no matter how hard he tried to resist them, they would enter his soul. In the line up, they had to shout out the words, they had to shout them out loud, louder, I can't hear you, louder, over and over until it seemed as if those words were God.

"Number one!" the big man named Cleft shouted so loud it rang in their ears, pounding his chest hard as if he were beating it into his heart, "I am your priest, your father, your only authority, understand? I am Sergeant Cleft, and my colleagues and I, your superiors in every way, are here to drill you until you break. We are not interested in bolstering your gutless egos. We are not interested in making men out of you. You are the worst kinds of boys imaginable, every one of your families has disowned you, and we intend to break you down as far as is humanly possible to go. Then, if you have what it takes, you will build yourself up from the tools we give you here. Right now, this is Hell to you. But when we are through grinding your bones and spirits, this will be heaven. I don't want any quitters, either. You never give up, do you understand me, grunts? Never ever give up! This isn't a camp for sissies and pansies, and you aren't here because you have been good little boys! You got sent here because you are headed for destruction! You got sent here because you couldn't cut it like others your age! You got sent here before someone sent you to jail! Before you destroyed your families! Before you could keep up your stupid anti-social ways!" His barks sailed over them, for by dawn, even the terrified ones were ready to put up some resistance, even Ralph's tears were dry and he spent the time imagining how to escape from this island in the middle of nowhere, how to get a message out to the authorities that he'd been kidnapped against his will, and then he was going to sue his parents for kidnapping, endangerment, and trauma. He looked at Cleft with cold eyes, and wished the big man dead. Cleft was musclebound, large, a baton in his beltstrap, pepperspray too, and something that looked like a stungun looped at his back. Ralph glanced around at the others, the twenty-three boys, all with dark-encircled eyes, all looking scrawny from a night of no sleep and dreadful fear, and he shouted inside his mind. How could they do this? How could all these parents do this to their children? What kind of world was this?

Morning had come too soon, and they'd been roused and tossed in the open showers (like the Jews, Ralph thought, remembering the show on The History Channel, like the Jews being thrown in showers and gassed, or hosed down before they started on their backbreaking labor, treated not like people but like cattle), and then they all had been given uniforms, and the boys had complied. It struck Ralph as strange how everyone accepted it all; as if this was the Hell they were all consigned to, and there was no way around it. The uniforms were brown like shit, that's what Cleft had told them, "Like you, you are shit, and you will look like shit until we make men out of you!" Then no breakfast, but barrels of water just outside the showers, and each boy, if thirsty, had to stick his head in the barrel like an animal and drink. Some didn't, but Ralph did. He wanted water badly, he wanted to drink the entire barrel despite the other boys' spit he saw floating in it, and the insects that had fallen in. The bugs were everywhere, from sucking mosquitoes to huge dark winged beetles that flew at the screen door on the barracks. And what kind of island was it? Where? Was it the Caribbean? Ralph thought it might be off the coast of Mexico some-where, something about the light of the sky, something about the water, but his experience was limited. He knew the island was flat where they stood, raised like a plateau. There were cliffs diving down to the sea, he'd seen them when the helicopter had brought him in the night, when the blindfold had slipped slightly and he'd glimpsed the rocky cliffs and the crashing waves far below.

"Grunt!" Cleft shouted, and Ralph looked up. Cleft pushed his way through the front line of boys in their shit-colored uniforms, and found him. Cleft looked like a parody of a marine, a steroid joke, a pit bull-human love child, and when he stood right in front of Ralph, Ralph wished he would wake up. Just wake up, he told himself. It's a dream. It has to be a dream. Piss your pants. Roll out of bed.

Cleft barked, "You worthless sack of owl dung, you keep your eyes on me, you understand? I seen a lot of boys come through here, and you are the sorriest-ass piece of shit I ever saw. You hear me?"

Ralph kept his gaze forward, staring at a place just below Cleft's eyebrows, not *in* the eyes, but between them.

"I said, you hear me?"

Ralph trembled slightly, feeling his knees buckle. Hunger grew from a place not in his gut, but in his extremities, his fingers, toes, the top of his head, it was like a spider tingling along his skin, squeezing his nerves. His mouth felt dry.

"I hear you like to set fires, Pig Boy," Cleft almost whispered, but a whisper that boomed across the heads of all the other boys. "I hear you did something really nasty to another boy back home. I heard you—" Ralph shut his eyes for a second and in his mind he was flying over all the others, he was going up to the cottony clouds. He felt hunger leave him, he felt tension leave him, he felt everything fly away from his body.

With a sickening feeling, he opened his wet eyes.

Then Cleft glanced down from Ralph's face to his chest, then his crotch. Cleft laughed, a nasty sound. "Baby Pig Boy here has pissed his panties!" Cleft clapped his hands together. "He's pissed his panties like a big Baby Pig Boy, haw! You can put out a lot of fires with that piss, can't you Pig Boy?"

Then, Cleft shoved him hard in the chest, so hard Ralph fell backwards on his ass. He looked up at the big man, the bulging muscles, the sharp crewcut, the hawk nose, and gleaming teeth. "Let me show you how to put out a fire, men!" Cleft laughed as he spoke, unzipping his pants and Ralph screeched at first, like an owl, as the piss hit his face. Cleft continued shouting, telling him that to be a man, one had to first prove himself worthy of manhood, one had to accept humiliation at the hands of one's superior, one had to take what one deserved whether one liked it or not, one had to know one's place—"You like to set things on fire, grunt, but you need a man to put out the fire inside you!"

Just kill me, Ralph thought. Just kill me.

We are just like the Jews in the concentration camps, Ralph thought, glancing to the others who still had their eyes forward, their lips drawn downward, looking scrawnier and weaker than boys of thirteen to sixteen should look, looking like they would all have been happy to not have Cleft pissing on *them*, happy that Ralph was the first sacrifice of the day, happy to just die.

Just die.

«« — »»

It became a routine that they neither looked forward to, nor complained about, and the others who had sat up with Ralph the first night never spoke together again. Ralph would give Marsh a knowing look, and Marsh would return it, but for a millisecond before his eyes glazed over in what Ralph came to think of as "Clefteye." It was the zombie-like way they were all getting, Ralph included. When he lay asleep in his lower bunk, he could hear Hugh weeping in his sleep, then whimpering like a puppy, and sometimes Ralph stayed up all night listening for Hugh to cry, and it would help him fall asleep if only for an hour or two. Food got better, but not good. From the first two days of water only, they went to bread and water. By the end of the first week, they were having beans, rice, water, bread, and an apple. By the second week, it was beans, rice, water, bread, milk, apple, and some tasteless fish. Ralph noticed that his diarrhea had stopped by the third week, as did most of the boys'. The labor was grueling, but Ralph didn't mind it because while he hacked at the logs, or while he chipped at stone with what seemed to be the most primitive of tools, he remembered his family and home and his dog, and it was, after awhile, almost like being with them until the workday was over. The maneuvers began at night. Cleft, and the six others who ran the camp, had them running obstacle courses in the stench of evening when the mosquitoes were at their worst, when the mud was hot and slick, when the sweat could almost speak as it ran down his back. Wriggling like snakes beneath barbed wire, climbing ropes to dizzying heights, leaping from those heights into mud, running across narrow, stripped logs, piled end to end, it all became second nature after the initial falls and screams. Foghorn, as they called a large boy in Hut D, fell and broke his leg the first day of the obstacle course, and Jesus, the little boy that Ralph had never heard say so much as a word, got cut on the barbed wire, badly, across his shoulders, and then got an infection when it went untreated. After the third week, none of the boys saw Jesus anymore. Some said he'd been sent back home. Some said he'd died. Some said he'd run off. Some said it was all bullshit and he was probably back with his dad in New York City, lucky bastard, with a scar on his shoulder, and an excuse for not being in Camp Hell.

Rumors circulated that Jack and Marsh had been caught jacking each other off. The next time Ralph saw them, he also noticed bruises around their eyes and on their arms. Boys had ganged up on them, but Ralph didn't want to know about it. He was somewhere else. He didn't need to be among any of them, he was in a place of family and fire in his head, and although his muscles felt like they were tearing open when he lay down in his bunk at night, he knew that he was growing stronger both inside and outside.

And then, one day, Jack came to him.

«« — »»

"Got any more matches?"

Ralph opened his eyes. It had to be four a.m., just an hour to First Call.

The shadow over him gradually revealed itself in the purple haze of pre-dawn.

"What the—"

"Matches?" Jack asked again. "You're like the fireboy, right?"

"No."

"Liar. Come on, wake up. We have something to show you."

"I don't care. Leave me alone." Ralph turned on his side, shutting his eyes.

"He pissed on you. Don't you hate him?"

Ralph kept his vision dark. If he didn't open his eyes, it might all go away. "I don't care."

"You will care," Jack said. The next thing Ralph knew, it was morning, the horn blasted, the rush of ice cold showers, the sting of harsh soap, the barrels of water and then chow. Out in the gravel pit, shoveling, someone tossed pebbles across Ralph's back. He looked over his shoulder.

"Leave me alone," Ralph spat, the dirt sweat sliding across his eyes; he dropped his shovel, looking back at Jack.

"You set fires back home, I know that," Jack whispered. "We all know it. It's all right. It's what you love. Don't let them kill that. We need you."

"Yeah, well, we all did something. What did you do to get you sent here?"

Jack said nothing for a moment.

Then,

"We found Jesus," Jack said, and tears erupted in his eyes. Ralph wanted to shout at him not to cry anymore, there was no reason to cry, that he was weak to cry, just like Cleft said—

Ralph asked, "Where is he?"

"Dead," Jack said. "They killed him. They killed him and they hid him so we couldn't find him. Did you know he was only ten years old?"

"Bullshit," Ralph gasped. "He's thirteen."

"Ten years old and his father sent him here after he left his mother. His father sent him because his father didn't give a damn about him. You, Ralph, you set fires. And me, I maybe did some stuff I'm not real proud of. But Jesus, all he did was get born in the wrong family. And they killed him."

Ralph closed his eyes. Tried to conjure up the vision of his family and home again, and the beautiful fires he had set at the old shack in the woods, the fires that had made him feel weak and strong all at once and connected with the world. But only darkness filled his mind. Opened his eyes. Jack's face, the bruises lightening, his eyes deep and blue, the dark tan bringing out the depth of the color of those eyes, a God blue. "Dead?"

"Yep." Jack said this without any hostility.

We are all zombies here. "How?"

Jack glanced over at Red Chief and the Commodore, the two thugs disguised as Marine-types who stood above the gravel pit, barking at some of the slower boys. "Keep digging, and I'll tell you, but do you know what I think we're digging?"

Ralph cocked his head to the side, trying to guess.

"Our own graves."

«« — »»

"Me and Marsh been trying to find a way out every single night. We wait till three thirty, when the goons are asleep with only one on watch, and we get mud all over us, and we do the snake thing and Marsh and me get away from the barracks until we go out on the island, and we see that there's no way anybody's getting off this island without killing themselves, that's why security ain't so tight. It's a nothing island, maybe two square miles at the most, with nothing. The thugs' huts are in the east, and between those and ours and the workpits, there ain't a hell of a whole lot. But we find this thin crack opening between these rocks just beyond the thug huts, and we squeeze in—that's all the bruises—"

"I thought you got beat up."

Jack held his temper. "That's what we said, dumbshit, so nobody would know."

"I thought you two…"

Jack cut in. "We spread that story, fool. So we squeeze through the opening, and it's too dark to see, and this cave that we're hoping will take us out ends within six feet of entering it, only we feel something there in the dark, we feel something all mushy and stinky and only when Marsh falls on it and screams does he realize it's a body."

«« — »»

It was Jesus DeMiranda, the littlest boy at camp, dead not from an infection but from something that smashed his hands up and his knees, too. Ralph heard the rest, tried to process it, but it made him sick. "Where the fuck are we?" he whispered, leaning in to Jack.

"All I know is, I think we're all dead."

"All?"

"I think," Jack said. "I think they're going to just kill all of us. I don't

51

think any of us are leaving." Jack stuck four small rocks in the back of Ralph's shorts, and then put some in his own pockets. Ralph looked at him, but Jack betrayed nothing in his eyes. "Later. They'll be useful," Jack said.

"Just like the Concentration Camps," Ralph whispered, and then Commodore shouted at him, and he returned to shoveling while the blistering sun poured lava on his back.

"I said get up here, you worthless Pig Boy!" Commodore yelled.

By the time Ralph made it up from the pit, crawling along the edges, he had scraped his knees up badly, and he was out of breath.

"Something you want to share with the rest of us?" Commodore said, his eyes invisible behind his mirrored sunglasses. His head was completely shaved, and he had green camouflage make-up striping across his face. "I saw you chattering down there, Pig Boy."

"Don't call me that," Ralph coughed, his breathing becoming more tense.

"Something wrong?"

Ralph covered his mouth, hearing the balloon-hiss of air from his lungs. "Asthma," he gasped. "I don't have...my inhaler..."

"It's all in your tiny brain, Pig Boy, you don't need some inhaler like a mama's boy, you just need to focus. You need to be a man, Pig Boy." Commodore laughed, and shoved Ralph down in the dirt. Ralph felt his windpipe closing up, felt his lungs fight for air. He could not even cough. His eyes watered up, and he opened his mouth, sucking at air.

Commodore lifted him up again, bringing his face in line with Ralph's. Eye to eye, Commodore snarled, "Breathe, damn you!"

Ralph gasped. He knew he would die. He knew his lungs would stop. His vision darkened until all he could see were the man's brown eyes. He thought of little Jesus, dead, his hands smashed into bloody clay. Dust seemed to fill his mouth.

"Breathe!" Commodore continued, and reached over, pressing his hand down hard on Ralph's chest. "You want to be a man, Pig Boy, you breathe like a man, open up those lungs, make 'em work," and suddenly, air whooshed into Ralph's mouth, he gulped, gulped again. The darkness at the edge of his vision erased itself into the light of day.

Ralph sucked at the air like he was starving for it.

"There," Commodore said, and pushed Ralph back down in the dirt. "You boys, you think you can create the world in your own image. That's your problem. You think you can keep from growing up. Well, growing up means accepting the burden just like the rest of us. Accept it, accept the truth, and you'll thrive. Keep doing what you've been doing, and you'll die."

Ralph sat on the ground, staring up at the man. The air tasted pure. He gulped it down, feeling his lungs burn.

«« — »»

TO BE A MAN
YOU MUST KILL THE CHILD
YOU MUST BURY THE CHILD
YOU MUST GROW UP
YOU MUST ACCEPT RESPONSIBILITY FOR YOUR ACTIONS
YOU MUST TAKE ON THE RESPONSIBILITIES OF OTHERS
YOU MUST BURN
YOU MUST FREEZE
YOU MUST GIVE YOURSELF TO US

They shouted it in the morning, still shivering from the icy waters that erased their dreams, standing in the shimmering day, a mirage of day, for in their hearts, they never felt dawn. At night, Last Call, the bells ringing three times, running for the piss trough, running for a last cold shower, running for two minutes in the latrine, and then Light's Out.

«« — »»

"He's under the Hut," Jack said. He'd gathered Hugh, Marsh, a boy named Gary, a boy named Lou, and Ralph wanted to see, too, to see if they were telling the truth about Jesus. At three a.m., they all hunkered down, crawling like it was another maneuver under barbed wire to get out of the Hut unnoticed; then under the Hut's raised floor, down a narrow tunnel that might've been dug out by jackals. Jack and Marsh had dug an entrance that led down into a larger hole, and there, in the dark, they all felt Jesus' body, smelled it, some vomited, others gagged. Ralph reached into the dead boy's pocket and drew out the last match, the one he'd given the little boy the first night they'd met to keep him from the dark.

Ralph struck the match against a rock, and it sputtered into crackling light.

They all looked at Jesus, at the rotting, the insects already devouring his puffy face, the way his hands were bloody pulps, his kneecaps all but destroyed.

"Holy—"
"—Shit"
"They did it," Jack said.
"Mother—"

"Yeah—"

"Holy—"

"Is that really him?" Gary asked.

"It has to be," Marsh said.

"Who else?" Ralph said, and then the last match died.

Sitting in the dark, the stink of the boy's corpse filling them, Ralph said, "If we let this go, we all are gonna die. You all know about concentration camps in World War II. You all know what happens. This is just like it."

"Yeah," Lou said. "They killed him. Man, I can't believe it. I can't believe my mom would send me here. I can't believe…"

"Believe," Jack said. Ralph felt Jack's hand give Ralph a squeeze. "Maybe our folks don't know what they do here. Shit, I doubt Jesus' father even knows."

"I can't believe it either," Ralph said. "They're monsters."

"They aren't human, that's for sure," Marsh added.

"What are we gonna do?" Jack asked the darkness.

"What can we do?" Ralph countered.

"Someone should do something," Gary moaned.

Then, they crawled out of the ground, up to their Hut. The diffuse moonlight spattered the yard, lit the barracks and huts and showers and the boy's faces were somehow different in the night, flatter, more alike than Ralph had remembered them being. Before they went inside, Jack turned to Ralph and said, "Too bad you wasted that match. We could've set fire to this place with it."

Ralph said almost to himself, "I've never needed a match to set a fire."

«« —»»

In the morning, a quiet permeated the camp, and when the boys trooped out to shout their pledge of allegiance to the dawn, their mouths stopped up as if their tongues had been cut off.

On the side of the barrack wall, the words:

TO BE A GOD

YOU MUST KILL THE ENEMY

YOU MUST BURY THE ENEMY

YOU MUST NEVER GROW UP

YOU MUST BURN THEM

YOU MUST FREEZE THEM

YOU MUST GIVE YOURSELF TO THE CAUSE OF JESUS

There, besides the hastily scrawled revision, written in rough chalk, the body of Jesus DeMiranda, held up by barbed wire twisting like vines around his limbs and torso.

Ralph glanced at Jack, who laughed, and then to Marsh who had a tear in his eye. Behind them, Cleft came striding, whistle in his mouth, wearing a green baseball cap and green fatigues."Into the showers, you pansy ass bitches!" Cleft shouted, blowing the whistle intermittently, and then seeing what they'd done, the writing, the body,—the whistle dropped from his mouth. He reached up and drew his baseball cap off, dropping it.

And then the rocks. Jack had made sure there were enough, just enough, for ten of the boys, Ralph included and they leapt on Cleft, stronger now, their own biceps built up from weeks of labor. Cleft tried to reach for the pepperspray, but he had to raise his hands defensively to ward off the blows. Cleft was like a mad bull, tossing them off to the side, but the rocks slammed and slashed at his face, tearing his hawk nose open, a gash above his eye blinding him with bloodflow, and as the red explosions on his face increased, Ralph felt something overpowering within him. He became the most ferocious, ramming at Cleft with all his weight, cutting deep into Cleft's shoulder with the sharp edge of a rock, loving the smell of the man as he went down on his knees. Ralph grabbed for Cleft's belt, tearing it off the loops, holding up the pepperspray and stungun and baton. Tossing the gun and spray to others, he lifted the baton in the air and brought it down hard on Cleft's skull.

It hit loud, a crack like breaking rock when a pickaxe hit, and blood flowed anew.

And then all of the boys were upon Cleft.

«« — »»

"YES!" Ralph shouted, high-fiving Jack, running like a pack of wolves with the others, across the muddy ground, through the steamy heat, rocks held high, Cleft's pepper spray in Ralph's left hand. Jack held the stungun, and Marsh, the fastest runner of them all was in the lead, waving the baton that still had Cleft's fresh blood on it. They shrieked the words of rebellion, twisted from the Wall. Several of the boys had taken down the body of Jesus DeMiranda and were carrying it like a battering ram between them as they flew to the sergeants' barracks. They caught the masters in their showers, mid-coffee, shaving, cutting at them with their own razors, scalding them, beating them, until two more were dead, and the others unconscious. But the last thing Ralph remembered was the feeling of all of them, all the boys together, moving as one, storming the island, like lava overflowing a volcano. The rest was nothing to him, the hurting and maiming and all the rest, all the war cries and whoops and barbaric *ki-yi's* that stung the air—it was nothing to him, for his mind was overflowing.

When it was all over and night covered them, Ralph leaned forward to Commodore—the man was tied to a chair, his great muscles caught in wire. Ralph held out a cigarette lighter—a souvenir from a downed sergeant. Stepping forward to Commodore, Ralph struck the lighter up, the flame coming forth.

"Arsonist, murderer," Commodore said, his eyes bloodshot, his face a mass of bruises.

"Shut up or I'll cut out your tongue," Jack laughed. Ralph looked back at him, and wondered if, like Jack, he was covered with blood as well. He heard the shouts of the other boys as they raided the food supply.

"We didn't kill that little boy, you dumbfuck," Commodore said.

"Okay, here goes the tongue," Jack said, coming up to the bound man, clippers in hand.

"Liar," Ralph said, twisting the lighter in front of Commodore's face.

"One of you must've done it, " Commodore spat, but it was the last thing he said, for Jack had the clippers in his mouth. Ralph couldn't look, it wasn't something he enjoyed, but Jack had that glow on him, his whole body radiated with his joy.

The man didn't even try to scream.

Ralph looked at the blood on Jack's hands.

"Jesus, Jack," Ralph said, feeling the spinning world come back to him, the world of sanity that had somehow gotten out of control. "Jesus, Jack."

"What?" Jack laughed, dropping the clippers, clapping his red hands together.

Ralph looked back at the man, his mouth a blossom of bright red.

The man's eyes did not leave Ralph's face.

Ralph was amazed that the man didn't cry out in pain, that he kept his eyes forward, on Ralph, not pleading, not begging, but as if he were trying to let some truth up from his soul.

"Jack," Ralph went over to his friend, his blood-covered friend, his friend who had helped him get through this time in Hell. "Was he lying?"

"Yep," Jack said, averting his gaze. The blood ran down his face like tears. "He's one of them. They always lied to us."

"You sure?"

Jack closed his eyes. "Yep."

Then, "Did you and Marsh kill Jesus?"

Jack opened his eyes, staring straight at him. "If that were true, would it change anything? Jesus is dead. He came here. They did all this."

Ralph felt his heart stop for a moment, and then the beating in his chest became more rapid.

"We're just like them," Ralph whispered, mostly to himself.

"No," Jack grinned, blood staining his teeth, "They're weak. We're strong. Their time is up. Ours is just beginning."

"What did you do that got you sent here?" Ralph asked for the last time.

"Nothing," Jack said. "Nothing that you need to know about."

"You killed someone, didn't you?"

"It was nothing, believe me," Jack smiled. "And you've done some killing yourself today, haven't you?"

"I wouldn't have if—"

"You'll never know," Jack slapped Ralph on the back. "But it's okay. I understand."

Later, the man they called Commodore died.

Before morning, Jack came to where Ralph sat on a bench outside the barracks. He put his arm over Ralph's shoulders and whispered, "Now we can go home. We can go home and make them all pay."

"Are we men yet?" Ralph asked, feeling an icy hand grab him around the chest, under his skin, closing up his throat until his voice was barely a whimper.

"No," Jack said. "We're better than men. We're gods. Come on, let's play with fire. You'll feel better after that, won't you?" He stood, drawing Ralph up by the hand. "You're good at fires, Ralph. We need you. I need you."

"I don't know," Ralph said. "Yesterday it was one thing. It seemed different. Jesus was dead. They were like the Nazis."

"I need you," Jack repeated, squeezing Ralph's hand tight, warm, covering Ralph's fingers in his. "You as you are, Ralph. Not what they wanted. As you are. I want you."

Ralph felt his fingers curl slightly under the weight of Jack's. He looked down at their hands and then up at Jack's face. "I can't."

"No shame," Jack said, "Let's set it all on fire. Glorious fire. Let's make it burn all the way up to the sun."

"That's my dream," Ralph whispered, a shock of recognition in Jack's words, a secret between the most intimate of friends. "How did you know my dream? My first night here, I saw it in my mind, a fire going all the way to the sun."

They stood there, frozen for a moment; then, Jack slowly let go of Ralph's hand, leaving in his palm a silver lighter. "Go set fires across the land."

Before the sun rose from the sea into an empty sky, the fires got out of hand. Ralph realized, putting aside other considerations, that it was the most beautiful thing he had ever seen in his young life, the way fire could take away what was right in front of his eyes, just burn it away with no reason other than its own hunger. Jack told him it was the best day he'd ever had, and when the burning was done, the boys went and had their showers, all except for Ralph who went in search of something new to burn.

FLIP FLAP

I believe in magic. Who don't? Have you looked around yourself, up and down Coney Island's Bowery and lanes where men with pigeons make them disappear and reappear inside red silk scarves and women in Turkish gowns look into crystal balls and see your future filled with pretty children and lots of money? Didn't you hear how in July Teddy Roosevelt cast himself a spell on them Spanish on San Juan Hill and they just dropped down dead? You ever seen one of them Vitascope shows, where the ghost of a beautiful lady dances on a white screen and some train runs from one side of the room to the other without so much as smoke or noise? They call it "movin' pictures," but it's magic. Magic is everywhere, though some don't believe it. It's common as loose milk and mutton. 'Cause what is magic, but the power that makes something happen that you want real bad to happen?

«« — »»

"Open your eyes."
I didn't open my eyes.
"I said open your goddamn eyes!"
There was a sharp pinch on my shoulder. I

ELIZABETH MASSIE

opened one a tiny bit, the one closest to Victor so he would think I was enjoying myself, but all I could see was a blur of whites and blues and a tangle of faces and flowered hats below me. I hated heights. They made my stomach flip like a cake on a griddle.

"Ain't this great?" Victor asked cheerfully, knowing full well to me it wasn't.

I nodded, a lie, one eye closed, and one eye open to a slit. My fingers clutched the rope reins as tight as they could. Beneath me, the great weight shifted back and forth. Any moment I knew I'd slide off and get trampled to death by those huge, flat feet.

The smell of the elephant was ripe and strong. The saddle we sat on was made of rough leather, stitched around with blue lacing. It was made for ordinary people, and so it didn't fit me or Victor right. The rope reins were just for show; we didn't have no control. A boy in a turban and bloomers led the animal, with us atop, through Sea Lion Park.

"I asked ain't this great, Mattie?" Victor's voice had lost a bit of its cheer. He didn't like me nodding or shaking my head to answer him. It had to be with words.

"I like it, Victor," I managed. I was already swooning, my head filling with thick cotton and my throat crawling with ticks. Victor knew how I was feeling. I heard his satisfied grunting next to me. Victor always liked what I didn't like. He liked that I didn't like those things he liked, because they made me feel faint and weak. When I got faint he'd scoop me up and hurry me off to our dime-a-day room behind Stauch's and have his way with me real hard.

The elephant continued along another minute. I clutched the reins and my feet strained to reach the stirrups. I tasted blood in my mouth where I'd bit my tongue. We wobbled around by the lagoon where Captain Boyton was doing tricks with noisy sea lions for a cheering crowd. The sun was hot on the saddle and on my arms, and the stale lagoon stunk like an East River fishing boat. I heard the snapping of the American flags in the August wind, brand new, crisp flags Boyton had hoisted along the perimeter of his park once he seen Tilyou had done the same over at Steeplechase.

Then the elephant stopped short. He snorted and shook off a nest of flies that had trailed him on our little ride. Victor pinched my shoulder again and both my eyes opened.

"What you waitin' for? Get off," he said.

The boy in the turban watched me slide off the saddle and onto the stone stepping block. He didn't help me off the block, as short as I was. Like most people, he didn't seem to care to touch a midget. And a midget with bandaged hands clearly had him nervous. The boy turned away, pulled a little flag from his waistband, and waved it in the air to draw in more customers. "Come! See! Ride Tiny the Elephant!" he shouted above the din of sea lions in the lagoon, the brass band outside the dance hall, the rattling of the Flip Flap car going up its lift hill, and the rumble-swoosh of the boats hurtling down the Shoot the Chutes. "Ride just like the kings of the jungle or the queens of the Far East! Only a nickel!"

Victor slid off Tiny on the other side, came around to me, and stood wiping his forehead and rubbing his nose. He was nearly as tall as the elephant's back, a good six-feet-eight or more. He was dressed in his everyday clothes—white shirt, blue vest, gray trousers and a bowler that had seen better times. We were "taking the afternoon off" as he liked to put it. Usually, he dressed like Abraham Lincoln and made me dress like a miniature Southern belle in white cotton mittens with blue embroidered flowers that covered my hands until it was time for the big unveiling which costs customers an extra five pennies. We performed along the Bowery six days a week, ten to twelve hours a day, up and down the lane to catch as many customers as we could. Victor called our act "Honest Abe and the Wee Woman of Lies."

I stood, wobbling, on the stepping block. My arms were wet beneath my shirtwaist. My forehead was damp beneath the band of my broad, flat brown hat. My skirt, which I had tried to keep unrumpled as Victor had shoved me up onto the elephant's back, was creased and plastered in pachyderm hairs. One of my stockings was torn. I needed to sit down to catch my breath. But Victor just whipped me up off the block and carried me out of Sea Lion Park like a bundle of laundry, and took me to our flat behind Stauch's for the rest of the afternoon's entertainment.

He didn't want me to catch my breath. This was how he liked me, when he liked me.

«« — »»

I liked Edward the Great. He was a midget, too, smaller than me by about two inches. He wasn't born with fused fingers the way I was. His hands were perfect and strong. He had a real job with a real regular wage as part of the Troupe Minuscule in Steeplechase Park. The troupe was made up of midgets and dwarves who did tumbling, magic, and impromptu tricks on those who came to see their performance. Their little theater was at the far end of the park, close to the beach and underneath the sharp southern turn of the Steeplechase course. Edward grumbled as to why Tilyou built the theater there because every four minutes the wooden horses would come flying down the tracks and around the bend, clattering like an angry giant's dentures. The walls of the little theater would rumble and shake, and it was almost impossible to hear what the troupe was singing or saying. But the audiences didn't seem to mind the interference. Who wants to hear midgets anyway? People want to see them, not listen to their little voices. The theater was decorated real pretty, with painted bench seats, a little raised stage, and electric lights strung along the ceiling. Colorful plaster flowers were all over the walls, making it like a fairyland except for that blasted rattling from above. I never seen it myself, but Edward had told me all about it. Edward did magic in the act. He made coins come out of ladies' ears and made hoops float in the air.

Edward and the troupe worked from ten in the morning until the park closed at midnight. But he got time off for lunch. Every day at two he would leave Steeplechase, buy himself a paper cone of clams on Surf Avenue, then come to find me and Victor along the Bowery. He would stand in the shadows near the door to a gambling hall or postcard shop, eating his clams and watching us perform our morality play to whoever was willing to part with a nickel.

Our customers were an odd and silly crowd, some factory girls, some college boys, some middle-aged farm couples with wide eyes and tight purses, others immigrants as green as snakes who couldn't understand a word we said. Victor told me that once Coney used to be the playground of the very wealthy, that the very spots on which the vaudeville theaters and the hootchy-kootchy tents and the postcard booths now stood once held elegant hotels, ballrooms, fancy restaurants, and bathhouses. But as the politicians and crooks got their sticky, fat fingers into them money pies, the whores and morphine traders and cock-fighters got a whiff and signed on for their own little piece of them pies. Some of them fancy hotels burned down or got tore down to make room for an array of the pavilions and amusements that the bosses now controlled. The rich folks ran out to Manhattan Beach, but every once in a while you'd see a couple of them tippy-toeing around, hoping to have half the fun the poor folks were having. Captain Boyton built himself Sea Lion Park in 1895, and put a fence around it to keep out the riffraff and pickpockets. Then Tilyou got the same idea and in '97 built himself Steeplechase Park the same way, filled with amusements and food and shows and wrapped up in a big old fence. They advertised that this was good entertainment for good, wholesome people, and it worked. It drew in church-going couples and families with children who now felt safe coming to Coney for a day.

Most families were cautious of the Bowery and the lanes, though. They stayed clear except to cross through to the beach. Sometimes children would stop to look at Victor and me in our costumes, and say, "Mama, I want to see them dance!" Horrified Mamas would tug on their childrens' hands and drag them down to the ocean.

Victor and me didn't work as many hours as Edward, but I think we worked just as hard. Victor wore a sign saying, "Hear the truth for just 5 cents!" At some point a man with a cigar in his teeth would wag a finger at Victor and ask to hear the truth. The customer was usually some old drunk or young boy trying to impress the new girl on his arm. Victor would straighten to his full height, tip his top hat, and say we needed five people to pay for the truth. Sometimes five others standing nearby would ante up nickels. Sometimes they wouldn't. Didn't matter, we'd do the show for five cents. Victor would put his hand inside the front of his Abraham Lincoln jacket, recite the "Four Score", a little bit of the Bible, and then say how, as Americans, honesty should be everyone's favorite virtue.

"Virtue brought the South to its knees and united our great Nation! Truth gave us the grace of God over other infidels in other countries!" he'd spout.

There would be a chuckle or two until Victor pointed at me, the Wee Woman of Lies. "Do you want to see what telling falsehoods can do? How it manifests itself in the soul and on the body?"

I'd raise my mittened hands on cue. There would be a short hush, followed by more laughter and someone saying, "Thought she was your daughter! What you got there?"

I'd tip my head up, and they'd see under my hat I was no girl but a grown woman of twenty-four.

A drunk might say, "I'd pay to see something else, sweetheart!"

I wouldn't reply to that. I'd recite in my best Southern drawl, which wasn't no good since I came from New Jersey, "My, my, I used to always lie, but one morn I awoke, I witnessed nature's joke. I was forever changed, my hands were rearranged, and now I bear the mark. A lie is not a lark."

Victor's fingers would strum the air, demanding another few nickels. By now, the folks were ready to see what was beneath my cotton mittens. A few more coins were deposited into Victor's coat pocket. Off came my mittens. There were gasps and sounds of disgust. After a moment, someone would ask to touch my hands. The touches were brief and awkward. The men—for it was never women wanting to touch—would spit and turn away. The show was done and the mittens went back on. We'd go on to the next corner, to the next, fresh batch of gay holidayers.

«« —»»

Victor and me met on Coney when I'd come to apply for a job with the Troupe Miniscule in May. I'd been working as a maid in New Jersey for a Mrs. Maude Anderson. I hated her and she hated me. I didn't have friends. There weren't any suitors my size. What did I have to stay for? I read in one of Mrs. Anderson's newspapers that Steeplechase Park was adding a new carousel, a giant seesaw, and a troupe of performing midgets for its '98 season.

Oh! I packed my bags faster than a horse gobbles grain, and bid Maude Anderson no farewell but only left a note saying she was a mean-hearted old widow and I was glad to be shut of her. I got to Coney a day later and went to see the park's manager. There was a whole line of midgets and dwarfs already there, waiting in cue in the early morning rain. There was a nice-looking midget who introduced himself as Edward. He bowed to me and produced a white carnation out of nowhere. I thanked him and put the flower in one of the holes in my hat.

When it was my turn to talk to the manager, I told him I could sing and dance. The manager was young and curt, with a sharp mustache and straw boater. He said, "Let me see those hands." I took off the wraps and he said, "We ain't got a freak show. Maybe Tilyou'd like a freak show. Let me ask him." I said I wanted to sing and dance not show off my hands. The man said, "Go away, then. Get yourself a job as a hussy on the Bowery."

I was angry. Angry enough to go without food for three days and to sleep under the pier. Then I met Victor, who had just lost his waiting job at Feltman's. He said he had an idea of how we could make money. I was too tired to argue. He still had his black waiter's jacket from Feltman's. He let his beard grow and bought a cheap top hat from a gambler he knew. Victor was good to me the first week or so, buying me ice cream and offering to pay my way up the elevator to the top of the Iron Tower to see the sights or to take a ride on the Switchback Railroad along the beach. I accepted the ice cream but not the ride up the Iron Tower or on the Switchback. My body, it can't tolerate heights.

By mid-June we were a show, me and Victor, making enough to pay for a cheap room, some food, and an amusement now and then. By the end of the month Victor was beating me when he got drunk and forcing me to go on rides I didn't want to go on. I tried to fight at first but he was so big it just wasn't no use. I'd just get banged up and have to go, anyway. The Iron Tower. The Switchback Railroad. Shoot the Chutes. I would close my eyes and get faint and then Victor would take advantage of me.

Victor got drunk almost every night. Then he'd go out to gamble. That's when I'd go out walking. I'd hide under my gray hat, hoping to be mistaken for a little girl, although there were men who wanted little girls instead of women. It was nice to be alone, when there was hardly nobody around except whores, sailors what hadn't gone to Cuba, and coppers on the take. The great rides were still and silent after midnight, poking up at the sky like skeletons of the dead begging to get into heaven. The air was sweeter. I could see the stars blinking down at me. Stars are magic, you know that? I read that people wish on them and sometimes their wishes come true.

By chance I met up with Edward one hot night in July out on the pier. We walked down to the beach together and stood in the waves where neither of us would dare to stand in broad daylight. I clutched the guide rope and Edward clutched me. Salt water and foam filled our mouths and hair. I fell in love that very night.

After that, I'd wait anxiously in bed every evening, pretending to be asleep until Victor left. Then I'd go out to be with Edward.

Our favorite spot was a little amusement shack called "Shoot the Babies". During the day, men paid to fire rifles at stuffed dolls made out of burlap. They looked like devil babies to me, those dolls, with painted eyes and pointed teeth. "Shoot three babies and win a prize!" was the sign on the front. At night, the place got locked up tight.

There was a shuttered window in the back of the shack. Edward could pick its lock without so much as a sound. Then he'd hoist me in and climb in after me. We'd lie on the sawdust and make love. Being screwed by Victor hurt. Making love with Edward felt like Jesus, God, chocolate, and everything else good rolled together. Edward even kissed my hands and held them to his face. The tingle in my heart made me know then and there that magic was real.

«« —»»

The Coney season ended in September. With fall coming on, Edward told me one time, the winds started to blow big and the air got brisk and frosty. Didn't nobody want to stay out riding coasters or eating ice cream in the cold. Boyton and Tilyou made enough money from May until September to cover theirselves real good until the next spring. The men who owned the independent shows and rides just hoped they'd make enough to open up the following year and not have to sublease their little plots to some other idiotic hopefuls. The Troupe Miniscule had to decide what to do for the next nine months. Edward suggested to Steeplechase's manager that Tilyou build a miniature, midget town inside the park where the troupe could live and perform throughout the summer and live and keep an eye on the park in the off-season. Tilyou wouldn't have to hire extra men to patrol when the park was closed. Wouldn't that be a good thing? Edward said. The midgets and dwarfs would do it all for room and board. The manager turned up his nose and said Tilyou would fire him for such a stupid idea and to get the hell out of his office.

Edward and I lay together in the dark of the shooting gallery one night during the last week of August. Edward wasn't his usual dapper self. He was tense and quiet. I undressed for him and unpinned my hair, hoping it would cheer him up. I rubbed my body against his, but he only lay in the sawdust with his clothes on, staring at a box of burlap dolls. I sat up and crossed my arms over my breasts.

"What's wrong?" I asked.

"Coney closes in a couple weeks. Got nine months ahead and no work," he said simply. "I would guess the same goes for you?"

I shrugged. "I don't know," I said.

"Haven't you been thinking?"

I hadn't been thinking. I knew the Honest Abe act would be over in September. I hadn't thought much past that. I guess I'd believed Edward would take me away somewhere nice.

Edward picked up a piece of gravel and threw it against one of the dolls in the box. It struck the doll between the eyes. "Winner," he said dully. "Where's my prize?"

"Edward," I said, pulling my clothes back on. I suddenly felt ugly out of them. "Aren't you going to marry me?"

He turned to me, and looked surprised. Then he smiled. "Dearest bird, I would love to marry you. But I won't have enough work to support a wife."

"I don't want you to support me. I've always worked, since I was six, cooking, cleaning, shoveling coal. Ain't nothing I can't do."

He took my face in his hands. "If I were a rich man I would carry you off and make you happy." Then his smile faded, and he said, "But there is your giant. He will not want to lose you, and the income you'll provide. I cannot fell a giant. He would snap me like a dry branch."

"What are you...?"

"I have been in the gambling halls at night after bidding you adieu," he continued. "I have hid in corners and listened to Victor's inebriated boasting of his plans for you."

"What plans?"

"He says he will rent you out to carnivals in the South. Florida. Georgia. Some place where the winter isn't so hard and the season runs longer. He's planned a new identity for you, my darling. He will bill you as the offspring of a woman who was mangled by the claws of a monstrous crab. And not only are you to be an exhibit, he says he will charge extra for customers to...to..." Edward stopped, rubbed his face, and said only, "He sees you as his slave, my heart, a beast of burden."

"Dreadful!" I said. I didn't mind being the Wee Woman of Lies, but wouldn't be rented or bartered for like no cow or mule! "I'd like to put him in a show," I growled. "I'd like to make him go where he don't want to go and do what he don't want to do! I would show him how it feels!"

"I know you would, Love."

"You got to save me, Edward!"

"He is a giant, Mattie. I am a midget. I am no David, yet he is surely a Goliath."

"Use your magic," I said. I put my hands on his chest and leaned my face against his vest. He was warm through the fabric. "Save me with your magic!"

Edward shook his head. "I have no magic. It's an illusion. It's fakery."

"No, it isn't. I've seen what you can do."

"And what can I do? Reveal a rose through sleight-of-hand? Create a brief distraction in order to pull a penny from someone's ear? That is all the power I have."

"Don't lie to me!"

"I don't lie."

"Don't...lie..."

"Darling, I don't lie."

I felt cold then, colder than I could ever remember. Colder than the winter night Mrs. Anderson banished me from the house to the barn for posing in her shawl in front of the mirror. If Edward would not—could not—do magic, what was to become of me?

"Edward," I said, pulling away from him, my head tipping forward and my loose hair covering my face. "I need you."

There was a long silence. Outside the tiny window, I heard late-night revelers in the lanes, singing lewd songs, throwing bottles against buildings, and belching. Victor might have been among them, bragging about the midget he would rent out as a freak and whore in Florida.

Then a hand brushed my hair back. Edward whispered, "I'll give you your magic, sweet. Do you hear me? I'll give you your magic. Come to Sea Lion Park tomorrow at eleven o'clock with your giant. I will meet you there."

I didn't know what Edward had planned, but I trusted him completely. And when I went back to our room, I found Victor already in bed and snoring. There was a naked woman sleeping next to him. Victor would have her to pester if he woke up, and would leave me alone. That might not be magic, but it was good, anyway. I curled up on the floor and slept.

«« — »»

"You want to go to Sea Lion Park?" Victor was not a little irritated. "Why you want to go there?"

I didn't know what to say, so I said, "I heard that Boyton is looking for new acts."

"New acts? What do you mean?"

"He's worried Steeplechase is taking in more money than Sea Lion. He wants to line up new acts for next season."

"I can't imagine Boyton'd want us. Tilyou wouldn't give me the time of day." He straightened the black bow tie at his neck, smoothed down his long black jacket, and stared at himself in the tarnished mirror on our wall. I stood at the window, staring out at the Bowery. The morning sun was already blindingly bright, painting the lane in swatches of orange and gold. Weary belly dancers, sluggish waiters, and rumpled boys who sold cigars out of shoulder boxes shuffled about, heading to their places of employment.

"It might be worth it, just to see?" I pressed.

"You're soft in the head," Victor scoffed. "Next year. Who knows next year?"

"It could mean regular money for us. Not only wages, but tips. People pay tips in the parks when they like something. Even the sea lions get tips. We could make twice as much, Victor."

There was only one thing Victor liked more than sex and drink and that was money. So he said, "All right. But let me do the talking."

Sea Lion opened its front gate at 10 a.m. Victor didn't want to waste a moment, so we were there with the rest of the mob, waiting to get in. A young man in an admiral costume appeared inside the gate a few minutes before ten but did not move until a gong sounded inside the park. Then he unlocked the gate and opened it wide enough to let one person through at a time. Each dropped a nickel into a tin box as they entered.

Victor tossed our nickels into the box and demanded of the admiral, "Where's Boyton?"

The admiral wrinkled his nose and said, "I don't know. Maybe his office."

"Where's his office?"

But the admiral ignored Victor, his attention moved on to the hoard pressing forward to pay.

Victor stalked on ahead of me, his head whipping back and forth above the crowd like an American flag in the wind. "Where's Boyton's office?" he mumbled. "Where's it at?" We walked around the lagoon, past the brass band, which was warming up with a slightly off-key "Yankee Doodle." There was the bloomered boy by the stone stepping block, tapping Tiny with his cane and calling for riders.

Victor strode up to the boy, grabbed him by the shirt, and roared, "Where's Boyton's office? Tell me now!"

"I…" said the boy, his neck straining up to look Victor in the face. "He got an office by the Flip Flap. But he ain't there now."

"No?"

"No, sir."

"Where is he, then?"

"He don't come until noon, when he does the first sea lion show. I'm sorry, sir."

Victor shoved the boy back and stormed off, heading toward the front gate, pushing against the crowd. I trotted after him. "What, we got two hours 'til we can talk to the man?" he called back over his shoulder. "We ain't leaving, then, until he comes. I ain't paying another ten cents to get in again."

I tripped on my skirt but caught my balance. A little girl nearby giggled as I stumbled, then stared hard at me when she saw my face.

"We're going to catch that fat yok when he comes in," shouted Victor. "We're going to impress the hell out of him."

"All right!" I shouted over the din.

We stood inside the gate until well past eleven. Victor didn't move a muscle, but stood with his arms crossed and his top hat perched on his head, staring at each and every man who passed through. I wanted to sit down. I was tired of studying faces. I was tired of the heat. Where was Edward? Where was his magic?

Suddenly, I was poked from behind with a stick. I whirled about to see Edward dressed in a frilly harlequin suit. I put my hand to my mouth, trying not to shout out or laugh. What was he up to?

Edward jabbed Victor in the back. Victor spun around, teeth bared, one hand lashing out as if to grab Edward by the throat. But Edward was quick. He leapt back with a manic laugh.

"Sir!" cried Edward. "I've a wager for you!"

"Go away, midget!" said Victor.

"A wager. Five dollars to you should you win."

"Get away before I break your neck."

But Edward only skipped and hopped, then poked Victor again with his stick.

"You little idiot!" Victor shouted, and he swung a fist at Edward. Edward jumped back again, then again, as Victor tried to strike him. I was surprised at how fast Edward could be.

"You want five dollars?" chided Edward.

"I want your stinking hide!" said Victor.

"Five dollars!"

Victor struck out again and missed. "I'll smash you to bits, you little demon, then have Boyton throw you out on your ass! We are Boyton's newest act, did you know? We're going to replace you!"

"I think not," said Edward. "As I'm Boyton's nephew."

Victor's fist froze in midair. "What?"

"Boyton's nephew, Randolph. He would never replace me, and not with the likes of you. Pah!"

For the first time since I'd known him, Victor was at a loss for words. I could guess what was rolling around in his brain. If he smashed the midget, as he so wanted to do, Boyton would never hire him. If he made good with the midget, which was an utterly repulsive idea, perhaps Boyton would give him a job.

Edward smiled and winked at me. I could feel the magic rising up.

"Okay, yes," said Victor, his nostrils flaring but his voice now calm. "I'd like to wager for five dollars. I wasn't really going to hit you, you know that?"

"I know what I know," said Edward. "Follow me!"

Edward lead us to the southwest corner of the park, where the Flip Flap ride stood like a steel cobra ready to strike. A handful of women with parasols and men in bowlers were gathered by its base, watching for any riders willing to have a go. The ride operator stood beside the track, dressed in a beret and striped shirt. His hands were in his pockets.

"Are you brave enough?" asked Edward, dancing on his toes. "If so, you shall win five dollars! If not, you will owe me a nickel."

Victor barked, "What bravery does it take, fool?"

I knew what bravery it took. The Flip Flap was a coaster ride, with a tall lift hill, a rapid steep decline, and then a tight circular loop through which the car would careen, held in place only by force and speed. Tiny had been frightening, the Iron Tower and Switchback Railroad had been terrifying, but I could not think of a word to describe the horror I felt when looking at the Flip Flap. I had heard rumors that people sometimes had their necks whip lashed in the loop, and were pained for days afterwards. It was no wonder more people preferred to watch than to ride.

"Five dollars?" Victor said. "Just to ride that contraption?"

Edward nodded.

"All right," said Victor. "Find the money, fool, for it will be mine in just a few minutes." Then Victor grabbed me by the hand and dragged me toward the Flip Flap car.

"No, Victor!" I shrieked. "I can't! It's too high, it's too fast! The loop...!"

"You go where I go," said Victor.

I looked at Edward hoping he would save me from the terror of the coaster. But he only grinned his harlequin grin. Did he not care for me, then? Didn't he love me anymore?

The ride operator situated us in the car, side by side. It was a tight squeeze for Victor to get his feet inside. The operator made some joke about never having such a tall man ride before, that he'd scrape the clouds at the top of the hill, but Victor just grabbed for the front of the car and said, "Let's go!"

I closed my eyes and Victor pinched me. "Open them!" he insisted. I opened them. The car began its ascent, dragged up the lift hill by clanking chains. With each clank my stomach bubbled and churned. My heart thundered and I knew it was going to bust right there in my chest. At the top of the hill there was a little turn, and then we were facing straight down and into the loop.

"Edward, help me!" I cried.

Victor looked at me as if to ask, "Who the hell is Edward?" when the car pitched violently forward and we were racing down the steel frame against the wind. My mouth opened to scream but the wind forced the sound back into my throat. My fused fingers clutched for something to hold, but there was nothing but Victor's arm and the side of the car.

We reached the bottom of the hill. Before us was the loop, and then we were in it. My eyes closed and I felt the sickening swoop as we followed its perfect circle up and around.

Then I knew. With my eyes shut, with my wrapped hands grasping for something to hold on to, with my stomach trying to fly out of my mouth, I understood Edward's magic. Yes! Yes! Victor would disappear in the circle! Like a vanishing pigeon in a red silk scarf or a coin from nimble, magical fingers, Victor would evaporate into thin air! Praise the Lord!

"Praise Edward!" I sang out as our car raced down and out of the circle. It made a left turn and then slowed at the end of the ride. My heart beat wildly, but no longer from fear. It was joy! Edward and I would be free!

I opened my eyes.

Victor sat next to me, his hat long gone, his hair plastered back, his mouth bobbing up and down as if he wanted to say something.

Edward's magic had failed.

"Damn," whispered Victor, though he didn't seem to be talking to me.

I was a fool to believe there was hope to be rid of Victor.

Edward ran up to us, and helped me out of the car. My legs tried to give out beneath me, but Edward held me tightly. His harlequin collar scratched at my face.

The ride operator tried to coax Victor out, but Victor didn't move.

"Hey, chum," said the operator. "Maybe somebody else wants a turn? What, you wedged in so tight you can't get out?"

Victor said, "I can't move."

"Ha!" said the operator. "Need a crowbar?"

"I can't move!"

And he couldn't. Seems that as tall as Victor was, his neck did not whiplash in the circle. It snapped completely. Under Boyton's direction, he was removed from the car by two strong men, and placed on a stretcher to get him out of the park quickly before others might see him and fear the ride wasn't safe.

«« — »»

Edward and I joined up with the winter carnivals in the South. We became quite the toast of the circuit, and were for many years. We made enough money to buy a little house outside of New Orleans. Edward even got a fishing boat. We billed ourselves as "Mr. and Mrs. Little and Their Big Baby Boy." Children and their parents loved our show! They thought it sweet that such little parents could love such a hulking child.

Victor couldn't do anything about it. He could only move his chest enough to breath and his head enough to eat and look around. We dressed him in a gigantic baby bib and bonnet, and pushed him about in an over-sized baby carriage. We'd stick a bottle in his mouth. That always made the crowds laugh. We told Victor if he ever complained during the show, we'd let him go without food or a changing for a few days. He never challenged us. He didn't dare.

Magic is everywhere. And I know it's real. 'Cause what is it, but the power that makes something happen that you want real bad to happen?

ITSY BITSY SPIDER...

The moon was high before Toby spotted the first one. A hairy hunter—the hunters only came out at night. He hadn't seen this one before. Big, but not thick and bulky like a tarantula. Its sleek body was the size of a German shepherd; its eight long, powerful legs spread half a dozen feet on either side, carrying its head and abdomen low to the ground. Moonlight gleamed off its short, bristly fur as it darted across the back yard, seeming to flow rather than run. Hunting, hunting, always hungry, always hunting.

A cool breeze began to blow through the two-inch opening of Toby's screened window. He shivered and narrowed it to less than an inch, little more than a crack. It wasn't the air making him shiver. It was the spider. You'd think that after a year of watching them every night, he'd be used to them. No way.

God, he hated spiders. Had hated them for the entire ten years of his life. Even when they'd been tiny and he could squash them under foot, they made his skin crawl. Now, when they were big as dogs—when there were no dogs because the spiders had eaten them all, along with the cats and squirrels and woodchucks and just about anything else edible, including people—the sight of them made Toby almost physically ill with revulsion.

MEGGAN C. WILSON & F. PAUL WILSON

And yet still he came to the window and watched. A habit...like tuning in a bad sitcom...it had become a part of his nightly routine.

He hadn't seen this one before. Usually the same spiders traveled the same routes every night at about the same time. This one could be lost or maybe it was moving in on the other spiders' territory. It darted to the far side of the yard and stopped at the swing set, touching the dented slide with a foreleg. Then it turned and came toward the house, passing out of Toby's line of sight. Quickly he reached out and pushed down on the window sash until it clicked shut. It couldn't get in, he knew, but not being able to see it made him nervous.

He clicked on his flashlight and flipped through his spider book until he found one that looked like the newcomer. He'd spotted all kinds of giant spiders in the last year—black widows, brown recluses, trap door spiders, jumping spiders, crab spiders. Here it was: Lycosidae—a wolf spider, the most ferocious of the hunting spiders.

Toby glanced up and stifled a scream. There, not two feet away, hovering on the far side of the glass, was the wolf spider. Its hairy face stared at him with eight eyes that gleamed like black diamonds. Toby wanted to run shrieking from the room but couldn't move—didn't *dare* move. It probably didn't see him, didn't know he was there. The sound of the window closing must have drawn it over. Sudden motion might make it bang against the glass, maybe break it, let it in. So Toby sat frozen and stared back at its cold black eyes, watched it score the glass with the claws of its poisonous falces. He had never been this close to one before. He could make out every repulsive feature; every fang, every eye, every hair was magnified in the moonlight.

Finally, after what seemed an eternity, the wolf spider moved off. Toby could breathe again. His heart pounded as he wiped the sweat from his forehead.

Good thing they don't know glass is breakable, he thought, or we'd all be dead.

They never tried to break through anything. They preferred to look for a passage—an open window, an open door—

Door! Toby stiffened as a sudden chill swept over him. The back door to the garage—had he closed it all the way? He'd run some garbage out to the ditch in the back this afternoon, then had rushed back in—he was terrified of being outside. But had he pulled the door all the way closed? It stuck sometimes and didn't latch. A spider might lean against it and push it open. It still couldn't get into the house, but the first person to open the door from the laundry room into the garage...

He shuddered. That's what had happened to the Hansens down the street. A spider had got in, wrapped them all up in web, then laid a huge egg mass. The baby spiders hatched and went to work. When they finally found the remains, the Hansens looked like mummies. Their corpses weighed only a few pounds each…every drop of juice had been sucked out of them.

The garage door…maybe he'd better check again.

Don't be silly, he told himself. Of course I latched it. I've been doing the same thing for almost a year now.

Toby left the window and brushed his teeth. He tiptoed past his mother's bedroom and paused. He heard her steady slow breathing and knew she was fast asleep. She was an early riser…didn't have much to stay up late for. Toby knew she missed Dad, even more than he did. Dad had volunteered for a spider kill-team—"Doing my civic duty," he'd said—and never came back from one of the search-and-destroy missions. That had been seven months ago. No one in that kill-team had ever been found.

Feeling very alone in the world, Toby padded down the hall to his own room where even thoughts of monster spiders couldn't keep him from sleep. He had a fleeting thought of the garage door—yes, he was sure he'd latched it—and then his head hit the pillow and instantly he was asleep.

«« — »»

Toby opened his eyes. Morning. Sunlight poured through the windows. A year or so ago it would be a day to go out and play. Or go to school. He never thought he'd miss school, but he did. Mostly he missed other kids. The spiders had made him a prisoner of his house, even in the daytime.

He dressed and went downstairs. He found his mother sitting in the kitchen, having a cup of instant coffee. She looked up when she saw him come in.

"Morning, Tobe," she said and reached out and ruffled his hair.

Mom looked old and tired, even though she was only thirty-two. She was wearing her robe. She wore it a lot. Some days she never got out of it. What for? She wasn't going out, no one was coming to visit, and she'd given up on Dad coming home.

"Hey, Mom," he said. "You should have seen it last night—the spiders, I mean. One crawled right up to the window. It was real scary; like it was looking right at me."

Fear flashed in her eyes. "It came up to the window? That worries me. Maybe you shouldn't sit by that window. It might be dangerous."

"C'mon Mom. I keep the window shut. It's not like I have anything else to do. Besides, it can't break through the glass, right?"

"Probably not. But just play it safe, and move away if one looks like it's coming near you, okay?" She grimaced and shivered. "I don't know how you can stand to even look at those things."

Toby shrugged and poured himself some cereal. They were running low on powdered milk, so he ate it dry. Dad had stocked the whole basement with canned and freeze-dried food before he left, but those wouldn't last forever.

When he finished he turned on the TV, hoping there'd be some news about a breakthrough against the spiders. The cable had gone out three months ago; news shows and *I Love Lucy* reruns were about the only things running on the one channel they could pull in with the antenna.

At least they still had electricity. The telephone worked when it felt like it, but luckily their power lines were underground. People whose power came in on utility poles weren't so fortunate. The spiders strung their webs from them and eventually shorted them all out.

No good news on the tube, just a rehash about the coming of the spiders. Toby had heard it all before but he listened again.

The spiders...no one knew where they came from, or how they got so big. Toby had first heard of them on the evening news about a year and a half ago. Reports from the Midwest, the farmlands, of cattle being killed and mutilated and eaten. Then whole families disappearing, their isolated houses found empty of life and full of silky webs. Wasn't long before the first giant spiders were spotted. Just horrid curiosities at first, science-fictiony beasties. Local governments made efforts to capture and control them, and hunting parties went out with shotguns and high-powered rifles to "bag a big one." But these weren't harmless deer or squirrels or pheasant. These things could fight back. Lots of mighty hunters never returned. Toby wondered if the spiders kept hunters' heads in their webs as trophies.

The Army and the National Guard got involved and for awhile it looked like they were winning, but the spiders were multiplying too fast. They laid a couple thousand eggs at once; each hatchling was the size of a gerbil, hungry as hell, and growing all the time. Soon they were everywhere—overrunning the towns, infesting the cities. And now they ruled the night. The hunting spiders were so fast and so deadly, no one left home after dark anymore.

But people could still get around during the day—as long as they stayed away from the webs. The webbers were fat and shiny and slower; they stretched their silky nets across streets and alleys, between trees and bushes—and waited. They could be controlled....sort of. Spider kill-teams could fry them with flamethrowers and destroy their webs, but it was a losing battle: Next day there'd be a new web and a new fat, shiny spider waiting to pounce.

And sometimes the spiders got the kill-teams…like Dad's.

Toby didn't like to think about what probably happened to Dad, so he tuned the TV to its only useful purpose: Sega. *NHL Hockey* and *Mortal Kombat IV* were his favorites. They helped keep him from thinking too much. He didn't mind spending the whole day with them.

Not that he ever got to do that. Mom eventually stepped in and made him read or do something "more productive" with his time. Toby couldn't think of anything more productive than figuring out all of the Mortal Kombat warriors' secret weapons and mortalities, or practicing breaking the glass on *NHL Hockey*, but Mom just didn't get it.

But today he knew he'd get in some serious Sega. Mom was doing laundry and she'd just keep making trips up and down to the basement and wouldn't notice how long he had been playing.

As the computer bellowed out, "Finish him!" he heard a cry and a loud crashing sound. He dropped the controller and ran into the kitchen. The basement door was open. He looked down and saw his mother crumpled at the bottom of the steps.

"Mom!" he cried, running down the steps. "Mom, what happened? Are you okay?"

She nodded weakly and attempted to sit up, but groaned with agony and clutched at her thigh. "My leg! Oh, God, it's my leg."

Toby helped her back down. She looked up at him. Her eyes were glazed with pain.

"I tripped on the loose board in that step," she said and pointed to the spot. "I think my leg is broken. See if you can help me get up."

Toby fought back tears. "Don't move, Mom."

He ran upstairs and dialed Dr. Murphy, their family doctor, but the phone was out again. He pulled pillows and comforters from the linen closet and surrounded her with them, making her as comfortable as possible.

"I'm going to get help," he said, ready for her reaction.

"Absolutely not. The spiders will get you. I lost your father. I don't want to lose you too. You're not going anywhere, and I mean it."

But her voice was weak. She looked like she was going into shock.

Toby knew he had to act fast. He kissed her cheek and said, "I'm going for Doc Murphy. I'll be right back."

Before his mother could protest, he was on his way up the steps, heading for the garage. The Murphy house was only a few blocks away. He could bike there in five minutes. If Dr. Murphy wasn't in, Mrs. Murphy would know how to help him.

He could do it. It was still light out. All he had to do was steer clear of any webs and he'd be all right. The webbers didn't chase their prey. The really dangerous spiders, the hunters, came out only at night.

As his hand touched the handle of the door into the garage, he hesitated. The back door…he *had* closed it yesterday…hadn't he? Yes. Yes, he was sure. Almost positive.

Toby pressed his ear against the wood and flipped the switch that turned on the overhead lights in the garage, hoping to startle anything lying in wait on the other side. He listened for eight long legs rustling about…but heard nothing…quiet in there.

Still, he was afraid to open the door.

Then he heard his mother's moan from the basement and knew he was wasting time. Had to move. *Now or never.*

Taking a deep breath, he turned the handle and yanked the door open, ready to slam it closed again in an instant. Nothing. All quiet. Empty. Just the tools on the wall, the wheelbarrow in the corner, his bike by the back door, and the Jeep. No place for a spider to hide…except under the Jeep. Toby had a terrible feeling about the shadows under the Jeep…something could be there…

Quickly he dropped to one knee and looked under it—nothing. He let out a breath he hadn't realized he was holding.

He closed the door behind him and headed for his bike. Toby wished he could drive. It'd be nothing to get to Doc Murphy's if he could take the Jeep. He checked the back door—firmly latched. All that worry for nothing. He checked the back yard through the window in the door. Nothing moving. No fresh webs.

His heart began to batter the inner surface of his ribs as he pulled the door open and stuck his head out. All clear. Still, anything could be lurking around the corner.

I'm going for Doc Murphy. I'll be right back.

Sounded so simple down in the basement. Now…

Gritting his teeth, he grabbed his bike, pulled it through the door, and hopped on. He made a wide swing across the grass to give him a view of the side of the garage. No web, nothing lurking. Relieved, he pedaled onto the narrow concrete path and zipped out to the front of the house. He scanned the front yard: clear. The only web in sight was strung between the two cherry trees to his left in front of the Sullivan's house next door. Something big and black crouched among the leaves.

Luckily he wasn't going that way. He picked up speed on the asphalt driveway and was just into his turn when the ground to his right at the end of the driveway moved. A circle of grass and dirt as big around as a manhole cover angled up and a giant trapdoor spider leaped out at him. Toby cried out and made a quick cut to his left. The spider's poisonous falces reached for him. He felt the breeze on his face as they just missed. One of them caught his rear wheel and he almost went over, almost lost control, but managed to hang onto the handlebars and keep going, leaving it behind.

Toby sobbed with relief. God, that had been close! He glanced back from the street and saw the trapdoor spider backing into its home, pulling the lid down over itself, moving fast, almost as if it was afraid. Toby started to yell at it but the words clogged in his throat. A brown shape was moving across his front lawn, big and fast.

Toby heard himself cry, *"No!"* The wolf spider from last night! It wasn't supposed to be out in the day. It was a night hunter. The only thing that could bring it out in the day was…

Hunger.

He saw it jump on the lid to the trapdoor spider's lair and try to force its way in, but the cover was down to stay. Then it turned toward Toby and started after him.

Toby yelped with terror and drove his feet against the pedals. He was already pedaling for all he was worth down the middle of the empty street, but fear added new strength to his legs. The bike leaped ahead.

But not far enough ahead. A glance back showed the wolf spider gaining, its eight legs a blur of speed as they carried it closer. It poisonous falces were extended, reaching hungrily for him.

Toby groaned with fear. He put his head down and forced every ounce of strength into his pumping legs. When he chanced another quick look over his shoulder, the wolf spider was farther behind.

"Yes!" he whispered, for he had breath enough only for a whisper.

And then he noticed that the wolf spider had slowed to a stop.

I beat him!

But when he faced front again he saw why—a huge funnel web spanned the street just ahead of him. Toby cried out and hit the brakes, turned the wheel, swerved, slid, but it was too late. He slammed into the silky net and was engulfed in the sticky strands.

Terror engulfed him as well. He panicked, feeling as if he was going to cry or throw up, or both. But he managed to get a grip, get back in control. He could get out of this. It was just spider web. All he had to do was break free of these threads. But the silky strands were thick as twine, and sticky as Krazy Glue. He couldn't break them, couldn't pull them off his skin, and the more he struggled, the more entangled he became.

He quickly exhausted himself and hung there limp and sweaty, sobbing for breath. He had to get *free!* What about Mom? Who'd help her? Worry for her spurred him to more frantic squirming that only made the silk further tighten its hold. He began shouting for help. Someone had to hear him and help him out of this web.

And then a shadow fell over him. He looked up. Something was coming but it wasn't help. The owner of the web was gliding down from the dark end of the funnel high up in the tree, and oh, God, she was big. And shiny black. Her abdomen was huge, almost too big for her eight long spindly legs to carry. Her eyes, blacker spots set in the black of her head, were fixed on him. She leapt the last six feet and grasped him with her forelegs.

Toby screamed and shut his eyes, waiting for the poisonous falces to pierce him. *Please let it be quick!* But instead of pain he felt his body being lifted and turned, and turned again, and again. He was getting dizzy. He opened his eyes and saw that the spider was rolling him over and over with her spindly legs, like a lumberjack on a log, all the while spinning yards and yards of web from the tip of her abdomen, wrapping his body in a cocoon, but leaving his head free. He struggled against the bonds but it was useless—he might as well have been wrapped in steel.

And then she was dragging him upward, higher into the web, into the funnel. He passed the shriveled-up corpses of squirrels and birds, and even another spider much like herself, but smaller. Her mate? Near the top of the funnel she spun more web and attached him to the wall, then moved off, leaving him hanging like a side of beef.

What was she doing? Wasn't she going to kill him? Or was she saving him for later? His mind raced. *Yes. Save me for later.* As long as he was alive there was hope. Her web was across a street…good chance a kill-team would come along and clear it…kill her, free him. Yes. He still had a chance…

Movement to his right caught his eye. About a foot away, something else was hanging from the web wall, also wrapped in a thick coat of silk. Smaller than Toby—maybe the size of a full grocery bag. Whatever was inside was struggling to get out. Probably some poor dog or raccoon that got caught earlier.

"Don't worry, fella," Toby said. "When the kill-team gets me out, I'll see you get free too."

The struggle within the smaller cocoon became more frantic.

It must have heard my voice, he thought.

And then Toby saw a little break appear in the surface of the cocoon. Whatever was inside was chewing through! How was that possible? This stuff was tough as—

And then Toby saw what was breaking through.

A spider. A fist-sized miniature of the one that had hung him here emerged. And then another, and another, until the little cocoon was engulfed in a squirming mass of baby spiders.

Toby gagged. That wasn't a cocoon. That was an egg mass. And they were hatching. He screamed, and that was the wrong thing because they immediately began swarming toward him, hundreds of them, thousands, flowing across the web wall, crawling up his body, burrowing into his cocoon, racing toward his face.

Toby screamed as he had never screamed in his life—

«« — »»

And woke up.

He blinked. He was paralyzed with fear, but as his eyes adjusted to the dawn light seeping through the window, he recognized his bedroom and began to relax.

A dream...but *what* a dream! The worst nightmare of his life! He was weak with relief. He wanted to cry, he wanted to—

"Toby!" His mother's voice—she sounded scared. "Toby, are you all right?"

"Mom, what's wrong?"

"Thank God! I've been calling you for so long! A spider got into the house! I opened the door to the garage and it was there!"

The back door! Oh, no! I didn't latch it!

"It jumped on me and I fainted. But it didn't kill me. It wrapped me up in web and then it left. Come get me free!"

Toby went to leap out of bed but couldn't move. He looked down and saw that he wasn't under his blanket—he and his bed were webbed with a thick layer of sticky silk. He struggled but after a few seconds he knew that he was trapped.

"Hurry up, Toby!" his mother cried. "There's something else in here with me all wrapped up in web. And it's moving. I'm scared, Toby. Please get me out!"

Panicked, Toby scanned the room. He found the egg mass attached to his bedpost, a few inches from his head, wriggling, squirming with internal life, a many-legged horde of internal life.

We're going to end up like the Hansens!

"Oh, Mom!" he sobbed. "I'm sorry! I'm so *sorry!*"

And then the first wolf spider hatchling broke free of the egg mass and dropped onto his pillow.

Toby screamed as he had never screamed in his life.

But this time he wasn't dreaming.

The Questions of Doves

A Brackard's Point Story

It was warm enough to have the kitchen window open. Carma and I sat at the table, scanning the paper and talking over orange juice. Mourning Doves asked sorrowful questions from the cherry tree out in the backyard: *Oooh-weee? Ooh? Ooh? Ooh?... Oooh-weee? Ooh? Ooh? Ooh?*

They built a nest there, took turns watching over the eggs. They, like us, were starting a family. Perhaps they asked the same unanswerable questions we did of ourselves and each other at the time: *Is the baby going to be okay?—do we know what we're getting ourselves into?—are we going to be good parents?—will they grow up to despise us?—will they have a better shot than we did in life?* Questions, always questions. No answers ever forthcoming.

Carma threw the paper down in disgust, asked if I heard about the bank robbery.

I had. It happened less than a half-mile from our home, down at the bottom of the hill. Two tellers were killed. She passed me the paper. I scanned the article. No leads, nothing new.

"That's messed up," I said.

"Messed up? I'll say. What's it all coming to, if you can't even go to work without getting taken out?"

GEOFF COOPER

SHIVERS III

At the mention of the last word, our mutt, Rhea, stood up from under the kitchen table, placed her paw on Carma's lap and whined.

Carma laughed, rubbed Rhea's ears. "I wasn't talking to *you,* silly."

Now, of course, Carma *was* talking to her—and so Rhea began to bounce and grin and wag her tail even more. She ran, toward the door, then back to us. Then back to the door.

"Oh, God," I said. I had not yet finished my orange juice, did not much feel like walking her. Of course, I would wind up doing it anyway.

Carma was five and a half months pregnant at the time. She *could,* of course, walk Rhea. The physical activity of walking the dog around for a few blocks would not put undue stress on her or the baby, but I felt an obligation to do trivial things like that for her—especially since she became pregnant. I am sure a shrink would read deep into my behavior and come up with some psychobabblic one-hundred hundred-eighty-dollar-per-syllable diagnosis to explain my behavior. I had a simpler one: I loved her, and wanted to help out. Just not before I fully awoke.

"Can't it wait?" I asked the dog.

Rhea cocked her head at me, came bounding back from the door again. She jumped up, placed both front paws on my lap.

"I'm taking that as a 'no,'" I said. "All right, fine. Fine. Just let me finish this and get my shoes on, okay?" I stood, polished off the last swallow, and went to find my sneakers.

"Hey, why don't you take her down to Xelucha's?" Carma suggested as I tied my laces. "That way you can get one of your frou-frou coffees, get her a doggie treat…"

"And oh…let me guess…get you one of the scones, right?"

Carma had developed a thing for Xelucha's scones right about the time she became pregnant. Going there was becoming a daily occurrence. Could be worse, I supposed. She did not ask for anything disgusting like caviar, pickles and ice cream, or asparagus. I would have fetched these things for her too, if she asked, but would have been less enthused about doing so.

"Well, being as you brought it up…if you don't mind. You know. While you're getting your frou-frou coffee and all."

"Ain't much frou-frou about a 20 ouncer with 4 shots of espresso slung on top," I countered. Carma was right, though. One of my friends in San Francisco got me started on this whole ridiculous latte thing. From time to time, I have spent five dollars on a single cup of coffee but I did not like to admit it. Not when you walk into your average Starbucks, and see a bunch of 19-year-old kids writing poetry on laptop computers. I tried to disassociate myself from such idiocy, but I still liked those quad-shot coffees.

"Whatever," Carma said. "But if you go, can you get my scone?" Her scone. Already claimed. It was a foregone conclusion that I would return with one.

"Maybe," I tried to say with a straight face.

She pouted. "Pleeeeze?"

I would. Of course I would. She carried our baby. I could deny her nothing. She could have asked me to walk Rhea up to Buffalo and come back with some of the town-famous chicken wings, and I would have done so cheerfully, but I still said, "maybe."

I was not going to admit I was completely pussywhipped, even if we both knew it was true. I had standards to maintain, after all. I was shop foreman at this little 6-bay garage on the corner of Lake Road and Route 9W in Congers. The responsibilities were sometimes a drag, but after fifteen years in the business, it was finally starting to work out. I had to work Saturdays, because they were generally the busiest, but got Sundays and Mondays off. No one else at the shop got two days in a row. At work, I was top dog—and the top is a nice place to be. It would have been great to be top dog at home too, but a guy could not have everything. So I was a little mushy—big deal. I had it good and I knew it.

Carma was the afternoon deejay at WRLK, *The station that puts the* Rock *in Rockland County.*" While on air, she was "Carmen Miranda," and always hung up on people after saying, "You have the right to remain silent." At home, she was my Carma. And she was pouting at me to go get her a scone from the café.

"Of course," I said. "Anything else?"

"Nope." Her put-on pout evaporated into a grin. "Go walk The Dogma."

Dogma...that was her name for Rhea. The Dogma. She was The Carma, the dog, The Dogma. Tacky? Silly? Perhaps, but it was our thing. You had to be in the relationship to appreciate or understand—only then would it make perfect sense.

As soon as I grabbed the leash, The Dogma bounded toward the door. I clipped her on, gave Carma a kiss, and stepped outside into the unseasonably warm morning. It felt as if a late spring day had gotten lost in the calendar's inexorable march, and somehow wound up on a Monday in late October by mistake (wrong turn at Albuquerque, perhaps?). We walked, listening to the constant questions of doves.

A little girl was walking in the same direction—toward the café. The girl followed The Dogma and I for two blocks as we made our morning rounds: *stop, sniff here, squat there.* I thought the girl must be meeting a friend nearby to walk with to the schoolbus stop. She was maybe eight or nine, with beautiful auburn hair and a pink jacket. Under her arm were tucked a few textbooks. In the other hand she carried a small brown paper bag.

Rhea saw her too, thought she was wonderful. The Dogma loved kids—boys, girls, no difference to her. To Rhea, kids (whether they were friendly or not, the loving, trusting fool she is) were cooler than a fresh puddle of St. Bernard pee. The girl was too far away to play, so Rhea let out a doggy sigh and continued on, every so often looking back to see if she had caught up with us and entered petting range.

We were halfway down to The Café Xelucha when it happened.

A bird swooped down from nowhere. Literally: nowhere. Not from the rooftops, or an overhanging tree branch; it was as if it materialized out of the very air it traveled through. I was watching the girl walk quickly up the sidewalk toward us while Rhea paused to sniff a mailbox. One instant, above her head, there was nothing—the next, a cruel little bird that squawked and chattered insanely as it nipped and clawed at tender, pale skin.

I watched, momentarily stunned, as the bird looped back for another run. I could see its sharp little beak and black, shiny eyes honing in on her. Again, it attacked. The girl flung her books across the sidewalk to cover her face with her arms. The brown bag lunch sailed onto a neighboring lawn as she curled into a small ball. A small, auburn-haired little ball with a pink jacket that screamed.

Rhea let out a single "wuff," and her hackles stood on end. Her tail wagged slowly, sweeping the ground in a low, wide arc. Her every muscle quivered tight—a wound spring at the end of her leash. *Unclip me,* her stance said. *Unclip me. I'll get that bird.*

I'm not nuts. I've had my dog since she was a puppy—I know damn well what she wants when she wants it. If I have to explain, well...you've never loved a dog—it's as simple as that.

I unclipped her leash.

When she heard the release's metallic *click,* she lurched forward, then turned to look at me: *is it all right?*

I snapped my fingers, pointed toward the bird.

The Dogma ran. Forty-five pounds of goofy mutt barreled up the sidewalk.

The bird swooped and dove, clawed at the little girl's neck and shoulders, ripped away small parts of delicate, pale skin. With each piece, it squawked in triumph. End the thrill of the chase. Begin the joy of the kill.

Allow me to say that Rhea's predatory instinct has long been domesticated. The Dogma has never won a fight—not with another dog, not even an ornery cat. She has never won because she *always* backs down. Aggressive? *Her?* The idea is laughable. At most, she would bark and growl and carry on like she's Queen Badass, until someone stands up to her. Then, she'll immediately duck for cover, tail between her legs.

Rhea is a nice dog. She's a sweet dog, a good, loving dog, but she's a whimp. Once, when she was a pup, a cat rose its hackles and hissed at her. Rhea rolled on her back and peed herself as she whined pathetically. My old neighbor, Tracy Phillips, had this little tiny pound-and-a-half thing with pop-eyes and a ridiculous underbite. I called it a rodent on a rope. Tracy, however, *insisted* the butt-ugly creature was a dog. Once, she had me wait while she went inside to retrieve her AKC book so she could show me its picture. It had a *pedigree*, she said, and was quick to offer the papers of its lineage up for my inspection. I declined, because to my way of thinking, that thing's papers did not make it anything other than an *expensive* rodent on a rope.

Regardless of its species, this...creature, I guess you would call it, growled at Rhea (who could, even then, chomp it down in one bite), and the big doofus hid behind me, thumped Morse Code for "Please don't hurt me" on the ground with her tail.

Considering her lack of aggressiveness, the way she launched herself at that bird, four feet off the ground, a picture of grace and power in the air, impressed the Hell out of me. I nearly clapped as she snatched it in mid-flight, thought for a moment that I ought to paint her tennis balls black and give them little wings, because she can never catch those: they would *bonk* right off her head. It actually looked like she was a natural, there, for a moment—as if she knew what the Hell she was doing. That moment, she was Defender Of The Pack, saving The Pup from The Enemy.

The Enemy—the bird...

Birds are fragile—light, hollow bones. There is really not much to them.

Rhea killed it. Her jaws cracked the bird in half. When she dropped it on the ground, it lay folded back upon itself. She nosed it around. Her long tongue smacked against her rubbery lips, as if she had a bad taste in her mouth or a feather stuck between her teeth.

The bird did not move.

I turned toward the girl. "It's all right, honey. It's okay."

She did not rise. For a moment, she merely sat there, sobbing. Several scratches and small chunks of skin were missing from her neck. Against her pale skin, her blood was bright. Too bright. Too bright and too much of the wrong shade of red with her auburn hair and that glaringly pink jacket. All that red everywhere, but this shade—her blood—clashed horribly.

Rhea was sad because the girl cried. She whined, head down, walked in nervous circles. She crept forward, licked the girl's hand, until I heard this magical, soul-warming laugh.

"Yikes! It tickles!" the girl said. Both her little arms flew out, clamped The Dogma in a tight hug.

Rhea yelped, backed away, tail between her legs, head down low. I thought the girl hugged Rhea too hard, maybe pinched her collar. I stepped around to soothe The Dogma's nerves with a comforting pat. Her muscles quivered beneath my hand.

Re-enter the wuss, I thought.

"You're dopey," said the little girl, and giggled when Rhea cowered from her high, sweet voice.

She was not telling Rhea anything new. I was just glad to see the little girl was all right. I clipped Rhea's leash back on. She did not notice at all. Usually, Rhea would look up at me when she heard the click of the latch, but not this time. She stared at the girl's face, and shook.

The girl's face rose toward mine. She looked at me.

The eyes Rhea saved…

My mouth went dry. They were *black.* Pure black, impossible to distinguish between iris and pupil. There was no white in them; they were two dark holes in the upper third of her face. I tried to look away. I wanted to look away. I could not. I had no choice *but* to look. To see.

Silence between us, as I stared into the dark windows of its soul. My lungs locked around the breath I took, would not let it go. I would have welcomed a shiver, but could not move.

It spoke: "I need my books."

There were two voices. The little girl's for the ears, and the one that resonated with irresistible power deep within parts of my being long thought vestigial and dormant. The command could not be ignored. I gathered the books from the neighboring lawn, the sidewalk. I straightened the pages and readjusted the dust covers before I handed them over.

"Good dog," it said.

Not to Rhea.

It laughed that beautiful laugh cleverly disguised as a little girl's, rose, and skipped down toward the bus stop.

It looked both ways before it crossed the street.

Two Mourning Doves asked their eternal question: *Oooh-weee? Ooh? Ooh? Ooh?* from the power lines overhead. As that thing with auburn hair and a pink jacket approached, they asked again: *Oooh-weee? Ooh? Ooh? Ooh?*

Black, soulless eyes squinted at the birds overhead. It shifted its books under its arm and whispered a single word in answer.

They fell, dead as stones.

It looked back at me and said: "It's a girl."

Our baby. I knew she was talking about our baby. We did not know the sex. We did not *want* to know. Both Carma and I wanted to be surprised. They asked us when we had the ultrasound if we wanted to know whether we were having a boy or a girl. We told them no, we did not wish to know at the time. It was a private question, one we often pondered, but did not want answered until its time came.

We certainly did not want it answered by this little bitch standing over the corpses of two doves. Part of me wanted to strangle her, but that part was put in its rightful place by intense, irrational fear. I thought that if I touched her, my flesh would rot on my bones, if she chose it to do so.

"Going my way?" she asked, as she nodded up toward the café. Her body posture was nothing short of lewd.

Rhea and I backed up a few steps. Going her way? Not likely. "The fuck are you?" I asked.

Rhea tugged at the end of her leash to draw me further away.

"Omega and Alpha. The last and the first."

That's backwards, I thought. *Isn't it the other way?*

Revelation came back to my head and realization flashed across my face. She saw the comprehension settle in my features and snickered.

"My God…"

"Not yet."

It snickered as I backed away.

Rhea's self-preservation kicked in, and by virtue of holding her leash, I was to be taken with her, whether I protested or not. I did not, was merely too overwhelmed to react appropriately without a bit of assistance. She lurched, yanked my arm as she tried to flee. Her toenails scraped the sidewalk as she strained on the end of the leash, her collar dug into her neck. I could hear her starting to choke, yet still she tried to drag me away.

By the time the thing's snicker became a full-fledged laugh, I had joined in with Rhea and bolted for the house. Having only two legs, I could not move fast enough for The Dogma. She dragged me along the sidestreets to the perceived safety of our home.

I hurried to open the front door, Rhea looked back to see if it had followed. I could not bring myself to glance over my shoulder. I was afraid I would see it there. As soon as I opened the door, both Rhea and I rushed into the living room. I slammed it, locked the deadbolt behind me—something I *never* do during the day. I stood, back to the locked door and tried to regain my breath as Rhea sat at my feet. We both panted—she less so than me.

"Back already?" Carma asked from the kitchen.

It took me a moment to catch enough wind to answer her. "Yeah," I said. "I…I didn't go. To the cafe."

I heard the tap water shut off. "Why not?" she asked as she entered the living room. After she looked at me, she asked, "What's wrong?"

"I just…" Just what? *Just ran into the weirdest frigging thing I've ever encountered, and by the way, honey, we're having a girl? The antichrist told me so. Sorry about not having a scone for you, sweetie. It kind of slipped my mind…* I let the sentence die.

The more Carma looked at me, the more her face softened from annoyance to concern. "What happened? Are you all right?"

"Yeah," I lied. "Just kind of freaked out, is all." That's me: master of understatement.

"You didn't see *them,* did you?"

"Who?"

"The guys that robbed the bank?"

"The bank?" It took me a moment to figure out what the Hell she was talking about. I'd forgotten all about reading the paper with her—though it happened less than twenty minutes before. "Oh! The bank! No. Don't worry. It's…nothing. Seriously."

She gave me *the look.* Every man has been on the receiving end of *the look* before. I don't care *who* you are—you've tried bullshitting your way around some sort of obstacle, and a woman—your mom, your wife, your sister, the chick at the return counter at S-Mart the day after Christmas—pulls her head back, points her chin down, arches an eyebrow, and looks at you with a stare so powerful, so sharp and penetrating, that it slices through your bullshit and taps on the guilt center of your brain. Only women can master this look. I have often wondered if they taught that stare during sex education at school, when we were taken into another room and given a list of reasons why good little boys did not leave the toilet seat in the upright position.

I did my best. I held my ground for 3.2 nanoseconds before I told her everything that happened.

Carma, of course, thought I was out of my fucking mind.

The rest of the day, conversation between us was brief in verbiage and shallow in depth. *"Do you* really *want a scone?" "No, it's okay." "What's wrong?" "Nothing."* Shortly after noon, she announced she had to do some errands. When I inquired *what* errands she had to do, she said, "Oh, just stuff."

I gave her my version of *the look,* but it failed. Instead of spilling the proverbial beans, she collected her wallet, checkbook, and car keys, and told me she would return around dinnertime.

Alone in the house, I sat on the couch and pretended to be interested in the television commercials and the shows that accompany them while Rhea curled up next to me and slept. I made myself a pot of coffee, and, as I went for the fourth refill, I felt a pressure building in my bladder that required release.

I left the toilet seat up.

After another half-hour of watching television commercials, Rhea nudged me with her nose. She wanted to go back out.

The Dogma apparently did not remember the events of the morning. I did, thus was less than enthusiastic about taking her for another walk. She, however, was persistent, and—I shit you not—gave me *her* version of *the look.* I'm telling you: it's a female thing. And Carma was— according to the thing with the pink jacket—carrying a girl. I began to feel vastly outnumbered.

"Fine," I said, and put on my shoes.

Rhea tugged my arm, as usual, as soon as the door was opened. We stepped out off the porch into the driveway. It had cooled down, almost October again. The doves had either tired of asking the unanswerable or received a response that satisfied their curiosity. I hoped it was one they liked hearing, if that was indeed what had happened.

Carma's Saturn was parked behind my pickup.

I froze.

She took her car keys. I remembered her taking them. I tried to think back, see if I remembered *hearing* the car depart. I could not be sure. I placed my hand on the hood. It was cool. I looked inside the driver's side window.

The keys were in the ignition. Carma's pocketbook lay spilled across the passenger's seat and floor, as if it were hastily cast aside. A tube of her lipstick lay half-buried under a single smooth feather.

A thousand scenarios crowded my mind, choked out all thought. A thousand envisioned horrors strobed through my vision all at once, and my head began to spin. Numbness slid through my veins, sluggish and cold. I stood, dumbfounded, dimly aware of Rhea on the leash as she walked in nervous circles, holding onto the car's roof for support.

I stood there, head down, eyes closed, to steady myself. A moment or two passed before I opened my eyes and looked around. Should not have wasted the effort: my yard revealed no clues to Carma's whereabouts. I scanned the hedge, down along the fence, moved my head so I could see a little bit more of what might lie behind the cherry tree. There were no birds in sight, no sign of the thing in the pink jacket. I called for her, *"Carma? Carma?"* but knew as soon as I heard the question in my voice she would never answer.

Keeping an eye over my shoulder, I led Rhea back into the house. Once there, I forced myself to calm down. I did not want to sound like a lunatic when I called the cops. I told the operator that my wife was missing—vanished from my driveway. I told her about the feather and the way the purse was scattered over the Saturn's interior. I told her Carma was thirty-one, pregnant, that she was five-five and, at least before she was pregnant, a hundred twenty-five or so (even if Carma owned up to only a hundred fifteen of them). I told the operator everything—almost.

The cops came and looked over the car, then asked their questions. They were suspicious, grilled me as if I were a suspect. Asked me if there was anyone—a former lover, perhaps—that I could think of that might abduct her. I told them no. They asked if I—or she—had received any threatening, anonymous phone calls. I told them no. They finally left me with a business card to use in case something came to mind (an insinuation I resented), and with the feeling that I had wasted valuable time.

By then, it was well past dark. Dinner time had come and gone. I paced all over the house, muttered to myself and wrung my hands. Rhea thought I was nuts, and hid under the desk.

"She ain't coming back," I said to the dog.

Rhea peeked out, looked at me with large, sad eyes.

Then again, she looks at me with large, sad eyes when I'm holding a stew bone. She's a dog. They do that.

Thump.

My first thought was someone threw a rock at the window. I ran over there—thinking that it might be Carma, wanting to be let in and not having her keys, or that it might be the little bitch in the pink jacket, and I could get my hands around her delicate neck and start crushing. I was wrong.

A dove stumbled around on the outside of the window sill. It looked dazed, terrified. Large eyes pleaded with me from the other side of the glass. It opened its beak wide, and screeched. At first, I thought it would fly away soon after—that the screech was something out of pain, or that it felt threatened by me lunging for the window as I did, but it did not fly. It stood, favoring one leg, and continued to screech.

From the cherry tree in my back yard, I heard a terrible cackling of chirps and caws. The branches hung heavily with thousands of grackles. As one, they left their perches and swooped down toward my window. Angry eyes and screaming beaks, lice-covered feathers obscured my view. I thought they would all attack the window, throw their bodies at it until the glass shattered and the house was theirs, but their plan was not that at all: they fell on the wounded dove, flybys with extended talons, dive-bombing beaks.

The hurt dove fell off the window sill to the yard below. I saw it scrambling on its back as it tried to right itself and failed. Its only protection was a few blades of grass. It had no chance. The grackles ripped it to shreds in moments.

The Dogma was going nuts. She stood on the chair, barked at the birds on the other side of the glass, teeth exposed, ears as erect as she could get them, her eyes intense and wide. The sense of *deja-vu* was beyond strong: it was overpowering. Maddening. Dog barking, birds screeching…dead doves this morning and one mutilated by the beaks of its brethren in my yard, my wife and daughter gone, this thing in the pink jacket…

"Fuck it. Go get 'em!" I said, and ran across the room to open the front door.

She was standing on my porch, waiting for us. She smirked, giggled to herself. "May I come in?"

I growled. Rhea ducked behind me. "Where is she?"

"Oh. You want to discuss her, do you? Your girlfriend?"

"Wife," I corrected, but with the sense that I was being played. This little bitch knew I was having a girl—surely she knew Carma was my wife. "Where is she?"

The birds ceased screeching in the yard by now, and had all settled in behind her: an army of a thousand Grackles in neat ranks and files on my front lawn. A few could barely contain their bloodlust. With clicks and chirps, they hopped from foot to foot. Blood spattered on their beaks. Bits of wet meat clung to their sharp claws. They tittered and cawed and each bird's black, soulless eyes were fixated upon me.

The only difference between their eyes and their master's was the skull that held them.

"Let me in."

That voice struck a chord deep inside my being. I took one step aside for her to pass, but Rhea growled and blocked my retreat. She would not let her in. I took courage from my mutt, who had apparently found her backbone yet again.

"No. Where's my wife, you little bitch?"

"You kiss your mother with that mouth?"

I drew back my fist, and was ready to break this little-girl-thing's nose when the birds rustled their feathers as one. Rhea, from behind me, let out a single, low growl.

"Where's Carma?"

The thing in the pink jacket laughed. "Carma…*ha*! How adorable. This is your pet name for her, Carma, yes? Oh, how *quaint*! How *dear*!"

"Fuck you. What did you do to her?"

"I did nothing."

"Lying to me…"

"I repeat: I did nothing to her. I only gave her a dove and asked if she could love the dove as much as she did you. She lied. So she's gone. She did it—not me."

"Where did you take her?"

"I took her nowhere. She lied. *That* took her."

"Oh, fuck this," I said, and stepped toward her. The birds behind her rushed forward to meet me. The Dogma barked a barrage of canine fury and snapping teeth.

Glaring up at me with those black eyes, the thing in the pink jacket waved her hand, signaling her troops to fall in line. They obeyed.

"You want to find her?"

"What do you think?"

"Then take this," it said. "Take this dove and answer me: can you love this dove as much as you do your wife? Answer carefully, for that is the only way you have a chance of finding her."

I did not see the dove before, but I was becoming accustomed to such minute shifts in reality. Like the brown bird from this morning, it was not, then, it was. I wondered if the bird attacking her this morning was a friend of the doves somehow, or if it was all a setup.

The dove cooed, and fluttered toward me. I reached for it, but before it could land on my outstretched arm, Rhea leaped, and snatched it in mid-flight. She chomped and I heard the breaking of hollow bones as she thrashed her head from side to side. Blood slung out of the dove's chest to stain wing, carpet, and muzzle alike.

"Rhea, no!" But instinct had her, and its command could not be dissuaded. I fell to my knees, tried to steady her by force, but she wriggled out of my grasp. Another moment later, she dropped the dove. I watched it fall from her mouth to the floor. There, I watched it shift from a matte grey to a dull black. It was no dove. My eyes had deceived. It was a Grackle, and it let out these tiny cries of either hatred or pain as the malevolent lights in its eyes faded.

I reached for the bird, but Rhea snapped at my hand. She'd never done that before. Ever. So shocked was I that I lunged backward at the cost of my balance. I fell on my elbows, stared at my dog in surprise. She leaned over her kill and panted, but showed no signs of aggression as long as I made no move toward the dead bird.

"Dumb fucking dog!" the thing in the pink jacket said, and stepped closer to the threshold of my home. "Let me pass."

Rhea snarled.

"I said *move*," the thing's voice lowered four octaves at the last word, and rumbled with dark power. Legions of birds outside tittered and cawed.

They stared at each other—my dog and the pink jacketed thing. Rhea did not retreat. The little bitch did not advance. Three, four, five heartbeats passed, and neither moved.

"Stupid animal," the thing said, and flipped its auburn hair back over its shoulder as it turned to face me. "Put her away and let me in."

"I can't."

"Can't? Can't? You can't even tell your dog what to do? Did your bitch wear the pants in the house or what? Let me *in*."

Yes, Carma wore the pants in the family. I was only the Top Dog while at work. At home, I was there for Carma and our baby, and Rhea. Now that Carma was gone, I guess Rhea was top dog.

"You'll have to ask her," I said, and pointed to Rhea.

Rhea showed her fangs, dared the thing in the pink jacket to step through the door.

It did not get a chance. I slammed the door in its face and engaged the deadbolt.

It stood outside and screamed for a while, demanding to be let in, but I ignored it. The Dogma and I went back to the couch, to the television and the commercials, and increased the volume. I did not turn the sound up to drown out the thing on my doorstep. I did it so the thing on my doorstep would not hear me crying.

Rhea pissed on the carpet sometime that evening. I was not about to take her out. She did not even bother whining. Instead of sleeping on the couch with me, she curled up at the front door.

They were gone by morning. Only a few stray feathers and a bunch of bird shit on my pickup's windshield remained.

«« —»»

Carma—and my baby's—disappearance broke my heart. I've sat up countless nights since then in tears, wandered down every street in this town looking for her, most of Starson, Congers, and Nyack, too. Got jumped once on Franklin Avenue. Rhea bit the guy's arm. That's the fourth time she saved me.

It's been a year—she's still gone. Rhea is still here.

If I ever find my Carma (a hope that is dim, at best), I know the first thing out of my mouth will be: "What did you answer?"

I like to think I could believe her. My Carma would never lie to me…would she?

Would she?

The nest in my cherry tree is abandoned. I do not know what came of the eggs. I wonder if the Grackles got to them.

Some days, as I'm having my coffee and petting The Dogma's ears, I hear the Mourning Doves. They call from trees, power lines, elsewhere in the neighborhood, but not my backyard anymore. It sounds as if they're asking a question.

Oooh-weee? Ooh? Ooh? Ooh?

It sounds as if they suspect the answer is not one they want to hear.

SHIVERS III

Oooh-weee? Ooh? Ooh? Ooh?
What did you answer, Carma?
What did you answer?

Originally published under a different title and in an altered form as "Walking the Dogma: A Brackard's Point Story," in *Darker Dawning II: Reign In Black*, Dark Dawn Industries, 2002.

This is the first time the story has been published in this form.

HEDGES

I thought, *Will I finally belong?*

I passed the boy at dawn on my bicycle. He was standing in the middle of the road, his backpack slung over one shoulder, the way students do. He was reed-thin and tall, a little hunched at the shoulders, with a cranberry colored baseball cap on backwards. Grinning slightly, ironically—again, the way students do.

There was no danger of hitting him, but I wondered why he was standing in the middle of the street. Then I saw the school far ahead on the left, set back off the road, in the middle of a cleared field. There were lights on in the windows that looked like they had burned all night. They may have been bright in the darkness but now, with the sun rising behind the school, they looked defeated and dim. After giving me a smirk as I passed, the boy slouched toward the school.

I peddled on.

Before the school on either side was a short packed line of small houses, bordered by a thick hedge. Suddenly the dawn was banished back to night. Overhead were crouching, overarching oak trees, their branches brushing like the fingertips of lovers.

The hedges grew thicker to either side, a wall

AL SARRANTONIO

of April green buds on winter-sharp branches. It was dark gray as midnight, and the air had cooled. I was suddenly tired, and I slowed, and then the bicycle, urged by my slowing, tilted to the right and leaned me over against the hedge.

It held me, pricking, a wall of sharp sticks and tiny faintly perfumed wet buds, and I heard a faint voice I could not make out. It sounded like it said, *Yes*. The voice was very close. I pushed myself away from the hedge, my hands sinking momentarily into it, branches scratching, and something else, something that felt almost liquid and very cold, drew over my hand and then away.

I pulled my body back in disgust and fumbled at the bicycle, which caught against my straddling leg and again moved me over into the hedge.

The voice was right next to my ear, whispering, *Yessss*.

I flailed back, pushing my left foot against the bicycle pedal as I straightened the machine with a scrape and pushed off, back out into the road—

A car passed, close by in the gray darkness, horn bleeting. Its lights were dimmed, swallowed by the encroaching gray, and a pale oval face, hairless, lit with a green inner light, peered out at me from the rear window as it drew roaring away.

The hedge was next to me again.

I heard the whisper and felt cold pushing toward me and lurched back, dragging the bike sideways, making its tires scrape with complaint. My feet fumbled and found the pedal and then I was off again, straightening the front wheel.

But now in the grayness I saw the hedge narrowing in front of me.

I began to fight for breath.

The oaks had disappeared overhead and the hedge had grown up around into a crowning arbor. The air was chilled, damp, sick-sweet smelling.

The hedge narrowed into a closing dead end; I heard beyond it the fading roar of the car I had seen with the pale green face staring—

I thrust my feet backwards against the pedals, making the bike stop with a screech, then forced it around. Already the hedge had grown down from above, almost touching my head.

It was narrowing on all sides ahead of me, like a closing wedge.

With a shout I hit the pedals hard, keeping low, and shot through the narrowing opening even as it closed. I felt the scrape of budding branches like grasping bony fingers on me, and smelled something wet and lush and fetid, and heard what sounded like a sigh—

Gasping for breath I tore ahead, blinded by sudden sunlight. Ahead of me on the left was the school, its windows filled with rising sunlight now, the field in front of it full of milling students.

The loud blare of a horn made me stop short; in front of me was a school bus grinding to a halt, its brakes squealing. The driver was shouting at me behind the huge windshield set into the massive yellow front.

In a daze, I moved the bicycle off to the curb as the school bus ground into gear again. The driver glared at me as he drove past, then pulled into the long driveway toward the front entrance of the school.

I looked behind me.

The street, dappled in tree-shaded new morning sun, stretched straight behind me, lined to either side by a row of neat houses, cape cods and cute ranches. There was no sign of a hedge as far as the eye could see.

In the far distance was a cross street, a busy one by the look of the traffic at the intersection.

I felt a tap on my shoulder.

"Wha—"

An equally startled face peered back at me: a crossing guard, an older woman with a white cloth bandolier across her jacket holding a small red stop sign.

"I'm sorry," I began. "I'm new here, a Chemistry teacher, I start today—"

"You could have been hit by that bus," she said, concern and scolding in her voice. "You were tearing along in the middle of the street—"

"Can I ask you something?" I interrupted. "Has there ever been a long row of hedges in the street back there?" I pointed to the spot from which I had come.

"Hedges?" She looked confused.

"I'm sorry," I said, and began to pedal away, turning in toward the school. "I'll be more careful."

"Do that," she said, the scolding tone coming back into her voice. "There are children around here, you know…"

«« —»»

"So how did it go?" Jacqueline asked, with, as always, neither concern nor interest in her tone. A fresh vodka tonic in a clear tall glass lay on the kitchen table before her. Beads of cool perspiration freckled the glass. She did not offer me one but instead sipped her own, looking out the kitchen window to the backyard, a riot of green trees and untended bushes.

"About as expected," I answered.

"You mean like all the rest?" There was a undercurrent of venom in her voice now. *I told you so* and *I knew it* and *Here we go again*, her tone said, without her saying it.

I tried anyway. "Have you ever felt, Jacqueline, that you just didn't fit in? The children in this school are even worse than normal. They didn't show any interest at all. It was like I was talking to thirty sacks of potatoes. And the Vice Principal was almost unfriendly. I have the same bad feeling, Jacqueline. Just like all the other times. Like I don't belong. Haven't you ever felt that way?"

She sighed heavily, and turned her near-perfect face, framed in long black hair, slowly away from the window toward me. She pinned me with her violet eyes. "I've *always* belonged, Howard. The only question I've ever asked myself is why in hell I married you."

I opened my mouth but she turned her attention back to the window and her drink.

"The back yard needs tending," she said, tonelessly. "Every one of these houses we've rented, in every one of these rotten little towns, always has an overgrown backyard. This one's worse than the rest. Do something about it."

I said nothing.

As I turned and left the kitchen she called out casually, "I'm going out for dinner. There're TV dinners in the freezer if you want something. And I'll need the car again tomorrow."

««—»»

The next day was no better. When I entered the classroom all the desks were facing the back of the room. The day before, every student had been staring intently at the ceiling, which made me look, too. The boy in the cranberry colored baseball cap was among them. From that moment on, when they all broke into laughter, they had me. Today was no better. I should have made a joke, but nothing came to mind.

I tried to teach the day's lesson, to ignore them, but instead they ignored me, kept their desks turned around.

Soon they began to talk and joke.

The chalk trembled in my hand. I closed my eyes, leaned my forehead against the cool blackboard and then turned around, trembling with rage.

"This isn't right!" I stammered hoarsely, but they ignored me.

I dropped the chalk and walked out of the classroom.

The assistant principal was there in the hallway, and I almost ran into her.

"Having a bit of trouble?" she asked, and I couldn't help but detect the near-disdain in her voice.

"Yes. I—"

She moved around me and stuck her head in the classroom door.

"That's *enough*!" she shouted. "Get those desks back where they belong!"

There was instant quiet, followed by the shuffling of moving furniture.

The assistant principal confronted me again in the hall.

"Just treat 'em like animals," she said, giving me a smile that told me what she already knew: that I wasn't capable of treating them like animals, or anything at all.

She turned on her heels and marched off.

When I walked back into the classroom the talking began again. By the end of the period they had all faced their desks toward the back of the classroom once more.

«« — »»

I took a different route home, the same I had ridden that morning. There had been no trouble then, but this time as I left the school behind me, turning my bicycle into a wide street with houses set well back on manicured lawns, a wall of hedges suddenly thrust up in front of me. I drew to a stop. The wall was rushing like a living wave toward me. I turned my bike only to see another behind me. To either side the houses began to disappear, sharp green buds pushing out from their trim fronts, doors and windows and shutters, devouring them. The hedge drew in on me from all sides. I felt cool wet green and smelled rich oxygen.

"*No!*" I shouted in panic.

There was a driveway to my right, still clear of obstruction, and I drove the bicycle that way, the hedges closing in on me as I did so. As the driveway reached the side of the house branches pushed out of the siding toward me. The house disappeared in a blanket of green. The hedges pushed the bike to the right, where another wall of green awaited me. I felt the caress of soft buds and a whisper in my ear.

Yesss...

I screamed, driving the bicycle forward. There was a free-standing garage in front of me bursting into green before my eyes, the hedge closing in from both sides in front of it. But there was a slim opening to the left leading to the backyard and I peddled fiercely at it, pushing through as the branches like cold hands sought to pull me in—

And then I was through the suffocating hedge, the bike shooting forward into the clear backyard and toward a well separated line of forsythia bushes which marked the backyard boundary between houses.

I stopped, skidding on the grass, and turned around.

The house was as it had been—neat, trim, unblemished by green limbs and tiny leaves.

The hedge was gone from the driveway, from the far street.

I turned and dismounted the bicycle, rolling it through a gap between forsythias and into the abutting backyard and then to a new street and eventually home.

‹‹‹—››

I tried one more time.

"I just don't fit in."

Jacqueline laughed. "You've never fit in," she said, her voice slurred, and then she laughed shortly again. "And I do mean that in every way."

She was disheveled, the front of her dress buttoned incorrectly. She had obviously had much more to drink than the vodka in front of her. Her lipstick was smeared and her eyes unfocused as she bobbed her head around to regard me.

She smiled.

"I'll need the car tomor—"

"Have you ever felt physically smothered?" I asked, ignoring her.

She looked at her vodka tonic. "All the time."

"No, I mean physically. For *real*. Like everything, everything you've tried and failed at, your whole life, all your unhappiness, was literally closing in on you. As if…hedges, actual green hedges, were pushing you in from all sides and wanted to swallow you whole—"

It was her turn to interrupt. She laughed and then hiccupped, then brought her drink to her lips before putting it down again.

"Harold, you *are* a moron." She got unsteadily to her feet, forgot the drink, pushing it aside. It tipped over and fell from the kitchen table, breaking in a pool of clear liquid and glass shards.

She moved past me unsteadily, pointing languidly at the refrigerator.

"TV. Dinner," she said. "I'm…out. Need the car…tomorrow. Ride your bike again…"

She walked to the front door, leaving it open behind her, and in a few moments I heard the car door slam and then the engine start.

In the empty house I looked out through the kitchen window at the backyard, overgrown with weeds and bushes and what looked for a moment like a rising tide of hedges, which abruptly vanished.

‹‹‹—››

I took a third route the next morning. After Jacqueline had left the night before, the assistant principal had called and told me the school had decided it wasn't working out and that I should not continue teaching.

Would I please come in the next morning to sign some papers and pick up a check for two day's work.

The new route was out of the way but clear. In effect, I was riding in a wide circle to get to the school. As I turned onto an unfamiliar street which would bring me back in the right direction, the boy with the cranberry colored baseball cap was crossing the street in front of me.

He leered at me as I went by and shouted, "So long!"

I put my head down and rode faster.

When I brought my head up, I gasped.

"No!"

Hedges were pushing in at me from all sides, and the sky was quickly blacking out from a lowering cloud of green.

Buds burst from the street below me, snarling the spokes of the bicycle and then stopping it dead.

Branches twined around the handlebars, the seat, yanking the bike out of my grasp.

I felt a cold wet touch slide across my fingers, my face.

Yessss.

When I tried to scream, hedge shoots snaked over and up my body and deep into my mouth.

I was pushed onto my back and lifted in a cocoon of branches and leaves.

I gagged, and then the voice sounded close by my ear.

You don't understand.

I continued to thrash, to fight, watching the last glimmer of the world, a tiny hole of blue sky, blotted out above me by a tiny green wet leaf.

Think...

"No—!"

And then, suddenly, as if a switch had been thrown in my head, I *did* understand, and I stopped fighting.

"Yes!" I cried.

The hedge enclosed me, into itself.

Yesss.

My fingers are cold and wet, with green fresh buds at the ends.

I belong.

THIS, AND THAT'S THE END OF IT

Madsen kept visiting the hospital two weeks after his mother was dead. He'd get halfway through the main doors and see the security guard's shoulders hunch up beneath his tightly-fitted gray uniform. The two tiny Asian nurses at the administrative desk would whisper and watch closely, all eyes and long black hair and immaculately pressed bleached uniforms, and Madsen would suddenly remember he wasn't supposed to be there and turn around.

He'd wind up facing the massive five-tiered parking structure across the street, trying to remember where he'd left his Mustang. The snow continued to fall and was already nearly six inches deep, with plows and sanders coming through the area every fifteen minutes. They didn't help much and you could hear the sound of harsh crushing slams of metal striking metal from the highway overpass a couple of blocks away.

He watched the ambulances, police cars, and people huddling around their own dying children. Some kind of a bomb scare in the pediatric oncology ward had forced them all to congregate in the main lobby, but the dining area had closed hours ago. Kids in wheelchairs, left with only clots of burnished hair, throats and chests swathed in

TOM PICCIRILLI

bandages, sat wide-eyed as the cops poured past. Madsen looked up at the windows of the north and south wings and sucked air through his teeth, wondering what he ought to do.

The bomb squad didn't seem put out by the fact that he stood along with everybody else. German Shepherds trained to sniff out C4 sat barking at the terrified mothers trying to keep warm in the overcrowded waiting area. Nurses in sweaters flitted past carrying coffee cups around the corner of the building.

He stepped outside and let the roughly hewn moonlight slam across his back. The snow swirled around his feet and he tried hard to find something to do, at the moment and with the rest of his life. Madsen couldn't quite remember who he'd been before his mother had become so ill, and everything ahead remained hazy, foggy. It annoyed the shit out of him. He'd once had a distinct goal that seared fiery outlines into his dreams, but in the last few days it had faded until he couldn't remember what it had even been. A sense of relief was marred by the vague feeling of regret.

A young cop stormed past, giving him the slow once-over. Around twenty-two, new to the uniform, with a blond buzz cut and an aura of self-importance. Madsen cocked his head curiously, knowing a confrontation was inevitable.

"Who are you?" the officer asked.

"Madsen," Madsen said.

"Do you have a kid here?"

"No."

"Then clear out. What are you doing?"

He still didn't have an answer, two weeks later. He had nothing to say for a second and then it came to him. "My mother just died."

"What room?" the cop asked.

"What the hell difference does it make?" Madsen said, feeling the warm anger flood his belly. It brought back some calm and then there he was, ready for whatever might happen next.

"You should leave, sir, there's been some trouble."

The cop vanished around some vending machines and a dog wandered closer, nosing into Madsen's crotch. One of the kids giggled and his mother, a broad lady with features as bland as a shopping bag, shushed the boy. Madsen winked hoping he didn't appear to be a child molester. He held the back of his fist out to the dog and one of the bomb unit guys pulled the animal away and stomped down the hallway.

Tires scraped against spikes of jagged ice, coming off the exit ramp, and another screaming ambulance appeared at the corner, swaying as it turned too sharply and clipped the curb. Madsen took a step towards the doors as if he might…what?…protect anyone near him. Sometimes you acted without realizing the meaning behind the movement, or how stupid it might be. The ambulance slowed and coasted past, heading around to the other side of the building. The emergency room.

His stepbrother Bobby had died four weeks earlier and Bob's ex-wife still hadn't so much as notified a mortuary yet. They'd only hold the body for another few days, Madsen remembered, and then...what the hell would they do? He wasn't sure whether he should bother going and claiming it himself, giving the name of *Chapey's Funeral Home*, half a mile up the road. No matter what you thought you knew, the art of dying proved how incompetent you were.

He walked back across the lobby and the guard perked up once more. Madsen ignored him and went to the elevators. He already knew where the morgue was because he'd missed his mother's death by forty-five minutes and been forced to say his good-byes while she lay on a gurney shoved up against the wall. Chewing through his tongue and trying not to be distracted by her nakedness beneath the sheet, with her eyes a quarter of the way open, scowling at him.

He got in and pressed the button, held himself in the corner while the elevator lurched to a stop and the doors opened.

The lights were dim down here, one end of the corridor being remodeled. Wires hung in a colorful lump from the ceiling and a wooden ladder stood with stained cans and tools placed on every other step. He hadn't seen a wooden ladder in years and it reminded him of his father, the man's thick hairy arms speckled with paint. Yellow caution tape had been strung across the width of the passage.

Madsen decided to go the opposite way and continued along the corridor past half-open doors until he reached an empty desk blocking the vestibule. Like in high school, some monitor asking you for a hall pass.

A woman appeared in the room beyond, staring through the doorway at Madsen without any expression. Not a nurse or doctor, just a middle-aged lady wearing a prim brown business suit and tan shoes that didn't go. Jesus, maybe she really did want a pass, a doctor's note. *Please excuse Johnny from algebra, he has to go pick up his brother's remains.* Her pursed lips were covered in a heavy wax lipstick, the kind women didn't wear anymore. Madsen almost liked the look, mainly because it was old-fashioned and made him think of when he was a kid and his parents threw big holiday parties.

"Yes," she said abruptly, as if answering a question he hadn't asked. "And why are you here?"

The offhand, curt manner of the woman drew him forward another two steps until his knees were pressed against her desk. "My brother. Robert Harrington."

"Yes?"

"His body is still here. I'd like to make arrangements."

"How so?"

"If you'll let me use the phone I'll call information, get the number of *Chapey's*, and finalize details."

"And you are...?"

So it was going to be like that.

A shudder went through him as he tried to find a more patient resolve, not clamber over the side. "His brother."

"I'll need to see identification."

He pulled his driver's license and laid it on the metal desk top that was so shiny it startled him to see his face, the reflection of his own hand coming up at him.

"Just a moment, please," she said.

"Sure."

She disappeared into the room beyond, where he watched the shadows play against the open door but never saw anybody go past. He waited, realizing that he wasn't supposed to be here and had, for reasons unknown, thrown the place out of sorts by showing up. Sometimes all you had to do was breathe to ruin somebody else's day.

But on occasion you could take pride in being the stranger who's willing to cross a line, even if you didn't see it there or know what it meant to be on the other side.

It took her fifteen minutes to return with a small box.

"Mr. Madding?"

"Madsen."

A capped tooth impatient leer, as if he spoke his name only to be difficult. "Oh, I'm terribly sorry. Mr. Madsen then. You say you're the brother of the deceased?"

Okay, he was about to be pressed to another wall. That was fine. You almost got used to it. "Yes."

"But his name is Harrington. Robert Harrington."

"His step-brother."

"You said *brother*."

What did these people know about blood, really? "His step-brother. He has no other family."

"I was told there was a wife and children."

Who the hell was there to tell her that? Mom on her deathbed? "An ex-wife who doesn't care and two teenage sons who don't know him."

"I'm sorry, but they are the immediate kin and we can't—"

"What's in the box?"

She drew her chin back until it almost stuck out the other side of her head. "His ashes, of course."

"But—"

Since when did the hospital cremate bodies, and without so much as a signature from somebody? Madsen's back teeth ground together as he looked at her again, taking further stock. She enjoyed his puzzlement, comfortable and squarely settled in that knowledge of all matters of mortality. Working in a morgue could make you feel like the queen of the dead.

"I'm afraid you simply don't have the authorization needed to—"

"Sure."

His hands flashed out in a blur of motion and he had the little box. The significance of his brother's history had been obliterated down to less than three pounds.

Madsen walked around the desk, past the waxy lady and into the room. He expected to see shining steel drawers packed row upon row with corpses, jars filled with clear liquids and cancerous mutant organs. He thought there would be eyes watching from the tops of shelves, optic nerves still attached.

Instead, the room was empty except for well-catalogued files and envelopes and trays of bone dust, a scale and a phone on top of the counter. Flourescent lights hummed above and made the edges of Madsen's vision burn brighter.

No windows down here, nothing to do with Bob's remains unless he turned around and made a break for it. Madsen just wanted to get rid of the ashes and be done. The responsibility wasn't his and perhaps he shouldn't have taken it in the first place. Let them dispose of the man however they saw fit, what difference did it make to Bobby?

But maybe it did. Too late to back off now, Madsen's course had been set by his frustration. His scalp began to prickle and the heated rush of blood filled his cheeks. Chilly sweat stood out on his upper lip and along his hairline. He wanted to apologize but the lady wasn't even in the room with him.

"Hello?" he called. "Listen, I—"

That just made it worse, she was probably already calling security. He had to move in some direction, do what needed to be done. He pulled open the lid and poured his brother's ashes among the contents of all the other trays, a little at a time. Let Bob make some new friends, get taken home by other folks because his own family didn't want him and never had, alive or dead. It was good enough, and maybe the gesture would mean something later on.

Madsen spun and saw the woman turning the far corner of the hall beyond the caution tape. What'd she do, hop it? Her footsteps echoed down the corridor with a stern uncompromising cadence. He moved to the elevator and hit the button, wondering if a couple of guards would be ready to take him in the moment the doors opened. It perked him up, thinking of that. The muscles in his arms and back tensed. He wanted someone to test him in some capacity, whatever it might be. A beating would be all right, so long as it took a while.

When the elevator arrived it was empty. Madsen relaxed and both his shoulders cracked loud as gunshots. He climbed in and hit the button for the lobby. The doors slid shut just as the lady down the corridor called, "Mr. Madding?...did you...?"

"Thanks!"

In the lobby, dog fur floated past on the draft as snow piled in through the main entrance, the electric doors held open by thick rubber wedges while the police and families spoke quietly together.

Madsen left the hospital, crossed the street and hunted around the mammoth parking garage looking for his Mustang. He spent forty minutes roaming around the place and couldn't spot the car. It happened to him every time he'd come to visit his mother while she was sick—getting lost here for an hour or so before making his way home. But this felt different. He had no memory of where he might've parked the Stang and finally had to rest against a railing. He crossed his arms tightly against his chest, trying to hold in the confusion. Bobby would've been making jokes the whole time, drinking from a flask and eyeing every woman who passed by. The moment lengthened until Madsen wanted to let out a growl. The urge was more powerful than he'd expected and it panicked him some.

Madsen couldn't quite decide whether he ought to just leave the Mustang and call a cab or keep looking. In this weather it would take hours to get a taxi, if anybody could get through. He moved to the stairs and kept heading up until he was on the top tier and could look down at the rest of the area. The blizzard had grown much worse even while he was searching for his car. No cabs would be coming out tonight. He could see the cars stacked up along both sides of the highway, some alone and others crushed together in mangled black masses that were already partially covered.

He wasn't going home.

The walk back across the street to the hospital seemed a failure of some sort, as if he couldn't let go of the place even now that his mother was buried and his brother ashes had been...liberated. They were both gone so why couldn't he leave? The question came down to *When the fuck am I going to get out of here*?

He stood in the middle of the road, staring at the upper floors of the hospital as the snowdrift heaped against his knees. If there had ever been a reason for him to keep coming back, maybe he'd find it tonight. Sometimes you only had to think you had a larger fate than going back to the apartment and eating mac and cheese in the glow of basic cable and it might come true. If you believed enough, maybe you could force the issue.

Trouble was he could never believe in anything that much. By the time Madsen started moving again he was nearly buried where he stood. His hair was covered with ice crystals and he finally noticed his nostrils were freezing over.

Inside again, and the bomb squad had finished clearing the area. The kids were allowed back to the pediatric oncology wing but most of the parents and doctors still didn't feel safe and just stood around wondering aloud who'd play such a sick joke. The guards and nurses at the administrative desk had switched out and new faces peered at him. Somebody gave Madsen a Styrofoam cup of lukewarm coffee. He drank it without thinking and wandered off again.

He'd done this a lot while his mother lay dying. Like everyone here, he didn't exude much of a physical presence and he knew it. You didn't speak in these halls, didn't walk as upright as you normally would. The overbearing weight of illness made almost everybody gape at the floor and speak in whispers. You didn't make much eye contact, and when you did it was fleeting and sort of shameful. You hated the doctors and their shortcomings and mistakes and money, and they hated you for not dying quietly or quickly enough.

Madsen glanced down to see he was still holding the empty cup. There was no place to throw it away so he crumped it and stuck it in his pocket. He had no idea where he was and looked at the wall to see a green line running parallel to a red one. What'd that mean? He thought he'd walked up at least one flight of stairs. Christ, had he been this bad before his mother had gotten sick?

An explosive crush of noise burst from ahead. People walking quickly away, not running. He waited and saw a couple of the bomb squad dogs tearing down the passage followed by more young cops. He stepped back to the wall and watched them go by. The hell? It was like in high school when you were out on the soccer field and a thunderstorm made everyone rush back into the gym. The teachers wouldn't know what to do and you'd just hang around the place, hop on the vault, girls dancing in the corner, fights breaking out on the wrestling mats, guys making chicks under the bleachers, finding your friends on one side of the room, eyeing your enemies and waiting.

So there he was staring after them when he inched around another corner and a squat guy with powerful arms spun toward him, holding a pair of needle-nose pliers and wire cap connectors. A custodian, somebody doing electrical work. Pants riding too high, showing off old brown socks, even though they hung low on his thick hips.

"Now what's happened?" Madsen asked.

"There's been another bomb scare."

"Christ."

"This time in ICU. They're trying to evacuate all the patients but most can't be moved. Besides, where they gonna go? There's a blizzard out."

Madsen used to think of things like this while he sat with his mother, rubbing her hand. He always figured there'd have to be some kind of precautions set up to deal with troubles like these—power outages, a hurricane. But really, what could anyone do? How could they move people in the last hours of their lives, seven IV drips pumping into their bloated bodies?

"Is there anything I can do to help?" Madsen asked.

It caught the custodian wrong and he started to glare, putting heat into his cloudy eyes. They could really turn the poison on when they wanted to. "Who are you?"

"I'm—"

"Why are you here? You'd better go. Go on."

There was nothing to argue about so Madsen left, watching more police sprinting past him. None of the cops seemed to even notice him, and it made Madsen want to say something. Hold up a hand, ask if they could even see him.

His mother had been in ICU at the end, where he held onto her bruised and yellow arm, with the firm and frightening resolve that if he should let go, for a moment, she would leave him. The monitors kept careful scrutiny of her dwindling heart rate while the respirator forced jerking, heaving breaths into her lungs.

The IV drips—seven of them—filled the room with the sounds of water torture. The anticipation in waiting for each new drop drove Madsen into a silent rage. Every so often someone at the other end of the floor would burst out in a low groaning laughter until Madsen wanted to get up and strangle anybody he could find. You could easily lose your mind on the deathwatch.

It was almost a blessing—a kindness—that Bob had died first, and quickly. Cirrhosis of the liver and Hepatitis B had taken a strong grinning womanizer with a scotch in his hand and, within a few months, stripped him down to an angry alcoholic bleeding from the ass. Bob wore adult diapers with pants three sized too big, but he never let go of the bottle.

Madsen hadn't been around much at the time and had missed most of the transition, but he'd caught the tail end of Bobby's descent. His stepbrother on the busted couch, sallow and scrawny and scheming against his own children. His ashes, at least, hadn't smelled of booze and sour milk.

"Hello?"

You had to find your solace where you could.

"Hello?"

Madsen looked down to see a girl, maybe twelve years old, touching his wrist. Tufts of course gray hair stuck out in odd cusps and notches across her otherwise pink and scabbed head. She still had chubby cheeks though, and her hesitant smile brought out a heaviness of lines from the corners of her face. Bandages swathed her throat and forehead.

"Yes?" he said.

"My father—he hasn't come back." The dark angles of her ardent face drew together to form an exhausted shadow. She swooned and Madsen had to leap forward to catch her as she collapsed. He felt all the dense layers of gauze wrapped around her tiny frame beneath the bed shirt. He scanned the corridor for a doctor, hearing the dogs barking somewhere distantly, but saw no one.

"Hey!" he shouted toward the nurse's station, except there wasn't a station there. No one had ever been around for his mother either, except in the middle of the night when they huddled close, trying to explain to him, in mostly indecently placid tones, why she was dying.

"I'm sorry," the girl told him. "Sometimes I forget I can't walk too far anymore."

"Let me help you back to your room."

She pointed to the doorway and he hefted her into his arms. Maybe seventy pounds. She snuggled there for a second, chin pressed into his chest, while he tried to hold onto the moment knowing it was already gone. He placed her in bed where three sets of heavy sheets were carefully peeled back to reveal her small but deep indentation on the mattress.

"He left to get our car. From before. When we were supposed to leave, but it was snowing bad, and when they said we could all go back to our rooms, I did. But he hasn't come back yet, and he wouldn't have gone far."

"No, of course not," Madsen said. "He'll be here soon."

"My father—"

All of us, we're always searching for a family that's no longer there. "The blizzard has tied up traffic all over. He probably went out to—" Come up with a good one. "—get something…for you…to eat. The dining area's closed and he didn't know how long you'd be camped out in the lobby. I'm sure he's trying his best." Maybe the guy was out there in one of the wrecks, freezing to death on the side of the expressway.

Vases of flowers lined the sill, the girl's drawings taped over her bed. She had a good eye for detail, perspective, light and silhouette, distinctly textured realistic grimaces and smiles and sneers.

"These are wonderful," he said, and meant it.

"I'm okay so long as the pencils are sharp." Her voice had a pleasant sleepiness to it that made Madsen suddenly feel tired, in a good way. "I can't use ink or charcoal that well, and it's hard to keep the pencils pointy enough, even with a sharpener."

"Yeah?"

"Blunt edges turn everything ugly."

He let loose with an odd noise, and it took a second to comprehend that the sound was his own laughter. It had been a while since he'd so much as chuckled, and perhaps he'd lost the knack for it. Here she'd said something that had some *style—blunt edges turn everything ugly*—that rolled off the tongue, and he'd been self-involved enough to apply the words. Madsen shook his head.

Her small fist snapped out and caught him by the wrist. He sat on the edge of the bed and petted the small knot of colorless hair just over her right ear.

"You're cold," she said.

"Just my hands."

"What's your name?"

"I'm Madsen. What's yours?"

She ignored the question and kept gazing at him almost longingly, with a mixture of pity and adoration. It was how his mother used to look at him. "Will you stay with me for a while?"

"Sure."

"Just until I fall asleep."

"As long as you want."

"My father does that most nights, when they let him."

She closed her eyes and sighed, and he kept patting her hair with the same intense, obsessive need that had consumed him while he rubbed his mother's hand at the end. There's something about this, he thought, that warrants an unholy amount of care and attention. He glanced up at the faces on the wall, searching for her father, but saw only beautiful women and unsightly little boys. He wanted to ask who they were.

Snow pounded at the window, like dust—the dust of ancestors—craving notice. Damn, it got you thinking too hard. After more than an hour he got up and left the room. As he stepped into the hall he heard her, shifting in bed and saying softly, "Come back."

He wanted to but it was already too late. Madsen knew that now, without fully realizing why, and yet it didn't make the walking away any easier. There wasn't much left to do, but still, something had been left unfinished. He understood that more clearly than anything else that had occurred in the last couple of weeks. He hadn't accomplished the task at hand, whatever it might be.

Madsen came across an alcove filled with a few chairs, a new but worn couch, pay phone. At the end they tell you to go call any family members who might want to visit one last time. Like you ring them up while they're watching one of their yuppie sit-coms, sitting around in sweat pants, one-year-old napping in the bassinet, and they'll come charging into the night.

Somebody there now, crimped in the corner.

He started to walk past.

Someone on the phone, whispering in a monotone peppered with hideous titters that Madsen had never heard outside of his nightmares. Jesus, it stopped him cold. He swung around and watched the back of the man's head bobbing toward the mouthpiece, his heavy overcoat covered with ice crystals. The guy trembled there, hands quivering so badly that his knuckles snapped against the metal ledge of the phone and knocked over carefully placed stacks of coins.

"You—" Madsen said.

The guy—Christ no, the kid—wouldn't turn all the way around, arching his pink, peach-fuzzed chin just enough so he could give Madsen a sidelong glance.

"You. You're the one who's calling in the bomb threats."

The teenager coming around a bit more now but still not wanting to look into Madsen's face. Not a teen really, maybe pushing twenty-one, old enough to have already lost whatever there was to lose. Madsen moved to the other side of the pay phone and saw the kid's face had been viciously scarred—left eye gone, the socket crushed and matted with dark tissue.

He thought that might be what it was all about. Kid is in a wreck, holds a grudge against the hospital. Who died with him? A girlfriend? His granny? We all handle our broken hearts so poorly. So he's calling from inside the hospital and they can't trace him? The hell's up with that? Fifty cops and dogs running around the place, and nobody can find him, stop him? Now you're getting down to the grit, the dirt in the corner, knowing something even worse is going on, and you'll never know what it really is.

"You've got a beef?" Madsen asked, the rage coming up in him fast. First just a few drops of bile, and then all the rest of it just flooding in. He slapped the phone from the kid's hand and grabbed him by the neck.

Two sticks of taped together dynamite fell out of the guy's coat pocket. They hit with a hollow thud, sounding fake, but Madsen had never been around dynamite before and had no idea whether it was real. He had to follow through.

"Okay, bastard, let's get this over with."

The words had barely cleared his lips when a gleam of light drew his attention low, to the bomber's right hand. He knew what was coming but couldn't quite get himself out of the way—same old story, when you got right down to it. Hey now, here it comes.

The blade caught Madsen low in the belly but didn't go in deep. He tried to hold himself steady, laughing because it felt good to be doing what was right. No chance, though, he fell back to the other side of the hall and bumped a gurney shoved up against the wall—with a dirty sheet covering it—

Friggin' kid moved forward, terrified and fighting as if in self defense. He accidentally stepped on the dynamite and those two sticks cracked loudly—*plastic*—spilling ball bearings. A low whining moan crashed up through his chest.

The knife brushed Madsen again, and once more, but there was no pain. He brought the back of one fist up into that ruined face. The guy's nose went with an almost gentle snap and he started to scream. Madsen hit him in the same place again. He swept aside and stuck the kid's inner shoulder with the meaty part of his palm, driving deep into the bone, wanting to break the fucker's neck. An insane fury was on him but it only emerged second to second, with repulsive moments of clarity between them.

He kept at it for all he was worth as the blizzard continued, out there and in here. Howls echoed all around, perhaps the wind or maybe the dogs.

At last, the bastard swooned and tumbled backwards, stepped on the ball bearings and his feet went up from under him. It appeared like a perfectly choreographed move as he hung up there in the air chest high for an instant, before coming down flat on the back of his skull.

Madsen checked him. The bitter kid wasn't out yet, laying there chewing his own blood and breathing shallowly. His one good eye tried to focus.

The knife was still in his hand. Madsen kicked it away.

Skittering off, splashing drops on the tiles as it spun, all four inches of the blade were wet.

"Hey now," Madsen said, a giggle lurking at the back of his throat. He reached down and felt his belly squish aside as he touched it. His hands came away completely red and he realized he'd been nearly disemboweled.

"Who are you?" the kid whimpered, asking with a real interest. "What are you doing here?"

Always a good question. Madsen waited as the guy clambered to his feet and then punched him in the mouth once more with everything he had left. The kid went down hard and lay in a heap.

The blow had set Madsen off-balance and he went to one knee. Blood gushed from his stomach and poured over his shoes, but it still didn't hurt. He stood again and confronted the gurney behind him like a long-lost resentful friend. The shape under the cloth was as familiar as any obscured face would be, his own or another.

How much less of himself was there now? When they ground him down into ashes, what would the scale read? Would he be more than a handful for somebody to take home?

This I want to see.

His fingers trembled as he reached out to touch the soiled sheet.

"I'm not dead yet," he whispered, and the conviction of his own voice gave him strength. "I am not dead yet!"

Maybe it was true. His crimson fingerprints covered the cloth and bled through to what was beneath.

"Madsen?"

He wheeled and in doing so lurched wildly and kicked the gurney. It creaked and slowly rolled away.

And the little bald girl at the other end of the hall, swathed in gauze as if she'd been flung into fire many times before, smiling and beckoning him forward, the blunt edges of his life growing more and more ugly now, even as he was running, stumbling, and then finally crawling to meet her.

PANTHEON VERSION 2.0

This is how it started.

I woke up, looked out the window, and dead rock stars were climbing out of a hole in my backyard.

Blinking, I fished away an eye boogie. They were still there. Kurt Cobain brushed clots of soil from his hair while a left-handed genius named James Marshall Hendrix helped John Lennon and Cliff Burton haul Mama Cass out of the ground.

They didn't *look* dead.

Hendrix and Mama Cass didn't have that ashen hue from their autopsy photos. Burton wasn't squashed. Cobain still had *all* of his head, and Lennon didn't have holes in his chest or shoulder. Cobain fussed over the dirt in his hair, which I found odd. When he'd been alive, his hair looked like he washed it in a grease trap.

"This is fucked." The sound of my voice made me feel better—more real. I kept the blinds parted with my fingers, and scratched my ass through my boxers with my free hand.

As if the dead rock stars weren't spectacular enough, I then saw something *amazing*; Merle Haggard and Tupac Shakur clawed through the soil, then shook hands like old friends.

I'd predicted the rap-metal invasion long

BRIAN KEENE AND MICHAEL T. HUYCK JR.

before Limp Bizkit and Kid Rock made it cool. Back before the Run DMC-Aerosmith collaboration and the Anthrax-Public Enemy team up. But *rap* and *country*?

I don't think so.

Immediately, my mind swam with possibilities. Garth Brooks' "Rodeo" infused with KRS-One. One of Johnny Cash's prison songs dubbed over the bass and keyboards of Dr. Dre's "Stranded on Death Row." Maybe Ice Cube's "Until We Rich" layered with some Shania Twain rhythms.

That's the way my mind works. Writers see an altercation at the mall and they turn it into a story. Engineers visit Manhattan and design bigger buildings. I'm a DJ, and when I see the godfather of country and one of gangsta rap's most infamous icons shaking hands, I start mixing music in my head.

That's why I didn't freak out right away. My brain wasn't processing it; a defense mechanism of sorts, because dead musicians couldn't be crawling out of a hole in my backyard.

Nope, the brain said, *not happening. Must have been the E you took last night, during the gig. Make some coffee, take a shower, brush your teeth (in that order) and, when you're done, they'll be gone.*

I had that happen to a friend of mine once. Kris sang for this band called Suicide Run. He started fucking around with the occult and next thing you know, he was trying to summon demons on stage. He got killed in a stage diving accident that, in turn, caused a massive riot. Lots of people were killed and injured and that was it for Suicide Run.

Dumb ass. Should've listened to his brain.

That's what I did. I shuffled out to the kitchen. We were out of coffee filters, so I used a paper towel. Then I found out that we were out of coffee too. I cursed Storm, dug around in the trashcan for yesterday's grounds, put them in the microwave to dry them out, and then used them again.

I noticed that the trailer was getting messy, and made a mental note to bring some girls home from tonight's gig. If Storm and I treated them right and promised to call them, we could usually convince them to clean the morning after.

Coffee brewing, I chewed some aspirin to break the post-E headache and stumbled towards the shower. I soaked, lathered, rinsed, and repeated—all the time humming Willie Nelson's "You Were Always On My Mind" to an internal dance beat.

I was just getting out of the shower when I heard the knock at the door.

"Storm," I called. "Can you get that? I'm in the shower!"

There was no answer from his bedroom. This didn't surprise me. He'd sucked the better part of a fifth of scotch the previous night, and he could sleep through a war when sober. Fucker passed out at Ozz-Fest once. Slept through Disturbed's entire set.

The knocking was more insistent now.

I grabbed a towel and dried quickly. As I was stepping into my boxers, the knocking changed to somebody pounding "Shave and A Haircut, Two Bits."

That's when I got pissed. I fucking hate "Shave and A Haircut, Two Bits."

"Hold on a second!" I picked the least dirty pair of shorts and a slightly clean Fear Factory shirt. Then I went to the door.

I opened it and the King of Rock and Roll smiled at me, peering overtop his gold-plated shades. He had fresh grass stains on his white suit. The undead Music Hall of Fame crowded behind him.

My brain had been wrong. Faced with this knowledge, I finally freaked out.

I slammed the door in their faces. Screaming, I ran down the hall, burst into Storm's bedroom, slammed his door against the wall, and landed atop him on the bed.

"Dude, get the fuck up!"

He stirred, mumbling "No, s'okay. I'll still respect you in the morning."

Then he grabbed my ass.

I punched him in the head and ripped the blankets off. He was on his feet in three seconds.

"Dude!" he screamed, looking around.

"Rock stars! Zombie rock stars!"

"What the *fuck* is wrong with you, Rage?" he moaned, rubbing his head. "It's only—Jesus Christ on crack—eight o'clock!"

"Zombies crawled out of the backyard except that they don't look like zombies 'cause Kurt Cobain doesn't have a hole in the back of his head and Tupac is chilling with Merle Haggard and there's an Elvis impersonator at the door and I don't think this one is from Las fucking Vegas!"

I stopped for breath. Storm groaned.

"Rage, I told you not to take any more Ecstasy. That little Goth chick led you wrong. Go back to sleep. And …"

Something that sounded like a Keith Moon drum solo pounded on our door. I flinched, and made a silent promise to never do drugs again.

"Do me a favor, then, and get the door?" I whispered.

Grumbling, he stomped down the hall in his underwear. I followed along behind him, peering around the corner. My heart was pounding harder than a Prodigy bass line.

He flung the door open and froze.

"Hey little buddy," came a distinct Memphis drawl. "You must be Storm, and I think we briefly met Rage just a minute ago. Can you fine gentlemen entertain us a second?"

Storm shook and nodded his head at the same time.

"Then we, me and my friends, can come in?"

Storm stepped aside, the color draining from his face.

"Thank you," said Elvis. "Thank you very much."

«« — »»

Jimi Hendrix sat on the couch, staring at the stack of Pringles in his hand. He ate one, spun the form-fit pile of chips around, then ate another. Finally he shook his head.

"Cool. Hey Jelly Roll! C'mere. Look…Albert Fish is at it again. He's eating wieners and buns in Indiana. They got him on the news!" Hendrix's eyes drifted back towards his chip stack. Jelly ignored him and studied our stereo.

"What the *fuck* are they doing here?" Storm whispered.

I could only shake my head. My feet felt glued to the tile in the entryway.

I counted thirty-six, but the front door opened every ten minutes or so to let in another. Steve Took and Marc Bolan came together on the last knock. No small surprise.

"I repeat…why is our living room filling up with dead rock stars?"

"Did he say Albert Fish?" I hissed.

"Yeah, Albert Fish. He was in 'Barney Miller', right? I didn't know he was dead."

"That's Abe Vigoda, and I don't think he is. Albert Fish was a serial killer that kidnapped, killed, and ate kids. He died a long time ago—around the Depression."

"You're a regular fucking history book."

"I know my serial killers; it's a hobby I picked up from that Michelle chick I used to bang."

"The one that ordered a clip of Jeffrey Dahmer's hair on the net?"

"Yep, same one." Then a thought occurred to me. "Dude, if there's a house full of dead rock stars here, you think there's a house full of dead serial killers sitting around in someone else's living room?"

"Yeah, probably at your crazy ex's."

I headed for the kitchen, grabbed a beer out of the fridge, and offered it to Storm.

"We haven't even had breakfast yet."

"So?" I took one out for myself.

"You're right. Gimme that."

"Rock stars. Serial killers. Hey, you suppose there's movie stars and politicians, too?"

"Sure…why not? Could be house painters and fry cooks, for all I know. You see 'Night of the Living Dead'?"

"Yeah, but these don't act like zombies. They act alive. And every one," I stuck my head into the dining room and looked around, "*every one* of them is famous. Guess the same thing would go for the serial killers."

"He only said Albert Fish. We don't *know* that murderers are coming back, too."

Toscanini walked in, his staff clenched in one hand. "Wine?" he asked.

Storm opened the refrigerator and pointed at the five-liter box on the top shelf. Toscanini knitted his brow and walked back out.

"So why are they coming to life and why the hell are they in our living room?"

Storm shrugged. "They just are. The question, is how can we make this work for us? I mean, fuck, The King is sitting on our love seat! I wish I had cleaned house yesterday, instead of fucking around with the Playstation."

"The King. I can't believe it. And he's sitting next to Marty Robbins."

"You think Don Ho will show?"

"He's not dead."

"Damn…I love his 'Tiny Bubbles'. Mixed it to Eminem one time…"

Cliff Burton wandered in, my Metallica black disc in his hand. He seemed sad.

"They replaced me? Replacing Mustaine I could understand, but…"

He wandered away again.

I finished my beer and tossed it at the trashcan. "Hey, let's watch television."

"Huh?"

"Look, Jimi Hendrix said…I can't believe I just said *Jimi Hendrix said*…Jimi said Albert Fish was cooking again. He must be watching CNN or something. Let's go learn something."

We walked back into the living room and hovered on the fringes of the crowd, like wallflowers at a junior high dance. John Lennon was discussing something with Sid Vicious, but when I tried to eavesdrop on them, I couldn't understand either of them. They sounded like the chimney sweeps from 'Mary Poppins'. Storm must have been thinking the same thing because he asked me if Dick Van Dyke was alive or dead.

Biggie Smalls and Easy E. were going through our CD's, while

Robert Johnson watched with confused interest. The legendary blues-man handed one to Jelly, who tried putting it on my old turntable. Biggie and Easy E. found this hilarious, and started laughing. Then Easy announced that he had to take a piss and stumbled down the hall.

Jerry Garcia flipped through the channels with the remote, and Hendrix and Janis Joplin giggled in delight.

"Damn, Jerry, how are you doing that?"

"Remote control. They didn't have these when you guys left."

"Groovy."

"Here's something that will really flip your lid."

He paused on MTV, waited, and finally scowled at the television.

"When did they start doing sitcoms? They're supposed to be showing videos!"

As he spoke, the MTV News logo popped onto the screen.

"Turn that up," Elvis commanded and when he spoke, the room fell silent.

Storm drained his beer and whispered to me, "I've got to piss."

"So go piss."

"I can't. Easy E. is in there."

The room full of dead musicians were glaring at us.

"—in case you're just joining us," the newscaster was saying, "we repeat, rocker Ozzy Osbourne has suffered a heart attack on the set of *The Osbournes*, after the family's home was invaded by a Randy Rhoads look-alike."

"I was wondering where Randy got to," Cliff Burton mused. "He was a good guy. Couldn't play Asteroids worth a shit, though. I beat him all across the country when we toured with them. Wonder if Randy Castillo will be showing up too?"

"Great drummer," Bon Scott replied, "but I doubt Castillo's belief levels were high enough. Probably not enough energy to summon him yet."

"Hush," Freddie Mercury snapped at them. "Listen."

"—authorities say the intruder surprised the heavy metal singer at the door, and then entered the home, insisting that he was Rhoads, Osbourne's original guitarist who died in 1982. No word yet on Ozzy's condition, and sources have been unable to determine which hospital he was admitted to. Authorities have taken the imposter into custody. This is just the latest incident today in what seems to be a rash of deceased celebrity impersonators—"

"Bollocks," muttered Lennon. "This is a piss-up, innit? You want us to break him out?"

"No," Elvis shook his head. "We don't have enough time. The war will start soon. We'll have to do without him. Jerry, see if you can find some more news."

He sighed, raised his leg, farted, and then looked at us. "I don't reckon you'd happen to have some peanut butter and banana sandwich fixings in the kitchen would you?"

"Um," I stuttered, "I'm afraid not. We've got Ramen noodles, though."

The CNN newscaster drowned out the King's reply, and everyone's attention turned back to the TV. As Jerry Garcia had said, it was enough to flip your lid. John F. Kennedy had shown up on the White House lawn, demanding to see the President. Marilyn Monroe was entwined around him, purring seductively at the befuddled Secret Service agents. In the background, Richard Nixon was insisting that *he* wanted to see the President first. The two of them began to argue, while Marilyn and the men-in-black watched.

In England, Princess Di arrived at Windsor, asking for her boys. John Wayne stormed the doors of a cigarette manufacturer's headquarters, and Gandhi preached from the rooftops in Bangladesh, pushing for disarmament between Pakistan and India.

Those were the surreal. Then came the horrific. Ted Bundy and Jeffrey Dahmer had been sighted in Milwaukee, cruising in a black van with tinted windows. The gas station attendant who reported it said somebody was screaming in the back. In Ohio, the Reverend Jim Jones served his trademark purple drinks to an entire daycare center. Al Capone made a withdrawal from the Federal Reserve, leaving sixteen people dead. The governor of New Mexico had been assassinated by William H. Bonney, alias William McCarty, alias Billy the Kid. In Germany, Hitler was forming the Fourth Reich with an army of neo-nazi skinheads.

"Hullo, George!"

John Lennon distracted me from the news, rushing to the door to greet his old band mate. When I turned back, the newscaster was a *Breaking News* logo on the screen.

"We repeat, if you're just joining us, convicted murderer Charles Manson has tried, unsuccessfully, to commit suicide in prison. Sources tell us that Manson was behaving erratically, and stated that he, quote: "wanted to become a New God too", end quote. Here with us now is Doctor Sherman Oliveri, of the Johns Hopkins Psychiatric Hospital…"

There was another knock at the door, and this time Storm answered it.

"Hello. I'm Johnny Cash."

"Dude!" Storm fell to his knees and wept.

"You boys look a might confused," Elvis observed. "I reckon we'd better explain. Sit down."

He folded his hands, admired his rings, then looked at us and smiled.

"Gods don't come from books, be they the Good Book or otherwise. Gods come from here." The King pointed at the top of his tall hair. The widow's peak emphasized his age, as did the extra hundred or so pounds he was carrying. Still, he was The King.

Storm played with his own hair, pulling at the front and twisting it up to stack it.

"They, we, come from the brain."

"An' the 'eart. We come from the 'eart. Not jus' every bloke's piss'd noggin." Sid Vicious sat down on the couch arm beside Elvis. Side by side, I could see where the early Clash came from, and after them, the Stray Cats.

"On the money, Sid."

"You're a bunch of gods? Dead gods?" I sucked another sip of warm beer. It didn't taste right, what with the sun barely being up and all.

"Not dead," Janis said, putting one arm around my waist. "Not anymore, lover boy."

"I don't get it," Storm said.

"Humanity loved us," Cobain took over, "because we were larger than life. They were willing to overlook our faults because of that idolization—that worship. Those belief levels have kept us all in a spiritual and spatial limbo since our deaths. You still look confused..."

"No," Storm got to his feet, "I think I get what you're saying. I just never took you for the metaphysical type."

"It's kinda like the media is Johnny Appleseed and we're his apples," Elvis continued. "Only thing is, now we never go away. We just get bigger and redder and better. Everything and everyone made big by culture is up in arms about now, and I don't need the tube to tell me that. You have sports stars and Hollywood stars and stars of every type of media there is today. Here, in your living room, you have your musicians. We're some of the New Gods, the new, uhm..."

"...Pantheon," finished Monteverdi.

"Yup," said Elvis. "We're a pantheon. The time of the Old Gods is over. This is our age."

"Question, Mr. King. No...Mr. Presley. Why are you guys here? The killers, the movie stars, the politicians and sports heroes, they're spread out across the world. You guys are all here. Out of my backyard and into my living room. Why?"

The King leaned over, speaking so softly that I could barely hear him over the din. "Because we have plans, boy." He sat back and raised his chin to yell up at the ceiling. "Wladziu!"

Liberace, candelabra in hand, came over from the far side of the couch. He nodded his million-teeth smile.

"Wladziu here is our PR guy. He knows all about making a name, any name, commonplace in the home. With me in command and him on the media, we'll be in charge and the rest of them," Elvis waved at the television, "will just be annoying. If I can, I'll figure out a way to send 'em back where they came from."

"But he's Liberace." I couldn't get my eyes off his smile.

"Exactly. You didn't know his real name is Wladziu, did you? See what I mean?"

Storm leaned over and whispered "no" in my ear.

"And us?" I asked. "Why Rage and Storm Productions? We're just disc jockeys—clubs and bar mitzvahs mostly. What do we have to do with this?"

"We need priests and heroes. That's what Monteverdi here told me. He's the thinker in this group." Liberace nodded, his smile frozen wide and toothy.

"Priests and heroes?"

Monteverdi nodded solemnly. "You will take court with Pelopidas and Lycurgus and Dion. You will champion us to the masses as the New Gods most fitting of this day and age."

"Along with Wladziu here," Elvis added.

"Did he mean *Celine* Dion?" Storm asked, still whispering, "or Deon Yates?"

"Neither, I think." I finished the rest of the warm beer in one gulp and went after another; the realization that we'd literally just sold our souls for rock and roll starting to sink in.

««—»»

In retrospect, I should have figured that these were the Gods of Hell instead of Heaven. Why else would I have been damned to work hand in hand with Liberace? He's like a campy Mr. Rogers with cartoon eyes. And that smile. Damn. It's like his lips just *can't close.*

I'm still not certain that they're from Hell, because I'm not certain there *is* a Hell. Or a Heaven. Those are figments of what's now known as the classical religions. Christianity and its franchises have been subtitled as classical religions. Same with Islam and Buddhism and every other damn herding of the mumbling masses that used to run amuck on this earth. That's Elvis throwing the hard cases a bone, but don't expect it to last. In another five years or so, after their ranks have dwindled, he'll go about stomping them out. You watch and see.

All in three months. It's all happened in three months. But they've been *long* months, the last one the longest by far. Why?

SHIVERS III

Because it was on the first of April that I buried Storm.

Today's the first of May. May Day, we used to call it, but now it's Tim McGraw Day. Not that Tim should think he's special, because every day's named after a musician now. Next year we're thinking that we'll keep the same assignments and just get rid of the months and dates. Maybe even the days of the week. All we need is 365 good musicians and one so-so one for what used to be February 29th. Elvis hasn't made up his mind yet.

Storm. We'll get to that story.

It was early February when they all clawed their way out of my back-yard. By the end of the day Storm got some leg off of Janis Joplin and Buddy Holly damn near tore down the front door with a bloody Randy Rhoads in tow. Said he took out six cops on the getaway and they stole a plane together. I never figured Buddy for the action hero type, but the fact that either of them had the balls to get in a plane again said a hell of a lot more. But hey, they're gods, right?

That first day, the day we met The King, was the last day that I called that house my own. The Gods of Music took it over, making it their head-quarters. It took two or three more days for the reality of it to sink in, and then, for a little while, I was caught up in it. Swept away.

It began when Sonny Boy Williamson started hooting at the televi-sion. He hadn't left the couch once since he'd joined us, because the "talkies" in a box entranced him. Somewhere in all the milling and nos-talgia and soapboxing and planning we'd forgotten that there were other gods walking about. It hadn't occurred to the King that someone *else* might try to take over the world first.

Leave it to Bundy.

Before we go there, though, let's touch on the rest of them. The actors and politicians (yes, some politicians *did* become gods—but then Kennedy always knew he was one) and the incidentals. Babe Ruth was living naked in Central Park and chasing off joggers with an enormous Samurai sword. Howard Hughes applied to an Astronautical Engineering program at Purdue, announcing at the time of his application that he would be building the largest rocket ship ever after he graduated. The Rosenbergs were picked up and taken directly to Leavenworth, prompting Sing-Sing to sue for custody of their most famous couple. And that's just in America. All around the world celebrities of every manner created chaos and turned the world on its ear. Each of them had a priest or a hero, counterparts to Storm and myself. And each of them had a con-gregation—converts to the New World Orders. Storm and I did our best to preach to the masses huddled on our front lawn. We'd had a few groupies from our days of playing clubs and parties, but nothing like this. Storm's favorite move was to sleep with several women in one night, while preaching the doctrine that by having sex with him, they would grow closer to the gods.

While we were getting laid and the rock stars were partying and planning, Bundy beat Elvis to the organization thing. Their headquarters was a house in Bakersfield, California, and their priests were an F. B. I. profiler that had loved his job a bit too much, and an S&M queen. They set up a news conference; Bundy smiling in the middle, Dahmer passive at his right hand, and Gacy chewing on a huge, raw steak and mugging for the camera. Before them lay a Monopoly board.

"We're doing you a favor here, people. The world's leaders are ineffectual. They've *always* been ineffectual, compared to us." He put both hands down on the game board. "So now it's ours. The whole world—from Mediterranean Avenue to Boardwalk. Y'all will be worshipping at my bloody altar. Excuse me—*our* bloody altar." Bundy winked and nodded and Gacy waved a big flap of flesh at the end of his fork. Dahmer didn't budge.

That's when Liberace grimaced, and Liberace's grimace puts a whole new swing on the term. It still looked like a smile, but his eyebrows were evil. He looked like a clown.

"They've got a leg up on us, Elvis. It's time to get in gear."

Most of the rock stars were gone by then, dispatched as diplomats towards every corner of the world. Elvis, Liberace, and Monteverdi remained in our house still, planning and scheming and sending Storm and I off to do Heroic things like laundry and pizza-fetches. Something was afoot—we both knew it. Something big. But that's all we knew. These three kept their world domination plans close to their dead chests. Sure, Elvis had a plan, but all I knew so far was that his plan involved a little schmoozing with the Joe Q. Public. Working up the angle that they were back from the dead to make the world a better place for music lovers everywhere. They never talked about taking the country by storm or any coup d'etat. At least, not until the serial killers drew first blood.

"Who's in Washington, Monte?"

"Michael Hutchence."

"Ring him up. Tell him to notify Kennedy, Reagan and the other Presidential Gods that we're moving now. We can't wait. If they want in, they need to let us know. Wladziu, you put the sleepers into gear. Start with the old-school killers first, just to make sure the crematory approach works. Tell Morrison it's time for a Fish fry. We'll give it three days. If it's good, we go after 'em whole hog. If not, we take 'em on the politico way. Storm, you get more bananas and more butter. And some chocolate syrup. This is it, guys."

"What about me?" I asked.

"You're my media man, Rage. Set me up with Howard Stern for tomorrow. Can you do that?"

"If you make the call it'll get through. I can take it from there."

"Right. Let's get it in gear, troops. This is war."

The crematory approach, as The King called it, did work. Very well. All of the New Gods had one weakness. If they didn't have a body, they couldn't be *there*. The King lined up a collection of living hit men with New God counterparts and gave them instructions to, on his command, go after their named targets with gasoline and matches. Jim Morrison was the first, what with his love of fire, and the killer he took out was Albert Fish. Jim traced Albert to a gardener's shed on Michael Jackson's Neverland estate and swarmed the old bastard with two dozen stoned high school metal-heads. They burned him to cinder, taking out the shed, part of the house, several large fiberglass flamingos, and an unnamed chimp. No elephants were harmed. The important part is that Albert didn't come back. Not one whiff of him.

That first "shot" went down near the end of February, making March the beginning of what I called the God's War. Or what the media called War of the New Gods. They must get paid by the word.

There were other battles. Bon Scott and Billy the Kid played high noon on the streets of Dallas. Marvin Gaye and Roy Orbison cornered Timothy McVeigh skulking around Oklahoma City, and fried his ass a second time.

The Presidential Gods had taken over Washington by that point, and the Holy Trinity of Kennedy/Reagan/Lincoln formed an alliance with the King, and in collaboration with Winston Churchill, Princess Diana, and Gandhi, sent a large group of coalition forces, led by Douglas MacArthur, to take out Hitler's new Germany. Everybody got in on that one, except for Joan of Arc's France—which surprised nobody. When MacArthur finished with Germany, they allowed him to take over France as well.

As for the other dead celebrities, some of them went back to wherever they came from. Grace Kelly dropped off the front page of the papers like she'd never come back from the grave in the first place. One day there were six dead Popes whispering in the live one's ear, the next day he only had his Cardinals to talk to him. I'm guessing that the revving hostilities between the musical/political camp and the serial killer/dictator camp took everyone's mind off the rest of them. With no one paying them any attention, they just faded away.

Kind of like Storm...

Jesus—I mean, Elvis—it hurts to think about him. He was my bro, my partner—my friend. There was nobody I'd rather thump a club beat with. And now he's gone.

They sacrificed him.

The war broke out on all sides, spreading into the actors and other celebrity pantheons. There was a lot of bloodshed, both human and god. Eventually, the treaty between the Political Gods and the Music Gods disintegrated, after Nixon had the plane carrying Buddy Holly and the Big Bopper shot down.

They died in flames.

All sides took a heavy toll, and eventually, someone decided that the best way to rule the Earth would be for humanity to decide. Whichever group could garner the highest belief levels would stay in power. The others would simply fade away.

Armageddon took place in Southern California, and that was the only part of this whole affair that never surprised me. All of the gods gathered in Los Angeles, along with their priests and their heroes and their most fervent followers, and pleaded their case to the world via satellite.

The Kennedy/Reagan/Lincoln trinity promised humanity democracy and the American Dream. The Actors pledged that every day would be a magical, Technicolor day, that no one would ever grow old, and that everyone would be beautiful—just like a movie star. The Serial Killer & Mass-Murderer's Union proposed a world built upon Aleister Crowley's "do what thou wilt shall be the whole of the law."

But when Elvis' turn to speak came, he beat them all. For the King so loved the world, that he gave up his only begotten Kurt Cobain; that whosoever believed in him, would not perish, but have eternal life. They crucified Cobain next to the Hollywood sign, and so he wouldn't have to go it alone, they added two more crosses, upon which were hung a devoted groupie—and Storm, Cobain's most beloved priest.

The King's gift to the world won humanity over, and when the pictures of Cobain's anguish upon the cross, and his tortured cries of "Elvis, why have you forsaken me?" followed immediately by his death and resurrection, were carried live on television and radio and the net into every home, there wasn't a dry eye on the planet.

I cried too, but not out of joy. I cried for Storm. And I swore revenge.

I went underground after that, preaching a return to the classical religions. My dogma of the evils that the media and our social values had unleashed upon us got me labeled as a heretic, and they've been hunting me ever since.

They've caught up to me now, as I finish this story on a yellow legal pad, sitting in a dark motel room in New Jersey. I can hear them outside, the believers—human like myself. Mortal. The King doesn't dispatch his gods to handle things like insurrection anymore. They have their congregation and their priests and heroes to do that for them now. These days, the Pantheon are content to walk the land, soaking in the adulation of the masses. In Graceland, the King sits upon his throne, and Cobain sits at his right hand side. The gods hold a big concert in the sky four times a year, and the whole world watches it.

The crowd is right outside the door now. Any second, they'll bust it down. Don't know what they'll do with me. Stoning probably, or maybe burn me at the stake. I'm going to hide this under the mattress. If you've found it, and you've read it, then you've got to believe me. You've got to believe. And you've got to tell others and make them believe too.

Because if enough of you believe, then maybe—just maybe—I can come back too.

I'm Rage, the best damn D. J. in the tri-county area, and for just a brief moment, I was a star.

I want that star to shine again.

I wish I had a beer.

Here they come...

CELEBRATE WITH US

The October wind teased its way along the country lane, stirring up dried leaves and rattling dead branches, passing over the heads of the two children who waited outside the old stone home. They ignored its cold breath, no shiver going through their quiet forms, not a hair ruffled beneath their masked faces. Their hands were pale, clutching orange and black treat bags.

Eyes unblinking.

Inside the house, a man stared outwards, matching their gaze with a look of dread, pure and unrelenting. Jim Kussen, electrician by trade, felt the skin over his cheeks tighten, the lines of age and worry grow deeper, the stressed heart within his chest pound harder. A pair of trick-or-treaters—on normal occasion a comfortable sight, viewed within its proper, given season.

Halloween.

Except that it was three days before All Hallow's Eve. And they were in front of his house, along a mostly unused country road. Without parents, standing silent in the premature twilight. And they had been there before, every night since October had wakened from slumber, spreading autumn's chill magic across the land, preparing it for the black nights of winter soon to come. And

PAUL MELNICZEK

upon closer inspection, details were revealed which dispelled any fragment of the idea that things were the least bit normal.

Their figures wavered in the brisk air. Clothes were singed and browned. The treat bags were torn and empty. They remained there before the house.

Standing in silent accusation.

And coming nearer each evening.

Jim could sense them before they even appeared. He knew their purpose, had known of it upon seeing them the very first time. They would leave him messages.

Mostly in his head. Some not. What would it be tonight?

Jim waited.

The cloak of darkness eagerly descended, and still he waited. He forced his eyes to stay open. Willed himself to take in every measure of their small bodies. Features were impossible to describe. One wore a nondescript mask, pale white, almost a sheath of extra skin. The other was a soldier of some type, rough with camouflaged paint. He shuddered to think what they looked like beneath those masks, prayed he would never see the pain and horror behind them.

Jim struggled against the strain, his eyes now watering.

Please don't do this to me, for the love of everything...

He blinked. They were gone.

He drew in a deep sigh of relief, but the terror remained, clutching his heart and mind. It lingered and would not be driven away. Then he noticed something. A crumpled sheet of paper that had not been there a second ago. With much reservation, he hurried to the door, prying it open with trembling fingers. Outside nothing moved save for dried leaves, which scuttled across the pavement like agitated crabs. Jim rushed over to grab the paper. He picked it up, uncrinkling the stained sheet. It was cold to his touch, and he nearly dropped it. The handwriting was spidery and wandering, just like a child's. Three words were scribbled on the front.

North Ternh Church.

His mouth opened, and he lifted his head, staring blankly into the night. The place had been revealed.

A sudden gust of wind lashed across his face, snatching the paper from his hands and sending it spinning away, quickly disappearing into the surrounding woods.

Gone. Had it ever really been there?

Jim remained standing, knowing that things had been set into motion, events out of his control. Terrible things. And he was the catalyst to bring life to them. A puppet, but one of his own doing. He retreated, going back to his house, which was no longer comfortable, no longer safe. There existed no havens with walls high enough to protect him.

For what walls could shield him from the dead?

«« —— »»

October 29th

Jim walked up the cement steps leading into the modest town hall. The sky was sullen, gray with the threat of rain. A few people scampered along the sidewalks of the shopping district, but they seemed to be only vague shadows in Jim's mind. He tried not to think of the path which lay before him, one which would end in something beyond his control.

He opened the door, shuffling inside and moving down a dimly lit hallway. Fluorescent lights buzzed annoyingly over his head, and he stopped before a closed door. Rapping lightly, he entered before any response came from within. A small desk sat inside, a large man seated behind it in a worn brown swivel chair. On the desk was a white sign, with the words *Mayor Grimler* on it.

Jack Grimler looked up as Jim entered, frowning when he saw who it was.

"Hello, Jim. I'm pretty busy. What do you want?"

"You still haven't answered me about the Halloween party." Jim waited before the mayor's desk.

Jack adjusted his glasses, the wispy hair on his wide head damp with sweat. "Well, there's the Ladies Auxiliary event going on that evening…"

"More excuses, after all that's happened? It's for the kids. The *kids*." Jim peered down at him, his eyes smoldering, his throat parched.

"Damn it…don't talk like that." The mayor rose, his heavy frame bumping the desk as he moved to close the door. He reached into the pocket of his suit, pulling out a handkerchief and patting his forehead.

Jim was silent, content on watching the other man.

"Gail might *hear* you." Jack pointed towards the neighboring office where his secretary worked, the sound of typing echoing from behind the door.

But Jim prodded him further. "A few children are gathering, and they expect to have the town major leading them in the party festivities. It's the least you can do, you know." Jim moved back a pace, leaning against a wall, rubbing the dark circles under his eyes. "I have trouble sleeping…it's worse lately."

"So do I," Jack whispered, returning to his seat. He slid open a drawer, taking out a small flask and sipping. "Care for some?"

"No." Jim shook his head. "It's not the answer, although I'm tempted."

"You have to move on, try to forget it."

Jim grew angry. "Forget the deaths of six children? Never…"

"It was an accident."

"Don't try that argument anymore, *Jack.*" He slumped against the wall, his weary body finding the solitary chair. "You knew, and did nothing."

"So did you. But that still didn't cause the fire." Jack took another swig.

Jim slapped the wall with his bare hand. "I should have rewired it on my own. But for you to tell me to hold off because of the lack of money…is unforgivable." He paused. "At least I admit my mistakes."

Jim remembered the deadly flames which had consumed the old wooden cottage, an historic piece of property which sat next to the small schoolhouse. It had been used for holiday events and school gatherings, an informal meeting spot which adequately served the teachers and parents alike in various functions. The fire had licked upwards towards the stars that fateful Halloween night, the universe itself turning cruel as it displayed a brilliant, cloudless evening, a stark contrast to the horror which erupted below.

Six children waiting for their teacher to return from the school building. Trapped in the basement. The investigators pieced together a theory for what had happened to them. One of them probably had locked the door, attempting to scare their classmates. A spark had caught somewhere above from the fireplace, quickly spreading along the aged floorboards and transforming the cozy rustic cottage into a blazing inferno. The children never had a chance.

Jim felt like crying, but the tears had long since dried up and abandoned him.

He'd told the mayor about the wiring problem on a routine inspection, giving him the estimated cost for repair. Jack held him off, claiming a lack of current funds. Told Jim to wait a few months, as surely nothing would happen. The investigators had blamed the disaster on the fireplace itself, on a chance spark. The parents had blamed the teacher for leaving the children alone, and she'd been fired the following week, subsequently disappearing without any forwarding address. But Jim knew the truth, and it had consumed him completely.

And that was before the real dead had started to visit him.

Jim finally looked up, breaking from his grim reverie. "I expect you to be there. At eight, in the *North Ternh Church,* in front of the side building. A bunch of kids are having a Halloween party, and they were told that the town mayor would be the host. A small gesture, if nothing else."

"You act like it happened on purpose." Jack scowled. "An accident, hear me? Not our fault. And they never proved that it was anything else."

"Do this for the kids, Jack."

Before they drive me mad.

"The kids, please."

They're killing me.

The mayor put the flask back in the drawer. "Oh, all right. I'll be there."

Jim nodded, turning to leave. He mouthed a silent prayer as he walked through the doorway.

Please save us both.

««——»»

October 30th

The autumn sun shone brilliantly overhead, the day a living testament to all the good things which existed in nature and the hearts of men. People seemed genuinely cheerful, and the elementary school Halloween parade was in full swing, the little goblins marching down main street in a wash of ghoulish traffic. Mr. Milton opened the doors of his country store wide, placing tables on the cracked sidewalk filled with caramel apples, candy corn, and cups of steaming hot apple cider. The smell of honey roasted peanuts was strong, and he prepared a fresh batch for the excited children and teachers alike, more than one parent creeping up and giving him that 'may I please have one' look?

The mayor stood on the balcony of his office, an orange and black banner flapping before him in its harvest glory. Jim watched the events from a distance, as he stood across the street and partially down a side alleyway. But the sight of the mayor heralding the parade made him feel sick to his stomach. It had taken the small town many months to heal, but the process would never completely be finished. Families were scarred for life because of the terrible fire. Children still woke up from youthful sleep, nightmare wings plaguing their once-peaceful rest.

Jim waited until the last child disappeared around the corner, fading into the slate gray afternoon. He then left, returning to the water tower where he'd been working for the past two days. Keeping occupied was the only defense he could muster against the phantoms which visited him in the cool evenings. Stay busy or go mad.

He whistled absently to himself as he drove out to the patch of woods which housed the water tower itself. Grabbing his tool pouch, he climbed the tall ladder which led up to the top of the structure, where the security lights needed to be replaced. Not normally afraid of heights, he was uneasy as he moved higher, rung by rung, his hands feeling moist from sweat beneath the tough leather.

Three quarters up he glanced skyward, freezing as a figure appeared at the top. He blinked, swallowed heavily, but there was nothing there. Anxiety crept over his chest and he stopped. He was a tormented man, and it didn't take much for him to become suspicious of anything. Visions of spectral children swam before his eyes, and sinister thoughts stirred within his mind. Another visit? In daylight yet?

After a few moments he went upwards again, slowly and cautiously. When he reached the top, he half-expected to see a pair of costumed trick-or-treaters waiting, but there was nothing, only chipped paint and scattered leaves.

He quickly unpacked the necessary tools and concentrated on the task at hand, banishing all dark thoughts from his head.

Keep busy.

He spliced the exposed wires, cutting the insulation with his pocket knife. Without warning, a sudden gust of wind whipped through the tree tops, and the sun scurried behind a cloud. The temperature seemed to drop instantly, and his blood ran cold as two figures appeared from the corner of his eye.

He tilted his head in that direction, his worst fears materializing. Two costumed children stood there, one dressed in a black cape, complete with witches' broom. Except the outfit was tattered and scorched, the broom nothing more than a shriveled stick. The other child was a clown, missing half of its face, with a cracked metal horn, partially melted, in one small hand.

The dead had returned early this day.

The first child lifted a hand, pointing towards Jim. The gesture had a horrible effect on him, and he felt as if a lance of steel had pierced his chest. They were finally claiming him as their own, he thought. He didn't move for a long moment, and the sky seemed to grow even darker. But then he noticed something—maybe the child had something else in mind as the object of attention, pointing to his own hand.

The one holding the knife.

"You want me to kill myself?" He choked in horror. The clown child shook its head.

Images poured through his mind then—hints and suggestions, ones which he'd come to recognize as their way of communicating to him. Whispers rustled through his inner thoughts, and he understood two ideas, or words, in particular.

...pumpkin carving...

He was to bring his knife tomorrow. For carving.

Tears stung his eyes, causing him to blink. When he did, the children had vanished, leaving him alone on the water tower. He bowed his head, feeling as if he were the only one left alive in a forsaken, dead world.

And maybe he really was.

«« —»»

All Hallow's Eve

It had all come down to this.

Jim stared into the night, watching the bonfire which he'd started about half an hour ago in front of the aged *North Terhn Church*, its walls stained brown with moss, the rectangular windows vacant and desolate. He'd gathered the kindling, prodded on by the incessant chattering of the lost children, who seemingly at will could invade his mind, chase down his vulnerabilities, resurrect his guilt, and corner him. There was no escape for him.

Cinders smoldered, ashes sparked like screaming fireflies. Dried sticks crackled, consumed by the angry blaze. Jim continued to watch, and wait, his cold gaze unblinking. Waiting for the children to arrive.

And they came.

In pairs, from the surrounding trees. First starting as mere suggestions, the skeletal branches quivering over their shimmering forms, then growing more substantial, half-shadows, something indefinable and extraordinary. They moved across the barren ground mechanically, the faces costumed, all of them carrying the treat bags. Jim could not have imagined a more desolate and terrible scene. It was Halloween, and the earth was unleashing its lost ones, ghosts and goblins from the very bowels of despair.

They approached the fire, encircling it, stretching out their hands to one another, clasping in an unbreakable grip which could transcend the gap between life and death. Jim remained motionless, knowing that his past had fully awakened, had found its way to the present, rearing its grisly head to full height, and now was taking action.

And in what dark form would it take shape, what will be my cursed role in the monstrous climax?

The children were locked hand-in-hand, and Jim could see their features in the murky firelight. The scorched flesh, gleaming bones, a reminder as to the fateful events of a year ago. And they were together again. Soon it would be time.

A pair of headlights appeared from the nearby road, and Jim knew that Jack had arrived as promised. And Jim had kept his own promise to the children. He wondered then about their hold over him. Jack had obviously not suffered the same horrendous nightmares which tormented him, the calling which could not have been denied. Jim knew the answer. The mayor still admitted no real guilt, blaming the fire on freak circumstance, ill fortune. A granite denial, with no wrong-doing in his mind.

The vehicle came into view, a new four-door sedan, now churning into the church driveway. The car entered the tight parking lot, coming to a stop several dozen yards in front of the fire. Jim watched the door open, the mayor's husky figure trudging forward in the twilight.

The fire cackled gleefully, sending a fresh shower of sparks into the maw of darkness pressing eagerly downward from the autumn night. The wind stirred from slumber, catching the dead leaves and lifting them across the grass, tumbling, skipping, and twirling.

How they dance to the rhythm of death.

Jack cautiously approached the fire, looking curiously at the church in the distance. Jim watched in fascination as the mayor continued onward. Incredibly, Jack seemed completely oblivious to the spectral children, who still remained standing with hands clasped together. It was the most frightening vision Jim had ever experienced. He was terrified beyond belief as Jack was now right behind one of them, a girl wearing a ballerina dress, the outfit singed and ruined, her golden locks stained from soot and ashes.

"Well, when does the party start? I don't have all night, you know." Jack frowned, stepping towards the blaze and rubbing his hands together. Two of the children separated, letting the mayor pass through their terrible ring. When he'd gone another few feet further, the children moved closer, completing the bond once again. And still Jack was unaware of their presence.

"Are the kids inside? I'll take a quick swig if they are, need to warm my bones." The mayor pulled out his small metal flask, snapping off the cap and swallowing deeply.

Jim broke from his silence. "Can't you *see* them?" He gestured with his arms in a sweeping motion.

"Hmm?" The mayor wrinkled his face in confusion.

"Behind you—all around the fire. It's them…the six children." Jack moved closer, stopping just short of their dim figures, terrified and bewildered.

"What are you talking about?" Jack growled. "Is this some kind of a sick joke? I came out here as a favor—"

"Are you blind?" Jim shook his head in disbelief.

"And are you crazy?" Jack stared at him suspiciously, the glare from the bonfire making his face appear ghastly. "Why did you tell me to come out here anyway? Is there a party or not—don't waste my time with any of your misplaced guilt. I'm getting really tired of your attitude. It wasn't our fault!"

"You don't feel anything inside, do you?" Jim grew angry—the emotion was strong, overcoming even his fear of the six who waited patiently before him.

"Give it a break. I'm done arguing with you, Jim. Go on and live with your own guilt then. Of course I feel horrible, but my hands are clean in this. What do you think I am, some kind of a monster?"

Jim's eyes glazed over with hatred. "Yes..."

...our pumpkin...

"I do."

...celebrate...

A look of surprise crossed Jack's face and he stepped backwards, the children looking on silently. A knife appeared in Jim's hand.

"You're insane," the mayor gasped in fear, clutching his chest and stumbling backwards.

Jim thought he heard the sound of gleeful laughter, but he couldn't be sure. He lunged forward swiftly, raising the knife high into the air in a dreadful arc. Jack failed to move, immobilized by his numbing terror. He never had a chance to run, and couldn't have escaped regardless.

Jim clenched his teeth.

I'll cut them a fine Jack-o-lantern...

As Jim slashed the mayor with the blade, he thought several of the children nodded their heads in approval.

He couldn't be sure though, as he carved his guilt away with the knife.

««——»»

Jim cleaned up his gruesome handiwork. He found a fresh grave in the cemetery which sat alongside the old church. He doubted anyone would notice anything unusual, as the ground had been recently dug up in that spot.

The children were gone, once again banished to another world. Jim felt better now, at peace with himself. Cleansed. The first such positive feelings he'd experienced in a long time. He didn't consider himself a murderer, but only a tool of justice, a provider of overdue retribution.

And he always felt this way once the act had followed to its dreadful conclusion. There had been other towns, other faces and names. He couldn't remember them all anymore. Jim only knew one thing, and that was to move forward, keep the unquenchable fires which raged inside his heart at bay. At least for a while.

There would always be a need for people like Jack, unwilling associates to his terrible longing for violence. A vessel to transform the guilt from himself to another.

It was the only way he could still live with himself and not go totally mad. Jim whistled cheerfully as he drove home, the harvest moon grinning at him from above.

He grinned back.

THE LINGERING SCENT OF BRIMSTONE

The first thing Emily Doyle thought when she took the phone call from her mother shortly before 4:45 p.m. on Tuesday afternoon, July 6, 2004 was *Oh my God, no!*

"I've already called the police," her mother said, her voice strangely calm despite the severity of the situation. "I've sent the Baker boys out on their bikes in the hope they see where he went but—"

"I'll be right there, I'm leaving now!" Emily blurted, fighting back tears as she slammed the phone down and grabbed her purse.

Her co-worker, Lisa Wheatland, looked up, her pretty features concerned. "Everything okay?"

"I've got to go, somebody just took Amy." Emily could barely speak; already she could feel the fear and the shock hit her, freezing her up.

"*What?*"

Emily headed out of her cubical and made a beeline out of the office, ignoring Lisa's questions, only one thing on her mind.

Oh my God I can't believe this is happening, I can't believe this is happening, please let it be a mistake—

Somehow she made it out of the building and into her car, where she threw her purse on the pas-

J. F. GONZALEZ

senger side bucket seat. She slammed the door and started the engine, peeling out of the parking space and heading out to Route 372.

She had to force herself to be calm as she drove home, her heart racing. Her mother's voice echoed in her mind as she made the normally twenty-five minute drive home in ten minutes.

Emily, it's mom. You have to come home right away. Somebody snatched Amy while she was playing outside with the Baker kids.

What?

I called the police. I saw it happen and I tried to stop it but he was too fast. He just grabbed her and threw her in the car. It happened so fast—

What are you telling me, mom, are you trying to tell me somebody kidnapped Amy?

Yes! Somebody grabbed her while I was sitting on the front porch watching her! Now please come home! I've already called the police, they're on their way over and—

The conversation replayed in her mind as she raced home.

By the time she pulled into her neighborhood her nerves were shattered.

The first thing she saw were half a dozen police cars parked in front of the house, lights flashing.

She pulled into the driveway and was out of the car, stumbling in her haste to reach the front porch. She was barely aware of the humidity, fragrant with the scent of newly mown grass. She was barely aware of the policemen gathered around the front porch as she headed straight to the front door into her mother's arms.

"Where is she?" she babbled, unable to control the shakiness of her voice. "Have they found her yet? Have they—"

"Calm down," Mom said, taking her by the shoulders and trying to get her to sit down on the sofa. "They're out looking for her."

The living room spun before her as a uniformed officer sat down beside her and gently assured her he had the entire Warwick Police Department on the case. The state's Amber Alert was in affect with a description of the kidnapper's vehicle—a beige Cadillac, late seventies model—and a physical description of the kidnapper (white male in his late thirties, wearing tan Dockers and a white sport shirt). Emily felt her world collapse as her eyes focused on a stuffed animal on the sofa—Amy's favorite, a green teddy bear with dark eyes. *I can't believe it, I can't believe it, I can't believe—*

"We're going to find her," the uniformed officer told her. He was in his late forties, balding, watery blue eyes set in a hound dog face. "The kids got a good description and your mom got a partial on the plate and we got the State Police on it. Every cop has this guy's description. We'll get him."

Emily wasn't paying attention. All she could think about was Amy, wondering what was happening to her.

At some point she lost her composure and broke down.

The next thing she was aware of was her husband Jeff, holding her. She blinked, becoming aware of his presence as the sound of his voice came through. "…I appreciate everything. I know we're going to find her. Amy's a tough little girl and we've gone through all the safety precautions about what to do if a stranger were to lure her into his car. We're going to find her."

Emily took a deep breath, her mind focused on what Jeff just said. *We've gone through all the safety precautions about what to do if a stranger were to lure her into his car.*

We've gone through all the safety precautions—

—all the safety precautions—

Dear God…

Jeff led Emily away from the throng of police officers that had gathered in the living room. She had no idea when he'd arrived home, but it must have been a few minutes ago. Her mother was sitting at the kitchen table, looking shocked. A detective dressed in black slacks, a white shirt and black tie was sitting at the table with her, jotting something down in a notebook. "I'm going to get Emily something to calm her nerves and get her to lie down, okay?" Jeff said to the detective.

The detective looked up and nodded. Emily tried to make eye contact with her mother, who looked down at the table. She noticed the time—six-thirty p.m.

How long have I been out of it? Oh my God!

The cop with the hound dog face approached them. "Mrs. Doyle…Mr. Doyle…"

"Did you find her?" The words flew out of Emily's mouth before she could stop them.

Hound Dog Face shook his head. "Not yet, ma'am. We're chasing down several leads and the local news is on the case. Thought you might want to know." He gestured outside. "There's a couple reporters and a news van outside. We can keep them at bay if you want."

"Yes, officer, please," Jeff said. His grip on her shoulders was comforting, familiar. For the first time in years she noticed how different his grip felt with his missing left pinkie finger; gone now almost as long as Amy had been alive. It had been so long since he'd lost it that its loss seemed normal now. He squeezed her shoulders gently. "Thank you for everything."

Hound Dog Face tried to look encouraging, but Emily knew he was troubled. She knew the statistics of stranger abductions; she knew that despite their rare occurrence it still happened. They had never been worried about anything like that happening, but they'd still done what every conscientious parent would do and enrolled her in self-awareness and self-defense classes. They'd done everything they could to protect Amy—they'd moved from the mean streets of Los Angeles to this little town in rural Pennsylvania to be closer to Emily's mother, hoping to provide a safe haven for Amy to grow up in, away from the dangers of the big city. They'd taught Amy all the necessary drills—don't get in a car with a stranger; if a stranger asks you to help him look for a lost pet tell him no and run away; if a stranger grabs you rotate your arms and legs like a windmill and scream; fight and yell, kick and scratch, aim for the eyes and the crotch. They'd taught her other things too: don't take unnecessary risks; listen to your instinct; if you believe something is dangerous, avoid it. They'd taught her all this and somehow they knew that it might not be enough so they'd taken extra precautions, somehow believing nothing would never happen, especially *this*.

But it had.

The beginning of a nightmare.

«« — »»

Emily Doyle didn't know how she got through the night, but somehow she did. With her mother and Jeff beside her, she was able to maintain some vigilance of strength. They would find her daughter. She was alive. She had to be.

A squad car sat outside the house at sentry duty for the remainder of the night while the Warwick Police department joined forces with the Pennsylvania State Police and conducted a search. A description of the vehicle and the perpetrator went out over the wire and the latest updates were relayed to Hound Dog face, who had been assigned to stay with the Doyle family until the nightmare was over.

Emily didn't sleep.

She couldn't. Not with her nerves wired with worry, not with her mind constantly wondering if everything was going to turn out okay. She traded silent glances with Jeff and knew he was worrying about the same things, but they remained quiet. Emily's mother went through bouts of crying, chastising herself for not doing enough to protect Amy, and Jeff finally convinced her that she'd done all she could. She had done everything right. Finally Laura fell into a light sleep on the sofa, occasionally twitching in her sleep as the visions of what happened tormented her dreams.

At seven a.m. Hound Dog Face's cell phone rang.

He answered it, his eyes bloodshot, his jowls slacker now with lack of sleep. "Yeah?" He listened for a moment and Emily noted the sudden change in his features from fatigue to a slow warming of hope. "Are you serious? Oh that is good news! I...yes, let me tell them. They're right here—"

Jeff and Emily were up in a flash. "They found her!" Emily gasped.

Hound Dog Face held up his hand and nodded, still listening. He looked hopeful and serious as whoever was on the other end filled him in. Emily was frantic with hope and a new found joy. *They found her*!

"Okay...yes, I'll tell them. Yes, I'll bring them over." Hound Dog hung up the phone.

Emily couldn't stop the tears. "Is she okay? Where is she? Can we see her? What—"

Hound Dog Face took her hands and addressed both of them, his features still bearing the good news but Emily detected an undercurrent of something that troubled him. "We found her. She's okay, she's alive."

Emily felt her knees threaten to buckle. She fought to remain standing and she could feel that Jeff had similarly been overtaken by this sudden emotion of good news. She heard him draw in a breath, sniffling back tears of joy. "Where is she?"

"They're taking her to Ephrata Community Hospital to look her over," Hound Dog Face said, still looking shell-shocked at this news himself. "She's...the officer I talked to examined her personally and...he said she didn't appear to be hurt but..." He licked his lips nervously. "She was covered in blood."

Emily gasped. *Oh God*!

Jeff stiffened beside her, reacting to this news.

Hound Dog continued. "She was found in north Lancaster County wandering along 272 about six-thirty this morning. A trucker spotted her and called the police. When the officers arrived they identified her and...questioned her." Hound Dog swallowed and Emily could tell he was nervous. "She seemed to be fine but in light shock and she was able to tell the officers where...where she was taken. She described a motel and a squad car was dispatched there and found the vehicle, parked in front of a room at the end of the building." Hound Dog's face looked hesitant, as if he didn't know how to finish the story. "The perpetrator...what was left of him...was...well...he was pretty badly mangled, let me put it that way. Cliff, the guy who called, basically described the room as resembling an abattoir."

Emily was horrified. She could tell that Jeff was having the same reactions, but she tried to calm her sense of shock and horror in favor of letting her gratitude and joy that her daughter was alive and safe show through. The tears that were streaming down became a flood as she melted into Jeff's embrace. "I want to see her! I want to see my baby!"

Jeff held her, trying to be strong for her, and Hound Dog Face nodded and told them he was going to drive them to Ephrata Hospital to see their daughter.

«« —»»

Laura rode with them to Ephrata Community Hospital. Emily could barely contain her emotions. She wavered between crying and trading worried glances with Jeff, who sat on the driver's side in the back seat looking out the window, his features silent and stony during the fifteen-minute drive.

When they reached the hospital Emily had to resist the urge to run inside and demand to see her daughter. She let herself be led down the hallway and up an elevator. Another uniformed officer met them and led them to a room in the pediatric wing where Amy was seated on a paper-covered hospital bed dressed in a white hospital issued gown.

"*Mommy!*" Amy's face brightened instantly at the sight of her parents.

"*Amy!*" Emily and Jeff rushed to their daughter and Emily felt a sudden sense of elation as she swept the little girl into her arms. Amy began to cry, her small shoulders quivering with sobs. "It's okay, honey, it's okay," Emily cooed, holding her daughter, stroking her hair. "It's all over now, you're safe, mommy and daddy are here."

Jeff was holding both of them and she felt Amy shift in an attempt to include her father in her embrace. Behind them, Hound Dog Face and the other uniformed cop stood by the door uncomfortably. "We'll leave you alone for a minute," Hound Dog Face said. He exited the room with his partner, leaving the Doyle family alone.

The family continued to huddle close together, whispering to their daughter in soothing tones. Eventually Amy's cries trickled down. Emily held on to her, eyes closed, thankful that her daughter was alive and safe.

Jeff stepped back, running his hands over Amy's head and face. Emily stepped back as well, performing a visual inspection of her daughter. Her hair was damp, as if she'd just had it washed. "Are you okay honey?"

Amy nodded her head, her eyes wide, still red with tears.

"You weren't hurt anywhere?"

Amy shook her head. "No. I'm…I'm okay."

Emily and Jeff traded a glance and Emily knew from looking at her husband that he was thinking the same thing. *They said she was covered in blood and that the room her abductor checked into was spattered with it…that there wasn't much left of him. That must mean—*

"You weren't cut anywhere at all honey?" Jeff asked Amy.

Amy shook her head and began to cry again. "What happened to me? I don't remember what happened!"

"It's okay, honey," Emily said, pulling her daughter close to her. "It's okay. You're fine. You're safe and you're fine and that's all that matters."

"I don't remember anything," Amy said, her voice sniffling. "I...I tried to fight him off but he handcuffed me in the car and then...we got to that...that hotel and he got me into that room and then...*I don't remember what happened after that!* The next thing I remember I...I was walking outside, wandering around and...I was...*covered in blood!*" She broke down, sobbing quietly.

Emily and Jeff traded another glance and Emily felt a heaviness settle in her chest. Was what happened so horrible that she'd blocked it out?

Jeff was holding his daughter. "It's okay, sweetie. Mommy and daddy are going to take care of everything. Don't worry...everything will be fine. The only thing that matters is that you're safe."

Emily joined him in trying to calm Amy down and after a few minutes their daughter's sobs trickled down. Amy sat morosely on the bed, her gaze far away and dazed. She was going to need help at some point. The most immediate concern now was getting her out of the hospital and getting her home; the next was trying to keep the police from questioning her further. They would want to, Emily was sure of it, but she didn't want the questioning to damage Amy further. She traded a glance with Jeff, who nodded at her. It was like they were telepathically connected at this moment, reading their thoughts, making silent plans to resume their lives in peace and quiet the way things had been before somebody had tried to shatter it.

There was a soft knock at the door and then a doctor wearing a white lab coat poked his head in. He appeared to be in his mid-forties and wore glasses on a round face. "How's our patient?" he asked.

"Fine," Emily said, standing up, feeling a hundred percent better now that she had seen and touched Amy, confirming she was alive. "She's a little fighter."

"She is," the doctor said, smiling. He introduced himself as Dr. Knoll and flipped to Amy's medical chart. "Physically, Amy's fine. Emotionally she's been through a shock. I'd like to prescribe a sedative to help calm her nerves for the next several weeks, and then I'd like her to follow up with Dr. Jascowski, a child psychiatrist in the Denver area. She's going to need some help coping with what she's been through."

"Will the police want to talk to her?" Emily asked.

"They tried but they couldn't get anything out of her," Dr. Knoll said. "They'll probably want to try again once she's entered therapy. In the meantime, I'm sure they'll have plenty of other potential witnesses they could question to help explain what happened."

The rest of that morning was a blur; leaving Amy for a few more hours of observation in the hospital while Emily and Jeff went to the

Ephrata Police Station to answer questions. As the morning unfolded they learned the identity of the man who had abducted their daughter—thirty-year-old Ken Banning, a computer programmer with no prior criminal record. As the pieces were put together, a very sketchy chain of events was put into place with several large holes threatening to make the entire theory collapse were it not for the actual physical evidence—a very alive but shaken eight-year-old girl, and the scant remains of Banning.

The motel clerk who checked Banning in reported he had done so late that morning. After checking in, Banning was gone for a good four or five hours. He returned just past four-thirty—the clerk saw the car pull past the front office and around to the back where he had rented his room and he didn't think about him again until this morning when he showed up for work and the place was overrun by cops.

Based on what the police had been able to get out of Amy and the children she'd been playing with, as well as the motel clerk, the crime was both pre-meditated and impulsive; pre-meditated because Ken had already secured a motel room in which to commit his crime in privacy, impulsive because he wasn't familiar with the area and the kids that were playing with Amy reported they had seen him drive by twice before he'd stopped a third time, left his car running, got out of the vehicle and simply grabbed Amy off the sidewalk and made a beeline for his car. He'd thrown her into the car, quickly handcuffing her to the door handle of the front seat and driven away. Emily shuddered at what the police told her they'd found in the blood spattered motel room—leather restraints and a ball gag.

Amy had screamed and struggled during the ten-mile ride to the motel, and she claimed that Ken produced a gun at one point and threatened to shoot her if she continued struggling. A handgun was recovered from the vehicle but this proved to be fake. Nevertheless, it had the desired effect and Amy was compliant until they reached the motel. When Ken tried to usher her in to the room she became combative again and Ken quickly gagged her, uncuffed her wrists from the door handle, and carried her into the motel room.

Amy didn't remember what happened after that.

The next thing she remembered was walking along 272, dazed and covered in blood. She didn't remember how long she'd been wandering—she'd started off when it was dark and then it was dawn and then she was found by that trucker. She didn't remember how the blood got on her, and she didn't see what happened to the man who'd kidnapped her. Dr. Knoll explained that Amy's lack of memory in the hours between arriving at the motel and wandering near Route 272 in the early morning hours was due to shock; the mind's natural defensive mechanism to cope with what had happened to her.

The motel clerk claimed that he heard no violent sounds of struggle coming from the room. When pressed on the matter, he later claimed that he thought he heard screams, but he didn't feel inclined to investigate. "Nobody was screaming for help," he explained during questioning. "The people that check in here…they tend to rent rooms by the hour, you know what I'm saying? This guy, I just figured he wanted to play a little heavy duty by renting for the night, you know? Long as he paid and nobody called the cops, why bother?"

The pitiful remains of Ken Banning were still being examined later that day when Emily and Jeff took Amy home.

Deputy Sam Boyer—Hound Dog Face to Emily Doyle—watched the family leave in a silver Saturn station wagon. His partner, Don Hudson stood beside them. "She's one lucky girl," Don said.

"She is," Sam Boyer replied. "I can't imagine what she could have gone through."

"Neither can I."

"Have you heard from the coroner?"

"Nah. They're still trying to put the guy back together."

"Any idea what cut him to pieces like that?"

"If they know, they aren't saying yet."

Sam Boyer shook his head. What happened to Ken Banning was what had the department in a frenzy. On one hand it was a good thing that Amy Doyle was alive and unscathed physically…but something happened in that room that tore Ken Banning apart and Sam had no doubt that Amy saw what happened and it scared her so bad she'd blocked it out of her memory.

Don Hudson appeared to be reading his thoughts. "Think we'll ever find out what happened?"

"I imagine we will eventually," Sam Boyer said, turning to go back into the Lititz Police Station.

Don followed him inside, still chatting. "You know, something weird just occurred to me."

"What's that?"

"When I shook Emily Doyle's hand at one point I noticed she was missing one of her pinkie fingers."

Sam Boyer frowned. "I noticed that about her husband. Jeff's left pinkie finger was missing. I didn't think much of it at the time. Figured maybe it got lost in an accident. Emily's missing hers too?"

Don Hudson nodded. "Yeah. Weird, huh?"

"It is," Sam Brower agreed.

«« —»»

It had been a long time since they'd had a fight. They waited until Amy was asleep to let it all out.

Emily started by screaming at Jeff that this was his fault. Jeff countered by saying *she's alive, isn't she? She's alive and healthy and she's going to go through a lot of emotional turmoil, but she's going to get better. That's what matters, Emily. Our daughter is* alive. *If we hadn't done what we'd done, she'd be laid out naked and dead and alone in some farmer's field by now, raped and murdered.*

Emily started sobbing, knowing Jeff was right but still feeling angry at him—at herself—for what had happened. It was true—Amy was *alive*. She would have a chance at life that was denied to so many other children who'd faced similar horrors. But there was a price she and Jeff would have to pay now and she was sure Jeff knew that. He had to.

Surely he had to have noticed the smell by now.

She thought she smelled it late last night, when they were still waiting to hear if they'd caught the bastard who'd snatched Amy. It began as a faint tickle in the back of her throat that she first dismissed as tears—she'd been crying a lot—but it remained steady and constant. A steady smoky scent, pervading and unique, with an underlying tint of rotten eggs.

It remained with her the rest of that morning and throughout the day. There were times when she appeared to forget about it and not notice it was there, and then suddenly it would be almost enveloping, strong in its odor. Several times she found herself stepping outside her mother's house or the police station where they'd gone for questioning to see if she could see smoke but she never saw anything.

"Don't you smell it?" she asked, looking at her husband. She had settled down on the sofa, crying, and paused amid her sobs to look at him through tear-stained eyes.

"Smell what?"

"Just…sniff…" She sniffed the air. Despite her stuffed nose she could still make out the faint scent.

Jeff sniffed. His face flushed briefly. "I don't know what you're talking about," he said.

She could tell he was lying.

At some point during the argument the subject of packing up and moving came up. "What good would it do?" Jeff asked. He was pacing the living room, running his fingers through his thinning hair. "The cops would think something is up."

"How?" Emily asked. She was sitting on the sofa. Despite being tired, despite being up for over twenty-four hours, she was wired.

"We can't just pack up and leave!" Jeff protested.

"What are we going to tell them when they want to question Amy?"

Jeff paced the living room. She could tell he was thinking about it. "I don't know. We'll think of something."

Emily sat on the sofa, fidgeting. They'd never stopped to think about other consequences if this happened—or something similar. They'd been as careful as possible to avoid exposing Amy to danger. She told herself that she couldn't continue beating herself up over what happened. What happened wasn't their fault; the danger had come to *them*. Thank God they'd done something about it.

She paused at that thought: *thank God.*

God had nothing to do with it.

She became aware of the scent again, this time unmistakable, and she broke down again, weeping silently.

Jeff could only pace the living room.

«« — »»

Officer Sam Boyer came to see them three weeks later.

Emily knew this day would come. After their blow-up the evening Amy was found, she and Jeff agreed to think about it and talk about what they would do and say if the cops came around and started asking questions. In the meantime, they both agreed that they had to move. They loved living in their little town, but their idealistic dream of a small-town life had now been shattered permanently by what had happened. Jeff began quietly making plans to resign from his position at Braun and Sons and Emily made plans to transfer a portion of their savings account into bonds, something that would gain interest they could draw some income on. They'd made a tidy bundle on the sale of their home in California, and they'd been fortunate enough to not have to touch any of it. That bundle had grown in the five years they'd been in Pennsylvania and it would continue to grow a little bit each year, so long as they lived frugally for awhile.

Jeff began looking into real estate in New England. Specifically Maine and New Hampshire.

Emily doted on Amy and drove her to her daily therapy sessions where she seemed to be rapidly improving. The psychiatrist told Emily and Jeff that what she had witnessed in that motel room would no doubt live with her forever. "Fortunately she's suppressed that memory," he explained one afternoon. "It's in her subconscious, though, and there's no doubt we'll be dealing with this for some time, but for now her mind is handling this very well. She's not displaying any symptoms of depression or paranoia and she's sleeping well. My recommendation is she remain on the medication for the next year or so and I continue to see her every week, then maybe we can drop the visits down to bi-weekly, then monthly. At some point, preferably when she's in her early twenties, we're going to need to schedule some heavy therapy to draw those memories out gradually and deal with them. It will be catastrophic if they come out of her suddenly and without warning."

Emily and Jeff nodded, silently agreeing. Emily once again became angry with herself for allowing Jeff to talk her into this and once again her thoughts circled around to the inevitable. What they had done was the only thing they *could* have done. When Amy was born they'd made a vow to each other that they'd do anything to keep Amy safe from harm and they'd kept their end of the bargain. If they hadn't, their daughter would be dead, plain and simple.

But at some point the questions were going to come, either from Amy or the police, and they knew that it was going to be harder to try to fool the police. So they discussed their options and agreed on a plan of action.

And now it was time to act on it.

Sam Boyer stood on the front porch, alone. He was wearing his uniform and he nodded at Emily as she answered the front door. "Mrs. Doyle."

"What can I do for you, Officer Boyer?"

"Is your husband home?"

"Right here." Jeff appeared beside Emily.

"Amy home?" Officer Boyer asked.

"She's with my mother," Emily said.

"We need to talk," Officer Boyer said.

Jeff opened the screen door. "Come on in."

They offered Officer Boyer drinks and he declined. He sat down on the sofa and got right to the point. "The autopsy on Ken Banning has been complete and our investigation is far from over. There's…" he hesitated, regarding them both uncertainly. "…lots of unanswered questions. I realize that Amy doesn't remember anything about that night—"

"And we don't intend to put pressure on her to submit to hypnosis in an effort to find out what happened to that scumbag, either," Jeff said, sternly.

"I realize that," Officer Boyer said. He looked nervous. "Trouble is, I got the State Police breathing down my neck for answers. The Attorney General of Pennsylvania wants answers too. I realize that legally we're rather restricted in what we can do. Officially, Ken Banning's death is classified as a homicide and your daughter is the only witness. She's not considered a suspect because there's no physical evidence pointing to—"

"You were actually considering Amy a suspect?" Emily asked, her temper flaring.

"No, no, not at all!" Officer Boyle said, raising a hand. "She's a victim in this, but she's also a witness—and a good one, too, if she could only..." His voice trailed off.

"If she could only remember what happened," Emily finished for him.

"Yeah," Officer Boyer nodded.

Emily and Jeff glanced at each other and turned back to Officer Boyer. "I'm sorry we can't help you, Officer," Jeff said.

Officer Boyer continued as if he hadn't heard them. "The coroner stated that Banning could have died in any number of ways: blood loss, shock. It's hard to be entirely sure if he was alive when most of the mutilation took place because his heart was never recovered, although the amount of blood in the room indicates that he *was* alive for some time while he was being torn apart. Some of the...injuries he sustained appear to be from teeth...or claws from some kind of animal of some sort..."

Emily resisted the urge to gasp; she glanced quickly at Jeff who avoided her gaze. Officer Boyer was watching them and he noticed Emily's reaction. "Does this mean anything to you at all?"

"No," Emily said a little too quickly.

"I think it does," Officer Boyer said, gaze locked on Emily's now.

"Why would you think that?" Emily asked, trying to dismiss Boyer's allegations.

"Supposing some kind of animal got in that motel room and attacked Ken Banning, what difference does it make?" Jeff asked. "I mean, big deal! The man was going to rape and murder my daughter. Maybe Banning didn't check the place out too thoroughly when he got the room and woke up a bear or something that had slipped in through an open window or something."

"Forensics found no evidence of any animal or other people in the room aside from Ken Banning and Amy," Boyer said quickly.

"And since you said Amy isn't a suspect, you need to focus your investigation elsewhere," Jeff quickly countered. "You know we were nowhere near that motel—you were here all night with us. That leaves a third party."

Boyer's gaze was hard, stern. "There's something else I haven't told you yet."

"What's that?" Jeff said.

"We retrieved a knife at the scene," Boyer said slowly. "Banning's mother identified it as one her son owned. We found blood on it." He paused. "The blood on Banning's knife didn't match his blood type."

"So?"

"The blood was human."

Emily's heart pounded. She glanced at Jeff. *What is he talking about?* she wanted to ask.

"By process of elimination, we ran a test against the blood we drew from Amy a few weeks ago," Boyer said. "The blood on the knife matched."

Jeff opened his mouth, stunned. Emily's heart stopped; she felt numb.

"I know what you're probably thinking," Boyer continued. "It can't be Amy's blood. She sustained no injuries. Nevertheless, the sample from Banning's knife matched your daughter's blood type and I think we need to discuss this."

"Who knows about this?" Jeff asked, his voice raspy.

"Just the three of us, my assistant, and the coroner."

Emily's mind was racing, her limbs felt numb. She felt on the verge of faint.

"This needs to be explained because I have to submit our findings to the Prosecutor tomorrow. Do you understand what I'm talking about? You and I know Amy couldn't have killed Banning. We know *you* couldn't have done it. The prosecution is going to want some kind of case, though. We don't want a drawn out ugly court battle. I think you just want to pick up where you left off and get back to raising your little girl. Am I right?"

Emily could tell Jeff was stunned. This hadn't been in the script—no way were they prepared for this.

Boyer regarded them calmly. "I'm waiting."

Emily glanced at her husband again quickly and determined this latest revelation was too stunning for him—it had totally blindsided him. She turned back to Boyer and he met her gaze.

She nodded at him. "That's a lovely cross you're wearing Officer Boyer," she said.

"Thank you." Officer Boyer fingered the cross he wore around his neck on a slim gold chain.

"Are you a Christian man?"

"I am."

"Then you believe in Jesus...in God?"

"I do."

"Then if you believe in Jesus you believe in Heaven, correct?"

"I didn't come here for a Bible lesson, Mrs. Doyle."

Emily ignored him. "If you believe in Jesus and Heaven then you must believe in his adversary and the fiery pits of hell. Correct?"

"What does this have to with—"

"Please just answer the question, Officer Boyer!"

Boyer sighed. "Yes. I believe in Hell, Mrs. Doyle."

Emily continued, ignoring Jeff's nervous stare as he settled down in one of the kitchen chairs.

She also tried to ignore the scent, which had remained constant for the past three weeks.

"Do you have children, Mr. Boyer?"

"Yes."

"How many?"

"A son and a daughter."

"Do you love them?"

Boyer looked at Emily, his features uncomprehending. "Yes. I love them. Now please, what does—"

"How far would you go to protect your children, Mr. Boyer?"

Officer Boyer looked grim. "Mrs. Doyle—"

"Let me tell you a story, Mr. Boyer," Emily began. She could feel the shakiness in her voice and she pressed on. "Once upon a time there was a couple who tried and tried to have a child but they couldn't. For some reason, they just couldn't. They tried everything. Fertility doctors, various treatments. All to no avail. They prayed about it, and they kept trying and then finally the Lord blessed them with a child...a beautiful little girl they named Amy."

Officer Boyle listened. Jeff was sitting at the kitchen table, head bowed, not looking at them.

"When Amy was born her mother and father wept tears of joy. She was the most beautiful thing they had ever seen. They felt blessed. They swore to each other that they would love their child more than they loved themselves and that they would do everything in their power to protect and love and cherish and provide for her. You see, her mother and father never had that love and security when *they* were children. Her father came from a family of alcoholics that neglected him, and her mother never knew her father—she never knew her mother well either, since she was emotionally unavailable. They swore they would never put their daughter through what they went through as children. They would put their child first, above everything, even themselves. Their love for each other was still strong—in fact, it had strengthened with the birth of their daughter—but it was stronger for Amy. Do you understand their love for their child, Officer Boyer?"

Boyer said nothing; he waited for Emily to continue.

"A few days after Amy was born her mother and father sat up late one night talking. They talked about the uncertainty of the world and how worried they were about their child's future. They knew that they would be raising a healthy, happy, productive human being. They knew that their child would love them, would grow up to be a good person. They knew this with all their heart. But they were still afraid. They knew the world was full of...uncertainties...that they couldn't trust some people...they knew there would come a time in her life when their daughter would come in contact with people who would either wish to do harm to her or would unwillingly put her in that position. They knew that even if their daughter was as careful as they were going to raise her to be that they couldn't protect her from everything. They couldn't be there twenty-four-seven. So…" She raised her left hand, fingers splayed out; the pinkie was missing. "…they made a deal."

Boyer's eyes grew wide. He looked at Jeff, who was now looking at them, his own left hand held up, left pinkie missing. Emily watched him, noting the sharp rise in the Officer's breathing. "Do you understand what we're talking about, Officer Boyer?"

"I…" Boyer said, eyes darting from Emily to Jeff. "I don't know."

"I'll spell it out for you. You believe in God, don't you?"

"Yes."

"Jeff and I do too. But we also know that God…sometimes allows bad things to happen to good people. We've tried to understand why He allows this…and we both knew that if…something bad were to happen to our Amy that we would be devastated. And that God…wouldn't care. He wouldn't care about our suffering and anguish. I know that's probably blasphemous to you, Officer Boyer, hearing two self-professed Christians like ourselves saying God wouldn't care if he were to allow an innocent child to suffer. But…why does He allow so much suffering to exist in the world? Why does He allow children to step on land mines in Viet Nam, and why does He allow monsters to snatch children off the street, never to bring them back?" She faced Officer Boyer, the adrenaline running through her veins. "Why?"

Officer Boyer opened his mouth to answer and couldn't.

"Nobody can answer that question to my satisfaction, Officer Boyer," Emily continued. "Not my pastor, not a priest, not any minister I've spoken to. Nobody. Their answers ring false to me. And since we believed in God we began to…explore other options." She looked at Officer Boyer, left hand raised to emphasize her sacrifice. "If God wasn't going to care about the suffering of a little child, then we were going to do everything in our power to make sure nothing happened to our daughter. *Anything*."

Officer Boyer sputtered. "You mean, you—"

"We made a deal," Jeff said from the kitchen table, his face pale now, shoulders sagging with the weight of the dreadful implications of what had happened. "A protector for Amy who would only come to the rescue in the event she was put in imminent danger. Her life and soul for our souls. It would only become due and payable in the event…something like this were to happen."

Officer Boyer's face paled. "You…am I…are you telling me you sold your soul to—"

"The devil? A demon? Something like that, I suppose," Jeff said. Emily held back, her emotions running high. "It took months of research and prayer and…once we made the decision it was relatively easy. You can pray to demons just like you pray to God or Jesus or the angels. They answer your prayers the same way. But they do want…certain sacrifices." He held up his left hand, emphasizing the missing finger.

"You cut off your own *fingers*?" Officer Boyer asked.

"It's what they asked for," Emily said, her right hand caressing the spot where her left pinkie finger used to be. "It wasn't too difficult. Whiskey to deaden the pain, bandages to staunch the flow of blood when the ritual was over. We both used Jeff's electric bandsaw in the garage. Made it easier to explain to the doctors at Ephrata that Jeff slipped and fell while working in the garage and when I went to help him, I slipped and fell right beside him. They dismissed us as unlucky klutz's and patched us up."

"We told them we'd been in too much in shock to retrieve the fingers," Jeff continued. "That they'd fallen somewhere we couldn't get to them, that we realized we needed immediate medical attention and they worked with what they had. That made it easier to explain why they were missing when they couldn't be found later—rats, foxes, some small animal."

"They bought it," Emily said. "And we adjusted. It was a small sacrifice to make."

"And now we know that it was a success," Jeff said, his features grim. "The thing that protected our daughter that night…a dark demon created from our blood. That explains why you got a match."

"But—" Officer Boyer sputtered. "You're asking me to believe…*this*?"

"Do you smell anything odd, Officer Boyer?" Emily asked.

"Huh?"

"Sniff the air." She sniffed. "Smell anything unusual?"

Officer Boyer sniffed a couple of times. His brow furrowed in concentration. "Smells kinda like…it's really faint…but…" He sniffed a few more times. "It smells like…something's burning…like sulfur…"

"That's brimstone you're smelling Officer Boyer," Emily said, the tears streaming down her cheeks now. "You smell brimstone. We've been smelling it now ever since the day we were reunited with Amy, and everybody that's…that's been around us…has mentioned smelling it. It's…our mark." She broke down and wept silently.

Officer Boyer looked stunned. He turned to Jeff. "You mean…"

"'But the cowardly, unbelieving, abominable, murderers, sexually immoral, sorcerers, idolaters, and all liars shall have their part in the lake which burns with fire and brimstone, which is the second death.'" Jeff said. "That's from the Book of Revelations, Officer Boyer. It's a reminder that the bargain Emily and I made is now due and payable,"

And as Jeff put his arms around Emily in an attempt to comfort her,

Officer Boyer could only stand in their living room, his features still bearing a sense of shock. Emily wept, not caring what Officer Boyer did now. There was nothing he *could* do to them.

Officer Boyer turned away. "I'll see what I can come up with for the report I'm supposed to file to the Prosecutor."

Jeff's hand stroked Emily's hair. "Are you going to tell them what we just told you?"

Officer Boyer looked at Jeff and shook his head. "No. They wouldn't believe me."

"Do you believe us?"

Officer Boyer looked at them for a long time. Emily's sobs trickled down and she regarded him through tear-blurred eyes. "My rational side tells me I shouldn't," he said. "But…like you said…I'm a Christian man. And…"

Jeff and Emily said nothing. They held each other, watching as Officer Boyer came to grips with their revelation.

Officer Boyer's eyes reflected a sense of haunting. "I can't begin to imagine what you went through. To love your child that much to put yourselves…your *souls*…"

Officer Boyer shook his head and walked quietly out the front door. Leaving the Doyle family alone.

And as he drove to the station, trying to think of something to put down in his report that would explain Banning's cause of death, he couldn't get the lingering scent of brimstone out of his nostrils.

Run Away

The night absorbed the landscape around me, swallowing the terrain whole in a thick tapestry of shadows. Ahead of me I could see nothing but street lamps lining the freeway and ominous silhouettes of stalled cars laid out like gravemarkers, their occupants long fled or murdered. The only sounds were my own rapid footfalls, my own panting breaths, the disturbing sound of tearing flesh, and the snarls and growls of things pursuing me in the dark. The screams had stopped a few days ago. I feared I was the only thing left alive. It was all the incentive I needed to keep running.

I tried to stay beneath the streetlights. Slipping from one protective cone of electric sun to the next. Shadowy creatures lunged at me baring saber-like fangs and long gnarled claws, yellow luminescent eyes glazed with hunger. Gruesome things lived in the darkness now. I spun away from them, weaving and faking like an NFL runningback. I knew they couldn't catch me. Not as long as I kept running. They were slow, stupid, and every-fucking-where. There was just enough illumination between lights to allow me to see their silhouettes lurking there in the blackness, waiting to spring.

A car parked at the curb rocked and jerked

with violent activity as I passed it. A few weeks ago I would have thought there was a couple in there, fucking their brains out. Now I knew that whatever was in there wasn't copulating. It was eating. The wet smacking and sucking sounds, the grunts and growls and moans of ecstasy were not those of a happy couple consummating their relationship but of a feeding frenzy. I shivered and kept moving past. I still carried the axe I'd borrowed from a sporting goods store a few days ago when the cramps first began; the first indication that I wouldn't be able to outrun them forever. But whoever had owned that vehicle was past any heroics I could provide.

I hit a wet slick of dark liquid trailing out from under the car and nearly slipped; saving myself from a lethal fall by grabbing onto the next lamp post. I looked down at my running shoes already knowing that it wasn't motor oil that I'd stepped in. There was no time to wipe the tacky red substance from my sneakers. I had to get moving again. The car door was opening. Several long serpentine phantoms came slithering out tracking my scent, drawn to my heat. Had to run.

Human remains littered the street ahead. I would have to dodge the creatures while running the obstacle course of rotting carrion. Some of the bodies were still being fed on by the night things. I tried not to disturb their meal. I pumped my legs harder, as a herd of dark creatures rose from the gruesome maze of death and decay.

There had been all kinds of speculation as to where the things had come from. It had started with a few random attacks but soon swarms of the things began to pour out, covering the earth in a thick cloud of voracious evil. The best theory seemed to be that they had come from beneath the earth; roused from the bowels of hell by petroleum drilling equipment in search of hidden pockets of fossil fuel. The most popular one was that hell had unleashed its minions upon the earth. The end of times. Armageddon. Churches filled with parishioners begging the Lord for forgiveness. Many of them were eaten right on the church steps as they left, having made the mistake of worshipping past sunset.

Soon the wild theories and speculations began to peter off as thoughts turned towards survival and the theorists themselves were murdered in their beds. It seemed the entire human race was now under threat of extinction. Of course it could have just been happening in isolated cities and I'd just been unlucky enough to have run through every one of them. Or maybe it was just the West Coast? I couldn't be certain. My only concern now was with my own survival. I had to keep moving. I had to stay one step ahead of them.

I hurtled a couple of the night things as they burrowed in and out of a man who appeared to be about six-hundred pounds. Most of his girth was due to his body filling with gases as his organs decayed. He had obviously been dead for some time. The stench of the dead was overpowering. Nothing seemed to be alive anywhere except for the rapacious shadow creatures…and me. I tried to block out the thought that I might be the only living thing in the entire city to keep the panic from crushing the remaining air from my chest. I calmed myself as much as possible, concentrated on the road, maintained my heart rate at a steady even pace, still only slightly below panic level.

My lungs were burning and felt as if they would explode under the tremendous exertion. Still I maintained my pace. For the ninth day in a row I put in miles that would have awed the most dedicated ultramarathoner. There were still at least another three hours left before daylight and already I'd run twice the distance of the average marathon. But now my body was starting to rebel.

I was perhaps a day or two away from organ failure. I was losing fluids far too rapidly. And there was so little fat left on my body that my muscles were starting to consume themselves for fuel. Spots began to dance in front of my eyes as the oxygen in my blood continued to decrease, my lungs unable to keep up with the demand. But once again I could feel them expand a little farther to accommodate the strain and allow a few more breaths inside. The cramps in my legs and calves were getting worse. The blisters on my feet burst two days ago and the raw skin now rubbed against the synthetic leather of my broken down Tuned Air Max running shoes aggravating the tender flesh. Soon the sores would be infected and I wouldn't be able to run. I'd have to fight. But that was days away. Hopefully by then I'd be deep in the desert. Safe from the night things.

I jogged up the freeway entrance ramp dodging in between cars. As soon as I hit the freeway I knew that this had been a bad idea. The smell of death choked me and scalded my throat, churning a tidal wave of bile in my stomach. Even worse, the cars were too close together. If there were something inside waiting to lunge out at me, I had only inches to avoid it. But then again, if I managed to reach open highway where the traffic gridlock thinned out enough to allow a vehicle to pass through fast enough to avoid being attacked, I might be able to borrow one of the cars and give my legs a rest for awhile. I decided it was worth the risk. I kept running down the freeway, between the cars.

There were more lights on the freeway. Hardly any gaps between them. But where there were gaps, they were great expanses where the darkness seemed to stretch on for almost a mile before the light resumed. The pain in my calves, thighs, and feet was starting to slow me down, affecting my stride, and my lungs were starting to cramp again. I couldn't keep that pace up for long. I knew I had to make it to the end of the freeway.

I hadn't been awake during the day in nearly a week. I was too exhausted from running all night. If I could get a car and drive some during the night, then maybe I could wake up a little earlier and find out if anyone was still alive. Besides, I'd almost overslept two nights ago. By the time I woke up, the sun had already begun to set and the things had started crawling out of whatever dark pits they slept in. They were slithering into the apartment I'd slept in that morning, surrounding me. Luckily, I'd had the foresight to pick a ground-level apartment. I leapt out through the window with a herd of the things scratching at my heels and ran screaming down the street. I ran four city blocks before I could get my panic back under control and regain control over my breathing.

I was nearing the end of a long row of streetlights and there was about a quarter of a mile of solid darkness, pregnant with those voracious creatures, before I would reach the next light. I could see what looked like hundreds of the phantoms seething in the night that stretched out endlessly in between.

"The way out is not around but through," I could hear my counselor telling me after my first failed attempt at detoxification.

"There are no shortcuts."

"No shortcuts," I repeated to myself as I picked up speed and hurtled into the night.

Claws raked my flesh as the things tried to latch onto me. The sharpness of their fangs and talons worked against them now because it sliced right through my skin like a hot knife through butter and didn't allow them to grab hold and pull me down. I felt my skin shred as they slashed but I kept running, Olympian strides, until I could barely see them anymore. They were just blurs of dark flesh and fangs. I reached the next series of lights covered in blood and sweat, exhausted.

I had taken up running during rehab. The more health and body-conscious I became, the easier it got to stay away from the rock. I was only two months sober when I did my first 5k race; a month later I did my first 10k. I had been off the rock for six months when I finished my first marathon. Then the screams had started coming in the night. The bloody and dismembered bodies piling up in the morning. It had gotten harder and harder not to use.

My body was shutting down, failing. I could feel it. I was losing too much blood, exerting myself too hard. I had to stop. I stood beneath the light staring into the darkness, at the terrible things slithering and crawling around just beyond the light. This was the first instance I had ever taken the time to really look at them.

At first all I saw were claws and teeth, the flaming yellow eyes, then faces slowly swam into focus, familiar faces.

A shiver raced up my back as I recognized the face of the first kid I'd ever sold crack to. The thing's flaming yellow orbs began to soften and resolve themselves into those same big trusting eyes that I had taken advantage of all those years ago. Its fangs melted into a big dopey grin. Coiled beside him was a snakelike phantom that had once been a teenaged girl that I'd gotten hooked on crack so that I could have sex with her. She had only been sixteen years old. A church girl who thought she was too good for us street thugs. I had turned her into a crack whore in less than a month. I didn't even attend her funeral when she eventually died of AIDS. I had already moved on to the next innocent life.

One tiny creature was hurling itself at the cone of light as if it was an invisible force field that it could break through. The light would immediately scald its oily midnight flesh and it would shrink back squealing in agony only to attack again. I knew what and who it was even before I saw its face. I hadn't seen his face the night he died, not until I picked up the newspaper the next day. I had been driving too fast when I leaned out the driver's side window with the Tech-nine and let the Black Talons fly into the crowd of gangbangers. There was no way to see who I had hit, if anyone. The next day when I read that only one person had been killed, a six-year-old kid named Devon who'd been playing hide-and-go-seek with some friends when he'd been struck by one of my errant bullets, I didn't even cry. I smoked the largest rock I could find and went out again to find those fools I had missed.

There were larger creatures that began to push their way in closer to the light. They were more brazen and they got so close that their inky black skin began to blister and burn as they huddled in close. They knew that they couldn't get me as long as I stayed under the light, but they seemed determined that I should see them. They wanted to be recognized.

I looked past the gnarled and twisted horns and fangs and immediately began to put names to the faces. Donny, Tank, Warlock, Bean, Eddie, Malik. All rival drug dealers that I had murdered. There were other faces huddling in close to the light but I didn't recognize most of them. How could I? I'd never met half of the people whose lives had been ruined by what I sold.

Blood was starting to pool in my sneakers. I could feel myself getting light-headed from the blood loss. I had to get moving again before I went into shock. I had to find some open highway and a car.

There were six streetlights in a row and then beyond it another quarter mile of darkness. More of the things had amassed around the perimeter of the light. I would have to go through them again. I began to run.

As I sprinted beneath the last streetlight, preparing to charge into the darkness, I saw what looked like a wall of the fearsome night things raging amid the shadowy twilight between the streetlamps. Now I could make out all of them. The biggest mob of creatures, swarming directly in my path, were led by faces that I'd known most of my life. The Christians had been right after all. These things were not some genetic experiments gone wrong or the aftermath of some industrial accident. But they hadn't come from hell either. They were the most fearsome of all the demons, my own personal ones.

"The way out is not around but through," I whispered as I tucked my chin and hurtled right into them swinging the axe as I prepared to make my last stand. I saw demons with the faces of my mother and father lunge toward me and I prepared to cleave their heads from their shoulders. But I couldn't. I dropped the axe and ran, trying to dodge between them, but I was slow from injuries, exhaustion, and loss of blood, and there were too many of them. Their fangs and claws cut into my flesh and this time they hooked in deep. I couldn't break free, but I didn't slow my stride either. I dragged them along as I sprinted toward the light. My mother and father latched to my thighs and buttocks, slashing at my back. My sister, and brothers, my aunts, and uncles, and cousins, former friends, and ex-girl-friends, everyone who'd ever had the poor judgement to invest their emotions in me, were gnawing at my chest and stomach, working my muscle and fat free from my bones, and burrowing into my organs.

One of the night things, an ex-girlfriend whom I'd gotten pregnant and then coerced into having an abortion, scampered up my back and began biting and clawing at my throat, lacerating both my jugular and carotid arteries with its hooked talons and shark-like teeth. The spray of blood seemed to excite the demons already clinging to me and attract even more. I stumbled, nearly went down into the herd of rapacious shadows, then righted myself and continued to run. Staring at the cone of light just yards away, like an oasis in a desert of pain and death, I began to scream just before the thing on my back tore out my larynx, silencing me. Still, I kept running. It was what I had always done. The only way I knew how to deal with life. But now, my demons were catching up to me.

INITIATION

1

Five shapes. Tiny shapes, yet their long cast shadows reveal what exists underneath. The moon reaches its silver light between the rusted gutter-lined roofs. It snakes its way down and falls upon the shapes, illuminating smooth features. In a circle, they sit in silence. No one will speak out of turn. It is the way.

One figure trembles. He is uncertain. The moon reflects off eight eyes intently focused upon him. He wants to run, fear urges him to bolt, but he stays. He knows he has no choice if he is to survive.

Years of abuse have trained him well. His senses are acute, usually aware of every movement—only now there is none. The rats hidden deep within the stinking mounds of forgotten garbage twitch their whiskers nervously. The night is wrong. They are motionless. Mere feet away, rat-fed cats rest their bulk, unmoving. They sense it also. Feeding will have to wait.

Each figure sits cross-legged amid the stagnant pools left over from the previous night's rain. The sun barely reaches into the dark world of the back alleys. It is night twenty-four hours a day. They like it that way. Tense, unblinking eyes drill

DAVID G. BARNETT

the smallest figure—studying. The choice is important. It means life or death for him.

The still night is suffocating. *Run*, his mind screams. *You can't*, cries his heart, *you must survive*. The desire to live hushes the screams of his mind. His heart races as he waits. There is no other choice for him. He had tried the other options. Plans made for him without his input. What the fuck does a ten-year-old know anyway. He knows when he can take no more. He knows when to get out. And now, he knows when to stay. The bruises are painful reminders of a past he doesn't wish to return to. They echo the heart and tell him this is right. He has never felt more at home than he has here, hidden within the shadows. He has always been in the shadows, but now these were his shadows, warm and inviting. Gone were the mean and cold shadows of foster homes gone bad—of daily beatings at the hands of cruel children at the orphanage. Friendship was what existed for him now, and if all was right, soon a family. That's all he wants—a family.

Say something for chrissakes, he wants to yell. They have been sitting here for more than an hour. His legs have gone numb, and his ass itches. But he cannot move as the others study him, making their decision. *Don't show any signs of weakness*, he tells himself. *Don't even blink…*

The movement is quick. He has no time to react. Except for his eyes, which bulge with fear, he remains still.

Ed squats before the small boy, breathing slowly. He is the picture of sheer control. His thick eyebrows dip toward the center of his face, and he speaks. It is only one word, but it is the word that will decide the small boy's fate.

"Decide," Ed whispers, his eyes never leaving Runt's face.

Runt battles the urge to release his bowels. *Control*, he repeats to himself a dozen times. The moonlight shining off of Ed's long black mane is mesmerizing. Runt feels a slight bit of relief as his body relaxes. But the tension quickly returns. A voice from behind Ed sends a quick wave of nausea through Runt's body.

"No."

Runt suppresses his need to cry.

Never moving his gaze from Runt's face, Ed asks, "Why?"

Runt sees a shadow appear over Ed's back. The relaxing moonlight no longer reflects off the ebony hair. He shudders as Pep moves forward.

"He's too fucking small, Ed," Pep says, coming up alongside of Ed. He stares down at Runt, but Runt keeps his focus upon Ed's face.

Be strong, he tells himself.

"What's wrong with small?" Ed asks. "You were small once. We were all small once. Small means shit, Pep, and you know it."

"I say yes, Ed," squeaks a squirrelly voice from behind Ed.

"Figures," snorts Pep, rolling his eyes up in disgust.

A sudden movement brings Pep's eyes back into place, and he is quickly on guard.

"What the hell is that supposed to mean, you fuck?" Scratch comes into view, obviously irritated. Clawing feverishly at his arm.

Ed drops his face in annoyance. "Shut up," he says quietly. They do. "This is important, and if you two keep bitching at each other, I'll kill you." Scratch backed away, scared. Pep stood his ground, but fought to control a flinch. Ed didn't threaten, he promised.

"Tony?" Ed looked over his shoulder to the dark, heavy-set boy sitting quietly.

Tony waited for a moment as if pondering the meaning of life, then said slowly, "Sure."

Turning back to Runt, locking eyes once again. "I say yes."

Runt's heart jumped. He relaxed control over his body and looked up at Pep.

Disgust flashed in Pep's eyes, but he turned so Ed wouldn't notice. When he turned back around, Runt shit his pants. The howl that filled the silver night made him piss his pants.

"Welcome to the pack," was the last thing Runt heard. Then they were on him.

2

Time hadn't been nice to the warehouses on South Fermon Street. Too many businesses, not enough business had forced all of the buildings to be abandoned. Two years ago, the decaying, hollowed-out monsters were homes for many of the city's less fortunate. The owners didn't care; they only remember the buildings come tax time. So, if they didn't care, the cops didn't care.

Hundreds of homeless people filled the buildings each night, seeking shelter from the natural elements. But the rusting, corrugated walls that held those elements at bay couldn't do anything to stop the unnatural elements. Something had begun hunting the warehouse people, something unseen until it was too late. One by one, they began to disappear. There was no way to prove it to the cops. Homeless people just tended to up and move without a trace. What could the cops do? But the people knew it wasn't relocation that made these people disappear. They heard the cries that filled the night—cries that sent them huddling together for safety. Cries that made them pray that they wouldn't be the one to suddenly relocate.

At first, there was only one tortured howl that filled the night. Then there were two. Then three. With the addition of each night voice, came the disappearance of more and more people. There were rumors of quicksilver shadows that stalked the night. Rumors were all they were, because there was no proof. Only the thinning of the warehouse people's masses was the proof that something had gone wrong.

Each day, the masses departed in droves, as the people began relocating themselves around the city on their own. There were some holdouts, but without the safety of the ramshackle community, the holdouts didn't stick around for long. Soon, all the homeless were gone, but not all the life. The night voices remained, howling deep into the night. Time saw the addition of one more voice, and tonight there would be one more voice releasing its virgin song into the night and to the bright moon above.

«« — »»

The first pain had hit Runt like a truck. He fell to his knees and screamed. When the pain subsided, he chastised himself for showing weakness. He knew that Ed would have heard the scream, and he didn't want that. He wanted to be strong, to show Pep that he could handle anything. He could handle the pitch-black cooler that the others had put him in, but not the pain. It was unlike any he had ever experienced. It was even worse than the night when the others had decided to let him join their gang.

Following the frenzy that occurred after they had agreed to let him in, he had ended up with a dozen bites and three times as many scratches. The bites hadn't hurt, but only itched a little, so Runt didn't worry about it. Hell, he told himself, for an initiation, it wasn't all that bad. He had to laugh when he thought about the whole situation. Here he was glad to be joining a gang of little kids, of which he would be the littlest. What the hell would this do for him, he had asked himself over and over. There was no real answer, but Runt knew that the gang would help him to survive. For some reason these guys, who took him in when he ran away from the orphanage two weeks ago, survived. And did so very well. They brought him food every day, or at least Ed did. Runt knew it was out of pity, but fuck it, it was food.

The guys had never let him hang out with them once the night came, though, which was fine with Runt, because the last thing he wanted was to be out on the streets at night. But he had always wondered where they went. And one day he finally asked Ed. The question was simple, but Ed gave no answer. Instead, he offered Runt food, and said if he was strong, he would find out soon enough.

Runt poked at his arms, relaxing, confident that the pain was gone. He marveled at the smoothness of it. Only a day ago, he was covered in scratches and bites. Yet, when he had awoken the next day, all the marks were gone. He wanted to ask Ed why, but everyone had left him. Runt had found himself lying in the middle of a large warehouse. He hadn't gone to sleep there, and had no idea how he got there or where he was for that matter. After trying to figure out what to do, Runt had fallen back to sleep, and woke up ten hours later when Pep had shoved his foot into Runt's side.

"Wake up, Runt." Pep's tone was softer than it usually had been when he talked to Runt in the past.

Runt sat up and was amazed that he could see everything so clearly inside the dark warehouse. His excitement burst out immediately upon seeing everyone. "So, was that it? The initiation and all." Runt stood and held his arms out for all to see. "Shit, all the marks are gone. I don't know why, but...fuck it, that was easy."

With that, Runt noticed that no one was moving again. No one except for Scratch whose body was jittering up and down as he tried to stifle a laugh.

"Hey, what's the deal?" Runt asked. His excitement suddenly drained from his body.

Ed remained still as he spoke, "That wasn't it, Runt. That was the easy part."

"Yeah," interrupted Pep, his normal tone of disdain returning. "Now's when we see if you have the strength to be one of us."

"It's getting late," Ed announced and motioned to Tony. Tony moved toward a large metal door on the wall. "It takes a lot to be one of the pack, Runt. I told you all this before. Last night was just the beginning."

Runt let Ed's voice fall away while he watched Tony out of the corner of his eye as the chunky kid swung the door open wide. There was only darkness inside.

Ed's voice caught Runt's attention again. "This next part of the initiation is going to be the hardest. I ain't going to tell you what it is, because you need to find out for yourself." Ed moved to Runt's side and draped his arm around the small child's shoulders.

Runt could hear Scratch giggling, and constantly scratching at his arms. He slowly followed Ed's push toward the door.

"You're going to think this is going to suck, but you need to go in there."

Runt's step hesitated just long enough for Pep to notice and spit out, "Puss."

Something within Runt exploded. "Fuck you, asshole!" he screamed at Pep.

Pep only laughed, and said to Ed, "Looks like it's starting."

"What's starting? What the fuck are you guys doing? I can't go in there, there's no air."

"There's air," Ed assured. "Vents in the ceiling." He pushed into Runt's back again, and steered him closer to the cooler. "You gonna have to stay in there, alone, for a while. Got it?"

Runt looked up into Ed's cold face and knew that he would have to do what Ed said or he would die there. "Yeah." Then turning toward Pep, but not speaking at him he asked, "You guys aren't going to fuck with me, are you?"

Pep laughed again. "No, you little shit, we won't need to."

Scratch broke out into loud, nervous hysterics.

Runt felt a push at his back again. "Go on," Ed insisted. "The other guys are gonna go get us some food. I'm staying here in case you need me."

Ed's face never changed. Runt wondered if he ever smiled. Then he wondered why he would need Ed if he was just going to be locked in a dark cooler for a while. Suddenly a memory of the night before flashed into his mind. He saw Pep turning toward him. Only it wasn't Pep—at least not completely. Runt's heart started pounding a heavy, fast rhythm as more memories of last night flooded his mind. But as he tried to shake them into some sort of order, he felt a shove at his back and found himself hurtling though the doorway and into the chilled darkness of the cooler. The little light that managed to find its way into the cooler quickly disappeared as the door slammed close. But before it was closed tight he heard Ed say, "Just go with it, man."

«« — »»

Ed had sent the other three out. He would stand guard over Runt. He felt sorry for the little shit. Ed knew Runt might be too small, but he wanted to give him the chance. It was Runt's only chance really. Without it, he wouldn't last another month on the streets. But if he could withstand the change, then he would survive a lifetime.

It was the change that had Ed worried. It wreaked hell on the body. He wondered whether or not Runt could handle it. Shit, Ed thought, it almost killed me. But Ed had been sick when he first felt his insides catch on fire. He had thought it was the fever, but soon he had realized that it something more.

Ed's hand itched as he worked to control himself. He must remain in control, in case Runt needed him. The hunger was eating away at him something fierce, but the others would take care of him. That was the way of the pack.

Ed heard the first stirring about an hour after the others had disappeared through the hole knocked into the side of what was once the warehouse for Frank's Fish: Freshness Guaranteed. Ed had found the place to be of great use for the changing period. Pep had been the first. He had screamed his throat raw the night Ed had locked him in the 15x30 cooler. Ed hollered through the door that is was for the best, and after the first night, Pep agreed.

Ed sat directly in front of the door and waited. When he heard the first scream, he had closed his eyes and tried to disappear into himself, whispering *just go with it* over and over. He listened and wondered how long Runt's change would be. When the next scream came, an hour later, he knew it was going to be a long wait.

3

Space Boy wasn't happy. Not one damn bit. *Fuck Razor*, he kept saying just low enough for only him to hear. Why the fuck did he have to be out selling the shit. *Ain't right for Razor to be sending anyone out at night no more*, he thought.

No, Space Boy was an unhappy, little 'cid head. All he wanted was to be inside away from the streets—preferably inside with a nice tab quickly disintegrating beneath his tongue. Then everything would be all right. But no, not tonight. Space Boy had lost the draw. Seven years with Razor meant shit when it came to getting a deal done. Someone had to drop the money down the sewer opening on the corner of Ryan and 10th. This time it was Space Boy.

Just my fucking luck, he cursed to himself. Space Boy stopped and looked all around him as he had every minute for the past fifteen. It wasn't any different this time, than it was the other two times. Shitty streets, shitty alleys, shitty, fucking hole. It was all dark, and dark wasn't something that Space Boy wanted to see right now. Bright lights, and pure flowing motion was all he wanted. Pure ecstasy. But instead, he got darkness—pure black night. Half the streetlights didn't even work in the part of town Space Boy found himself in. Nothing here but burned out buildings, cars long ago abandoned, and dark, heavy night.

Sure, there was shit going on underneath the ground. Long tunnels of never-ending stench stretched for miles in every direction. But, down there Space Boy would be lost. At least up here he knew where he was going. He hated this shit. No car, only feet. Stick to the shadows. Didn't want no cops tailing his ass to the drop-off or pickup point. Franco wouldn't like that. No sir, Franco wouldn't like the cops knowing where his little underground, chemical factory was. And if any one of Razor's boys was to be stupid enough to get themselves followed, fucking forget losing one member every couple of weeks. There wouldn't be one fucking member left within twenty-four hours.

Too much to fear out here for Space Boy. "Fuck it," he said to no one. "Just, fuck it."

Space Boy continued his hurried pace to Alms and 20th—to the mailbox on the corner. By the time he would get there, the package of coke would have mysteriously found its way inside. He had his left hand shoved deep into his coat pocket, and had a tight hold of the key to the mailbox—one quick turn, grab, another turn, and he was out of here. Next time, it was someone else's fucking turn.

He rounded the corner of Alms and saw the mailbox sitting under an appropriately nonfunctioning streetlight. He also saw something else he didn't expect. Getting quite pissed, Space Boy moved quickly to the box yelling, "Hey, kid. Get the fuck outta here." He couldn't believe there was a little kid out here in this hellhole at this time of night.

"Didn't you hear me?" he asked, realizing the kid wasn't moving.

As Space Boy approached the box, the kid leaning against it slowly turned his head toward him and smiled.

"Who me?" he asked with a mild look of confusion.

"Yeah, you, ya little shit. What the fuck you think you're doing out here. Ain't you got a fucking home or something?" Space Boy came up close to the kid, and quickly got a whiff of him. "Shit, you fucking stink."

The kid looked up at Space Boy and sniffed the air, exposing his pure white teeth slightly. Then smiling, he said, "Yeah, you stink, too."

"Fuck you, you little shit." Space Boy wanted to beat the shit out of the kid immediately, but managed to restrain himself. He didn't need the hassle. *Just get him outta here, get the package and get home*, he told himself. He ran his right hand through his hair in frustration, keeping his left tightly wrapped around the key in his pocket.

"Look, kid. Just get outta here would ya. I got some business around here, and I don't want you nosin' around while I do it."

The kid shifted and swiftly moved away from the box. Space Boy lost track of where the kid was, he moved so sudden and quick. He moved his eyes to the left to try and get a good look at the kid in the dismal light.

The kid's clothes were big, way too big. He was kinda homied out, but this kid wasn't trying to be fashion conscious. He was practically wearing rags, big, man-sized rags and no shoes.

"What the fuck's up with you, home shit? You some sort of sewer rat?"

Space Boy tried to keep tabs on the kid as he moved back and forth in front of him. It wasn't easy, the kid moved too quickly. It was like he melted from one place to another, at times becoming one with the dark. Space Boy was getting the creeps bigtime.

"Look, home shit. I got business to do and you're bugging me." It was no lie, this little kid was bugging the hell out of Space Boy, and he wasn't liking it one bit.

The kid moved again and rested his back against the mailbox once again. Looking up at Space Boy, fixing him with an innocent smile and stare, he asked, "You gonna get the package inside."

"What?" Space Boy was stunned. This was all he needed. He reached out to grab the kid. There was a blur and Space Boy's hand found nothing but air.

"What's in the package?" the kid said from behind Space Boy.

Space Boy spun and saw the kid leaning against the useless street-light. "What the…"

"I saw some guy put something in the mailbox. Just wondering what it was. Not too many people use mailboxes out here."

You got that right, Space Boy thought. *Nobody should be out here, especially some creepy little shit like this. Especially me.*

"So what's in the box?"

"None of your fucking business. Now beat it." Space Boy was fed up and he turned to the box, deciding to just get this shit over with and get back to the car, his apartment, a tab, and ecstasy.

"Yeah," the kid said, disappointment in his voice. "That's what the guy over there said, too."

Space Boy stopped fumbling with the key immediately. "What guy?" he whispered softly, without showing too much alarm in case anyone was watching.

"The guy over there, in the alley."

"There's someone in the alley?"

The kid's face perked up followed by his body as he pushed away from the streetlight. "Yeah, big guy. Smelled, like you." The kid smiled and pointed to the alley about thirty feet down 20th.

Fuck, Space Boy thought. *Kill my ass as soon as I pick up the shit. That's just fucking great.* "You sure this guy's over there now?"

"Yeah," the kid assured and pointed to the alley again.

"Stop fucking pointing. The fucker's gonna know I know he's there," Space Boy hissed and slowly turned back toward the box, pretending that he was going to open it.

"He won't know."

"Yeah, whatever, kid. Do me a big favor would you, and get lost," he said turning back on the kid. But just as he turned he felt a slight breeze fly past his back. He spun to follow the black blur, but it disappeared into the darkness.

"Shit," he said. Space Boy was getting a full case of the fucking creeps now. He dropped the box-key back into his pocket and brought something cold and hard out of his other one. He dropped the gun to his side and slowly backed up against the building. Space Boy crouched down low, and cautiously inched his way toward the mouth of the alley. *Fucker's gonna get a full-on taste of some shit when I see him.*

As the alley came closer, and opened wider for Space Boy, he could feel sweat dripping down his back and into his ass crack. His jacket collar was rubbing against his neck, and to him it was the loudest thing in the world. Everything had gone into slow motion, except for his heart, which threatened to open his chest wide. Space Boy was aware of everything around him, and it wasn't like in one of his many trips. No, this time nothing was beautiful. Nothing was amazing, nothing was fucking cool. No, this time everything was fucking fucked. One hundred percent fucked. As he approached the alley, Space Boy got a full whiff of something bad, something real bad. His senses were so tweaked, that the stench was overpowering. He struggled to hold back bile.

Turn around now, his mind screamed. But he couldn't. If this fucker was hiding there to kill him as he went by, then this fucker was gonna get fucked. Plain and simple.

It took a few seconds for Space Boy to get it together enough to round the corner. It was quick. He jumped, coming in low. Gun aimed high. Take him in the chest or head. His finger pressed the trigger to breaking point. He wanted movement. Something to shoot, anything. But what he got hit him right in the face. A full blast of rank, fetid air. The smell of hundred gallons of dog piss, fifty rotting animals, and blood. Lots of blood. It was hard to make out, but he knew what it was, and he knew what it was that lay on the ground at his feet.

The head gave it away. It was whole, not like the rest of the body. The head sat upright on the ground wallowing in a puddle of blood, terror-filled eyes staring a hole right through Space Boy. Pleading, begging eyes. The mouth hung open in a twisted, tormented scream. A scream that told Space Boy to run. He looked at the body, what was left. The ribcage spread wide, ribs pointing in every direction. Inside the ribcage glistened with clean, white bone. Legs, arms, fingers lay strewn about like a ripped apart rag doll.

Space Boy's mouth hung open, and when his brain finally registered what he was seeing, the bile could not be stopped again. It came quickly and painfully, spraying his shoes, the sidewalk and the head. The head plastered with its frozen scream, the scream that Space Boy finally heard. The scream that said, RUN!

And Space Boy did. His legs were moving before he realized it and he stumbled into the corner of one of the buildings. He quickly righted himself and after a few awkward steps he was moving as fast as he ever had before. Down the sidewalk, around tumbled trashcans, crumbling furniture never picked up, burned out cars and into the street. Faster and faster, straight down the cracked asphalt, no obstructions there. His feet pounded the pavement as quickly as his heart pounded in his chest. He moved in one direction, away. Away from this night, away from this nightmare, away from a life he wanted no part of any longer. And away from the three shadows that crisscrossed in the street behind him.

4

Runt was slowly trying to recover from the sixth bout of pain that assaulted his body. He could no longer move. Every muscle, every joint, hair, tooth in his body ached. He had stopped trying to hold back the tears after the third attack. And soon there were no more tears to be held back.

What's wrong with me, he asked himself. He had never felt pain like this before. What did they do to me for chrissakes? Runt tried to stretch out, move his aching muscles. As he rolled on his back, a fresh shot of pain filled his chest. His body cinched into fetal form and he rolled around, scratching his flesh on the cold cement. Each scratch only intensified the pain. Even with all the pain, Runt hadn't gone numb—just the opposite in fact. He could feel every little grain of sand in the cement as it brushed against his flesh. Even the slightest touch sent a wave of new pain coursing through his body. His senses went into overload. Runt's heart sounded like the toy tom-tom drum he had when he was little—sounded like a hundred of those drums—each one pounding a separate beat. The noise was maddening. Runt tried to scream, but the sound that escaped his mouth was straight out of a nightmare. It cut off midway as Runt was shocked by the sudden animal cry that emitted from his lungs. He took a sharp breath of air and his body bucked from the increased scratching on his flesh. His heart continued pounding, unrelenting…merciless.

But the sound of his heart was nothing compared to the din that exploded right before the blinding light sent him scurrying to the far corner of the cooler. The metal click of the cooler door opening rang harsh in Runt's head. The scratching of the door across the cement floor produced bone-raking chills up his back. He tried to clutch feverishly at his ears, but every movement, every touch of his own hands on his body sent him flinching against the wall, which caused only more pain.

No, his mind screamed. He tried to remain still, eyes shut tight against the glaring light from the door. Ed's coming for me, he told himself. He prayed it was so. But there was only a quick succession of scuffling footsteps, low grunts, a hollow thump and the deafening sound of scraping metal across cement once again. But just before the light vanished, Runt thought he heard something through the pounding of his heart. "Just go with it, man." Then there was complete darkness again.

The sound of his heart boomed again. I can't stand it, he yelled in his mind. I'm going nuts. He wanted to scream again, but the memory of what came out the last time scared the shit out of him. It was as if every sense in his body had exploded. The dim light from the night outside had almost blinded him. It was like he could feel his hair growing, and with each little bit it grew his body burned. Runt wanted to be dead. He prayed for someone to come in and kill him. He couldn't take it anymore.

Then the smell hit him like a truck. It curled up through his nose, into his brain. What the hell? Suddenly the pain began to disappear. Runt slowly uncurled. He lifted his nose to the air and inhaled deeply. It was as if he knew what would stop the pain. The smell filtered throughout his body, wrapping around every nerve ending. It soothed every scrape, cut and bruise. It wormed its way into Runt's chest and slowed his heart. The pounding in his head ceased. Silence. Pure silence.

Runt found himself on hands and knees facing the cooler door. His nose high, he sought to eliminate the pain. Silence. Then noise. Faint at first, then a sharp gasp. Runt's ears twitched in tandem with his nose, both yearning for more. What did he hear? What did he smell? Runt stared into the darkness, through the darkness. Nothing was clear, but somehow, all was clear. He understood none of this, but something in his mind told him it didn't matter.

Movement. He could feel it in the air that touched his tender flesh. The tiny hairs covering his body danced as the air moved around him. He looked down at a hand that was no longer his. The hand that pressed hard and gnarled into the ground beneath him was covered with hair, long and dark. He followed the limb up and up, until it ended in his shoulder. He knew then that it was his arm that he was looking at. He shot a glance at his other arm, the same. He followed the arm to the shoulder, to his side, to his leg. Long, dark hairs. Thousands covered his body. His mind tried to shake the vision off. It's pitch black, how can I see this? It isn't real. But he looked down at his leg, the meaty thigh moving down into a firm, spring-loaded leg. He bounced on his new legs, contemplating his new design. Something in his mind said, this is crazy. But something else said, so what. He continued to stare at his new form in awe. Then his hairs moved again, and Runt glared through the black to the now clear form by the cooler door.

It moved. A rumpling sound of clothes filled the room and Runt's ears. Runt let lose a low growl, this time it went unnoticed to him.

"What...(cough)...what the fuck?" asked the lump.

The smell, the smell. Runt's mind began spinning as his rational side battled with this new, dark force that seemed destined to take over. He crept forward, oh so slowly. So carefully. No noise, no breath. Black on black. No, no, no, something in him whimpered feebly. But a louder, stronger voice burst past the cries for sanity. A voice that said, "Just go with it, man. Just go with it, man," over and over. And with a powerful explosion, Runt sent himself propelling forward toward the smell. The smell of blood.

«« —»»

Space Boy awoke to complete and utter darkness. This trip had gone one-way to fucked-upville. His head was ringing.

"What...(cough)...what the fuck?" He tried to sit up and quickly realized that was a big fucking mistake. When his head hit the floor, Space Boy saw a show in his head like he had never seen before, white and dazzling. When he opened his eyes again, and felt the shadow land on his belly and sink something hard and sharp into his stomach, Space Boy realized this was the last trip he'd be taking. And this trip had suddenly gone a brilliant red.

«« —»»

The scream came first. Then the howl. Then the muffled sounds of Runt ripping into the flesh of one of Razor's top men. Ed smiled for the first time that day. One more down, he said to himself. But even though the thought of one more ganger down made him happy, Pep had fucked up. Ed had told him no more gangers for now. Pep would have to have his ass kicked. Ed let the smile fall. He turned and came face to face with Pep's wide grin. Ed hesitated, and then decided to do something about it later. Right now he was hungry. The smile returned to his face.

"First flesh," Ed said softly.

"Best flesh!" they all yelled. And within seconds the night sky over the Fermon Street Warehouse district filled with the cries of many a man's nightmares. And for one more this night, that nightmare would too quickly become a reality.

END OF
THE LINE

T he subway train surged forward.
Then, braked.
A harsh screech rose like a siren, metal on metal burning, filling the air with its acrid stench.

Smith became aware of his nodding slumber, jolted awake. Found himself alone.

He looked around. The train was motionless. Dark walls encapsulated the windows, grease-coated cables snaking along them like unruly vines. He rubbed his face, senses muddy, refusing to accept the disconcerting truth: he'd fallen asleep, had missed his stop.

He let his hands drop to his lap. Twisted around to survey the barren territory of the NYC 2-Train car. Empty, save for strewn newspapers, coffee cups, dried gum circles on the floor. Above, cool air blew in from the vents, bouting the trickling sweat on his brow. He smelled the hours gone past on himself: the beer, the wine, the liquor, the fried hors d'oeurves from the party.

He stood up. Pressed a nervous hand against the dark window. He'd have to find his own way back to the hotel, despite his lack of NYC wisdom.

Park Central. 60th and Seventh Avenue.

He pinched the sleeve of his suit jacket. Peered at his watch. 3:15 AM. Where had the hours gone?

MICHAEL LAIMO

Tonight had been the con party, and he'd gathered with hundreds of other boatyard stewards, most of them strangers. Socializing. Eating. Drinking. Fanfaring their boatly triumphs, making business contacts for the future. It all seemed a blur now, and somewhere along the line he'd stepped away from the festivities, feeling ill or tired or bored, looking to call it a night.

The train jerked forward. The cables on the wall crawled upwards, giving way to pallid light. A station.

No identification upon its tiled walls.

No announcement from the PA.

Where am I?

The train stopped. A bell rang. The doors opened.

Smith made an unpremeditated decision to exit. Quickly slipped out onto the dusty platform. He looked right, and then, left. On either sides, the platform stretched unveeringly toward distant stairwells. Behind, the train remained still. Heavy. Like a mother minding a child at the bus stop on the first day of school.

Sweat flowed from his brow. The stench of puddling water and urine added to his discomfort. He switched his gaze back and forth, finding no solace in any potential choice of direction.

From the street above, he heard a pounding beat. A vibration. It sounded far away, like the muffled boom of stereo speakers from behind closed windows. He turned, looked at the standing train, thought about getting back in.

I'll take a cab, he decided. *Must be a thousand of them available at this ungodly hour.*

Slowly, he paced to the left. Eyed the steel-gray stairwell parallel to the rear of the train. The pounding beat outside grew louder. It prodded the walls of his stomach, thump, thumpa, thump. He tried to ignore the uncomfortable feeling, but it wouldn't go away.

He reached the foot of the steps, gripped the handrail, climbed them tiredly, one at a time, unconvinced of his decision to leave. *I should cross over to the other track. Wait for another train to take me back.*

He reached the top of the steps. Here, another barren NYC landscape awaited: lone turnstiles, an empty token booth, black-rusted entry cages. Smith glanced back down the stairs. The slumbering train's doors were shut. They didn't ring. *I didn't hear them sliding on their tracks.*

He looked forward. Ahead were a second set of steps leading to the street.

Thump, thumpa, thump.

I'll take a cab, he thought again.

He paced swiftly forward, up the steps. Into the outside world.

The streets were dark and desolate. Empty cars sat at the curbs like sleeping dogs. The storefronts were boarded-up and useless, sheathed in graffiti. He gazed quickly at the four street corners. A cool wind blew. The hair on the back of his neck stood on end.

No signposts.

No people to be seen anywhere.

But the sourceless beat played on. Louder now. Impregnating the hot summer air. He paced instinctually to his left. At the corner, he turned left again. Here there were no cars at all, parked or otherwise. The buildings lay in near-darkness. If not for the corner streetlamp to provide a pallid wash, Smith's world would have been black.

He started off down the street. His shoed footsteps augmented the beat—nothing else seemed to exist beneath the dark city sky: no distant car horns, no faraway shouts. No taxis.

Shaken, he began to jog. Then, he ran.

Through the slapping of his footsteps, he heard the distant beat rising. Thump-thumpa-thump. Louder now.

To his right, a door slammed opened in a brick-walled building, spilling out a loud slice of the incessant thumping.

Winded, Smith stopped running. Hands on knees. Panting.

He looked toward the open door.

A black man emerged.

They locked eyes, Smith contemplating the man under a sweat-soaked brow. A haze of fear washed over him. He shuddered.

The man was naked.

With no warning, the man reeled toward Smith. Arms outstretched. Squealing.

Smith took a step back, then whirled and fled. His heart pounded with fear, exhaustion. *Jesus, Jesus, Jesus,* he repeated in silence, seeking support from a historically unreliable source. He peered over his shoulder. The naked man had quickly gained on him. Bare feet slapping the pavement. Eyes wide and rolling. Tongue lolling doglike from a blood-red mouth.

Smith's screams echoed those of his pursuer. Other than imminent death, nothing else seemed likely at the moment. His lungs burned for air; his mind struggled for a sliver of lucidity amidst the terror. He darted ahead, stumbled down into a concrete recess: stairs leading into the gated entrance of a building. Whimpering, he closed his eyes, pressed himself against the sewage grate at the bottom, feeling the release of wet bowels. *How effing ironic.*

The heavy slap of naked feet on asphalt ceased.

Smith waited. Anticipating an attack. Minutes passed in silence. Silence—except for the muffled beat, which continued on and on.

He opened his eyes, allowed the blur of fear to fade. He waited. Then, slowly, rose up. Peered around, body pressed against the concrete wall. The stink of his excrement sickened him, as did the stench of his dread. Cautiously, he crawled up the steps, hands scraping gritty concrete. He reached the top step. Looked. Saw nothing.

He stood, bones creaking.

From behind the gate, the naked black man leaped out. Growling. Swiping the air. Smith scrambled back against the building. Wedged himself against an empty steel trash can, peering up at his attacker. The black man's eyes were huge, rolling impossibly in their sockets. Mouth coated in white foam.

It stroked a monstrous erection with malformed clubs for hands.

Then, reached down and grabbed the trash can next to Smith.

The receptacle proved showfully easy to render in half, despite the deformity of its hands, the resulting jagged strips tossed yards away with swift jerks of its muscular arms.

It squealed. Reached its twitching clubs toward Smith.

From behind: a siren-bleep. A cop.

Jesus, thank you!

The man-beast darted around.

Through fluttering eyelids, Smith saw a cruiser. Sitting in the middle of the street. The driver's door opened. A cop emerged.

Like a bullet, the man-creature lunged at the cop, who'd had about three seconds to get a shot off. He performed his duty well, hitting the attacker once in the chest. A circle of gore appeared in its slick, naked back. Blood poured out in a gush.

But the man-beast didn't slow. The cop fell still, his attacker launching a clubbed fist deep into his sternum, blowing it apart. From within, it ripped free his still-beating heart.

Turned around. Displayed it boastfully to Smith.

Smith choked and gagged at the display. Blood spouted freely from the hole in the cop's chest, arcing as he fell to the asphalt in a trembling heap, face yellowed, gasping crazily for air.

Smith, writhing in his own bowels, screamed. Struggled to crawl away, resigning himself to certain death.

No way could one escape such a monstrosity.

First time in the big city. Everyone had told you to be careful. Said there were crazies running around.

Smith stood. Plundered down the street, legs like sodden tea-bags. From behind came the quick feet-slapping-on-asphalt noise of his pursuer.

And then, a mind-numbing blast against his shoulder. Smith succumbed to the ensuing pain. Fell, clawing at the ground. The man-beast was on him. Tearing his suit jacket, reaching for his leg. Smith turned

MICHAEL LAIMO

quickly. Saw the thing's blood red mouth opening, and then closing on his calf, rendering away the cloth of his pants. Blood oozed. Seconds passed before the pain caught up. He roared in agony. Made a final attempt to flee.

A loud whump sounded. Then, a blast of hot air. The thing loosened its grip on Smith, howling like a tortured dog. The furnace blast came again. Instantly, the man-beast was on fire, staggering away. Arms flailing recklessly, endeavoring to douse the blaze. Flames sprouted from its jerking body like offspring, smidgening the air with the unmistakable reek of burning flesh.

Smith collapsed flat against the street. Face touching blacktop. He could feel the continuous vibration of the beat in the earth. The beat. The cops' heart? He felt the want to pass out.

A pair of black military boots appeared alongside him.

From above, a deep voice: "Get up if you want to live."

He reached out, touched the worn leather boots. A calloused hand grabbed his wrist, yanked him to his feet. Smith followed the lead, legs tremoring. He meant to gaze at his savior, but couldn't get past the man-beast, melting in a fiery heap, thick plumes of black smoke rising, filling the air with its smoldering stench.

"Come," his savior said, pulling his wrist hard, "before another one shows up."

Finally, Smith turned. He looked at the stranger. Human on the outside. Black. Tall. Six-six, bursting with muscles. He wore a tank top and leather pants, both black. Holstered around his shoulder was a flame thrower, the blue pilot aglow in the barrel.

Smith staggered behind the man, led urgently toward the area of the sourceless beat. How long had it been since stumbling into this freakish world? His head spun with horrid confusion, unsure of the moment's reality. He faltered behind the man, unable to keep up, the bite in his leg firing jolts into his groin. He lost his step, fell down once, twice, the man silently lifting him over massive shoulders and carrying him away.

Feeling assured of his safety, Smith passed out...for only seconds it seemed, until he came to once again in another ghastly world of unfamiliarity.

«« — »»

He opened his eyes.

He lay on a tattered sofa, stenched with mildew. The incessant beat loomed from behind the stained and peeling walls.

A murmur of voices.

185

His vision cleared. A black woman with long braided hair came into view.

"He's awake," she announced, voice unusually deep. She came close to him. Full lips nearly touching his cheek. "It bit you, didn't it?"

Smith nodded, looked at his body. He'd been stripped naked. A towel covered his groin. The pain in his leg had subsided.

"Tell me what happened. How did you get here?"

Smith tried to speak, but his tongue was coated.

"Bring him some water, and another painkiller." A young boy appeared beside her, holding a paper cup and a white pill. He gave it to Smith, who chased the pill in three gulps. The cup was taken away. Refilled. He downed the second cup just as quickly.

Smith propped himself up on his elbows. Gazed around. The room was filled to capacity, twenty to twenty-five people staring at him. All eyes were upon him as he quickly explained his plight, from the moment he awoke on the subway, until he fainted in the arms of the flamethrower man. At the conclusion, he gazed down at his leg. It had been bandaged, only a spotting of blood seeping through the thick white gauze.

"You brought the demon outside," the woman said. "Now, we are forced to send it back in."

A chorus of groans filled the room. Smith looked about defensively, as though he were on trial. "I didn't do anything," he said.

"You did," Flamethrower Man said, stepping into view, weapon poised across his chest. "You stepped into the demon's world, delivering life onto a deadened street. They've devoured it, and now, they're awake. We must do something about it." He paced back and forth.

Smith straightened up. His leg reminded him of his injury. "What the hell is going on? What was that thing out there?"

The woman posed, arms on hips. Looked at him sourly. "You set them free…never thought it would happen. But it did."

Someone from within the crowd called out, "The beat is very loud. We have to take action now."

Bodies shifted in the room. Guns were checked and loaded. From an unseen point, Smith heard Flamethrower say, "There was a cop. The demon got him."

More groans. Curses. Headshakes.

"What the hell is going on?" he pleaded, tears filling his eyes.

"Their tribe is in ceremony. They want to take our territory. But we won't let them. No. This is our turf…the turf of the Angels. The Demons are trying to take it away from us."

"Jesus," Smith cried, "Is this a gangland issue? Because if it is, I just want out—"

"Shut up!" Flamethrower yelled. "We saved your ass. Now, you gotta help us burn the Demons." He leaned close to Smith, cigarettes and whiskey on his breath. "Consider yourself an honorary member of the Angels of Life."

"I don't think I can—"

"You've no choice. We purified the street at midnight: no cars, no signs, no people. When you stumbled in, you breathed life into their ceremony. Just what they were praying for. And now, they'll take to the streets."

Smith gazed at the room's occupants: all of them, wearing black. Tank tops. Black bandanas knotted around their necks. Sweat coated their faces.

"Can I have my clothes back?" Smith asked.

The boy who'd brought the water returned with Smith's pants and shirt. They were damp, cleaned of his release. Smith got dressed while the group murmured amongst themselves and loaded their weapons. The *Angels* were preparing for war against an enemy no human could outwardly defeat. Unexplainably, Smith felt an admiration for this modern band of martyrs, game to fight to the death in order to protect their interests.

A gun was thrust in Smith's trembling hands. "Jesus, I can't—"

"You can, and you will," a bald man demanded, shouldering a hunter's rifle. "Just aim for the head," he added. Smith recalled how the cop's shot through the heart resulted in the ruination of his own.

Flamethrower silenced the room with a howl. "Angels!"

Smith stared up at the towering man with awe and suspicion. *God help me,* he thought, *I'm going to die. I'm really going to die.*

"Angels—the time has come. We've organized ourselves for this day. The demons are loose...but we've got God fighting with us, may he protect our souls against the evil that defies us." A rousing battle-cry followed, drowning out the wall-filling beat, some people screaming, "This is our territory!" and "Protect our turf!"

They started filing toward the door.

The woman prodded Smith with the flat blade of a machete. "Move your ass, boy. There's strength in numbers."

Smith rose. Dizzied. Fatigued.

Imagined what it felt like having your heart ripped out of your chest.

«« — »»

Smith felt something in the air. A thickness, revealing itself with acrid smells, and a further dulling of the dark environment. Surrounded by the band of Angels, the braided woman held him close. She'd explained that the Demons sought to gain the streets, not only here in New York, but in other inner cities as well. They were humans, but in sinful prayer had transformed themselves into powerful beings capable of taking down entire neighborhoods. "They hadn't expected such a formidable enemy," she'd explained, speaking of the Angels. "The Angels are gorgeous creatures. We are close, bonded by soul. We will protect ourselves and our turf with our lives."

Flamethrower, leading the procession, stopped before the doorway from where the first demon emerged. Smith saw him sniffing the air. "They are frightened of us," he revealed. He closed his eyes and offered up a prayer to God, then screamed and kicked in the door.

Smith, carried by the throng, gripped his pistol with sweaty hands and allowed himself to be shoved inside the building. Ahead, the burst of the flamethrower drowned out the pounding beat and the subsequent howls of those caught beneath its torch. Inside the building's first floor (which had been shrewdly gutted, forming one large room), Smith caught sight of another demonic man, also black and naked and glistening, crawling up a support column like a spider. A barrage of bullets took him down. Flamethrower added the final blow.

Another shape approached stealthily from a distant set of stairs: a creature bred of man and canine, its snarling muzzle defiant of its attackers. Wounds were pounded into it until it lay wheezing in a steaming puddle. Smith could hear the settling of its wet injuries as bone and oily gristle seeped out onto the floor.

Someone yelled: "Look out!"

A deafening rock of dynamite quaked the room.

Smith dropped his gun, collapsed to the ground in a heap, along with many others. Needles of pain penetrated his head and teeth. In the booming silence that followed, someone uttered, "Ho-ly Shit."

Smith looked up. Saw a huge dark hole in the wall, surrounded by a halo of smoke. From within the hole, the beat emanated like a great heart, its source emerging from within its depths.

Smith's blood stood still in his veins.

In writhing lumps came a massive congregation of bodies, knotted together to produce a singular beating heart,

(thump-thumpa-thump)

a living, breathing entity gushing hungrily forward, sucking into its collective the closest members of the Angels tribe, ten—or more—bodies. Green smoke sputtered from its intricate surface like laval geysers, its agglomerated bulk thick behind it, hundreds of skinless hands reaching out, grabbing the torn wall, rooting itself into the hole. Human parts jutted at countless angles, hordes of swelling eyes peering out alongside naked bone. But not all its features were born of human genes: sharp pointed teeth melted into glistening organs; patches of fur and hide rode the transmuted surface like mossy growths.

Flamethrower tossed a fiery spew at the mass. People fled everywhere, forward, backward, sideways—lambs endeavoring one final opportunity to escape their slaughters. Bullets flew. The air in the room darkened and cooled, an icy frost coating everything and everyone. It penetrating Smith's skin as he fought his way backwards through the ensuing chaos. He chanced a look back at the gangs of Demons and Angels, the conflagration between them dwindling into a battle of one Goliath against a few weakened Davids, the likely victor swelling with the mutilated bodies of its enemy. He choked at the scene, fleeing bodies seized by writhing tentacles emerging from the bloody mass, gripping ankles and necks, hauling them in. Limbs twisted like fleshy ropes, blood bursting at the swelling pressure; bones, ground to silt, muscles and tendon to fibery pulp.

Smith, crawling toward the door, witnessed the lopping off of a man's head, the eyes exploding as it hit the ground just inches away. The braided woman crawled toward him, handless arms reaching out, gushing blood. The boy who'd brought him water lay gutted in the doorway, entrails seeping farther away from his body as he attempted to move. Smith crawled over him, looking back one last time, witnessing a bloodbath.

Why not me? he thought, stealing his way outside, into the heat of the night.

««—»»

"Sir…"

Dull pain lanced through his ribs. He opened his eyes. They burned from the light.

Above, a figure loomed.

"Get moving," the voice demanded.

Smith nodded. Then, sat up. His head swam with pain and noises. He rubbed a hand through his hair. Then, looked around groggily, pondering the reality of his thumping heart.

Rows of windows. Running adverts above. Vents blowing cool air.

Subway car.

The doors open.

He peered up at the figure, now in focus. Transit cop.

"Where am I?" Smith asked, tongue parched.

"Midtown. 54th Street Station. 2-Train."

He gazed around. Confused. The Park Central...it was at 60th Street and 7th Avenue. Not that far away.

A dream?

"The train is being taken out of service, due to mechanical problems. Sorry, this here's the end of the line."

"Thanks for waking me," Smith managed. He stood, exited the car, onto the subway platform.

On a bench, a man sat. Reading the Post. The headline: *Policeman Murdered In Cold Blood.*

Smith stared curiously at the headline. Then, leaned down to tackle an itch on his calf.

He couldn't get to it.

Something in the way.

A bandage...

From somewhere, a dampered beat emanated. A pervasive chill followed.

"Jesus Christ," Smith muttered, his breath suddenly visible before him.

The man on the bench lowered the paper and smiled.

Revealing to Smith his sheer nakedness.

And his wholly demonic intentions.

PLEASE LET ME OUT

"What's a woman to do?" Dee posed the question past her Packard-Bell computer. Her bleached-blond hair looked like bright straw. "Liars, cheaters—all of them. I've never in my life dated a guy who didn't run around behind my back."

Marianne, the redhead with a face reminiscent of a pug-nosed Meryl Streep, lamented in agreement. "Goddamn men, they got their brains in their pants. I mean, I never cheated on Willy, and let me tell you, I had plenty of opportunities. I gave that bastard my heart and soul, and next thing I know he's playing musical beds with half the barmaid staff."

Joyce Lipnick couldn't help but overhear these vocal ruminations: the CSS bug in Dee's intercom speaker was Joyce's ear to the outer office. She didn't consider this eavesdropping; she was just being careful. When you were a managing partner at the number-three law firm in the country, you *had* to be careful.

But the girls (Dee, her paralegal; and Marianne, the floor receptionist) were right. *What's a woman to do?* Joyce reflected in the plush, cherry-paneled office. Czanek, the sleazy P.I. she'd hired, had proved Scott's rampant infidelities. With full-color glossies, no less. How could Joyce ever

EDWARD LEE

erase those images? Scott, the love of her life, servicing his secret bevy via every conceivable sexual position. He left her no choice.

"I couldn't believe it," Marianne rambled. "I came home early one day, and there's Willy with that hussie from the first floor, and he's going at it like a lapdog."

Like a lapdog, Joyce pondered. Has Scott performed likewise? Czanek had verified at least five "steadies," but suspected four more. "Your man gets around, Ms. Lipnick, a real nutchase," he'd eloquented upon receipt of his $200-per-day fee. "Of course, a good-looking boy like that, it stands to reason."

Stands to reason. Joyce could've spit. *I give him a car, a beautiful home, money, credit cards, not to mention all my love, and he repays me by sowing his oats with a bunch of bimbos!*

"Yeah, you tell me," Dee reiterated over the hidden bug. "What's a woman to do?"

Joyce sympathized... But she herself had *done* something.

She pressed her intercom. "Dee, I forgot to tell you. File a health insurance termination for Scott. Right away."

The pause yawned over the speaker. "A termination, Ms. Lipnick? But I thought Scott was on vacation."

"No, Dee. He was fired. What good is a copy boy who's late every other day? And I want those deposition digests for the Air National case on my desk in an hour. I'll look pretty idiotic if I can't go into court and cross-examine those grapeheads on prior testimony. Oh, and remember, we only have a week to get out the preliminary jury instructions for the JAX Avionics appeal."

"Yes, Ms. Lipnick."

Joyce switched off and listened to the bug.

"Did you hear that shit?" Dee whispered to Marianne. "She fired Scott!"

"And he was so cute," Marianne lamented. "That face, and—Christ, did he have a body."

"Tell me about it." Dee's whisper lowered. "That guy could go all night. It was unreal."

"Dee! You mean you... With *Scott?*"

"A bunch of times," she giggled. "Let's just say that all my sick leave's used up for the year, and there're a lot of worn out beds at the Regency Inn."

"Dee!"

But even this news didn't dishearten Joyce. Not now. Not ever again, she resolved. *What's a woman to do, girls? I wish I could tell you, because I did it.*

And as for Dee... *Giddy little slut.* Joyce would trump something and fire her next week.

«« — »»

"Darling?" Joyce set down her litigation bag and unlocked the steel-framed bedroom door. She supposed it was fitting: that Scott's prison be a bedroom. Poetic justice with a twist.

He was waiting for her in bed. "God, honey, I missed you." His strong arms reached out for her. *He's just so sweet,* she thought. *How can I be mad at him?* She decided not to even bring up the business with Dee. That was over now. All of his infidelities were over. Instead, she kicked off her shoes, climbed into the luxurious four-poster, and was embraced by him at once. "I missed you more," she whispered.

"Uh-uh." His kiss devoured her: it took all the stresses of the day and banished them. It made her forget everything. In just seconds, she was so *hot.* His tongue roved her mouth. His hands—strong, assured, insistent—shucked her right out of the charcoal cardigan, then stripped off her white Evan-Picone silk blouse. Nimble fingers released her breasts from lace bra and stroked her nipples. *Oh God, oh my love,* came the helpless thought. His mouth sucked her breath out of her chest.

"Baby, he murmured. "Please."

Her own kisses descended then. Scott's hands peeled away her skirt as Joyce played her tongue over his nipples, then licked ever downward. "Sweetheart…" His fingers finnicked in her coiffed black hair. "Do you love me?" she asked and admitted his penis into her mouth before he could answer. He squirmed, moaning. She sucked slow and hard while her fingers explored testicles that felt large and heavy as hen's eggs. "Do you love me?" Again. "Do you love me, darling?" Again, again. "Yes," he panted. Her tongue traced around the gorged dome, teasing the tiny egress. This only heightened his squirming, as Joyce squirmed herself to get shed of her panties.

"Joyce—honey… I love you *so* much."

"Do you? Do you really?"

"Yes!"

"Then show me." She crawled up to poise herself, then placed her sex right onto his mouth. Her eyes rolled back at the instant flood of sensation.

"You taste lovely," he murmured.

«« — »»

Later—many, many hours later—Joyce lay sated and deliciously sore. She sipped Perrier-Jouet and watched him sleep. So beautiful, so loving. Czanek's photographs reared in her mind. And Dee? *Don't think about it.*

The little tramp. Joyce could scream thinking of Scott with someone else. Those strong hands, the broad sculpted chest, shoulders, and back, and that gorgeous curved cock. *With someone else?* she pondered. *No, never again.*

Who could provide for him better than Joyce? Four hundred thousand a year, a spacious house on the water, and anything else he'd ever need. *And love,* she thought. *Real, mature, guiding love.*

She'd never been with a man like him: so passionate, so deft.

His ability to sense her—her moods, her needs, her desires—was nearly psychic, and the orgasms he gave her—a dozen hot thrumming gifts each night—wrung pleasure from her nerves like warm water being twisted from a sponge. Often he'd make love to her till she simply couldn't move.

And he would understand the rest, in time. When he was older and realized that Joyce knew what was best for him. That's all that mattered. *The truth,* she thought.

Later, his whispers woke her. "Darling?" His hands traced her warm flesh. "Darling?" He nuzzled her breasts, stroked her back and buttocks. "Once more," he whispered.

Joyce's heart pattered against her fatigue. "I don't think I can do it again, honey. You wear me out!"

"Yes," he insisted. "Yes." He rolled over on top of her, pinned her arms above her head as his erection slid directly into her sex. "I love to make you come." The deep, gentle strokes, like a lovely derrick of flesh, drew expertly in and out of her. Joyce felt electrified. Her breasts filled, her nipples distended to pebbles. Oh, she could do it again, all right. Always. Always. Her hands plied his muscled buttocks as he rocked into her, and his penis—always so hard for her, so large and knowing—tilled her salt-damp depths without abatement.

Orgasms like sweet dreams unloosed in her, strings of them, carrying her away with their succulent spasms. *I'm in heaven,* she affirmed. *I'm in heaven every night.*

When he'd finished, Joyce lay immobile, shellacked in sweat and afterglow. His semen ran out of her, so much of it. Scott coddled her, soothing her inflamed breasts, kissing up and down her throat. "Joyce, I know I was bad before," he whispered.

No, she thought. *Please.*

"But I really do love you. I would never want anyone else again, ever. Please believe me, darling…"

Please don't…

"But it drives me crazy, sitting here by myself all day waiting for you. Each hour you're gone feels like a week."

Joyce was wilting.

"Oh, please, honey. Please let me out."

She stroked his hair, touched the side of his handsome face. "I will," she promised. "I will."

But the promise, like many made among lovers, was a lie. She knew she could never, ever let him out.

《《——》》

Their morning ritual: breakfast in bed. Nude, they fed each other languidly—Eggs Benedict, Iranian caviar on toast points, chickoried coffee—as their bodies pressed. Then she showered and began to dress. She always dressed slowly, knowing his fascination for watching her. It made her feel sexy, delightfully lewd.

"You're so beautiful," he said. His clear baby-blue eyes fixed on her from the bed, "I might have to touch myself."

"Don't you dare," Joyce said behind a sly grin. Of course he touched himself; all men did. But did he think about her when he did it? Facing him, she snapped her bra, then teasingly drew her stockings up her legs. "I want you to save it for me, all of it. Every drop."

"Well…" His grin cut into her. "I'll try."

She fastened her floral waist-skirt, then buttoned up the placketed Jacquard top.

"Give me something," he said.

"What?"

"Give me your panties."

Joyce blushed. "Scott, I can't go to work without—"

"Yes you can. I want them with me, so I can think about you sitting there at the office with nothing underneath. I'll think about your beautiful pussy all day, and how bad I want to taste it."

God! Joyce's blush deepened. When he talked dirty like that, she was helpless. She slipped off her panties and tossed them to Scott, who plucked them out of the air and held them fast to his chest.

"I love you," he said.

"Not as much as I love you," she assured him, and then she assured him even further when she left the bedroom and locked the heavy hardwood door behind her.

《《——》》

It was for his own good, anyway. Cruel, yes. Extreme, certainly.

But left to his own devices, Scott would cheat on any woman he became involved with. *What kind of life is that?* Joyce inquired. *What would he become?* All Scott had were his looks. Little education, and less drive. Without Joyce's guidance, he'd be a drifter all his life. *I'm saving him from himself. He'll thank me someday.*

Joyce idled the Porsche into the firm's underground lot, then strode, Bali heels clicking, to the elevator. *Of course, keeping a man locked in your bedroom presents some legal problems.* But why worry? The windows were Lexan set into steel frames, the doors were all locked, and the great waterfront house stood so remote he could yell till his face turned blue and no one would hear him.

"Good morning, Ms. Lipnick," Dee and Marianne greeted in unison when Joyce entered the front office.

"Good morning, girls." She repressed the urge to frown at Dee, whose large breasts threatened to erupt from her blouse. *If she ever has a child,* Joyce postulated, *it'll overdose on milk.* "Don't forget those Delany 'rogs, Dee. I want them out today."

"Yes, Ms. Lipnick."

"And those JAX instructions—today."

"Yes, Ms. Lipnick."

Blond ditz. Thinks she can steal away any man with those big boobs. In her office, Joyce contemplated her own breasts in the mirror. They looked fine now—the $5,500 implant job had taken care of the sag. And as for her dreaded cellulite, good old Dr. Liposuction had made short work of it. Scott being so handsome, Joyce felt the maintenance of her own appearance was an obligation. *You're fifty-one now,* Joyce, *and you're not getting any younger.* Soon would be time for another lift, or a chemical peel. Thank God for plastic surgeons.

But the two fresh young girls outside inhibited her. She pressed her intercom. "Marianne, come into my office please."

"Yes, Ms. Lipnick?" said the receptionist a moment later.

"Come in please, and close the door." Joyce stood up, mildly befuddled. "This may sound silly, Marianne, but I'd like your opinion about something. Your honest opinion."

"Sure."

"Am I..." The question drifted. "Do you think..."

"What is it, Ms. Lipnick?"

"What I mean is, do you think I'm pretty?"

The young receptionist fidgeted at the question, "Well, of course, Ms. Lipnick. You're a very attractive woman. In fact, I heard some the associates talking the other day, and they were saying how they couldn't understand why a woman so attractive wasn't married."

Joyce brimmed. "Ah, well. Thank you, Marianne. It's very nice that you related that to me. But please don't tell anyone I asked."

"Of course not, Ms. Lipnick."

Marianne left. Joyce reseated herself and thought, *There, see? Nothing to be paranoid about...* Nevertheless, she turned on the bug.

"Dee! You'll never guess what the Ice-Bitch just asked." Joyce's jaw set. *Oh, so it's the Ice-Bitch is it?* "She asked me if I thought she was *pretty!*"

Dee chirped laughter. "What did you say?"

"I'm not stupid, I told her she was very attractive." Marianne chirped a bit of her own laughter. "I even made up a lie about how the associates thought so too."

"I still can't get over that boob-job she got. Thinks no one noticed. One day they're like pancakes hanging to her waist, and the next day she's Dolly Parton."

"What an old bag!" Dee whispered.

An old bag, huh? Joyce smirked back her ire. Pancakes. She'd trump something up on Marianne and fire her next week, too. Then the two little airheads could stand in the unemployment line together. See if their youth put food on the table. See if their big tits paid the rent.

«« —»»

That night Scott spread Joyce Lipnick out like a feast. A feast of passion. A feast of warm flesh. Her orgasms rushed out of her, each a torrid spirit unleashed by her lover's ministrations. It was like this every night now: any pleasure Joyce could imagine was made manifest in the locked room's gossamer dark.

Via mouth, hand, or genitals, Scott left no orifice untended, no anticipation unslaked. Time passed not in minutes, nor hours, but in the repeated pulses of her bliss. His love consumed her, it carried her away on angels' wings to a demesne of passion and indefectibility that was theirs and theirs alone.

It would be like this, she knew, for the rest of their lives. Till death do them part. Scott's imprisonment was really his salvation, his *freedom* to love and to be loved to the ultimate limit of truth. What could be more wonderful, or more real, than that?

Later, they embraced, laved in sweat, lacquered in joy. Joyce fell asleep, content by the feel of his copious semen in her sex, and the trail of its aftertaste glowing down her throat. But she also fell asleep to his whispers, and the night's ever-faint plea:

"Please, Joyce. Please let me out."

«« —»»

Weekends unfolded in sheer hedonism. Rich meals in bed, between frenetic bouts of love. Once Scott ate Steak Tartar out of the cleft of Joyce's bosom. Another time he'd poured an entire bottle of Martell Cordon Bleu over her body and licked it off. Salmon roe was daintily eaten off of genitalia. Sashimi was lain out on abdomens. Once Scott had even filled her sex with baby Westcott oysters—flown in fresh from Washington—and plucked each one out with his tongue.

Was this so bad, so cruel, to share with him life's delicacies? To enjoy each other in unbridled abandon? What difference did it make that the door was locked? Between hard and heavy love-making, they'd loll in the jacuzzi, sipping champagne from Cristal d'Arques flutes. Swirls of warm bubbles cosseted them. Joyce couldn't resist; any proximity to Scott lit a lewd fuse in her that never went out. Frequently she'd fellate him beneath the water, gentling stroking his buttock's groove. Scott shuddered amid the luxurious swirls, then Joyce would coax out his climax with her hand and watch the precious curls of sperm churn away in the foam…

Week-mornings shared the same feasts of the palate. "I've got to keep my baby well-fed," she'd say. "You'll need the energy tonight." Then he'd watch her shower and dress—in total adoration. Giving him these images of herself kept her aroused all day. To hell with what those silly tramps thought? If Joyce wasn't really beautiful, then why was Scott always so hot for her? Sometimes she'd make love to him just before leaving: fully dressed but for panties she'd straddle him amid the covers, and just ride him until his climax answered the demand of her loins. Or she'd service him orally, and swallow up his need. "That should tide you over till I come home, hmm?"

This particular morning, though, he repeated his former request just as she would leave. *My darling fetishist,* she thought.

"Give me something," he said.

"Hmmm?" Joyce coyly replied.

"Your bra," he decided. "Give me your bra."

"Oh, so it's my bra this time?"

"That's right. Take it off right now and give it to me." His smile teased at her, his awesome pectorals flexed as he lay with his fingers laced behind his head. "So I can think about you sitting at your desk all day long with your bare breasts rubbing against your blouse. I'll think about your beautiful nipples getting hard, tingling. I'll think about kissing them, licking them…all day…"

Joyce's face flushed. She'd get excited just listening to him! She removed her blouse, tossed him the sheer, lacy bra, and redressed.

Scott held the bra like an icon. "I love you," he affirmed.

"I love you too, and I'll show you how much when I come home."

And when she left, and locked the sturdy door behind her, Scott's eyes squeezed shut so hard that tears leaked out. His hands mangled the bra, twisting, twisting, as though it were not a bra at all, but a garrote.

«« — »»

Joyce's guilt frequently presented itself by midday. So she did what all good lawyers did with guilt: she rationalized it out of existence. *Look at what I'm absolving him from,* she attested. Shallow interludes, bogus relationships, disease. What she'd done was actually an act of love—a superlative one—and she knew that already he was beginning to realize that. Her mere sleeping with him was proof, wasn't it? At night Joyce locked herself in with him. She was open to him, vulnerable; in a sense, she was at his mercy every night. Scott easily had the physical capability to kill her if he wanted to. But not once had he even threatened violence.

Because he loves me, she realized, braless and musing at her desk. *Because he's finally beginning to understand.*

Without me, he knows he's powerless against the seductions of the world. If I hadn't taken the necessary steps, he'd still be out there cheating on me, wasting his life and disillusioning himself. Causing pregnancies. Catching chlamydia, herpes, AIDS.

He knows now. This is the only way.

Between deposition rewrites, Joyce turned on her bug. Dee and Marianne, the magpies, chattered away as always.

"Gary was such a dream. I mean, we were perfect together."

"Dee, Gary was a conniving, treacherous *cockhound.* He was putting the make on your mother, for God's sake."

"Yeah, and both my sisters, too. I hate to think how many women he went to bed with while we were engaged."

"They take everything for granted. The minute they find a good thing, they're snuffling around every skirt in sight."

"Men. Sometimes you could just lock them up."

Joyce nodded a curt approval. *Ladies and gentlemen of the court, the verdict is in, and the judgment in unanimous.*

She thought about Scott all day, her tingling nipples an interminable reminder of her bralessness. She imagined Scott's adroit tongue gingerly encircling the tender areolae, his heavenly mouth sucking them out. She imagined his hands describing the contours of her breasts—adoring them, worshiping them. And she imagined much more, till the urge to masturbate overwhelmed her. *No!* she demanded. *Wait.* Why touch herself when in just a few hours *he* would be touching her?

Marianne buzzed. "Ms. Lipnick? There's a man to see you.."

SHIVERS III

A man? Probably some counter-lit bozo from the JAX Avionics appeal. *Wants to settle now for five or ten mil. Don't hold your breath, pal.* "Send him in, please," she said.

Past the threshold stepped a tall, well-postured man in a fine pinstripe suit. Short sandy hair, blue eyes. *Handsome,* she thought. But something bland like a stoic chill set into his face. "Ms. Joyce Lipnick?" he queried. "My name is Spence."

Joyce stood up, hard-pressed not to frown. "Well, what can I do for you…Spence?"

"Oh, I'm sorry. I should say *Lieutenant* Spence."

Lieutenant?

"…District Major Case Section."

Joyce felt forged in ice—

Spence continued, "You are under arrest, Ms. Lipnick, for first-degree sexual misconduct, abduction, and sexual imprisonment, and those are just the trifling charges."

"Now see here, Lieutenant!" Joyce erupted. "What in God's name are you talking about?"

Behind the policeman, Dee and Marianne could be seen peeking in, their faces pinched, inquisitive. Spence looked like a well-dressed golem as he paused to assay Joyce's expression.

And then it dawned on her. *God, no. Somehow Scott got—*

"He got out, Ms. Lipnick," Spence informed her. "It must've taken him hours to pick the lock on the door—he did it with two bent bra-clips. Then he got to the phone and called us."

Joyce's nipples instantly lost their arousal. She could only stand there now, opposing this brazen cop as she felt all the blood run out of her face. "I—" she attempted. But the words dissolved. In fact, her entire being felt as though it were dissolving right there before the witness of the whole world. Eventually she was able to croak, "I had no choice. He was cheating on me."

"Well, you certainly took care of that inconvenience." Spence, for only a moment, spared a smile. "And it gives me great pleasure, Ms. Lipnick, to inform you that you have the right to remain silent, and that anything you say…"

«« — »»

Joyce paid no attention to the rest of the policeman's obligatory mirandization. Instead, paling, she thought in scorn, *The goddamn ungrateful bastard got out. I should've know he'd try something like this. How could I be so stupid?*

And what was that Spence had initially said?

—and those are just the trifling charges—

Spence, at least, had a lawyer's wit.

Dee and Marianne looked on, aghast. Joyce's face felt like pallid wax as Spence handcuffed her. "Don't you have anything to say, Ms. Lipnick?" the policeman inquired. "In my experience, criminals generally have a comment or two upon arrest."

"I think I will observe my right to remain silent," Joyce blandly replied.

"A commendable decision."

But as Joyce was ushered out, she couldn't escape the inscrutable image—Scott, travailing down the hall for the phone. Nor the final consideration: *I guess I should have cut his arms off too,* she thought.

WHAT THEY
LEFT BEHIND

"The rain is getting worse," Scott Soderman said as he stepped up to the open dock door. He focused his attention on the empty parking lot that sloped down toward the warehouse so trucks could back up to the loading docks. At the base of the incline were two large storm drains, both of them clogged with leaves, brush, and debris that had collected during the ten years the Timlico warehouse, office building, and factory sat abandoned. A long trailer with the Soderman Logistics logo painted on its side was parked at one of the oversized dock doors to Scott's right. More trucks with more trailers would be coming, despite the bad weather.

"Yeah, what a day for a move," George replied. George was a few years older than Scott, and he had grown up in some town in New Jersey that no one in the Soderman family had ever heard of before he proposed to Scott's older sister. Soon after that George came to work alongside Mary Soderman and her father at the family's warehousing business.

"I guess there wasn't much choice," Scott said. "The lease for the old place ends on Monday, doesn't it?"

"Correctamondo."

Scott flinched as jagged lightning flashed in

BRIAN FREEMAN

the distance, splitting the dark summer sky. Thunder rolled by a few seconds later. It was going to be a long day.

"Got a light?" Scott asked, pulling a cigarette from his pocket.

"I don't smoke. Are you even old enough?"

"I'm almost eighteen. It's all downhill from there, right?"

"You do know those things are going to kill you before you're fifty, don't you?"

"If I live that long." Scott laughed at his own joke and put the cigarette back in his pocket for later. "They calm my nerves."

"If you say so."

"I do. Anyway, there's not much I can actually do here today. I may as well get busy getting cancer."

"So why'd you volunteer then?"

"I guess Mary told you I'm not really into the family business?"

"Many times."

"Yeah, well, I knew I was going to be dragged along one way or another so I volunteered before my father could draft me."

George laughed. "Like the Army."

"Yeah, like the Army. Anyway, you guys are going to bulldoze the office building and the factory next week, right?"

"That's the plan. We only need the warehouse, not the rest of the complex."

"Well, I want to check everything out before the demolition. You know, try to find something neat that was left behind by the previous owners. A souvenir of sorts. It'll be cool."

George laughed again. "If you say so, Scott."

Mary was operating the forklift, and she sped by her fiancé and brother, sounding the horn as she passed. She was busy unloading pallets and crates from the trailers and moving them to the appropriate place in the warehouse while Scott and George tracked the inventory to make sure each delivery was recorded properly. Every hour a truck driver brought another trailer from the old warehouse where Ronald Soderman and the rest of his full-time employees were busy closing down operations. The driver then returned an empty trailer to the other side of town and the process repeated itself again and again. It would have been a long day even without the storm.

"Hey, you two," Mary said, stopping the forklift a few feet from where Scott and George stood watching the rain. The forklift's engine was loud, coughing black smoke, and the noise almost masked the sound of the thunder rumbling across the valley.

"Hey what?" Scott replied. Lightning split the sky outside, even closer than before.

"Dad called. The power went out at the old office and there's a good chance it's going to happen here, too. Someone needs to see if the generator in the basement still works."

"There's a basement?" George asked.

"Not under the warehouse, but under the offices. There's supposed to be a generator room down there somewhere."

"Sure, I'll go," Scott said. This was the opportunity he had been waiting for all morning long—an excuse to explore the rest of the building.

"Take this." Mary tossed a flashlight to her brother. "And watch yourself in there. You don't want to fall through any holes in the floor. Why don't you go with him, George? Make sure he gets back in one piece."

"Yeah, okay, I can do that," George replied.

Mary gunned the forklift's engine and rolled into the trailer to grab the next pallet, leaving a cloud of smoke hanging in her wake.

George and Scott walked across the enormous warehouse to the wide double doors that separated it from the offices. Tacked onto the wall next to the doors was a map of the complex, and at first glance the area resembled a maze, but the color code system helped bring some order to the chaos.

"Looks like the stairs to the basement are all the way on the other side of the building," Scott said, pointing at a square labeled MECHANICAL ROOM #7/BASEMENT ACCESS. "But it's a straight shot through one hallway, at least."

"Okay, let's go then," George replied. "I don't want to spend too long in there."

"Scared of the dark?"

"Don't ask."

"Too late."

They opened the double doors and darkness greeted them. They stared into a pitch black void while Scott swatted around the wall, finding mold and wetness and finally a series of switches. He flipped them. Some of the lights flickered to life.

"Holy cow," George said.

Only a few lights had come on, leaving the long hallway eerily cloaked in shadows, but Scott and George could still see the piles of discarded paperwork scattered everywhere, the secretary's chairs laying on their sides or upside down, the water stained ceiling tiles that were crumbling and covering the floor, and the colorful graffiti spray painted on the walls.

"Watch your step," Scott said, walking slowly, waving the flashlight back and forth to fill in the gaps of darkness between the functioning florescent lights.

"This place is trashed," George said.

"Yeah, from what I've heard punks break in to party all the time."

Scott stopped at the first office and aimed the flashlight into the small space barely larger than a walk-in closet. A high-backed chair was overturned behind a scarred desk, several framed aerial photographs of the property were smashed on the floor, and two filing cabinets were stripped of their drawers. Paperwork littered the office, along with discarded beer cans, used condoms, and broken needles. A steady stream of dirty water dripped from a yellowed ceiling tile in the far corner.

"What a mess," George muttered as he and Scott started navigating the hallway again. The further they went the quieter the growl of the forklift in the warehouse became, and soon all they could hear was the storm. Hundreds of offices, dozens of conference rooms, and numerous other hallways branched off to their left and right.

"Why'd they leave all this stuff?" George asked, pointing at another filing cabinet lying on its side. Yellowed and wet piles of paperwork covered the floor. "I mean why didn't Timlico take it with them when they closed up shop?"

"Shit, you don't know, do you?"

"Know what?"

"There was a freak fire about ten years ago. Some people were killed and the company closed down because of the lawsuits. There was no reason to take anything with them, I guess."

"How many people?"

"Nearly fifty."

"Jesus, how?"

Scott pointed at a MagCard slot. "See these panels?"

"Yeah?"

"The doors worked on an electronic passcard system, but when the fire started in the basement, the MagCard system locked. A bunch of people got trapped in their offices while the smoke was sucked through the ventilation ducts. They didn't burn, they suffocated."

"Jesus Christ. How'd the fire start?"

"Some kind of freak accident," Scott said. "A spark where there shouldn't have been one or something like that."

"Damn, this is creepy," George said.

They had reached the end of the hallway, where the door marked MECHANICAL ROOM #7/BASEMENT ACCESS—RESTRICTED ACCESS awaited them, and looking back, Scott agreed with George's assessment: the building was seriously creepy.

"This is like something from a slasher flick," Scott said, trying to sound like he was making a joke.

"Yeah, this might have been a bad idea."

"Do you want to go back? I can handle it myself," Scott said even though his nerves were beginning to dance in his stomach. The interior of the building really was more disturbing than he had expected. All those offices. The dark hallways. The empty conference rooms. The memories contained within the walls. Everything left behind. He could feel the darkness creeping around him; the thought was almost maddening.

Finally, George said, "No, let's just get it done."

Scott nodded and pushed the door open. The room's lights weren't working. He hit the switch a couple of times before giving up. Instead, he searched with the flashlight until he located their destination: a door marked BASEMENT ACCESS. They slowly crossed the room and Scott pushed the door open to reveal a narrow set of concrete stairs leading down to another door.

"I don't like the looks of this," George said.

"We should probably check it out anyway," Scott replied.

When they arrived at the bottom of the stairs, Scott tugged on the basement door's handle, pulling it open. He reached around the corner and found a switch. Several of the lights began turning on. Scott and George peered into the basement.

"Damn," Scott muttered.

The room was filled with lockers and desks and concrete support columns and equipment that neither of them could identify, but the first thing they really comprehended was the water. Six inches on this side of the room, at least. Two hundred feet from where they stood were a set of stairs leading up to a door marked GENERATOR ROOM, and the water was deeper on that side of the room, too. Scott could tell from looking at the waterline along the long row of lockers on the wall to his left. The difference in depth didn't make a lot of sense to him.

"Maybe the floor is sloped?" George suggested.

"Could be. I think we can handle it. It's not that deep."

Scott and George stepped into the cold water that splashed around their ankles. They hurried across the basement as the water slowly got deeper, rising to their knees. At one point two dead rats floated past them and soon after that they slipped on rotting papers and other things they couldn't see in the dark water. Doors along the wall to their right were marked TRANSFORMERS and AIR COMPRESSION UNITS and BOILER and MAIN ELECTRICAL SYSTEM CONTROLS.

Scott was studying the doors when a wave of claustrophobia rolled over him: the walls appeared to be closing in, bowing, sliding closer. He blinked, shook the thought away. He knew his imagination was playing tricks on him. The walls couldn't really be moving, right? But then the tremors in George's voice told Scott that he wasn't the only one seeing something strange.

"Hurry up," George said.

They were still a short distance from the stairs when the lights died.

"Shit," Scott muttered. He lifted the flashlight, shining it toward George. His sister's fiancé had turned toward him, and his face was very pale.

"Let's go back," George whispered. "I hate the dark."

"Why didn't you say that when I asked?"

"I didn't know it would be *this* dark!"

"The door is only a few more yards," Scott said, pointing the light at the stairs. It really wasn't that far, but the distance suddenly seemed to be forever and a mile. The light drifted back to George's face. He was shivering.

"The water's still rising," he whispered.

Scott looked down, startled. They hadn't moved, but the water was now above their knees. The coldness was soaking into Scott's bones and terror began to grow within him. The darkness was closing in on him, tightening like a vice, and tremors spread from his feet to his legs to the rest of his body. This was a bad situation that could only get worse, but it wasn't too late to turn back. And why were they trying so hard to get to the generator room in the first place? Why not just go back to the warehouse and call it a day? Couldn't make it, sorry, wasn't going to risk drowning just to keep the lights on. But they were so close now and some compulsion was pushing Scott forward...

"Let's get the generator started and then we'll haul ass out of here," Scott said. "We'll be quick."

George didn't look convinced in the spotlight of the flashlight, but he turned and started toward the stairs. Scott tried to keep the door in the narrow circle of light, tried to keep his eyes on their goal, but something was wrong.

Terribly wrong.

He heard splashing behind them, to their sides, everywhere.

Someone or something moaned. Or maybe a piece of furniture had shifted. How could he tell the difference?

Was that a scream in the distance?

No, it had to be thunder, had to be.

What about Mary? Was that her screaming?

No, she was all the way on the other side of the building.

Suddenly Scott's nose filled with smoke and he began to cough.

The stairs were only a few feet away, not much further now, but the water was nearly up to their waists and...

George dove into the water and started swimming. Scott followed suit, struggling to keep the flashlight out of the icy water. The circle of light swung wildly around the wall in front of them, up to the ceiling, and then back down to the stairs, which they climbed in a panic to the door marked GENERATOR ROOM.

"What the hell was that?" George muttered, spinning around to face Scott, his words turning to fog in the increasingly chilly air.

Scott was cold and soaking wet and his heart was beating a mile a minute. He turned the flashlight back to where they had just been: the ripples from their panicked swim still spreading across the water, but there was no smoke and no one to be seen anywhere.

"Just our imaginations," Scott said, forcing a tight laugh, trying to hold in his gasping breaths. "It's dark and our imaginations got away from us. Gotta be."

When George didn't reply, Scott tried the door. It slowly swung into the room. He had expected there to be a small generator like the one at his father's hunting cabin, but instead he found a large control panel and a locked door. The sign next to the door stated: #1 & #2 (BACK-UP GEN-ERATORS).

They stepped into the room, and the door swung shut behind them. Scott approached the control panel. There was a series of gauges and buttons and a few blank screens. The needles on the gauges lay to the left. Scott pushed the green ON button. Nothing happened. No sputtering. No revving of power. None of the gauge needles jumped.

"Damn," Scott muttered. "Should have figured as much."

"Broken?"

"Something like that. Maybe just no fuel."

"Let's get the hell out of here then."

"Yeah, let's do that."

Scott returned to the door, opening it with his free hand.

Instantly fear rose up and tightened around his throat as water came pouring in at his feet.

The stairs were now submerged, but that wasn't what stopped Scott dead in his tracks, and it wasn't what made the shriek escape from between his lips before he even knew it was coming.

He and George weren't alone. That realization paralyzed him.

Smoke filled the air.

Dark, billowing smoke.

And in the smoke, Scott could see the outlines of people. They were moving toward the stairs and the door, their arms flailing above their heads. Long-forgotten echoes of whispers and cries and screams filled the basement, bouncing off the walls and the foaming water.

"Holy mother of God," George said, his cold hand grabbing onto Scott's arm.

The contact snapped Scott's mental paralysis, and he pushed George back into the generator room. He forced the door shut as the smoky outlines of people reached the stairs. The flashlight slipped from his hand, hit the wall, and the bulb shattered. Darkness engulfed the two men.

"What the hell is going on?" George screamed.

Footsteps on the stairs approached the door. The cries and whispers grew louder.

"I think they're…ghosts," Scott said, his mind suddenly fuzzy. He felt almost drunk.

"Ghosts aren't real!"

"Maybe you should tell them that."

Scott stared into the pure black nothingness, and it was like being blind. Blind and intoxicated. Ghostly hands began to pound on the door, scratch at the doorknob. Hoarse screaming followed.

"Why are they coming after us?" George asked, his voice cracking.

"I don't think they are," Scott said, trying his best to maintain his composure even though every rapid beat of his heart was a jackhammer pounding the inside of his chest. Then came a moment of surreal clarity. "I think they're doing whatever they did when they died! I don't think they can hurt us!"

George didn't reply right away. Then:

"We're not alone in here," he whispered.

Scott started to open his mouth, then stopped. Something *was* moving from the other side of the room, from where the locked door blocked access to the generators. Scott could hear the wet footsteps; he could feel the little waves of water breaking against his ankles. The room was suddenly as cold as the inside of a meat locker, and it wasn't just from the icy water. There was a presence with them.

A loud clicking echoed around the room—and it instantly made Scott think about all the times he had absentmindedly played with his lighter, flicking at the sparkwheel, causing the flames to jump again and again and again. It was something he did when he was trying to think, and he could identify the sound in his sleep.

"Scott, what's that?" George asked, his voice trembling.

"A butane lighter…" Scott's words died in his throat. Goosebumps broke out all over his flesh.

The coldness was getting closer. There was a series of clicks, like someone was fumbling with the lighter and didn't know how to make it work.

A spark jumped in the darkness near the generators. Then another. Then another. Closer and closer and closer.

"We have to get out of here," Scott said, fear consuming him. There was another spark, even closer, and he flinched. He stammered when he tried to speak. Cleared his throat. Finally forced out some words: "Those things out there, I don't think they can hurt us. But whatever is in here…"

The thought trailed off and he reached for the door without finishing his statement.

"Let's go then, let's go fast," George whispered, directly into Scott's ear, making him jump again. He hadn't realized how close George was and his first thought was that the evil, whatever it might be, had reached him.

Scott and George pulled the door open, stepped out and dove over the steps, dove through the smoke, through the whispered cries of pain, and hit the water hard, beginning to swim immediately, coughing and choking and splashing in the dark. They swam side by side with absolutely no way of knowing which direction they were going in or how far they had gone. Their arms and legs hit desks and other objects in the water, but they pushed on through the blackness that was threatening to swallow them whole.

Scott remembered how the walls had been moving in on them a few moments earlier and how the ghostly outlines in the smoke had been crying in fear, and once again terror threatened to paralyze him. He forced himself to concentrate on each stroke, on making the next motion, on pushing forward as hard as he could.

But suddenly George was gone.

Scott stopped, his feet finding the concrete floor. The water level had risen to his waist. He stayed very quiet and nearly motionless as he listened to the splashing in the distance, to the whispered cries. The smoke wasn't nearly as bad, but still he violently coughed.

Then Scott felt movement under the water, just behind him. His blood turned to ice in his veins. Something broke the surface, splashed wildly.

"George!" Scott screamed. He reached out into the darkness, found an arm flailing in and out of the water. He grabbed onto George's hand and pulled as hard as he could. He felt the water move, he heard coughing and a loud gasp.

"Something pulled me under," George cried, spitting more water out. He didn't wait for Scott to reply. He dove forward and began swimming frantically. Scott quickly followed.

Soon their hands were smacking the floor and they stumbled to their feet and ran, the water sloshing around their knees as they stumbled into furniture and equipment, bruising their arms and legs.

They had no idea where they were, but they knew they were headed the right way because the water level was dropping. Still, they were running blind until Scott slammed face first into the wall of lockers and yelled in pain. George ran into him from behind, smacking him against the cold metal a second time.

"Follow me," Scott said, grabbing George's arm. He used the lockers as a guide to reach the corner of the basement near where they had entered. Soon they were at the door to the stairs that would take them back up to the offices. There were still muffled screams out in the darkness, but there was no more smoke hanging low in the air and the coldness seemed to be drifting away.

Scott threw his weight against the door and it popped open. He and George stumbled onto the stairs and Scott turned, slamming the door shut again.

"Jesus Christ," he whispered, his breathing heavy, his heart pounding in his chest, his eyes still trying to focus in the never-ending darkness. "Are you okay?"

"Something pulled me under," George said, sounding dazed. "The thing from the room, I think. It…I almost drowned. Did you feel it? Scott? Did you?"

"I don't know, but it was bad, whatever it was," Scott replied. "My mind. I couldn't think. Like my head was full of fog. Christ, let's just get the hell out of here."

They rushed up the stairs, holding onto the railing to keep from losing their balance and tumbling back to the bottom. Scott opened the door at the top of the stairs and they nearly threw themselves into the room labeled MECHANICAL ROOM #7/BASEMENT ACCESS on the maps of the building. They could hear the storm again, pounding at the building from every angle, and they eased their way along the wall, finally reaching the door to the hallway after what felt like an eternity. Scott shoved the door open, feeling a sense of growing euphoria at being free of the basement.

Off in the distance, beyond the end of the long hallway, he could see the lightning flash outside the open loading docks at the far side of the warehouse. The lightning would be enough to lead them to safety. They were going to be okay.

Scott and George held onto the walls to steady their trembling legs as they began walking. They didn't stop until they were standing at the dock doors in the warehouse, staring out at the raging storm. They told Mary there was nothing they could do about the generators, they explained that they had gotten wet in the basement and that no one else should go down there because it was flooding, and Scott apologized for breaking the flashlight. Mary went to call their father, and Scott moved to the edge of the dock and stood there, grateful to be somewhere safe from the things that lingered in the basement of the building. Lightning splintered trees in the forest around the warehouse and heavy drops of rain spit on Scott's face, but the wetness on his flesh actually felt good. Deep down, Scott felt like he had been born again.

"George, I think we're lucky to be alive," Scott said as he stared out at the storm and thought about what he had sensed in the basement. The presence in the generator room was pure evil and it wasn't to be messed with. He was certain of that…

…which was why terror exploded within in him when he turned and saw George with his head down, a shiny silver lighter in his right hand.

George's thumb flicked at the sparkwheel again and again until he did it correctly, and the flame jumped to life.

His glassy eyes were locked on the fire he held in his hand.

Then George looked up at Scott and grinned.

Scott's heart slammed against the inside of his chest and he wanted to scream but he couldn't. He realized too late what had happened under the dark waters in the basement and screaming wouldn't help them now. Screaming wouldn't help at all. That was what he had learned from the people in the basement, the shadowy souls in the smoke, the echoes of the workers whose cries were but whispers in the memory of the building. Screaming wouldn't open doors, wouldn't extinguish fires, and it certainly wouldn't put the genie or the demon back in the bottle. Scott realized all this, and something else, far too late to do him any good.

George had found what they left behind.

THE HOLE

The hole in the back yard appeared where the old, dead cherry tree had been cut down five years before. The stump had rotted from the inside out, until it was gone and a wide hole remained.

Ron stood looking out the kitchen window. It was March, and spring was on the way. Soon the bird feeder would be taken down, and the sparrows, grackles, doves, and squirrels would disperse. It would again be time to mow the lawn, trim the hedges, and perform his other outdoor chores.

Kate walked up, followed his glance, and echoed his thoughts. She tended the flower beds, but sometimes they strayed into each other's territory.

"That hole will have to be filled this year," she said. "I keep stumbling over it."

"Don't worry," Ron replied. "I already have it on my list."

His wife went away, but he kept staring, thinking where on the property he'd get the dirt to fill the hole. And that was when the sparrow disappeared.

He saw the little brown bird hop over to the edge of the hole, then down inside. It was looking for grubs, he thought, or was on a misguided search

JOHN MACLAY

for a nesting place. He'd seen other birds and squirrels investigating the hole.

But this one didn't come out. He was sure it didn't, because he was staring intently. He waited a full five minutes for the reappearance of the sparrow. But it never returned.

Ron was curious enough to put on his jacket and walk out to the back yard. He even came back in to get a flashlight so he could explore the hole. When he did, though, all he could see were a deep vertical space and several branching tunnels where the big roots of the cherry tree had been. There was no sign of the sparrow.

"What were you doing out there?" Kate asked when he returned.

He described what had happened.

"Oh, it's probably nothing," she said. "The sparrow probably hopped out while you were getting the flashlight."

Ron agreed. The next morning, though, it happened again.

This time, it was one of the grackles. Watching from the window, half-expecting a repeat performance, he saw the bird drop in. And not come out, although he waited fifteen minutes, making himself late for work.

"You're right," Kate said, after he brought it to her attention. "We have a problem. Maybe it's a gopher that's taking the birds."

"Not a gopher, silly," he responded. "A gopher is a small animal, and it's a vegetarian." He was suddenly struck by the absurdity of the situation. "Or maybe the root tunnels have become a subway to Bird Central."

"But it could be a fox," she persisted. "They've been seen around the neighborhood, and one of them might have made the hole its burrow."

That idea held more weight. But he had to dismiss it, too.

"If it were a fox," he said, "then the birds and squirrels wouldn't even come to the yard. Remember that time a hawk perched in the tree? Everything else left like a bat out of Hell."

She had to admit that. Still, the problem wasn't solved.

So Ron kept watching the hole. And, on the third day, a dove was taken in.

It was as though the ground were growing an appetite for bigger and bigger things.

He didn't have time to go out to the back yard before he and Kate left for their jobs. In the evening, though, he did, again armed with the flashlight. Neither in the shaft nor the tunnels was there any sign of the three birds.

Now he began to obsess about the thing. Why had this unexplained phenomenon suddenly invaded his yard, and his mind? Had he offended the cherry tree by cutting it down five years before, and had some vengeful wood spirit now returned?

But no, that was for George Washington. And besides, the cherry tree had been dead.

Ron felt a little better when, on the fourth day, he didn't see a single bird vanish into the hole. One or two of them approached it, but then hopped away.

It was as if the thing that had been drawing them had become temporarily sated. Or, he thought as he left for work, as if he'd been crazy to worry about it at all.

When he got home, though, he made one more, and hopefully last, check of the yard. And that was when he found the bones.

They were all there, all three carcasses, at the side of the hole. A small one, a medium, and a large, actually laid out in order. Picked clean and white, every scrap of meat having been removed. He felt a chill as he regarded them, and not from the March weather.

He lifted them by the clawed feet and carried them to the trash can, where he hid them under a bag. He didn't tell Kate this time, and in the morning, he was glad he hadn't.

When, just after she left the house, the hole took the squirrel.

This time, there were screams. And this time, in an attempt to save the terrified and obviously wounded animal, Ron ran out into the yard.

But he reached the hole too late. When he peered apprehensively down it, there was nothing but the brown-lined mystery of the tunnels.

He turned away, his heart pounding as much from his bafflement as from the late violent scene. But he was forced, sickly, to turn back.

When, in what he could only interpret as a taunt, the hole, or what was definitely in it, disgorged the denuded carcass of the squirrel.

He took that to the trash can, too. But now he knew his obsession had been well-founded. There was a problem, indeed. Some horrible, insatiable thing, something about which he sensed no book or authority would enlighten him, had taken up residence in his yard.

During the next few days, that thing also occupied Ron's every thought. He still tried to spare Kate, though, while he figured out what to do.

But that ended when she was the first to find out about the neighbors' dog.

"It's terrible," she cried when he got home. "Chippy is dead. He was, well, killed in our back yard. The children are really upset, and the Davises are a bit mad at us."

He didn't need to ask about the bones being found next to the hole. Her eyes told him everything.

"What are we going to do?" Kate pleaded, not even knowing as much as he did. "This can't go on."

Suddenly, it hit him. Her own words, at the beginning, had provided the answer.

"I don't know how I could have been so stupid," he said.

"I'll do it right now.

"I'll fill in the damned hole."

In the night, without even a flashlight so the neighbors couldn't see, Ron tended to the job. He took shovelsful of earth from the corner of one of the flower beds, and meticulously packed each of the tunnels. Although he was leery of the task, he did it well. He even went out to the street and got some loose gravel to fill the main shaft.

He was manually patting the gravel level, and even thinking about how much easier it would be to mow the spring grass there, when it happened.

There was a sucking, so quick and almost hypnotic that he didn't have time to pull his hand away. A sucking, felt as much as seen in the darkness. Of the gravel, first, and then of his hand itself.

And a biting. And pain, incredible pain.

And a tugging from which it took all his strength to wrench himself free.

"Oh, God!" he screamed when he reached the house. "Oh, Kate! Help me. Please!"

She ran out of the bedroom and downstairs in her nightgown. Seeing his bloody hand, she acted quickly. She grabbed a towel from the kitchen, put on a coat, and helped him out to the car. He dimly saw drops of gore, his, spattering the front walk.

At the emergency room, they gave him a tetanus shot and, after an interminable wait, tended to his hand. Three fingers bore inch-long gashes to the white bone, and many stitches were required. It was four in the morning by the time they were able to return home.

Ron called in sick to work, and stayed mostly in bed for the next two days. Although he'd been given pills to take, the pain returned more intensely than ever, making his head swim. It was true that the fingers were one's most sensitive parts.

In his delirium, he thought, although he tried desperately not to think, about the hole. And his yard, in fact his whole once-peaceful property, now assumed an alien, panic-inducing character from which he wanted to escape.

But to which he was also perversely attracted. There was now a hole in his spirit, in his soul.

When he was able to get about again, he stayed clear of the kitchen and all the rear-facing windows. He even had Kate drive them to a long weekend at a country inn, where he drank a lot and tried to forget.

But, when they returned home, the hole was still there. He had her take him out to see it, and the caved-in gravel, speckled with his blood, was unchanged.

There was the problem with his fingers, too. While the pain had lessened, they'd become infected, and the doctors didn't seem to know what antibiotic to use.

At his job, what had been a few sick days and a few vacation days became a leave of absence.

And in Ron's mind, what had begun as an absurdity now had turned into an all-consuming ill.

"You've got to leave this thing," Kate said to him one evening, when he was trying to watch television with her. "We could even move away, if that would help."

He looked at his still-bandaged hand. "But what about this? Would it heal this, too?"

"It might," she tried. "It could be mental."

"No, I don't think so," he said, conscious of his hollow-eyed, half-crazed stare. "I think I was bitten by an imp from Hell."

She regarded him fearfully. "But there hasn't been a bird, or a squirrel, or a dog sucked into that hole for weeks. I mowed the lawn for you today, and it looked just the same."

Spring had arrived, and he hadn't even noticed it. Still, he couldn't move on from where he was.

"That's because it's waiting for me," he concluded. "Its appetite grew to the point where only I could satisfy it."

He paused, while her mouth fell open. "I escaped once. But now I have to go to it, and solve this thing, alone."

Kate got up and, crying, left the room.

Late that night, Ron forced himself to walk out into the yard. The air was warm, but the chill remained in his soul. He didn't know what he meant to do anymore, whether it was to identify the monster, face his fear, or give himself over to it.

And courage wasn't even a factor. He was beyond that, and beyond everything.

He knelt at the edge of the hole. He stretched out his hand, his wounded hand, and touched the gravel. He moved his fingers forward to where the hollow place was.

He was seeking healing, he tried to think. But what he found was something else entirely.

There was something in life, he suddenly knew, that sucked certain people into horror. That began as innocuously as a rotted tree stump in one's back yard. That only fed on lesser beings, but that infected, and then consumed, a human, in a different way.

In the next few, amazing moments, Ron gave himself over to his fate. As if recognizing his resignation, the thing no longer bit, but only ate. First his hand, and then his arm was drawn into the hole and down one of the tunnels. He felt a coolness and a mystery he'd never experienced before.

Then, when his shoulder and his head were pulled in, he saw it. Just as it hadn't been hot, it didn't flicker with the flames of Hell. Instead, it was brown and murky like the earth.

It kept sucking him, whether it was the earth, or Hell, or the embodied monster he'd thought it to be. His torso was engulfed, leaving only his legs to kick above the surface. Then they, too, were gone, and so was he.

Inside, he knew his bones would never be disgorged. That was because there were others, as he now was, there, fully-fleshed shapes moving in a low-ceilinged darkness. Some might wear angels' wings, but this was his destiny.

The hole had been calling to him, all along.

Kate sold the house and moved away. She told the neighbors Ron had disappeared, explaining him as an abandoning husband. But, while she didn't excavate, she sensed where he might be.

The new owners looked curiously at the hole in the back yard, especially the apparent attempt to fill it and the wide gap that remained. They brought in more dirt and gravel, but still there was some sinking.

From time to time, Ron came up to eat a bird or a squirrel. He tried not to be obvious about it, so as not to attract undue attention.

During the years and decades that followed, though, he identified an occasional person above who was akin to himself and the others below. Someone who'd be receptive, or damned, or as he had to think, enlightened.

Then, he was obvious. Then, he enticed and sucked that person in to join them.

They moved through the root tunnels and the earth to new locations. And wherever a tree was cut down, or perhaps an excavation for a new house made, they waited to appear.

THIS HOUSE IS NOT MY HOME

The knocking at the front door was loud and insistent, punctuated only by the occasional lead-fingered mashing of the doorbell. It was somewhat more than Richard Wallace could take at this time of the morning. Somewhat more than he could take at this point in his life.

By the time he'd crawled from bed, belted on a robe, rubbed the sleep from his eyes and cleared the cobwebs from his head, he was steaming. He hadn't chosen to live this far out in the country, to distance himself from the herd, just so that his sleep, especially as rare as *that* was any more, could be interrupted by nosy neighbors, pushy salesmen, religion-peddlers…or whoever the hell this might be.

"Just a minute," he yelled as he slumped down the stairs while the pounding continued.

He didn't bother with peeking out past the drapes or through the peephole, just turned back the deadbolt with a vicious twist of his wrist and flung the door open.

He briefly registered that the unwanted visitor was a tall, thin, well-dressed middle-aged man sporting a fedora of some sort. Undeterred, Wallace began to launch into an angry spiel.

"Listen, dammit, I don't—"

ROBERT MORRISH

"Good morning, Mr. Wallace," interrupted the man, as if Wallace hadn't said a thing; as if he wasn't violating his solitude and tromping across his time of sorrow like a drunk through a graveyard.

"Not to me it isn't," answered Wallace, leaning into the doorway. And that was no lie: with everything he had on his mind, sleep was a precious commodity and happiness a drought-stricken flower. Not to mention that he'd tried to drink himself to sleep last night, and failed, with the only tangible result being a head that threatened to throb itself into pieces at any second. "I don't know what you're selling, but I'm damned sure not interested."

The man took a slight step backwards and allowed a small frown. "I'm sorry, Mr. Wallace, if I've caught you at a particularly bad time. I know what you've been through. But believe me, I'm not selling anything. As a matter of fact, I'm buying."

Wallace started to ask the man how the hell he could possibly understand what he'd been through, but then the rest of what he'd said sank in.

"Buying?" Wallace's weary features scrunched together in confusion. "Buying what?"

"Why, this house, of course. It is for sale, isn't it?" The man turned and pointed out to the yard.

Wallace stepped out onto the porch to see what the man was pointing at. Saw a "For Sale By Owner" sign in his yard. "What the…"

"I didn't put that there," he declared. "This house is not…" But when he turned back, the man was gone.

Then Wallace heard the sound of the man's footsteps.

Inside.

"What the hell do you think you're doing," asked Wallace, charging back into the house. *His* house. But the man had already turned the corner at the end of the hall and gone into the kitchen.

Wallace followed, as fast as his aching head and sizable paunch would allow. "Come back here," he demanded, getting no response.

He rounded into the kitchen, saw a flicker of movement from the corner of his eye, and then lightning exploded across the back of his skull.

««—»»

Wallace awoke to a brutal pounding. His first thought was that his head hurt much worse now, something that he'd barely thought possible. He'd had a concussion once, in college, and that was one of the most painful things he'd ever experienced. This was worse.

He wondered if his skull might be fractured. Wondered if this was what dying felt like. Realized he was probably being melodramatic, just like Carli had always said.

Still foggy, he thought that at least Carli could take care of him, doctor him back to health, baby him a little. But then he remembered that that wouldn't be happening.

Once he became familiar with the pain in his head, and the fact that it wasn't going away anytime soon, his brain sent feelers out, taking inventory of the rest of his body. His back felt like someone had pounded it here and there with a mallet. His arms were cramped and his ankles chafed.

When he tried to move, he realized, finally, that he was bound, hand and foot.

With a sound that was half-whimper, half-strangled-cry—as he realized that his mouth was taped shut as well—he forced his eyes open.

An open-raftered ceiling stared fuzzily back at him. His nose, beginning to work again, noted the musky, damp odor. He turned his head—having to pause for a moment when the movement sent sparks of pain across his eyeballs—and saw a concrete block wall. Twisted a bit further and saw the washer, dryer, and slop sink.

He looked down. His hands were duct-taped together, as were his feet.

Trussed up in my own basement. This is not good.

But so much better than it could be, his mind quickly added. The sonuvabitch apparently just wanted to rob him blind, not torture or murder him. There was that tidbit to be thankful for, at least.

But then he realized that being tied up and left in his own basement could ultimately be a form of torture and murder, after all. His prized privacy, his lack of neighbors or visitors of almost any kind, could wind up being the death of him. He had few friends, and none that dropped by unannounced. He'd taken a leave of absence from work, so no one there would be concerned by his absence. There'd be a meter-reader or some-such interloper eventually, but who knew how soon? Even the police had quit coming by to ask him questions.

No one was going to come to rescue him. He had to get himself out of here.

He tried to pull his hands free from the tape, twisting and straining until he felt beads of sweat popping out on his forehead like water bubbles at a full boil. Giving that up for the moment, he tried to roll onto his knees and then hop to his feet to look around for something sharp, but had to give up when his head threatened to explode. He fell back down, exhausted.

Right about then the pounding started up again.

When he'd heard it earlier, as he was clawing his way back to consciousness, he'd chalked it up as a manifestation of his aching head, but now…now it was obvious the noises were real.

They seemed to be coming from outside, but…the banging was literally shaking the house. He could feel the vibrations, could see dislodged dust drifting down from the rafters like snowflake skeletons. Wallace lifted his head again, craning his neck around, trying to see what was happening. But the laundry room was a walled enclosure in a corner of the basement. The door to the room was closed and, unlike the rest of the cellar, there were no windows tucked at the top of its walls.

Whatever was going on out there, it was completely hidden from him. And he from it.

His ears picked up a new sound. He strained…and could make out voices, people speaking or shouting. And he had to get their attention.

He worked his jaw, straining against the gag like a smothering boy fighting a pillow clamped down over his face. He tried to scream, to shout, anything. All that came out was a muffled moan.

After a while, he just lay there defeated, as the pounding continued, punctuated by the occasional, distant voices.

Eventually, as Wallace started to drift in and out of consciousness, the sounds stopped. Without the background noise, he continued to drowse fitfully.

Until the door to the laundry room started to slowly swing open.

Wallace looked up, felt a bud of hope blossoming.

But then the man—the *buyer*, as Wallace now thought of him—stepped through the doorway, a small, sad smile on his face, and a very sharp knife in his hands.

«« — »»

When the buyer stepped into the laundry room with the knife, Wallace panicked. His only thoughts: *Oh my God, is this what it's like? Is this how it ends?*

He tried to scoot back, to roll away. To do something. Anything.

"I'm not going to hurt you," the man said. "Now calm down."

Wallace tried, but with little success. His breath still came in rapid snatches, his eyes popping as if the pressure in his head was redlining.

Then the buyer stepped forward, knelt down, and unceremoniously yanked the tape from Wallace's mouth.

Wallace cried out, choked on the sudden inrush of air into his gargle-dry throat. Tried to spit, but only gagged.

Still trying to catch his breath, he cringed when he saw the buyer's shadow loom over him again, backlit by the naked, hanging bulb that gave the room its only illumination.

"Just tell me what you want!" Wallace pleaded. "Why are you doing this!"

The man didn't answer just stood there, knife in hand.

"What…what's the knife for?" Wallace managed. Better to confront it, he thought, than to let his imagination keep torturing him.

"To cut you loose," the buyer said finally. "What else would it be for?"

Wallace didn't respond to that. Instead, he asked: "What's all the pounding? What are you doing to my house?"

"You'll find out soon enough. Although I can assure you that there's no damage being done. In fact, we're adding value."

"Who's we?"

"No more questions."

The buyer started to leave the room.

"Wait," managed Wallace. "Hold on a second."

He paused and looked back.

"Yes?"

"Just tell me why. Why in God's name are you doing this?"

"Why? Because I know what you did, Mr. Wallace."

«« — »»

Deja fucking vu, thought Wallace, as he woke some time later to a pounding, this time seemingly only in his head, and the feel of tape upon his hands and feet. And a new feeling, even worse.

He'd been tied up for so long, he'd soiled himself. He shifted around as best he could, but realized that there was no comfortable position to be found.

He wished Carli was here. And Jenni. What a comfort they would be.

But no, he didn't *really* wish they were here. God knew what this madman might have done to them. It was better they were already gone, no matter how much he missed them sometimes.

And despite the misery their absence caused him, despite the pain in his head and the discomfort he felt over every inch of his body, Wallace offered a small prayer of thanks. At least he hadn't woken to some kind of torture. At least he'd *woken.*

He didn't know what the man was capable of, and he wasn't sure he wanted to find out.

"Oh, but you will, Richard. You'll find out."

Wallace screamed. Came as close to jumping out of his shoes as his bonds would allow. Jerked his head around, searching…

No one there. But how…?

The voice, the whisper, had seemed to be right in his ear, the breath almost tickling the small hairs along his lobe.

"Because it's your turn to find out just what people are capable of."

Again! Jesus! Where—?

Wallace whimpered. Tried to scoot himself backwards, get against a wall so at least no one could sneak up behind him…

But, then, before Wallace could give full reign to his hysteria, he heard the now-familiar sounds of stairs creaking and leather squeaking across the basement floor.

Wallace waited, holding his breath. The door swung open.

"Ah, we're awake."

Wallace grimaced but didn't reply.

"Don't worry, Mr. Wallace. We're almost to the end of this part of your journey."

"What the hell does that mean?"

The man ignored the question. "I'll be leaving you this," he said, tossing the knife to the floor behind Wallace, "so you can cut yourself loose."

"Until we meet again," the buyer said as he turned and walked away.

««—»»

It took Wallace longer than he expected to cut himself free. His feet had been relatively easy, but figuring out a way to cut the tape on his wrists had taken a little longer. He'd settled on jamming the knife upright in a drawer and holding the drawer closed with his knee while he rubbed the tape against the blade.

Once he was done, he massaged his wrists gratefully. Wiggled his numb toes.

Free.

His limbs felt like hammered sushi, his head a weathered anvil, and the feeling in his pants was pure misery.

But moving had never felt so good. He stretched, took a few more steps.

More than anything, he wanted to discard his filthy clothes in the slop-sink, but he couldn't allow himself that yet. First, he had to see if the buyer was gone. If not, he didn't want to face the man naked. He would somehow feel more defenseless that way.

He gave himself another minute to clear his head, walking in circles around the laundry room until some of the rubbery feel left his legs. Quietly splashed some water on his face from the sink.

Eased open the door and peaked out into the rest of the basement.

Dark, save for the bare light bulb at the bottom of the stairs. Night had fallen. But, most importantly, there didn't seem to be anyone else in the cellar.

Moments later, he was creeping up the stairs, taking care to step on the outer edge of each step.

The door at the top of the stairs was ajar. It swung open slowly in response to his touch.

The kitchen, dark and quiet. Beyond it, the hallway and the living room. He crept through the shadows, peering into corners as his eyes adjusted to the darkness, ears alert for any hint of an intruder.

He completed a circuit of the downstairs without turning on a light, not wanting to draw attention to his presence. Finally satisfied that he was alone on this floor, he started towards the stairway to the second floor, then hesitated. He had to check upstairs, but…the front door was so close. A breath of fresh air, a chance to step outside, to even flee if he wanted— these things suddenly seemed important. The upstairs could wait for a second.

There was a slight click as he eased open the front door, but no other sound save those from outside—the croaking of frogs, the hooting of an owl, the harmony of crickets. Wallace opened the door, exhaling in relief…

…and found himself staring at an evenly-spaced set of thick steel bars.

"What the hell?" Wallace heard himself say.

He reached out, grasped the bars. Solid. Very solid.

The banging…

He turned, hurried to the living room windows. Bars.

The kitchen window. Bars.

From there, he started almost running, forgetting his quiet caution.

And not until he'd checked every door and window, found the same bars on each and every one, pulled on those bars until his hands were raw and blackened…until he'd found that the garage, and the tools that resided there, was blocked off as well…until he'd searched fruitlessly for useful tools anywhere inside the house…until he'd investigated the attic and stared up the chimney…until he'd tried the phone line and the satellite Internet connection…until he'd exhausted every possibility he could think of…until he'd worked through stages of anger and denial and pure mystification…not until then did he slow down enough to really think about the essential nature of what that crazy bastard had done to him.

Made him a prisoner in his own house…and spent a helluva lot of time and money going to the trouble. Why go to all that time and trouble? Was he just insane? Or was it because…

I know what you did.

What did that mean? What could he know? Nothing. That was the bottom line.

Wallace sagged against the kitchen counter, exhausted. The only sleep he'd gotten in the last couple hellish days was due to the blow to his head,

At least there was plenty of food in the house, he'd checked on that, and the water hadn't been shut off.

God only knew when or how he'd get out of this, but at least he didn't seem to be in any immediate danger. It could be worse, he heard that annoyingly optimistic corner of his mind telling him.

Faced with no other recourse, he decided to clean himself and get something to eat. Wallace clumped up the stairs, distinctly aware of how his clothes were pasted to his skin.

After a few minutes of hot shower, he felt significantly better. His head still hurt, and he was still endlessly turning his situation over in his mind, trying to find an angle that made sense, but at least his body was clean again.

With beads of moisture still clinging to his skin, he waddled over to the closet to pick something out.

A couple steps before he reached the closet door, he heard someone laugh at him.

Startled, he whirled about like a naked spinning top, almost losing his balance.

The laughter grew louder. But there was no one there. And he couldn't tell where the sound came from.

"Who's there?"

No answer, just a slight titter as the laughter faded away. It had been a female laugh. Like the female whisper he thought he'd heard in the basement. Only this time…

…it sounded as if there might have been a second voice as well. A younger one.

He waited, shivering now in his nakedness, but was rewarded with only silence.

When Wallace was almost dressed, nothing left but his socks to pull on, the doorbell rang.

He froze for a moment, like a deer shined just before its death, not trusting his own ears. But when the bells chimed again, he dropped his socks and headed for the stairs, as fast as his legs could carry him.

Who? A neighbor, perhaps, alarmed by the banging earlier? A lost driver, seeking directions? Maybe the police, geared to ask him the same questions for the dozenth time. Even that would be a blessing.

"Coming," he shouted.

But when he yanked open the front door, his hopes flew away between the bars.

The buyer.

"Good evening. Mr. Wallace. You look like you're settling in nicely."

For a few seconds, Wallace stood there dumbfounded, searching for words but finding not even a syllable.

"What. Do you think. You're doing?" he managed finally.

"Ah, the caged bird sings," was all the buyer said. It was his small smirk that tipped Wallace over the edge.

"God-damned you! Why are you doing this? Are you completely crazy?"

At that, the buyer grew serious. "No," he said, slowly shaking his head. "I'm not the one who's made my own prison."

"Will you ever stop talking in riddles?" Wallace rattled the bars. "Just who the hell *are* you?"

"Does it matter?" asked the buyer, his gaze narrowing. "Does it really, truly matter?"

"It does to me."

"Fine. Call me a friend of the family." The buyer cocked his head slightly. "A friend of your wife, to be specific."

"You knew my wife? I'd never even seen you before."

"I wouldn't say I *knew* your wife. It would be more accurate to say I *know* her."

"You mean…" Wallace's voice faltered. "You mean, she's alive? Have you seen her?"

"Such games . We both know your wife and daughter are dead."

"That's not true! No one knows if they're dead. No one," said Wallace, his voice dwindling to a whisper. "They just disappeared."

"Disappeared," repeated the buyer. He turned and walked slowly down the porch, almost slipping out of Wallace's view. "Vanished off the face of the earth. Left this beautiful home, and their loving husband and father for no good reason."

"I love my family!" cried Wallace, his face pressed against the bars. "I would never hurt them."

The buyer turned back toward the door. "At least never *again*," he said quietly.

"Stop it," said Wallace, tears welling in his eyes. "Just stop it. They probably are dead. As long as it's been, I know that. But I didn't have anything to do with it, if that's what…"

He paused. "What did you mean when you said you *know* her?"

The buyer waved a hand dismissively, then turned and started down the stairs.

"Wait!" yelled Wallace. "Just what the hell do you want from me?"

The buyer paused and looked back. "I'm afraid you'll think my answer to be yet another riddle, but…it's not a question of what *I* want. It's what someone else wants from you. And you'll find that out soon enough."

«« — »»

It was four long, lonely weeks later that Wallace started to get hungry.

It was several days before that, however, that he began to get really and truly scared.

During those sluggish weeks, he went over every square foot of the house countless times, prying at bars, trying to punch holes through sheetrock and siding, pounding on the attic ceiling. And spent a lot of time gazing longingly outside, where the sunlight lounged along the woods and the breeze blew wherever it wished.

He had tried to plan for the long haul and dole out his food carefully, but it was hard. Sometimes he found himself eating out of sheer boredom. Sometimes in an effort to quell a swell of panic.

As the days passed, his stocks dwindled, and he began to calculate how long the remainder could last…provided that he conserved, of course, a provision that stayed forever just out of reach.

Soon, much sooner than he would have thought possible, he was reduced to guessing how long he could last after his food ran out and there was nothing but water to keep his body functioning. His new mantra became *at least I have plenty of water.*

Through it all, the buyer never reappeared, despite Wallace's series of alternating curses and prayers. Nor did any other soul grace his doorstep.

Total solitude. Just like he'd always wanted.

The electricity stayed on, proving that either the buyer was paying the bills or the electric company allowed a fair amount of debt to accrue before flipping the switch and demanding payment.

The phone rang on one occasion, in the middle of the night, but by the time Wallace reached it, there was no one there. Except perhaps a dry chuckle at the other end of the line, although he tried to convince himself that that was his imagination. When he hung up the phone and picked it up again, dreaming of a dial tone, there was nothing but dead air to mock him.

Wallace learned to live with, or at least deal with, the diminishing supplies, the endless isolation, the unyielding frustration and boredom.

It wasn't so easy to live with the fear, when it came.

Early on, he'd started talking to himself as he wandered from room to room, restless yet listless. It was probably no surprise that he came to miss his wife and daughter more than ever during these days upon days. Before long, he had started talking to them as if they were there with him, murmuring small tokens of longing and regret.

It was when they started to talk back that Wallace's world changed.

Tired and sweaty from his attempts to ram a chair leg through the exterior wall (the concrete-fiberboard siding had seemed like such a good idea when they'd installed it a couple years back, as had nailing it over the top of the old plywood siding for additional strength and insulation), he was headed for a nap in the guest bedroom at the back of the house. It was cooler there, buffered by overhanging trees from the Indian summer heat.

He was wishing Carli and Jenni were there with him, heard himself saying those words out loud, heard the whispered response *"we are here,"* stopped moving, stood stock-still, listened harder than he'd ever listened in his life, thought to himself—more hallucinations, now I've really started losing my mind—took another step, heard the words *"we're right here,"* in his ear, and lost control then, sprinting for the bedroom door and slamming it shut behind him and flipping the lock and pressing his palms against the door with all the force he could muster. He stood there, panting, straining but unable to hear much over the in-out tide of his breathing, willing those words he'd heard to go away, just go away; sorry for what he'd stupidly wished for, sorry for the veneer of nostalgia he'd allowed his loneliness to create, sorry for oh so much more than just that; wanting nothing, nothing, nothing more than just to have back his old life…

And then he heard the words uttered from behind him, within the bedroom:

"Did you really miss us, Richard?"

"How much did you miss us, Daddy?"

«« — »»

Wallace had never been the imaginative sort.

And so, once he'd recovered from the screaming fit that had sent him running from the back bedroom, careening about the house in mindless, panic-strewn loops until he finally fell, huddling and whimpering…once he'd recovered from that, he didn't waste much time trying to tell himself that he'd hallucinated the whole affair.

Hallucinations, visions, products of one's imagination…these were simply not the province of a practical mind like Wallace's. And he didn't have to spend very long at all convincing himself of that before he heard his wife and daughter speak to him again.

And this time, he didn't just hear them, he saw them.

And they were not pretty.

They looked about the way you'd think they would, not that most people ever allow themselves to think about such things, after spending months buried beneath the forest floor. Their hair was matted in dirt-clod clumps, festooned here and there with leaves and maggots, while their lips had pulled back from their teeth to unveil a gum-line sneer. Their clothes, and skin, were gone in many spots, decayed or eaten away, and their muscles and tendons, what was left of them, had drawn tight, pulling their torsos down into a pronounced hunch, and bending and twisting their arms and legs into contorted poses.

Aren't, he asked silently, tiptoeing on the edge of hysteria...*ghosts supposed to look the same way in death that they did in life?* So he would have assumed. But apparently the dead had no rules.

Somehow, maybe because he knew the futility of running in circles, he managed to keep a semblance of control, to not run screaming from the room. To watch, wide-eyed, as they came gliding slowly but steadily across the floor toward him.

As they drew closer, he could see that, compared to the rest of them, their eyes were surprisingly intact. And they only had eyes for him.

He felt himself edging backward and forced himself to hold his ground. There was, after all, nowhere to go.

They finally stopped, scant inches away, and just looked at him, the seconds stretching out until he realized he'd been holding his breath and couldn't hold it any longer, and let it out in a rush.

"If you miss us so much, Richard, then...why?"

"Yes, daddy, why? Why did you do it?"

"Why?"

"Why?"

"Why?"

"Why?"

The same question came, again and again, assaulting his ears, his senses, like a flock of birds slamming into a window, one after another.

He covered his ears, squeezed shut his eyes and prayed.

««——»»

When, some interminable time later, he'd finally found the strength to open his eyes, they had left him.

But not for long.

After that first occasion, they began to appear every few hours, although thankfully their visits were brief. They had few words to say to him, but those eyes...those eyes and their shadowed sockets had much to say.

Simply averting his own gaze was not enough. He'd resorted to hiding beneath blankets or burying his face in his hands, anything to avoid the accusations in those soul-dead stares.

No matter where in the house he slept, they would appear several times during the night, awakening him not long after he'd finally been able to get to sleep.

But at least, his mind tried yet again…at least they couldn't hurt him. They were only ghosts, wispy and ethereal. They could taunt and torture with their presence, but nothing more.

And at least he still had water, even if the first couple unexpected visits from his wife and daughter had led him to finish the last of his food in a stress-driven eating frenzy. At least there was still water. With that, he had several days left yet. Someone could still come. Someone could most definitely come.

At least he still had hope, even if he was slowly starving to death, imprisoned in his own house and tormented by the ghosts of his murdered wife and daughter.

Wallace would've laughed at that, if he still had the capacity to laugh.

And then, as if on cue, that very same night he got up in the middle of the night to get a drink of water, turned on the tap…

…and stood there, empty Dixie cup in hand, listening to the desperate, gasping pipes.

He stared at the fixture, as if willing it to produce, but after one more gurgle, it lay quiet. Finally, he went to the window, looked out at the well-head and the 5,000-gallon water tank, just visible beyond the corner of the garage.

Wallace realized, abruptly, that the buyer had probably shut off the well pump weeks ago. Since then, the booster pump had faithfully served up water every time Wallace requested it. But there was nothing more to pump beyond what had been in the tank.

The needless showers he'd taken. The frequent flushing of the toilet. He should've thought, should've known…

He leaned against the wall, slid down its surface as if he were suddenly boneless, as limp and insubstantial as his wife and daughter had become.

Wallace felt like crying. But he'd already cried more in the past few weeks than he probably had in his whole life. He wasn't sure if he had any tears left. And, besides, what was the point? There was no one to hear him and take pity.

One small sob escaped him before he could choke it off.

"Tears are a waste of water," came the voice from somewhere in the darkness of the bathroom.

And then, huddled there at the base of the wall, he felt a pair of hands fall roughly upon his neck.

«« — »»

He'd felt their touch upon his skin for hours afterwards, burning cold, as he cowered in the closet like a little boy, venturing out only when he could see the first hints of daylight creeping under the door. Not that the daylight provided any safe harbor, but it somehow seemed so much better than facing them in the dark. But when he came out, there was no sign of them.

And though the next few days found him shying away from shadows and peering around corners, his tormentors did not reappear. As his throat constricted to a sandpaper funnel and his stomach twisted in upon itself and he grew ever weaker, they did not whisper in his ear or thrust their tattered faces at him. He began to wonder if they had moved on, their work now done, but that seemed too much to hope for. Anything seemed too much to hope for.

He had nothing but time during those last days, and he spent much of it in a fevered half-sleep, dreaming of roads not taken and anger restrained. Once, he dreamed that the buyer showed up like a kindly warden, key in hand, to proclaim Wallace's time served. But even then, Wallace woke from the dream without hope, just lay there idly wondering who, or what, the buyer had been.

When Wallace had finally lost track of the passing days, had almost forgotten what it felt like to swallow, he opened his eyes and was not surprised to find his wife and daughter standing over him. He was too groggy to be scared, too delirious to be repulsed, and so he just lay there until he felt his eyelids start to flutter closed again.

But before his vision was gone, he saw them leaning closer. Before sleep took him, he heard his daughter say *"Is he ours now, mommy?"* and felt one of them touch him.

At that, he bolted upright, launching himself off the bed and past them with a strength he didn't know he had. He made it out the bedroom door, not knowing where he thought he was going, but not caring. Away was good.

But then, as he started down the stairs, something grabbed his foot from behind. He lurched and fell, hands flailing for and missing the balustrade. He went down sideways, landing on his shoulder with a sickening crunch and rolling twice before finally hitting bottom.

Stunned, he lay there at the foot of the stairs, unable to move, pain stabbing a signature across his shoulder and back.

Lying there, Wallace for the first time wanted nothing more than just to die. Wished for it all to end, for just a little bit of peace. He let his head fall back to the carpet, closed his eyes.

But then he heard sounds, growing closer: the rustle of frayed, threadbare clothing, the click of hardscrabble fingerbones, the squirming of hungry things in decaying flesh.

At that, Richard Wallace summoned what will he had left and rose to one knee. Pushed himself to his feet. Ran-stumbled to the front door.

Pulled it open, threw himself uselessly at the bars.

Screamed.

As long and loud and hard as he could.

When his voice was gone, when all his throat could offer was a piteous croak, he felt their hands upon him once again.

Their hands: two small, and two smaller.

Their hands, once loving, kneading, comforting. Now angry, raking, clawing.

He felt their hands, and then he felt their teeth, and then he knew that they were at least as hungry as he.